I0822798

It Might Have Been

And Other Stories

2nd Edition

A. K. Frailey

Hardcover ISBN: 979-8-9874047-6-8

Website https://akfrailey.com/

Amazon Author Page
https://www.amazon.com/A.-K.-Frailey/e/B006WQTQCE

Cover Photo credit egal (Elena Schweitzer)
Cover Design by A.K. Frailey and James Hrkach
Back cover photo credit: Freepik

The Writings of A. K. Frailey
Books for the Mind and Spirit
https://akfrailey.com/

Contact
akfrailey@yahoo.com

Historical Science Fiction Novels

OldEarth ARAM Encounter
https://amzn.to/2KLhlsN

OldEarth Ishtar Encounter
https://amzn.to/2OAkDQF

OldEarth Neb Encounter
https://amzn.to/3iGqGlQ

OldEarth Georgios Encounter
https://amzn.to/3v7w8oI

OldEarth Melchior Encounter
https://amzn.to/3nyfkEJ

Science Fiction Novels

Homestead
https://amzn.to/3DcTuhz

Last of Her Kind
http://amzn.to/2y1HJvg

Newearth Justine Awakens
http://amzn.to/2pq0vWN

Newearth A Hero's Crime
https://amzn.to/3S4rROI

Short Stories

It Might Have Been—And Other Short Stories 2nd Edition
https://amzn.to/2XXdDDz

One Day at a Time and Other Stories
https://amzn.to/2YFtQ5r

Encounter Science Fiction Short Stories & Novella 2nd Edition
https://amzn.to/3dq6q5l

Inspirational Non-Fiction

My Road Goes Ever On—Spiritual Being, Human Journey 2nd Edition
https://amzn.to/2KvF3Ll

My Road Goes Ever On—A Timeless Journey
https://amzn.to/3v5BlOM

The Road Goes Ever On—A Christian Journey Through The Lord of the Rings
https://amzn.to/3rtAy6S

Children's Book

The Adventures of Tally-Ho
http://amzn.to/2sLfcI5

Poetry

Hope's Embrace & Other Poems 2nd Edition
https://amzn.to/3cn22X8

Contents

Introduction

Writing short stories has been the best writer's workshop I could ever have imagined. I've learned more from wrestling with my characters and their chosen settings than any how-to book, lecture, or friendly advice I might have encountered along the writing journey.

Oddly enough, I had to unlearn a few bad habits. First was clinging to the ridiculous notion that I knew what I was doing. I had to accept the fact that my characters were quite proficient at telling a good story if I would just get the heck out of the way. The second was to shut up about two paragraphs before I was done.

The realization that the reader doesn't honestly care about the nitty-gritty details—explaining why Aunt Sarah is a nut case for example—but rather just focus on the story I am actually telling—took my proverbial pen into wonderful and terrifying territory. Suddenly, there were no longer words to hide behind. Meaning mattered. Heart-wrenching reality and glaring insight stomped onto the page and demanded its part to play.

Often, I'd find myself shuddering upon impact with a story that I never knew was inside of me. Perhaps it wasn't. Perhaps it rode on my shoulder and dropped onto the page when I started hitting the keys. It felt like that most days...

Who are you?

I'm a story trying to get told—do you MIND?

Oh, no, of course not. No worries. I'll just tap with a couple of fingers and eat these delicious (and nutritious!) peanut M & Ms and watch.

Fine. You do you. Just stay OUT of my way, hear?

Rather pitiful to be intimidated by my own storylines. But heck, they do the work, and I get all the M & Ms. And maybe, if I pay attention, I might just learn how to write a good story.

The Kingdom of If

Originally published on The Writings of A. K. Frailey
6/25/2012

Once upon a time there was the kingdom of IF (Indivisible Fiefdom – a bit of an oxymoron but as people liked it, so it was) and the people of IF had a king, King Oban, who was chosen by them because of his great popularity, and so they believed, as every generation before had believed, that he would be the perfect king.

When he ascended to the throne, they hailed him as both hero and savior, and he believed every word of their hearty proclamations (though why he should is a bit of a mystery for even a smattering of IF history should have warned him that no king served unscathed and more often than not was picked to pieces before he was ousted for a more promising candidate).

The kingdom had started out nobly enough. In fact, inspiring quotes like "I will live and die for the salvation of IF" were quite prominent in their early history. Young citizens of IF loved to thrust their little fists against their chests with hearty thuds and quote the luminaries who offered their lives in the service of IF, though in more modern times, this had gone quite out of fashion for everyone is well aware that it is a young person's primary duty was to live and die only for themselves.

But the Kingdom of IF faced a crisis, unlike anything they had ever faced before though, to be sure, they had faced and overcome many dire situations in their uncounted generations of existence. But now, the Indivisible Fiefdom was sorely divided between the Earth-dwellers and the Sky-dwellers, both of whom claimed the right to influence the king. But as it turned out, King Oban was heavily in debt to the Earth-dwellers (for his great-great-grandmother on his father's side was an Earth-dweller of immense standing, and she had quite a bit of money in very deep pockets) and this left the Sky-dwellers in a high dungeon for they felt left out of everything. In fact, every decision the king had to make was considered from these two opposing camps, but he overwhelmingly favored the Earth-dwellers.

The Earth-dwellers saw everything from a personal point of view. "It is my right!" was their motto, and "Save the Earth!" was another favorite axiom. The Sky-dwellers, on the other hand, saw everything as a matter for long consideration in relation to right and wrong. Though there were a variety of different clans in the Sky-dwellers dominion, still they tended to group around a vision of a "higher-calling" and this left the Earth-dwellers perfectly incensed, for they believed that no one had the right to tell anyone else what to do (except of course when they were telling the Sky-dwellers where to go and how to follow their laws), but the Sky-dwellers were also in the habit of telling the general population how things ought to be done though they argued, quite honestly that they were not preaching a singular individualistic doctrine, but the beliefs of their ancestors dating back time out of mind. Their favorite motto was "God really rules" (though there was some debate as to what God believed exactly), and they loved the ancient melody and lullaby "Tradition Still Has Meaning In Our Lives."

But the real danger facing the Kingdom of IF was not simply their divided nature, for they were always arguing, but rather that they did not look very far into their own future. For it was the will of the people of IF that when the king chose a side, he must stick to that side at all costs and listen not a word to the other side—even if they happened to be making humongous good sense.

So, the population of IF was dwindling into sad chaos. In fact, it was only surviving due to the charity of a few who still believed in the ancient prophesy that the Kingdom of IF was the best of all the kingdoms put upon the earth.

But there was another danger facing the kingdom that few seemed to realize. There was an enormous kingdom to the east known as DOOM whose motto was "Conquer without battle." And though they professed enduring love for the people of IF, they were secretly rubbing their hands in glee at all the in-fighting between the Earth-dwellers and the Sky-dwellers, for they were observing that all the work of destruction was being done quite efficiently for them. Also on the sidelines were the tri-kingdoms of Kab, Bab, and Dan. These three semi-allied kingdoms (always together except when they were at each other's throats) also professed an enduring love for the people of IF, though they would chant "Death to the King of IF" at every family gathering.

Besides the efforts of King Oban (who was himself a hard worker except when he was on vacation, which was at least once a week or every day that began with a headache and that was becoming rather more common), there were organizations of "Centralized Order" with highly trained worker-bureaucrats toiling ever so hard in the dark, dank libraries of great wisdom (though their words were drier than the parchment they lay upon) to keep the kingdom financially afloat. They had at that time finished volume P of laws and rules for tax regulation though they were now working on volume Q, but it had become stalled when the president/ CEO (and DMD for he pulled teeth on the side) of Rule-Keepers had to have an extended stay at Sunny-Shade, for his nerves had become rather undone in all the hairsplitting technicalities of tracing contradictory laws and rules and regulations to their origin and rewriting them in modern jargon.

But the people of IF saw not their danger.

There was, however, one child who had written a poem for her mother, who seemed to grasp the implications of the dire times. She had learned in school about their noble history, and her friends had all chosen sides. But one sunny day her little brother sat down beside her near a great old oak tree, and he asked her why she looked so sad. Though she could not answer her sibling's innocent question, she did think that a poem might relieve her pent-up feelings, so she wrote this quaint little prose, and she gave it to her mother, who was clearly too busy to read it.

But *you* may find time in your busy life to read it before the parchment crumbles into dust—for even questions from young people will fade if given enough time to wither and fall.

THE KINGDOM OF IF

If only we remembered from whence we came
And delighted in the goodness from above.

If only we grew our strength
From the victory of enduring love.

If only we realized, everything we have is a gift.
And that gifts can be taken away.

If only we toiled for that which lasts
And not so much for the day.

If only we lived lives of hope and not of dreadful dread-

We would know lives of joyful fruit
And not live as if we were already dead.

So, though the Kingdom of IF still stands upon its majestic past, and faces its future quite blindfolded, still it will not last forever, for nothing in this world ever does. But there is a quaint little plea in the child's verse that strikes deep into the heart—for history will record not only how well the kingdom rose but how badly it fell.

Yet may our world live long, inspiring hope and enduring faith in humanity.

If only...

Sanity

Originally published on The Writings of A. K. Frailey
12/2/2015

Mom liked to say: "Everyone is crazy, except thee and me. And I'm not so sure about thee." I knew she was joking, though there was always a shadow of pain in her eyes when she said it. Still, I'd laugh. Like I was supposed to.

I always got up early, when the world was still dark and cold. I'd get everything ready for school, eat a bowl of cereal, and maybe have toast scraped with butter. At promptly seven, I would get her coffee ready, spooning in plenty of sugar and creamer. I could practically taste the dark aroma. She was always pleased with my coffee, which always pleased me. Life was too hard not to make people happy when you had the chance.

On school days, I'd hike up to the bus station and wait, hugging myself, trying to keep off the morning chill. I'd try not to think too much about Mom and her troubles. I had troubles enough.

On the weekends, I would make Mom breakfast with her coffee: usually just an egg and toast. She had simple tastes. Then she'd get up and go about her business, and I would head outside to play, sniffing the fresh, clean air. I can't remember studying much. Maybe if I had studied harder, I would have been able to respond better. Maybe I would have understood what she was really trying to say.

It must have been Veteran's Day or something because I had the day off, and I stayed inside to help Mom make her bed. She was in a good mood; she hadn't been drinking lately, and she wasn't brooding over Dad so much. It felt good to pull the sheets tight around the mattress and then spread the blanket smooth. I remember I was wedged between the bed and the wall, the window behind me, when Mom stopped and stared right past me out the window.

I didn't want to know what she was thinking when she pointed her finger and giggled, an eerie giggle. I only felt cold ripples roll over my arms. She spoke in a hushed tone. "Well, now he's gone and done it! I didn't think it was possible."

I remember the soft sigh I heaved. I didn't want her to hear it, but I couldn't help it. It just escaped. She waited for me to ask. So, I asked: "What did he do?"

We both knew we were talking about Dad, but it seemed only I knew that it wasn't about Dad. Mom's voice projected a certainty that made me look out the window. "He's gone and turned himself into a Japanese man. Look there."

I don't remember what else she said. I just remember looking out the window and seeing no Dad and no Japanese man. I kind of hoped there would be one or the other.

A brown leaf fluttered to the ground, delicately, like sanity. "And I'm not so sure about thee."

James Milford Parker III

Originally published on The Writings of A. K. Frailey
4/17/2016

~Death~

James Milford Parker III stared at the gravestone with his name etched out in block print and realized that he would never be the same. James had seen tombstones before. Many times, in fact. But they had all been part of a set. His father had been a movie producer and his mother an actress of some renown in her early days. Now, they were just aging celebrities who lived quiet lives in as stress-free an environment as possible. They deserved some rest and fun. After all, they had given their best years to the world of entertainment. They ought to keep their golden years for themselves.

James stared and wondered why the stone in front of him did not seem real. He stepped forward and pressed his fingers against the marble slab in an attempt to dislodge it from its foundation. It did not budge. It was stone, all right. He could feel the firm, smooth foundation under his casual shoes. Patting the stone, he smiled, as if asking the stone if it could take a little joke. *You don't mind, do you? I had to make sure.* The image of a plastic tombstone being carried off in one hand by a prop man turned his smile into a grimace. *So hard to be sure, you know.*

James turned, got into his car, and drove twenty-seven miles home. He lived in the country on a sprawling estate. He never knew why his wife had insisted on having a place so far out, but he respected her wishes as he had respected everything about her. She was a good woman, and that was why her sudden death baffled him to the point of incomprehension. He got out of his car and looked around. Everything was very quiet. It was early autumn, but the days were still quite warm. California seasons change almost imperceptibly. It was hard to realize that anything had changed. But he knew the night would bring a chilling breeze, and he shivered at the thought.

I could use a drink, he mumbled to himself but brushed the thought away with a flick of his hand. He had suffered the pains of hell trying to sober up permanently. He wasn't going to risk a rerun of that life, not without Cindy. Cindy had been the bedrock of his sanity when alcoholism almost destroyed his will to live. It had cost him his job at the studio and many of his friends. Though his name alone would always assure him of a following, it would not always assure him of friends. There were very few people he called friends, and he just lost the best of the bunch four days ago. Shaking his head to ward off any other dangerous thoughts, James punched in his key code and then slid the glass door open and walked inside. The echoing silence nearly deafened him.

He scratched his head and wondered if perhaps he should have just one drink. After all, his wife had died, and no one would blame him for getting drunk. Standing in the middle of the foyer, he lifted his head, and his gaze fell on a small marble statue of the Blessed Virgin Mary that Cindy had installed in a little niche as you entered the house. Good Lord, how he hated the thing! He tried for weeks to convince Cindy that it made them seem like religious fanatics, like real provincials, but she had just smirked and said that at this point in her life, she didn't give a hoot what people thought. Maria, her maid, had given it to her just before she died from liver cancer, and she wasn't about to remove it. Cindy had said that it reminded her of something important. When James had asked her what was so damn important about it, she just told him that when he grew up, he'd figure it out. She said this with a smile, so James didn't take it as an insult, though as he thought of it now, he wondered if it was an insult — he'd just been too besotted to catch on.

He moved toward the expansive living room, all done up in wood paneling, shag rugs, and Native American themes. He found it rather revolting. His boyhood had been immersed in ultra-modern chromes and sleek metals, and this reversion toward mother-earth had struck him as somewhat barbaric, but once again, this was what Cindy wanted, and as he had his own place closer to work, he was willing to allow her decorators do their worst. *And they did. Oh, Lord, did they ever.*

James suddenly realized that he would have to sell the place, and he would need help. He considered several options for a moment. There were so many ramifications of Cindy's death that his head spun. Too much to think about. Ever since Thursday morning when he awoke and realized that Cindy, lying there beside him, was not moving, that she was too still and too cold, he had existed in numbed shock. He had called an ambulance and his personal physician, but it was too late at that point. He had then called his secretary, and after telling her the news, she had promised to clear his calendar. All his projects had been shoved to the side.

His father had said that he might come for the funeral, but as his mother hadn't been feeling well, she probably wouldn't be able to make it. James knew. His mother never liked Cindy, and it wasn't in her nature to do anything she didn't want to do. He was grateful for his father, though. He didn't have any other family to call, and Cindy's family was spread all over the globe. Her brother flew in from Texas, but that was it. Her father was in a nursing home, and her mother had died years ago. Cindy had wanted to go to her mother's funeral, but they had been in the middle of a big movie opening. James insisted that he couldn't break away, and since his sobriety was still in question, Cindy had elected to stay at his side. Later she told him that she felt like she had betrayed her mother by not going to her funeral, but James had just laughed.

"Good God, Cindy! The woman was cremated! What kind of funeral can there be for a pile of dust?" He had not realized how cruel he was at the time. Cindy had walked out of the room. It wasn't until a few weeks ago that she reminded him of the incident and asked him if he remembered. He said he didn't remember his exact words, but he supposed he had said something like that. She asked him if he still felt the same. He shrugged. "I don't know. I don't like to think about death. It was a long time ago,

Cindy; forget it." She seemed to. But it nagged at him now. It more than nagged at him. It felt like a hammer blow to the heart. How could he have been so cold?

James turned and walked toward the steps. *Well, if I can't have a drink, I'm sure as hell not going to stand around here thinking about the past. I can't change anything. It is – what it is.* He walked into his study and turned on a large screen television. He picked up the remote and began flipping through the channels as he pulled at his tie. He stopped at a news channel and then threw his cell phone on his dresser and tugged off his dress shirt. He began talking to himself. "Why did I go today? The funeral was yesterday. I didn't need to check to see if the stone was set. Totally neurotic. I could have sent Eduardo. Damn, I am such—"

James turned at the sound of his cell phone ringing. He snatched it off his dresser and stepped over to the window, only dressed in his casual pants and shoes. His chest was bare, and he allowed the sunlight to warm him through the window. "Yeah?"

It was Dalton, his friend and buddy from days long past. He hadn't heard from Dalton for years. Dalton explained that he had just heard about Cindy's death, and he was in the area. Would it be okay if he stopped by for a moment? He was on his way to a screening, but he really wanted to see him for a bit. James squinted, trying to remember what had happened at their last meeting. He had a vague feeling that their last conversation had not gone well, but he couldn't remember the details. He shrugged in the afternoon sun. “Yeah, sure. I’m not doing anything.”

James could almost feel Dalton’s relief. He stared out over the vast expanse of scrub brush and rocky hills and tried not to sigh. He wasn’t sure what would be worse. Sitting here alone or having an old friend come by and try to comfort him. Well, it was a moot point now. Dalton made sure of the address and punched it into his phone. He was as good as in his living room.

James pressed the end button and threw the phone back on his dresser. Well, so much for immersing himself in some stupid movie or another. He looked at the screen and scowled. There were images of his wife’s face and then scenes of the funeral. What? Couldn’t people ever leave them alone? Voyeurs and parasites! Then the screen blinked to the most recent war victims. It showed the fragmented remains of a school that had been bombed. Bodies were everywhere. The sound was muted so James couldn’t hear the grisly details, but he could see the reality for himself.

“Christ! Do they have to put that up all the time? Isn’t there ever any good news?” James looked for the remote, but he couldn’t find it. He began to scramble madly around the room, searching for it. He wanted to turn the bloody thing off, but in his confusion, he felt his face flush with fury. “Where the hell did it go? Damn it! Where—” He saw it under his shirt, and grabbing it, he squeezed the off button. When the screen turned black, he flopped down on a chair and buried his head in his hands. “God, Almighty! I just can’t take things like that. Not today.”

James sat there for a moment and then remembered that Dalton was coming. He tossed his used shirt into the over-flowing hamper, relieved that the cleaning woman would come in the morning. He tried to remember her name. Cindy was the one who hired and managed their help. He didn't know a thing about them other than they came and went like invisible angels of mercy. He supposed he'd have to find out what their names were. He opened his closet and pulled a casual shirt from the rack. He could smell a faint odor coming from the closet and realized that Cindy had come in the other day night before they were heading out to a party; she had practically reeked of perfume. *Funny I can smell it now. I didn't notice it this morning. I never smell anything anymore...* James realized that this wasn't helping him get ready for Dalton, so he strode to the bathroom, splashed cold water on his face, and returned to the first floor.

He meandered into the kitchen and decided he would fix a little something for his old friend. He took out a package of fat-free chips and a platter of cut vegetables that had been left over from the funeral, and he poured some ranch dressing into a container. He put these on the counter with some cold meat and cheese that had been carefully wrapped away, in case he got hungry, someone had said. Who had said that? James tried to remember who had been at the funeral dinner, but it was a blur.

James was about to open the refrigerator when his hand accidentally brushed against the counter and sent the chip bowl sprawling. He bent down reflexively to catch it and slammed his head against the edge of the marble counter. The blow sent lights flashing before his eyes, and he lurched backward from the sharp pain. He clasped his hand over his temple and realized with a shock that he was bleeding. He knew that head wounds tend to bleed profusely, and it did little to stem the rise of panic as he felt drops of blood slide through his fingers. He rushed to the bathroom. He looked at himself in the mirror and suddenly felt sick. Before he even thought out his next move, he found himself retching into the toilet. Grabbing roller-spinning wads of toilet paper, he tried to wipe his face and temple and stem the flow of blood. After a few moments, the dripping slowed, and he cautiously moved toward the living room. He plopped down on the couch and lay his head back with a muted groan.

Does it get any worse? James closed his eyes and tried to calm down. His stomach was empty now, and the blood was definitely congealing though he feared that if he got up, it might start up again. He lay as still as possible and tried to think. He should call Dalton and tell him not to come. He probably should call someone to take him to the doctor.

He envisioned Dalton forcing the door open and finding him in a pool of blood. He saw himself floating above his wife's tombstone ...also *his* tombstone. He realized that it was his now as much as hers. He would die, and he would lie there, and his body would never bleed again. He would never breathe again. He would never answer the phone or have old friends coming over to comfort him. He'd never make another deal or handle another movie project. He'd never give advice or slap down a stupid idea. He'd...

He saw Dalton entering the room, calling for him. He tried to tell Dalton that he wasn't here anymore, to go look at his wife's tombstone, but his tongue felt thick, and his mouth was glued shut. Someone was tugging at him. James grew frightened. He felt himself fighting, trying to slap with cardboard arms that couldn't move. He wasn't ready. He didn't know where he was going. He didn't want to die. He didn't know what death meant. He hadn't decided yet.

"James! James, for God's sake, wake up! Jenny, call the doctor! I think he's tried to kill himself or something!"

James' eyes fluttered open, and he saw a salt-and-peppered swatch of hair way too close to his face. He tried to lift his arm, but it was too heavy. He decided to scream.

Dalton heard the merest whisper brush against his ear. He stared at James lying prone beneath his inquiring gaze, and when he saw eyes staring back, he jerked backward. "Oh, James! Looks like something happened. You looked so bad lying there, and you didn't answer the doorbell. I got worried, and we just walked in. Hope you don't mind."

James tried to sit up, but the pain in his head throbbed him into submission. "No, not at all." He whispered. He tried to pull off the messy swath of toilet paper and found that it was glued to his head. He grimaced and pointed with his other hand. "I hit my head against the counter—stupid."

Dalton smiled, relieved. "Oh, I've done that a hundred zillion times. Hurts like hell, doesn't it?"

James grimaced his agreement. Jenny came over and inquired if she should call for an ambulance. James looked at the sleek blond in front of him with her large worried eyes and realized how bad he looked. He felt like a fool and wanted nothing more than to get them out of his house and take a hot shower and then crawl into bed. He envisioned some sleeping pills that his wife occasionally took. They were probably still in the cabinet. He waved his hand benignly.

Dalton got up from the couch and took Jenny by the arm. "Hey, honey, why don't you get James something to eat? It looks like something spilled over there. Maybe you could—"

Jenny nodded and turned to accomplish her domestic duty. Dalton turned back toward James and smiled. "Well, I know better than to ask if you want a drink. But perhaps a soda or something?"

James smiled at the incongruity of having a guest treat him to his own food. "Yeah, that'd be fine."

Dalton stepped away to perform his act of mercy. James forced himself into a sitting position and tried not to groan as his head swam. He pulled the tissue away from his head, tearing it, and was disappointed by how little blood was actually there. It was hardly the excessive bloodbath he had imagined. "Huh."

Dalton returned a moment later with a tray of drinks and the cut vegetables with the little ranch dressing poured off to the side. Dalton nudged the end table a little closer with his foot and set the tray down. Then he sat in a chair next to the couch. He handed James his drink and leaned in. "So apart from nearly smashing your head in and your wife dying, how've you been?

James merely mumbled something about the fires of hell, so Dalton accepted the mantle of charming host and continued talking.

~~~

Seven months later, James sat in his office, staring out a large bay window, his swivel chair facing away from his top aide.

Todd was gesturing enthusiastically as he outlined his newest great idea. "Do you know what the term 'forged by fire' really means? Some guy, Ignatius something-or-other wrote about it. I had no idea. I think that'd make a great title for a movie—don't you? How about if we take that surreal concept by that new writer - you know, the one who's always acting so damn deep - and throw that at her and see what she comes up with. It might be good - we can always add in some fast action sequences and a bit of sex to spice it up. Besides, *deep* is in right now."

James wondered if it would be considered first-degree murder to strangle an idiot. *Why do I let this man work here? Why do I listen to him?* James continued to stare out the window overlooking one of the highest-priced pieces of real estate in Los Angeles and heard the answer in his head. *Because he turns stupid ideas into multi-million-dollar winners.*

James turned and looked at the well-dressed man in front of him. Todd was sharp in the worst sense of the word, yet he also had a boyish charm that made even those who had suffered at his hands care about him. He really didn't mean any
~~~

harm. He merely had an incredible knack for taking the pulse of the movie-going public and serving up what they wanted. If they were obsessed with scary aliens landing on our shores, he found a script with the scariest aliens possible, and if New York had to be smashed to bits once again – so much the better. If the public was subconsciously feeling a little guilty, he didn't bother to know why; he just found a way to address that hidden psychosis through a cathartic heroic-romance, where even the worst sinner alive could feel a dash of patriotic hope. If they were looking for their lost childhood, he found a way to update one of the oldies-but-goodies. Todd was a gifted man, all right, but who he was working for, James was never certain. Todd was a natural chameleon. Perhaps that's what made him so good at what he did. He understood everyone because, in truth, he was no one.

James rubbed his chin. "Funny you should mention Ignatius. It's also the name of a priest. Ignatius of Loyola." James turned and stared at Todd's blank expression. "I only know because Martha, my cook, has her daughter dropped off at our house after school, and she studies in the kitchen until they go home at seven. The other day I went in to ask Martha something, and I saw the book on the table, so I asked the kid about it. She got excited telling me all about him – she went on and on. She goes to a Catholic school, and they fill her head with all sorts of stuff." James stared right into Todd's eyes. "The kind of stuff that you should steal and turn into a movie, maybe." James briefly wondered if Todd would jerk away, shielding himself like Dracula did when presented with a crucifix. Todd merely stared back; his mouth slightly open. Finally, he smiled and nearly giggled.

"Damn it, James, you had me going a minute."

James smiled. "Yeah, gotcha." He leaned over his desk. "Well, if that's all you have to cover, I think we can quit for today. I'd like to get home early. Jimmy wants me to attend his party tonight, and I need to get ready. Besides, I'm feeling kind of tired. I think I've been working too much lately."

Todd nodded, his appraising glance telling James more than he wanted to know. He already realized that a lot of people thought he was having some kind of breakdown. There was even a rumor months ago, that he was drinking again, but he had put that one down by showing up for work early and in perfect form every day for six months. He usually stayed over time, and he had never been as successful as he had been in these last months. Everyone was full of admiration for how well he had handled his wife's death. Until recently. Recently he had started to leave a little earlier and come in a little later. Though he still looked good and was at the top of his game, he realized, along with everyone else, that something had changed.

Todd shut the door quietly behind him after saying that he'd see him at the party – his parting shot to demonstrate that he was invited "everywhere" too. James closed his eyes and leaned back in his chair. *God, what's happening to me? What's wrong?* James realized that he wasn't merely speaking rhetorically. He was really asking a question of God—well, of Someone anyway. *When did this start?*

It started with the dreams. After selling the house and reorganizing almost his entire life, James had felt that he deserved a little break and a change, so he took a week's vacation. He went to a resort in Nevada that someone had insisted was just the place to get his mind off his troubles. It was the worst vacation of his life. He not only didn't get his mind off his troubles, he found he was being haunted by his grief, a grief he thought he had already worked through. He started dreaming about Cindy. He hadn't done anything she would have disapproved of, well, maybe a couple things, but she'd understand.

He was no longer a married man. He had his needs. It took him the better part of the week and three very unpleasant encounters to realize that his needs had changed. He may not be Cindy's husband anymore, but he wasn't the man of his youth either. There was no going back, only forward, but without some kind of a roadmap, he wasn't exactly sure where the future led. He cut his vacation short and threw himself into his work with a vengeance. It worked for a while. He was able to concentrate amazingly well while in his office, and he found himself arriving early and staying late. But then there was that incident with the cook…

James rubbed his face and tried to shake off his recollections, but before he realized it, he was staring into space again. It had been nearly four months ago when his life took the next unexpected bend in the road. His old cook had been a rather eccentric old fellow by the name of Filippo. James figured that he was Malaysian though when he'd ask him, Filippo would just smile and say that he came from a lot of places. James always felt like he was on the outside of a joke. But one day, Filippo didn't show up for work, and James was having a few friends over for an important get-together that night. He got pretty worked up about it. He ended up having to order some food in, and it wasn't nearly as good as what Filippo could dish out with a snap of his fingers.

The next day, when Filippo again didn't show up, James sent someone to his place to find out what the hell he was doing, and they reported back that Filippo had died in his apartment and no one had realized until the landlady had been alerted. James sat dumbfounded on his couch as he took in the news that his cook was dead and had laid there cold and stiff in his apartment for two whole days while he had secretly, and not so secretly, raked him over the proverbial coals for not doing his job.

It was when Filippo's daughter came to the house asking for any personal items Filippo had left behind, that the whole event began to really sink in. There was this beautiful twenty-year-old girl standing in his doorway asking with her big honest eyes if she could come in and collect her father's things. It was then that James realized that he knew absolutely nothing about the man who had worked for him other than the fact that he was a great cook. He stepped aside and let the woman in, and he followed her to the kitchen, opening the closet where Filippo usually hung his sweater and stored whatever stuff he had brought with him. It was there that James discovered that Filippo was Roman Catholic, for there, hanging on a little nail inside the closet door, was a set of rosary beads. What? Did the man recite prayers in between courses? James felt as if his head would explode.

He watched from the side as Filippo's last remaining worldly possessions were gathered into his daughter's arms. As she stepped over the threshold, James felt a resolution form in his core, and he decided to act on it at once. "Can I ask your name?"

She looked at him with those sad, sweet eyes and spoke so softly that James had to lean in to hear. "My name is Martha." James nodded, and before she could retreat into the outer world again, he put out his hand and stopped her.

"And what do you do for a living, Martha?"

She whispered, her eyes downcast. "I was training to be a cook, like my father."

James felt a spark of life flicker in his middle. "Really?" He appraised her. She could not be more than twenty. "How old are you?'

"Twenty-seven."

James' eyebrows rose. He was used to people undercutting their age, not adding to it. But—who knows. He leaned on the doorframe. "Why do you say, 'was'?"

"My father helped to pay my tuition. I cannot pay for it by myself. I have a daughter to raise."

James stopped leaning. "Where's your husband?"

"He is away."

James nodded. "Well, I just happen to be in

need of a cook. Do you think you might consider working here?"

Those luminous, black eyes stared into his soul, searching, and he stared back, uncertain of what she was looking for. She barely nodded her head.

Perhaps, James realized, as he propped his head on his hands in his silent office, perhaps he had been infatuated with those eyes and that perfect face. Perhaps he felt just a tad guilty for the way he had behaved toward Filippo and wanted to right some wrongs. Perhaps, he was just a mercenary jerk who just wanted to banish all grief and doubt from his mind. But as the weeks passed and as Martha came dutifully each day, he kept true to his resolution. He had decided that he would know more about the people in his life, no matter who they were. They could be the lowliest trash collector to the highest producer; he would ask more questions; he would get to know the people in his life.

He was never more surprised than when Martha's husband showed up one day asking for her, and she threw herself into his arms like some sticky, sweet version of a movie he had dubbed a failure to express real life. Apparently, the husband, Max, really had been away. He had been working in Alaska and was home, at least until he found another job. James discovered opportunities a little closer to home. Max was grateful to take one. So Martha and her daughter, Elizabeth Grace, and husband, Max, became members of James' household – though he never mentioned this fact to anyone. There was never any need. Not really. How does one casually bring up the subject that you've practically adopted an entire family?

But the dreams about Cindy never really stopped. Despite everything. James wondered about that, but he figured that Cindy would be pleased with him. She was always so kind to the servants. Really, she was very kind to everyone – especially him. James realized that now.

James got up from his desk and looked at his watch. He gathered up his keys and his cell phone. He didn't want to go to this party, and he really didn't want to have to appear happy. Wasn't he happy? James sighed at the question and moved across the room. The sudden image of a plastic tombstone being carried away made him stop. Counterfeits were such a part of his life; he had to wonder if he'd ever really been happy.

~~~

Five years later, on James' 47th birthday, when he was returning home from a long day at work, he saw, out of the corner of his eye, a minivan barreling toward him. In a split second, he realized he was not going to be able to avoid being hit; he realized that he was probably facing his final moments on earth. As he lay in the car, after the smashing, grinding impact, he could not think. Everything was immensely quiet. Then, just as suddenly, there was more noise and confusion than he could tolerate. As he blacked out, he hoped that someone nice had decided what death meant for him—he still didn't know.

When he woke up, he was on a hospital bed in a white-walled room with large vinyl curtains
~~~

blocking out the sunlight. He blinked and attempted to move his head. He discovered he could not move anything but his eyes and his mouth. He felt like his whole body had been frozen, but his face was still free. His brow furrowed as he pictured a man buried up to his neck. As his mind became alert, James started to realize what this meant. Frantically, he tried to remember what had happened. Panic began to rise as he felt his breathing becoming faster and shallower. A nurse bustled into the room, looking right at him with a laptop clasped to her chest. She saw the fear in his eyes, and she placed the laptop on the counter and moved to his side.

"Mr. Parker, it's all right. You'll be all right. You might feel rather numb right now, but that's from all the medication and the nature of your injuries. Most of your injuries should heal in time. Right now, you should just be happy you're alive. It was a close call." He knew she was patting his arm from the rustling of her sleeve against his hospital gown. He did not feel the pat. She bent closer and stared him right in the eyes. "Mr. Parker, it is very important that you stay calm. You're in good hands. I'll call Dr. Freeman and let him know that you're awake."

James wanted to say something to the effect—"Yes, you do that, and by the way, while you're at it, would you mention the fact that I'm practically dead? He might find that interesting as well." But he found his mouth was too dry and his tongue too thick to form articulate words. He just mumbled something that the nurse took to mean "Thanks." He watched as her upper half moved to the head of the bed, her arm adjusted his drip line, and then her shoulders and head moved away from him and bobbed out the doorway.

He imagined getting one of his men in here and whispering a desperate plea to pour a pint of whiskey into the drip bag. Todd might do it. It would be just the thing that might amuse him – offbeat, gritty realism. The only problem would be that Todd would need an audience, so he'd have to tell the whole floor of nurses, and they'd freak out, end of the scenario. James wondered if he could be arrested for attempting to spike his own drip bag. He closed his eyes. *Can it get any worse than this?* When had he thought that before? He couldn't remember. But he realized; he'd have a lot of time to play memory games. Lots of time to consider the direction his life was taking.

A white-coated doctor entered the room. He looked Indian; his smile seemed genuine. James swallowed and was relieved that he actually felt the sensation. He did not smile back, however.

"Hello, James. My name is Dr. Joshi. I was on the team that worked on you. It was a mighty good fight you put up. We were relieved when your heart started again. I just want to let you know that though you did sustain serious injuries, it looks like the worst is behind you. With some physical therapy and perhaps a couple minor reconstructive surgeries on your right leg, you should be able to get up and move around again. But right now, all you need to know is that your paralysis should be temporary, and you'll be feeling more like your normal self in a few days, though I don't suggest you attempt to do anything too strenuous too soon."

If James could have burst out laughing, he

would have at this bit of incongruity. Was Dr. Joshi blind, or was it no big deal that he had just about died? What did he say about getting his heart started again? Was returning to life just a mere blip in the day's events? Everything will be back to normal? Yeah, right! James merely blinked rapidly and attempted to shake his head. Dr. Joshi took that for agreement and smiled again.

"Your nurses will be close by if you need anything, and they'll check on you regularly." The doctor straightened and turned to the nurse, giving her directions that James could not understand, and he started walking away, his head bobbing slowly out of the room. The nurse checked James' drip line, took his pulse, did various other duties and then patted him on the arm. Rustle, rustle. She ordered him to get some rest. James didn't bother to watch her head bob out the door.

He stared up at the ceiling and realized that before long, he'd know exactly how many tiles comprised the ceiling and how many dots in each. This was life right now. Surely, they had a television, a way to listen to music...something to occupy his mind. James realized he felt very relaxed and sleepy. Apparently, he didn't need to spike his drip bag—they'd done it for him. Perhaps later, when the nurse came back, he'd ask a few questions. James would learn all about life here and find a way to survive. He closed his eyes.

He wondered who would care that he was here. His mother? She was slipping into another world—dementia at its best. He'd leave her to go gently into her private world. His dad? Yeah, his dad would come and be very pleasant and upbeat, trying to cheer him up so that no one need feel sad. Tears were just for critical moments in movies. Tears weren't intended for real life. If one got sad enough for tears, it was time to pack it in. There were those who took that way out. But Dad wouldn't be one of those. He would die cheerfully, pretending that death wasn't getting the last word, even when it did. James wasn't sure he wanted his dad's pleasant ignorance at this point. James sighed and was infinitely relieved when he felt his chest heave painfully. He wasn't quite as numb as he thought. He tried to feel some other part of his body, but it still felt still absent. *Damn. I'm living in a dead man's body.*

~~~

There were visitors those first days, mostly people from work and a policeman who wanted to go over the accident report with him. The friendly visits were painful as James attempted to do more each time to appear less disabled than he was, but he got through them with as much aplomb as he could muster. He assured everyone that he would fully recover and be back at work by the New Year at the latest. When the policeman entered, James felt the greatest flutter of excitement since he had first awakened. He told the officer what he could remember and then waited for him to explain what had actually happened. After the officer told him, James felt his spirit go as numb as his body.

A woman and child had been in the other car.
~~~

No one was exactly sure what made her drive into him, could be the slight drizzle obscured her vision, or she just wasn't thinking and didn't see the red light directly in front of her, but she rammed into his car full speed. She and the child died. Their names were Mrs. Carol Jones and Sylvia Jones. Sylvia had only been five. They think that Carol had been driving so fast because she was hurrying to pick up her son from soccer practice. Sylvia had been at tumbling class, and they had gotten behind schedule. James wondered at the value of his life when it had almost been snuffed out because of soccer practice. It wasn't until the officer mentioned that the husband was outside waiting to see him that James wondered if it would have been easier to simply die. He merely mumbled, "Yeah, sure, what can it hurt?"

The police officer had tapped his notebook closed and left the room with a nod, hoping that James would "get better soon." Mr. Jones entered the room slowly. His eyes had dark circles under them. His hands hid in his pockets as he moved to the side of the bed. The nurse had raised James' bed so he was in a semi-sitting position. James wasn't sure why this man had come or what on earth he was supposed to say, but he figured that he should be compassionate. After all, he did know how it felt to lose a wife, and the officer had said something about there being another child. So, along with everything else, this guy was a single parent now, and that couldn't be easy.

Mr. Jones shuffled his feet and then looked at James. "I just wanted to let you know how sorry I am that this happened, Mr. Parker. My wife was a good woman, and I know she'd never have wanted this. It was just some stupid accident and..." Mr. Jones' voice cracked, and his stricken eyes filled with tears.

James felt his own eyes ache. He realized that he was hurting inside in ways he had not admitted to himself and he did not want to face. He could not lift his arm well, but he could gesture feebly. He attempted to do so. "Please, Mr..." James tried to control his voice. "What's your name?"

"Eric."

"Listen, Eric, I know it was an accident, and it looks to me like you've suffered more than me. I've just got bruised up a bit, but you've lost your wife and kid. I lost my wife a few years back; I know how hard that can be. We never had kids... but I can only imagine the hell you're going through. So please, no apologies—"

Tears were flowing down Eric's face. "My son blames me. He said I should have gone to pick him up. I knew Carol was behind schedule, but I was at work and..."

James felt his breathing quicken. He couldn't handle this. He wasn't a therapist. He was a recovered alcoholic who made a living by faking reality. "Eric, your son is just lashing out at you because you're all he's got to lash at. Who else is he going to blame? God?"

Eric stood mute with tears falling freely. James stared at the ceiling tiles and tried to remember how many he had counted before he gave up. "Oh, God!" He looked back at Eric. "I can't help you, Eric. I don't know how. I wish I could. But if it means anything to you—I don't blame you or your wife. I don't blame anyone. I can't say why. But you and your son are still alive, and you've got to figure out how to live through this. Just like me. It's a hell of a world, and I'm the last person on earth to give anyone advice, but if I did, I'd say it'd be better to try to make the best of this rather than let it tear you to pieces."

Eric nodded, wiping his face with his arm. "I'm sorry I fell apart like this. I didn't mean to. It's just when I saw how bad you got hurt, and I remember… It just kills something inside me."

James shook his head. "Well, don't! Don't let it kill you. Not yet. Death gets its way often enough. Don't give it anymore."

Eric stuck out his hand and gripped James' free hand lying on his bed sheet. "I meant to come here and apologize for hurting you—but you've helped me—more than you realize. Thank you."

James watched as Eric left the room, and for one astounding moment, he realized that he thought of death as an enemy—one that must be avoided at all costs. Problem was, he knew he couldn't avoid him forever.

~~~

When James was sixty-eight years old, he was diagnosed with a severe heart condition and was hospitalized in the hope that he would undergo a heart transplant. But that transplant never took place. He died two days before the planned surgery. But the day before he died, an old friend came to visit—his cook's eldest daughter, Elizabeth Grace, now grown into a matronly
~~~

woman with four kids.

She had taken his cold, papery hand in her own and stroked it gently as she smiled through her gentle laugh. “Hey, Mr. James, how you doing today?” They bantered about her mother and brothers and sisters, about all the “goings-on” in the world, and recent events in the family they shared. James suddenly realized that with Elizabeth Grace at his side, he felt brave and comfortable. She looked at him with eyes that could peer directly into his lost soul, and she loved him anyway.

“Hey, my little love, I have a question for you. You were always so smart in school and read all those books about saints and heroes of old—”

Elizabeth stared at him, keeping his eyes held in her own.

James felt he could go on. “So, what’s death, anyway? I mean, where is it? What happens when the old, grim reaper shows up?”

Elizabeth’s eyes grew round, and her smile widened. “Wow, Mr. James, you always know how to surprise me.” Her smile faded as she saw something in his eyes that saddened her. “I don’t know anything about grim reapers and such, but you know, I was taught that death is a doorway—from this world to the next. It’s a chance to go home, really—if you want to.”

James shook his head. “I don’t get it. I’m home now. I mean, I want to go home to my place on the hill. I want to get back home—not leave it forever. Death is about leaving.”

Elizabeth Grace shrugged. “I guess; you can look at it that way. But my dad used to say that he never really had a home here. He wasn’t so worried about leaving since he knew that he'd be going to his real home later. I miss him, but I don't worry about him. He was right. He was a good man who loved a lot of people. His love didn't disappear—I think it just led him home."

James nodded. Then he squeezed Elizabeth's hand and closed his eyes. "I'll have to think about that. I've never understood death, but I like your version. I've tried to love more, to really care, and—it has led me home — already."

Elizabeth smiled as she let his hand go and then bent down and placed a kiss on his white cheek. "Good night, Mr. James. You'll always find a home in those you love."

James smiled as he drifted into a peaceful slumber. He still didn't know exactly what death meant, but he did know what happiness was. And he figured that knowledge would lead him past the tombstone.

The Key

Originally published on The Writings of A. K. Frailey
3/13/2017

When people say they're haunted, it usually conjures up images of ghosts and wraiths. But that's not how it is with me. Six words, a beard, and the tap of a hand haunt my days and nights.

I'm probably as ordinary as a person can get, living a typically mundane life. One particularly innocent day, my client asked me to run a few papers by a local nursing home. Easy? Sure. Safe? Not so much.

I was running a tad behind schedule when I pulled into the parking lot—a totally nondescript building with a colorful banner emblazoned with "We're so glad to see you!" rippling in the cold, February breeze. Turning from that cheery message to the field, not a half-mile away, I encountered a decided mood-changer—a prison yard.

Brushing dark comparisons aside, I hurried inside and ran smack into a large common dining room. Old folks milled about, aimlessly, it seemed. I spotted a nurse-type in her flowered top and waved my manila folder stuffed with my client's "important papers." A quick explanation and the flowered top flew off in hot pursuit of the needed signatures.

So, I just stood there, looking about, pretending I wasn't looking about. It got awkward—real quick. I perused the menu, listened to the laugh track playing on a large screen television, and studied the "Report Abuse

Here" sign. I turned around and surveyed the room. Any sign of abuse?

A couple old guys slumped at a table, one with his head down and his eyes closed, though his legs were in perpetual motion, the other chattered away undaunted by his less-than-enthusiastic audience. Several figures slept in front of the television, while a young man cleared tables nearby. Several old gals, the lively ones of the bunch, were looking my way. Oh no. One, with a crippled leg, limped toward me. Lord, did she think she knew me? What did she want? Where could I hide?

Too late. She'd seen me. Stretching out her hand, she reached for my arm. Would she fall? Tackle me? I searched wildly for a nurse, an aide; frankly, anyone under seventy would have been a Godsend at that moment.

I watched her hand reach out—and she patted my arm. I managed a squeak. "Need help?" After a brief smile, she limped on, her gaze focused on some mission up ahead.

"Nope. Just glad I can still get around." She sounded like she meant it too. I looked at my arm, where she had patted me. Had she seen my panic? Was she comforting me?

The flowered-shirt nurse trotted up, a satisfied smile alerting me to her success. "The director said you should come back next week for—" I hardly heard the next words. Next week? Come back? Here? Dandy. I marched to the double doors, shoved the handle, and promptly set off every alarm in the place.

The following week was as busy as a spring tornado, but everywhere I went, I saw that hand, felt that gentle pat, and heard those bloody, comforting words, "Just glad...." Life is a mystery. I thought I had accepted that long ago. But now, I was a mystery to myself. When the manila folder was thrust unceremoniously back into my hands, I drove back to that parking lot overlooking the prison yard.

Squaring my shoulders like a soldier facing combat, I marched myself through the doors, breezing right by some old guy sitting in a wheelchair by the front glass doors, his gaze searching the parking lot. Must be waiting for someone. Maybe a son with grandkids—something like that. Sure.

In a moment, I stood before the throng of elderlies, searched for the flower-topped nurse, but instead, a large man in blue lumbered over. Taking my manila envelope like a precious charge, he snail-paced away. Okay—so what's on the menu today? This week? Any card catalogs I could peruse? I skirted by the Elderly Abuse notice.

Weakening, my gaze traveled the room. Before I realized what I'd done, I had stepped further into the room. A woman on my right sat at a table and gazed up at me, her eyes wide and frightened. Was she afraid of me?

I looked away—fast.

A man rocked in his chair—back and forth—while another woman talked and talked though not a soul was listening. The woman on the right cleared her throat. She leaned in, shoulders hunched, using every bit of courage to speak. Without warning, her gaze plunged into my own.

"If you'd just give me the key—I could get out

of here."

My heart stopped. Or it jumped to my throat. It certainly wasn't where it was supposed to be, doing its job. I tried to say something, but no words would form on my lips. Desperate, she repeated her plea.

"If you'd just give me the key—I could get out of here."

Lord have mercy, I couldn't get out of there fast enough. I met the man in blue halfway across the room and bolted for the door. The old man didn't even flinch at the breeze from my passing, his gaze stayed fixed ahead, scanning the parking lot.

I spent the next week trying to rid myself of the echo in my mind, "If you'd just give me the key...." And the feel of my empty chest, where my heart should have been, the pat of a gentle hand, and the horror of knowing that the man in blue was going to wheel that old guy back to the common room—alone.

By the middle of the week, I needed serious therapy. But as that was not an option, I confided my hauntings to a friend of mine, Sammy, Sam for short.

Sam is a dear girl—woman—person, I suppose. In her own way. She listened patiently enough, and then she began her lament. It's the government's lack of decency, a selfish bunch of...causes all our troubles, religious zealots, insensitive relatives, you name it—Sam had a name to blame. When I finally admitted to myself that she wasn't listening, I went home to the tune of "If you'd just give me the key...."

In fact, I never intended to go back to that

nursing home. But in some kind of Christmas Carol twist, my client discovered one more signature was needed.

Fate, sure enough.

This time I came prepared. I ducked my head and shielded my eyes from the prison yard; I whizzed by the old man by the front door; I ignored the menu and practically knocked over a scruffy-bearded kid who loped along to the center of the room. Flower-shirt was back, and she didn't need to ask. She just plucked the manila folder from my grasp and suggested I sit and enjoy the live music before she trotted off.

Live music?

The kid who looked like he had slept on a park bench all night unslung a guitar off his back and sat down in front, smiling, nodding at people like he was having a good time. Joking even!

I leaned against the wall, prepared for nothing. The kid's dark, lanky hair, tattered jeans and threadbare jacket told their own story. He sang country stuff mostly, though he'd stop to answer a question or change tunes at a request. He and the old folks exchanged teasing jibes. Obviously, he'd been here before.

I gazed around the room. Most of the folks had gathered around. The sleepers stayed put—in their own worlds. Some folks rocked, some stared, a few drooled as was their way. But the woman from last week smiled up at the kid through shining eyes. No mention of a key. And the front-door guy had wheeled himself in, one foot tapping away.

Suddenly the manila envelope was thrust into my hands. But I wasn't ready to leave. Why? I don't even like country music.

It's been months now, and I've never gone back. But I am haunted, I tell you—haunted by a gentle pat and a scruffy young man—with a key.

Every Word

Originally published on The Writings of A. K. Frailey
3/31/2017

Lawry considered the long, red scratch on his face. "It'll leave a scar—that's for certain. Just the luck! Spiteful bush! Clip a few branches and wham—raked across the face. Well, I was never handsome, to begin with...."

Lawry dabbed the dried blood with a wet tissue and stumped past his unmade bed to his littered desk. A cup with dried fruit juice, a scattering of cereal flakes, and bread crumbs testified to where he ate a majority of his meals. Tottering piles of books crowded around his computer. He fell into his chair with a sigh.

His mom had knitted him a blue hat with his name in scripted, bold, red letters across the top L-A-W-R-Y three Christmases ago, but never having the courage to actually wear it, he had placed it jauntily on his stuffed monkey who adorned the top of his computer like a good-hearted, though rather mischievous looking, angel.

Maximus Monkey, Ruler-Of-All-He-Surveyed, was the main character in a series of comics that Lawry had been working on for years. A moldy orange rind had somehow landed on Max's shoulder. Lawry winced, and pinching the offending bio-matter in two fingers, he pitched it into an over-filled trash can. He tucked Max's arm against the wall for better support. Though the little monkey still leaned, at least he wasn't in imminent danger of careening to the floor. Lawry peered under his desk; his eyes widened. "Oh, wow! I really need to do something about this mess." He looked for a broom, but as none was in sight, he returned to his computer screen and hit the power button.

He checked his mail. Nothing but spam. No agents or publishers begging rights to any of his stories. He checked the news. "Yep—the world's going to hell in a hand basket—as usual."

He opened his recent story page and stared at the blinking cursor. What could he write about that he hadn't already written? What story was left to tell that hadn't been told a million times over in cyberspace—a universe filled with unread, unloved stories?

A light knock drew a grunt from Lawry's middle.

The knock tried again.

Lawry grunted again, a little louder, a little more articulately. "Yeah, what?"

A young boy, Jimmy, stuck his head through the opening. "Mom said thanks for cutting the hedge, and she's making—hey, you get cut?"

Lawry rolled his eyes. Jimmy had an exasperating habit of stating the obvious as if it was headline news.

"Yeah. It's nothing."

Jimmy took those three words as an invitation and crept into his brother's inner sanctum—holy ground—albeit a messy, holy ground. A badminton racket dangled from Jimmy's hand.

Lawry shifted his gaze away. He wasn't an outdoorsman as today's battle with the hedge surely proved. He sighed, his shoulders slumping even further. He leaned in towards the computer screen, tapping keys aimlessly. *Just look busy.*

"What're you working on?"

"Nothing."

"How about Maximus? He doing anything?"

Lawry's gaze shot to the skinny eight-year-old. How did the little twerp manage to stay so skinny? He ate at least as much as any ravenous jungle animal Lawry had ever read about, but he stayed stick-thin. *Metabolism.* Lawry shifted his heavy frame in the chair. *Damn metabolism.*

"Can you read me something?"

Red, hot blushing fury filled Lawry. It was ridiculously unfair. Here he'd written his heart out for three long years, read every book there was about the art and craft of writing comics, joined clubs, took online classes, worked at a stupid, menial job on the side just to pay his fair share while he still lived at home—yet nothing. Not one,

"Dear Mr. Lawry Lawrence,
We would love to represent you—"

Not even "—*like* to represent you—" Heck "—we'd *consider* representing you—" would be a joy. But no, week after week, he received: "Your work does not fit our needs at this time."

Lawry glanced at Jimmy's hope-filled eyes. He was a lonely little kid. *Doesn't seem to make many friends at school. Just hangs out with his stuffed animals, mostly.*

Lawry's hands dropped to his lap. "I don't have anything new—not really—"

"That's okay. I like all your stuff. How about

'Maximus Meets a Moon Alien?'"

"I read that a hundred times. It's—well—not one of Max's favorites."

Jimmy slid to the edge of Lawry's bed and leaned against it. A stuffed rabbit peeked out from his pants pocket.

Lawry tapped his fingers on his desk and stared straight ahead, unblinking. He cleared his throat. "Maximus doesn't have any favorites. Not anymore. Max is thinking about moving away. Maybe getting a real job—in the real world."

Jimmy's eyes widened, fear rippling across his face. "But Max can't go! He can't leave here. At least not till he saves his Monkey clan—like he's always planning...."

Lawry felt the lump in his throat rise before he realized that his eyes stung. "Maximus can't save anyone, Jimmy. He's really a rather unimportant little monkey. He's decided to settle down and stop all this adventure nonsense. Can't be a silly monkey forever, you know. Gotta grow up sometime."

Jimmy brushed back tears with the back of his hand, pretending he wasn't.

Lawry glanced out of the corner of his eye. He reached up, lifted Maximus off the computer, stared into Maximus' ready-for-anything eyes, and passed him over to his little brother. "You take him. Maybe with you, he can have some fun. He's tired of being stuck in down here every day. Go play badminton with him—or something."

Jimmy slid Maximus under his arm uncertainly. "We can't play alone...."

Lawry huffed a long, drawn-out sigh. "Oh, what the heck. We'll play together. Max can watch."

~~~

Two weeks later, Lawry sat at his computer desk. His face was almost healed, though he had been right, there was a scar. His desk was clean, the floor was swept, and his bed was neatly made. He placed one last sheet of neatly printed paper onto a stack and clipped it into a large, red binder entitled in bold blue letters:

THE ADVENTURES OF MAXIMUS MONKEY
By Lawry Lawrence
For Jimmy Lawrence on His Ninth Birthday

Lawry snatched car keys off his dresser and hustled outside with the binder snuggled under his arm. Jimmy was swinging Maximus from a long "jungle rope" in the backyard. Lawry smiled as Jimmy trotted over.

Jimmy pointed to Max. "He hasn't given up his adventures—see? He's back in the jungle and leading all the other monkeys to safety."

Lawry grinned. He could almost see the entire herd as they swung from branch to branch under the green canopy. He patted Jimmy's shoulder. "Listen, I gotta go to work now, and I probably won't be back until late—but I wanted to give you this. It isn't much, I know, but you always liked my stories. I figure they're best in your hands.

Jimmy hugged the binder—his eyes wide. "Wow! You sure? I mean—I can't believe it. Now I can read 'em whenever I want. I can read them to Max!" Jimmy scurried back to the tree, untied
~~~

Max's dangling arm, and showed the little monkey the cover of the binder. Max's face glowed.

~~~

Fifty-six years passed, and Lawry sat in a wheelchair near a bright window. His mind wandered endlessly after a severe stroke, and the ravages of diabetes took his body places he never intended to go. Speaking was a challenge now, but he could hear as well as ever. His ears were cocked for the light tread of his brother returning home in the evenings. *The shadows are growing long. Soon, he'll come. He'll sit with me awhile—he always does. Green day—almost feel—*

The door opened and Jimmy stepped in, heavier, stooped a bit, and gray hair crowned his head. "Hey, Lawry. The grandkids were going through the attic over the weekend, and guess what they found?"

A bald-spotted, dustier version of his former self, but still staring out of those read-for-anything eyes, Maximus Monkey landed in Lawry's lap. Lawry blinked. His hand, as well as his voice, shook as he lifted the adventuresome critter. "I—almost—remember—"

Jimmy chuckled as he scraped a chair near, into the dwindling sunlight. "Don't worry. I remember every word." Jimmy leaned in, patted Lawry on the knee, and grinned. "Once upon a time, there was a monkey named Maximus, and he had grand plans..."
~~~

Lilliputians

Originally published on The Writings of A. K. Frailey
4/14/2017

"It's the little things that tie us down—you know—like the Lilliputians."

Adam snorted; his eyes stayed glued to his phone. "Life's what you make of it, Grandma." His attention wavered. She said something he couldn't catch.

He scrolled. "Yeah, sure, whatever." There were three new messages, and he was itching to check his Facebook and Twitter pages. His stomach rumbled. He checked the time. Sigh. He knew his duty. "Hey, have you eaten yet, Grandma?"

Her puzzled frown annoyed him. It was a simple question; it shouldn't cause brain strain.

"I—I don't think so.... But don't worry. I'm not hungry. You go ahead and check your box now and then we can chat."

On autopilot, Adam scooted the kitchen chair out and sat with his arms propped on the table. There were a lot of posts to scroll through...and through.

A sudden bang snapped his head up. Grandma's stricken expression propelled him to his feet. She stood in the middle of the room, staring at the fallen teakettle as if it had flown through the window. A pool of steaming water slowly spread across the floor.

"You okay? Did you burn yourself?" The stovetop was glowing red, and the kettle spout smoked like a chimney. Adam gritted his teeth as a wrenching pain punched his gut. He led Grandma to the table.

"Here, sit down. I'll clean up. What were you doing anyway?" He grabbed a towel and tossed it over the wet floor. The twin pools of confusion and disappointment in Grandma's eyes sent another twist to Adam's gut.

"I just wanted to make us a cup of tea—for our chat." She plopped down heavily on a chair. Her right hand stayed fixed with the palm up.

Snatching a potholder, Adam conveyed the kettle back to the stovetop and turned it off. He plucked ice from the freezer, wrapped it in a paper towel, and handed it to Grandma. "Here, put this on your hand."

"Why?"

"Cause you burned it, see? It's red there. Might blister. Dang it, Grandma, you know you're not supposed to touch the stove! Just let me do it next time, okay?"

Grandma blinked back tears and straightened her shoulders. "I'm not a child—or a loony—you know. I can still make a cup of tea!"

"Sure, sure. I know. I shouldn't yell. Just Mom will get so mad that you got hurt under my—"

Adam's phone chimed. He snatched it up and stared. "Oh, brother! Some idiot just plastered a bunch of political slogans on my page." He barely glanced at Grandma. "Just a minute, I gotta—"

Grandma shook her head as she rose and returned to her tea-making.

An hour later, Adam looked up. Grandma's place was empty. A cold cup of tea with a slice of lemon balanced on the saucer and a little cookie sat before him. He stood and looked around. Her washed teacup lay neatly drying on the drainboard. Long evening shadows slanted across the tidy kitchen.

Adam tiptoed down the hall. “Grandma?” He peeked into her room. There she lay, sleeping peacefully on her bed, her hands folded over her trim waist. *She’s really a beauty—funny I never noticed before.*

~~~

Two months later, Adam sat beside Mom on the front pew at church. Grandma was laid out in her finest, and her hands once again rested in quiet repose over her neat, trim waist.

Mom’s shoulders shook as she covered her face with her hands. Dad wrapped his arm around her and leaned in. “You were always there for her, honey. Now, it’s time to let go.”

Adam stared straight ahead. All he could see through his parched, unfocused eyes was a cold cup of tea with a slice of lemon on the side. His phone vibrated in his pocket. But he only felt the sharp snap of strings breaking
~~~

Translator

Originally published on The Writings of A. K. Frailey
4/28/2017

To be honest, I thought she was a bag-lady. The long, scraggly, gray hair, the oversized, shapeless sweater, the dark circles under her eyes, and the haunted expression all pointed to one, obvious conclusion—a conclusion I was in too big a hurry to even pity.

The boys were due home at any minute, and the babysitter would expect me to have dinner ready. Julian hated to be late, and since we missed our date night the month before, I wasn't about to let anything mess with this one. I felt a head cold coming on, the refrigerator had gone on the blink, and I was struggling to maintain a civil, if not cordial, relationship with my boss at work. It had been a tough week.

So, when the disheveled woman appeared in line ahead of me, I wouldn't have bothered with a second look—if it hadn't been for the flowers. The incongruity of the scene struck me like a splash of cold water. I even dropped my fish fillets. There she stood, or stooped rather, hugging this glorious bouquet. A worn-out bag-lady with spring flowers. Crazy, right?

I rescued my fish, hurriedly emptied my cart, and watched with unabashed fascination as this odd spectacle leaned forward and whispered in Spanish to the cashier.

I rolled my eyes. I had worked as a translator long enough to understand exactly what she said, but I didn't really want to get mixed up in some crazy situation in the middle of a grocery store. I had more pressing matters to attend.

The cashier stared blankly and shook her head. "I don't understand." She looked beseechingly at the line forming and called to the other cashier. "You understand Spanish?"

The other cashier shrugged. It wasn't his concern. Realizing that doing nothing meant this situation would take longer; I volunteered to assist. "She asked how much." I pointed to the woman's bundle. "For the flowers."

This time, it was the cashier who rolled her eyes. "It's on the tag."

I translated and pointed to the aforementioned stub.

The woman's hand shook as she considered the cost. I sighed. *Lord, she probably doesn't even have enough money.* I had already opened my wallet, and though I had more than enough to buy my groceries and her flowers several times over, the principle of the situation rankled. What in God's name had she been thinking when she picked up those stupid flowers?

Almost as if she had read my mind, she blinked and answered my question. With a shaking hand, she pulled a tiny purse out of her shapeless sweater, and hugging her flowers even tighter, she pulled folded bills into the light of day, explaining all the while in her husky, whisper voice.

"Mi hijo…solo diecinueve…trajeron su cuerpo a casa hoy. Mi esposo está trayendo su foto, y tienen una bandera—pero—yo quería flores…."

My translation skills kicked in automatically.

My son…only nineteen…they brought his body home today. My husband is bringing his picture, and they have a flag—but—I wanted flowers….

She peered at me, her eyes brimming. "*¿Tú entiendes? Estaba en la flor de su juventud.*"

I closed my eyes, but I could not escape her meaning.

You understand? He was in the flower of his youth.

She smoothed the bills on the counter and nodded to the cashier, who snatched them up and efficiently offered her change.

The cashier and I both watched the lady over the threshold, even as we went about the business of packing my groceries.

"Thanks for helping out." The young woman peered at me. "What did she say?"

I opened my mouth, but I couldn't explain. My translation would miss too much.

The cashier forced her curiosity aside as the next patron stepped up. "Never mind. Just glad it worked out. I thought for sure she didn't have enough money."

I edged away, my eyes scanning the parking lot for a husband with a photo in his hand.

The cashier called after me. "Guess it shows—you never know, eh?"

I hefted my bulging bag into my arms and nodded. "You're right. We never know...

Native Elements

Originally published on The Writings of A. K. Frailey
4/12/2017

Cyril swore under his breath as he stared at the mounting black clouds sweeping across the mountain range. The pine trees swayed with warning sighs as the wind whistled through their branches. Crows whirled towards earth, out-flying the looming threat.

"Stupid weatherman never said anything about a storm." Cyril didn't realize he had spoken aloud until Jeanette curled her arm through his and clucked her disapproval.

"Weather*woman*, Cyrus. Not *man*. Besides, no one is perfect."

Cyril didn't doubt that for a moment. He had never really intended to invite Jeanette to his private sanctuary—but in an unguarded moment he had pontificated, "Kids today are out of their native element," and Jeanette, being his superior by two grade levels and French proficiency, had laughed. Smirked really.

She had sat across from him in the teacher's lounge, sipped her black coffee, nibbled her wheat crackers, and shook her curly-haired head. "Native element? What, pray tell, is a kid's native element, Sorrel?"

Cyril squeezed his eyes shut against the memory. His face flushed, as it always did when she mutilated his name. When she first practiced her ruinous arts at a teacher's convention— "Oh, good, here's Floral, so we're well represented—"

He had dared to object. "The name is Cyril—

not Sorrel, not Floral. Can you remember that?"

The flock of attending teachers froze in the face of his unflinching correction, but Jeannette merely grinned like a Cheshire cat. "Oh, *Creel,* don't get all flaky and fall to pieces."

His only retort had been a mute glare while his co-workers simply chuckled and wandered toward other entertainment. He had been bested. Clearly.

For two years, he waged a stoic campaign to keep his name unaltered, but Jeanette found myriad atrocious variations to spring on him—passing in the hall, at meetings, and even as she waved goodbye in the parking lot. In the teacher's lounge, she would rattle on about her latest date, fashionable clothes, a got-to-go-see movie, progressive teaching, antiquated traditions, and whatever else fueled her current passion while he doodled swaying pine trees on a memo pad and retreated into icy politeness.

Occasionally, he'd vary his day by hunting up extra resources for a struggling student, but most sixth graders hated math and made little attempt to hide their distaste for the subject in particular—or for him in general. Even when he lugged in architects' drawings, carpentry notes, checkbooks, and myriad other real-world examples of math's viability, he would still be slapped down with the oft-opined sentiment, "We're never going to use this stuff—it's a waste of time."

He might as well be forcing broccoli down innocent kids' throats. At least, Jeannette never made him feel like the enemy—a fool—but never an enemy. Perhaps that was why he accepted her question as a challenge and invited her to come to the mountains with him and experience the native elements herself.

Only when the muscled P. E. teacher, Mr. James, squeezed his shoulder and intoned the words, "Best of luck, ol' pal," did Cyril realize that staring down a pack of hyenas would have been a wiser option.

Their afternoon started more optimistically than he anticipated. Jeanette had met him in the parking lot decked out in cowboy boots, jeans, and a leather jacket.

He refrained from shaking his head and merely jiggled his keys. "Mind if I drive?"

Jeannette shrugged in utter nonchalance. "Might as well. You know where we're going—I suppose." Her grin widened wickedly as she added, "Series."

He sped up the winding road and, after arriving, started down the simplest and shortest trail. She bounced along at his side pointing out every squirrel and bird in hyper-exultation. When they returned to the parking lot, she deflated. "Is that it? I mean—that's all you got, Virile?"

Cyril's squinted at the lowering sun and considered his revenge—trail number five, meant for experienced hikers with a loud, splashing stream, a long, steep incline, two narrow passes, and one precipitous drop. His eyes narrowed as he returned to the forest.

They floundered across the bubbly stream and scrambled up the first incline when a warning rumbled across the sky. Distant trees swayed as a murmur rustled through the foliage. Cyril considered the low sun and a slight twinge shivered down his spine.

Jeannette scanned the waving branches with a frown. "How far have we come?"

"About halfway."

A brilliant flash of light made them blink as black clouds bundled together overhead.

That's when he spouted his politically incorrect fury on the weatherperson. He could feel her arm squirming around his; searching for something he was loath to offer.

"Half-way? Seriously, Cereus, what were you thinking—"

He felt the familiar, hot flush rise to the roots of his hair. Cyril shook Jeanette's arm away and snapped around like a wounded panther. "C-Y-R-I-L! My name is CYRIL!"

Jeannette blinked as the sky blustered overhead.

Cyril wrung his hands in a pantomime of strangling something—or someone—and bellowed. "Now shut up and quit acting like the stuck-up, little snob you always are, and let me think of the quickest way out of here." He looked up and down the paths and then pointed ahead. "Let's go on."

A fair imitation of a rock wall, Jeanette folded her arms and glared.

Cyril stomped away with a wave of his hand. "Fine. Be a smart-ass. See if that gets you over the stream again. Not that I'd go back that way. But enjoy the incline and don't slide off the edge of anything. There are about thirty minutes of light left—you might make it to a cave or something before night sets in."

He was nearly a quarter of a mile down the

path in the pelting rain when he heard her splashing steps. She charged into him, grabbed his shirt, and yanked, sending them both careening into the mud. With her limp hair streaming across her face, she rounded a slug on his shoulder.

"You stupid pig! Heartless idiot! Why I spent the last two years being nice to you is more than I can figure. But I never expected this!"

Cyril's eyes widened as he staggered to his feet and watched her slip and slide. "You've been *nice*? When was that? I must've missed it. I could have sworn you spent the last two years tormenting me with your cruel, twisted, little name-calling."

Lightning flared, and thunder crashed over their heads as Jeanette clenched her fists, facing him, bedraggled. "Always so high and mighty, aren't you? Always getting your pants in a twist when I try to add a little fun into your life. Can't climb down from your superior loft in the high and mighty world of algebra and advanced math. You think I couldn't teach math? I could. I just chose to do something a little more creative, something that means something TO ME!"

A deafening crack of thunder sent them pelting down the path. Cyril slipped and threw his arms out for balance. The downpour increased, but Jeannette raced on. Cyril snatched her sleeve and pulled her to a jog. "You'll fall, stupid. There's a drop coming."

Jeannette yanked away and raced ahead even faster. She shrieked as she started sliding down a steep incline.

Cyril grabbed her arm and pulled back,

sprawling them both onto the muddy path.

Jeannette's face twisted; she slapped his hand. "I'm not stupid!"

Cyril climbed to his knees, crawled under the shelter of a tree and let his head fall against the trunk, leaning back with heaving breaths. "Neither am I. Though every time you speak French, smirking as if I am too dense to understand, or when you mutilate my name—"

Jeannette rose shakily to her feet, slapped mud from her jeans, squared her shoulders, and started forward. She stepped into a dangling vine and yelped as a thorn scratched her cheek. She turned on Cyril, her voice low and menacing. "If you're trying to get revenge—mission accomplished."

Cyril rose and blinked at her silhouette in the dim light. He glanced at his muddy watch, sighed, and grabbed her hand. "Mission aborted. I'm an idiot, and we need to get out of here—now."

Jeannette pulled away. "Don't touch me!"

"You want to wander aimlessly in the dark under tons of swaying trees? Let's make a truce and get out alive, okay?" Cyril stretched out his hand.

Jeannette turned and charged up the path.

~~~

As they sat dripping and muddy in the school parking lot, a sickle moon peeked through the vestiges of drifting clouds. Cyril hadn't looked at her during the whole, miserable drive back to the city. She had stared straight ahead, silent as a tomb. When he parked, he expected her to bolt,
~~~

but she just sat there.

Finally, he broke the ice with the most inane comment he ever made. “Well, at least it’s Friday.”

She stared at him a long moment, shifted in her seat, and faced him. “Native elements? You want the kids to experience the wonders of—”

Cyril let his head drop back against the headrest, though he would have welcomed a brick wall. He took a long, cleansing breath. “I wasn’t expecting a storm of biblical proportions. I just wanted—”

Jeanette lifted her hand. “No, I get it. I just wish you’d have told me, not tried to kill me.” Her gaze dropped to the floor. “I was just joking. It was all in fun.”

The lump in his throat surprised Cyril. It was hard to swallow away. “Not so fun for me.”

They sat in silence, the school building a rectangular shadow looming in the background.

Cyril rubbed his dirty fingers together. “The woods—the natural world—it’s like God made it just for me. Thousands have been there before, but for a little while, it’s all mine. No forcing dreaded math problems on squirming kids—”

Jeannette sighed and wiped a stray strand of hair from her eyes. “Most kids think French is stupid. After all, who needs a teacher when there’s Google translator?”

Cyril folded his hands and shrugged. “Google would have me ordering snails for breakfast.”

The barest hint of Jeannette’s smile glimmered between the neon light posts and the black night. “To be totally honest, variables scare me. Letters smacked up against numbers, it seems wrong, somehow.”

Cyril never knew exactly what came over him, but he reached across the seat and lifted Jeanette's hand, lacing her fingers with his. "Actually, they can do amazing things together."

Jeanette tilted her head, the moonlight highlighting a teasing smile. "Like thunderstorms in native elements—Cyril?"

Cyril grinned.

Persian

Originally published on The Writings of A. K. Frailey
4/26/2017

"They don't think like us—you know that—don't you?" The fluffy, striped Persian with piercing blue eyes stretched lazily across the porch floor in a patch of sunlight. Two kittens batted the leaves of a potted plant like players in an obscure Olympic game.

A miniature Panther sat on his haunches and blinked at a passing farm truck. "But they're highly motivated; that's what troubles me. Their whole demeanor of desperate devotion hides an unscrupulous plot—a cunning trick—to be sure.

"Unscrupulous? You've been listening to the boy at his lessons again, haven't you?" Persian flicked her tail and eyed her kittens. "You give them too much credit. Most are as stupid as posts, though Clarabelle, now, she may have shepherding in her blood, but notice which critters she chooses to corral. Wouldn't mind nipping that puppy in the heels, I'd warrant."

Panther stretched. "You'd think the bipeds would sense the tension, but no, they just pat everyone on the head in the same enthusiastic way. The lady's the worst, repeating that stupid mantra—*My little loves*—revolting.

A little boy jogged to the bank by the roadside and watched a tractor rumble nearer. Clarabelle raced by in a blur, weaving close to the huge, revolving tires.

Persian rose. "She's at it again. One of these

da—"

The boy screamed.

Persian scrambled down the wooden steps and raced across the yard with Panther dashing close behind.

The tractor rolled down the road—oblivious. The boy scuttled down the embankment and trotted to the pavement. He lifted a limp, fluffy, little body off the blacktop. Clarabelle barked and raced in circles around him.

Persian yowled. "Darius!"

Panther shivered. "I wondered where he'd gotten to."

Tears streamed down the boy's face as he climbed the hill and jogged toward the house. A lady flew out the door and raced down the steps. She stopped and knelt on the freshly mown grass at the boy's side.

Persian cantered closer and swirled between them, meowing plaintively.

A pitiful cry issued from the limp kitten.

The woman looked from the Persian to the boy, one outstretched finger caressing the kitten's head. "Look, even his mama's worried.... I'll take him inside and see what I can do. You go off to Daddy. He's in the barn." She lifted the limp body into her arms.

The boy stared up at her mutely.

"Go on; he needs you. We'll see—" She turned and climbed the steps.

The boy watched her disappear behind the screen door, stuffed his hands into his pockets, and trudged away toward the barn.

Persian stood, glaring at the door. She trotted forward, scampered up the steps, and clawed at the screen.

Clarabelle sprang onto the porch and nosed her. “It’s no use. They’d just throw you out.” She sat on her haunches. “I tried to get in a few times, but—”

The Persian turned with a snarl and raked Clarabelle across the nose. The collie jumped with a yelp and trotted away with one baleful, backward glance.

Panther edged closer to Persian, eyeing the retreating figure. “Take it easy. There’s nothing you can do.” He stepped between the mother and the door. “The lady will do what she can. You better get back to the others before something else happens.”

Persian yowled. “He’s my kitten!”

“They think he’s theirs. No point in arguing.”

Persian darted down the steps and hurried away, a warning growl vibrating deep in her chest.

Panther trudged down the steps and headed toward the barn.

Clarabelle stepped in Panther’s way. “I was only trying to help. Darius would already be dead if I hadn’t been there.” Clarabelle lifted her nose to the wind as two other dogs galloped closer. “But I shouldn’t be surprised—Persian never liked me.”

Panther eyed the collie, blinked, and then turned. “Like as not, you pushed Darius under the wheels.”

Clarabelle sneezed and watched Panther amble away before the two puppies pummeled into her. She snapped at them. “There’s been a tragedy, fools! Quit acting like drooling idiots.”

The hound snorted. “You mean that ball of

calico fluff? Please, it's been wandering far afield since the first day Persian let him out of the barn. I always said, coyotes or cars—"

The beagle yawned. "Never did see the use of all these darn cats. Two would do the job just as well. Sides, they're so narcissistic!"

Clarabelle tackled the beagle and nipped him in the ear. "Awful big word for such a small quadruped." She cocked her head toward the barn. "I'm going to check on my boy. He'll be taking it hard. Always does."

~~~

The sun flickered between the tree trunks as it crested the horizon. The lady, the man, and the boy stood with bowed heads near a small mound of freshly dug earth.

The boy raked his sleeve across his tear-streaked face.

The man slapped a cap on his head and shuffled his feet. "It's just a kitten for heaven's—"

The woman glared at him.

The man knelt down beside the boy and squeezed his shoulder. "It's part of life on a farm, son; you gotta accept that."

The boy leaned forward and buried his face into the man's chest, his sobs muffled by the man's plaid shirt.

The man cleared his throat, glanced at the woman, and lifted the boy into his arms. He placed the child high on his shoulder and carried him away.

The woman sighed and picked her way across
~~~

the dewy grass to the house.

Persian trotted to the small mound, sniffed, and scratched the crumbly surface.

Panther ambled over. "You've got two left. Not bad—considering."

Persian's one eye pierced him with an icy glare. "You'll never understand."

Panther yawned and strolled away. "Not my job—understanding. I'm a hunter. That's why I'm here."

Persian closed her one good eye and sat on her haunches.

Clarabelle circled around and plunked herself down out of scratching range. She blinked at the rising sun. "Males don't think like us. Can't grasp what it's like." She rose and trotted over to another, slightly larger mound, covered in short grass and dandelions. She pawed at the mound and then stared at Persian. "Poison. It was a mistake—the man felt bad—but she died a terrible death just the same."

Persian's whiskers twitched. "You think you understand me?" Her yowl was incredulous.

Clarabelle shook her coat and trotted toward a car pulling into the driveway. "Someday, there will be mounds for us all."

Persian climbed the porch steps and was about to settle down in the sun when the woman came out and scooped her into her arms. She sat on the large, wooden rocking chair and smoothed Persian's ruffled fur. She tucked a stray lock of her gray hair back into her disheveled bun. "Ah, Lordy. It's not easy getting old; seeing so much hurt and loss and not able to stop a bit of it."

Persian couldn't help herself. She stared

across the emerald lawn, over the treacherous road, toward the concealing woods, and her whole body relaxed into the soft folds of the woman's lap. A vibrating purr began deep within her being. Someone understood.

The Visit

Originally published on The Writings of A. K. Frailey
6/23/2017

Autumn was cold that year, frigid by all accounts. But in Chicago, I hardly noticed since I couldn't see many signs of life on the Southside, much less the beauty of autumn that I was accustomed to from my Wisconsin upbringing. I felt cold most of the time I lived there, no matter the season.

I taught kids for as far back as I could remember. Now, I was getting paid to follow my passion. It was a good deal, except I felt like a fish out of water. My white skin didn't fit in, my naiveté often set me up for a fall, and my past haunted me.

Dealing with kids from broken homes kept me safe from dealing with my own broken life. Teaching assured me that I was in charge. Until a letter arrived.

My dad had been out of my life for so many years; I could hardly remember his face. I harbored no hatred. No guilt. Just a mountain of sadness. Sadness that kept me comfortable in its very familiarity. I liked walls. And a mountain makes a terrific wall.

During my second year in Chicago, I received a letter from my father. He was going to be on the North Shore, touring with his new wife. They were both highly educated, well paid, and living in another world. I remember the feel of the crisp, thick paper in my hand, and my surprise that it had actually traversed the distance from his home out east to my present abode. Quality paper like that hardly seemed real as I scanned the stained, cement sidewalk, the broken glass littering the street side, the scraps of candy papers blown by a forlorn wind.

He had asked if he could drop by and see me. A short visit, since he'd only spend the weekend in town. But would I mind? Seeing him. Visiting a bit.

I stuffed the letter in my jacket pocket and descended the apartment steps. Looking around, I realized there was nowhere for me to go. My lesson plans were complete for the following week; the afterschool kids had gone home hours ago; everyone I knew was gone for the day. Yet, I must go somewhere.

I trudged back to school with no object in mind. It was late on Friday afternoon; no one would be around. As I crossed the playground toward the redbrick building, I saw Mr. Carol. His stooped back bent over a broom as he swept up the latest mess in a continuous stream of litter and broken bottles. I wondered for the zillionth time where all the glass came from. Did vicious, little gremlins dance about each night and sprinkle broken bits like confetti? Hardly likely. But it was a better vision than the alternative.

I stepped up to the old man, though I realized anew that he wasn't really old. It was his clothes, his shoulders, and his demeanor that left the impression of elderliness. Oldness. Worn out like his faded jeans. "Hey, Mr. Carol. You're working late."

It was a stupid comment. He worked early, late, and all the time in between. A maintenance man's work was never done.

Mr. Carol turned, startled. He rarely spoke, and I never dared to break through his own private wall. But this time, he smiled. Looking me up and down, he seemed to see something that I didn't realize I was showing. With a wave of his hand, he pointed to the cement steps leading to the front door. "Hey, yourself, young lady. What you doing here?"

Feeling very much like one of the kids I taught, I shrugged. I didn't have an answer, except the one in my pocket.

He leaned the broom against the wall and lowered himself to the middle step and gestured. "Sit a minute. Keep an old man company."

I remember the burning tears that filled my eyes. I didn't want to cry. I didn't want my mountain to crumble. But I sat anyway. For a brief second, it seemed as if the world was perfect, as if everything were where it was supposed to be, and I was destined to be sitting on the third step with a man in faded jeans and a worn, blue shirt. I clasped my hands tight, hoping to hold my voice steady. "Do you have any kids, Mr. Carol?"

Mr. Carol looked off into the blurry distance and tented his fingers in steeple position as if in prayer. "Yeah, I do. A daughter. But I haven't seen her since she was a baby." He looked at me. "She'd be about your age by now."

The rightness of things settled into quiet conviction as I sighed. "I have a dad."

He smiled. "Most do."

"I haven't seen him for a long time." I pulled the letter out of my pocket.

Mr. Carol stayed very still as if he was afraid

of frightening a mouse back into its hole.

I tapped the cream-colored envelope. “He’s going to be in town and wants to see me. But it’s been an awfully long time. And he’s bringing his wife.”

Mr. Carol leaned back onto the second step and stretched his legs. “You know, I have thought of writing such a letter. Many times. Though I have no wife to bring along.” He sighed. “But, you know, my writings not so good. And my girl has got her own life now. Besides, I don’t have anything to offer. It’s too late to meet up and start over. But, still, I’d like to tell her something.”

The earth was rumbling under my feet. I could feel clods of dirt scuttle passed me as my mountain, and my voice, shook. “What would you tell her?”

“I’d tell her that I never stopped thinking about her. That I wish I had been a better man, a better father. A real dad.” He shook his head. “There’s no excuse, I know. I failed. I wasn’t there for her, and I’ll always be in the wrong about that.” He stood up and took the broom from the wall. “But, you know, I regret it. Deeply. I think of her every day.”

I stood up and crunched the letter back into my pocket. “You think I should see him?”

This time, Mr. Carol shrugged. “I’ve found that it wasn’t the things I done that I regretted the most. It was the things I didn’t do, the things I left undone. You know what I mean?”

I pictured the lined, school paper stacked on a shelf in my apartment; it wasn’t thick and fancy, but it was letter sized. “Yeah. I do.”

Mr. Carol returned to his endless sweeping as he nodded. “Good.”

Decorum

Originally published on The Writings of A. K. Frailey
8/4/2017

Josie hated going to parties though she often spent hours imagining what they would be like beforehand. This party, a fundraiser for her father's high school alma mater, involved an actual meal with fancy china, long-stemmed glasses, and two forks. She entered the reception area and instantly knew that she wore an invisibility cloak. Not only did no one look in her direction, two people actually bumped into her as they headed across the room, apparently thinking they could walk right through her.

She tugged at her black dress, trying to keep it from riding up her legs. It was already too short for her comfort, but her mom had insisted that it was the style nowadays. Yeah, stylish. That was Josie. About as stylish as a Jerusalem cricket on a potato leaf. *Sheesh. Couldn't anyone make dresses that fit a human body these days?* Josie crept to a corner and hoped that her invisibility cloak would hide her from her parents as well as the scintillating society of Riverside High.

~~~

Kendrick Murphy tugged at his tie, flapped his hands at his side, and wondered if it would be rude to put his hands in his pockets. Why on earth had he agreed to this? Yes, he did want to support a worthy cause. Yes, he had spent four
~~~

hideously bored years here, and he saw no reason to neglect the current generation's allotment of torturous education. But. Still. Well, at least Jane was having a stupendous time. She swirled around the reception room like a ballroom dancer. And all eyes danced with her.

Whoa! Was that Mac? MacMcDermit? The football coach? Why hell, the man hadn't aged a day! Oh, no, of course not. Too young. No wrinkles around the eyes. Oh, Lord in Heaven, that's his son. There he is, shuffling on the boy's right. Good, God! How he's aged!

Kendrick stepped closer, leaned in, and nodded his head. *Yep. This whole evening is some kind of retro-inferiority-complex come to haunt me.*

~~~

Jane's smile began to ache. Her gaze scoured the room. Where in the world was Josie? *She ought to be helping out. Oh, there in a corner, hiding, as usual.* Jane patted the arm of the lady in front of her, Sue Some-thing-or-other, and swayed over to the dark side of the room. As she drew closer, she wiggled two fingers expressively toward Josie.

Josie's eyes widened in terror. *Oh, no! She wants me out there. Where everyone is mingling, chatting, and pretending to have a marvelous time. Me. And. My. Invisibility Cloak. Out There?*

Jane laid a hand on Josie's shoulder. "You're too timid for your own good; now look at your father over there. He's chatting away with that old man and some young guy as if they're old friends."
~~~

Josie refrained from stating the obvious. She tried to disappear entirely, but her mom's hand would not let her dematerialize.

"Listen, I know how hard it is." Jane leaned in and whispered. "I hate these things too. I always feel like a fool, wondering what everyone says the second I turn my back."

Josie blinked as if someone had just shoved a light in her face.

"But listen, honey, it's part of life, part of growing up. We have to do these things. It's called social decorum. You need to get good at it."

Josie blushed and stared at her high-heeled shoes.

"All you have to do is walk around and introduce yourself. Say that your dad went here and that you—"

A tall man in his late fifties sauntered over, swishing a drink in his hand. "Hey, are you Gracie? You remember—"

Jane gave her daughter a little shove. "Off you go now. Be nice. Make friends."

Josie nearly tripped, but she tottered into the noisy room. Her dad was talking sports with the old guy. *Well, at least he's saved.* She looked back over her shoulder. Her mom had dragged the tall man over to a crowd of women, and suddenly there was a burst of laughter. Apparently, the tall man just met the *real* Gracie. Josie stood in the middle of the room and wondered how long until the appalling dinner and the hour of retreat. Her gaze fell on a thin, short girl about her age standing in the shadows—*her* shadows.

When Josie sauntered up, she met the girl's eyes as they fixed on her. Josie shrugged. "You here with your dad?"

The girl shrugged back. "My mom." She pointed. "Over there."

Josie glanced to the far side of the room. A short, plump woman with striking red hair and a tight dress exchanged laughs with a bubbly assortment of guests. "Well, at least she's having fun." Josie turned and stuck out a limp hand. "My name's Josie.

The girl returned the handshake, limp for limp, like two octopus tentacles passing in deep water. "Karen. Nice to meet you."

She has good manners. Wish I'd thought to say that. "Nice to meet you, too." Josie surveyed the bar on the right and realized that there wasn't a single soda bottle among them. *Hopeless.* "So, where do you—"

The lights flickered, and conversation stopped for a second before it picked up to the tune of everyone strolling toward the dining room.

Karen teetered on her heels, sticking close to Josie's side. As they entered the huge room lit by ornate chandeliers and arrayed with round tables decorated with flowers and fine dinnerware, Karen froze. "Oh, no. I don't know which fork to use. I meant to ask mom, but I forgot."

Josie grinned. She tugged at her dress and watched her Mom and Dad sit side-by-side looking into each other's eyes as if they shared a grim secret. Suddenly, she understood.

Decorum. Society. Two forks.

"Use the one on the outside first. But don't worry. No one will notice. They're scared too. Trust me."

Drama Trauma

Originally published on The Writings of A. K. Frailey
8/18/2017

Kelly shuffled forward in line at the Save-All Market and averted her eyes.

Directly in front of her, a woman with spiky hair and dangling earrings swatted a heavyset four-year-old as she tossed items on the counter.

The girl whined a long, high-pitched squeal.

The woman swatted again and flung an iPhone into the child's grubby hand. Gleefully, the child tapped the screen, and suddenly a Disney movie theme blared.

Kelly's gaze grazed the cashier's face in the midst of an eye roll.

A young man wearing an orange uniform and carrying a sweeper stepped near. He waved at the little girl and grinned. "One of my favorites, too."

The woman swung around and glared, one arm barring the child from leaning forward. "Get away from her, pervert!"

Kelly's eyes rounded as she watched the young man back away, hunch his shoulders, and with grieved eyes, begin sweeping near the restrooms.

"Twenty-five dollars and eighty cents." The cashier pushed her glasses up her nose and waited, her eyes fixed on the space above the woman's head.

As Kelly fumbled to unload her purchases, her gaze meandered to the newspaper selection. On the left, bold headlines screamed: "Aliens Alive and Menacing on Mars!" Before she had time to consider the possibilities, much less the syntax, a man jostled her arm as he snatched a magazine with a full-color picture of a terrorist holding a severed head with the headline: "World War III Imminent."

"Fourteen sixty-five." The cashier considered the state of her nails.

Kelly slipped her card through the scanner mechanically as the woman and child struggled for control of the iPhone. She could hear their sharp argument rise to hypersonic pitch as she scurried her cart to the door. Another swat set off a long wail.

Maneuvering her car across the parking lot, Kelly spotted a disheveled man with long, stringy hair and a tattered coat huddled on the corner where she had to turn. Kelly's heart raced. How fast could she pass him? Or should she stop and give him something? The man, in his forties maybe but roughly used, held a sign. "Out of work and going blind—Please help."

Kelly knew she had a ten-dollar bill in the front pocket of her purse, but it would take a lot of agility to get it out, steer close enough to hand it out, and not tick off the line of cars behind her. Kelly sped up.

Once on the highway, Kelly began to breathe a little easier. Then a series of red revolving lights caught her eye. She slowed and peered at a police officer waving traffic onto one lane. "Oh heck." Kelly blew air between her lips and tapped the steering wheel.

As she navigated to the left, she glanced over and saw a smashed truck cab and a mangled tractor. An ambulance siren wailed nearby, and a woman sat on the embankment, her head in her hands. She seemed to be sobbing. Kelly's attention snapped back to the road. The police officer waved her on.

When she finally picked up speed, Kelly darted a glance at her watch. She'd be late for class if she didn't hurry. Her foot pressed the pedal nearer the floor. She upped the volume on her favorite music and lost herself in scenes from a horror movie she had seen over the weekend.

When she slipped into her seat, her professor waved to a large screen in the front of the room. "Today, we will focus on the oppressive state of our culture and how we are destroying our world." Kelly tapped on her recorder. This would be on the exam—no doubt about it.

By the time she pushed her way through the front door late that night, Kelly's shoulders drooped, and she had a splitting headache. A light shone in the kitchen, so she wandered inside.

Her mom, wrapped in a garish orange bathrobe, sat plowing through a quart of chocolate ice cream.

Kelly tossed her car keys on the counter and nodded.

Her mom nodded back. "Lousy day. You?"

Kelly shuffled to the cabinet, snatched up a rumpled bag of broken cookies, and grabbed a spoon out of an open drawer. "Nothing new. You know—same ol', same ol'." She plopped down beside her mother, poured the cookies on the table, and dug in.

Visions of Grandeur

Originally published on The Writings of A. K. Frailey
9/1/2017

Loren crouched low as she snuck up behind the enemy, one finger poised over the trigger. She knew all too well the price she'd pay if she missed.

The enemy swarmed off to the right—they'd be beautiful if they weren't so dang dangerous. She had children to protect. Creeping ahead, she spied their base of operations.

Got 'em now!

Exhilaration pumped adrenaline into Loren's bloodstream. She rose to her feet, both hands braced over the canister, aimed, and fired. Direct hit!

The swarm didn't know what had happened. They dropped onto the porch floor and buzzed furiously until Loren swept them into the front garden bed with her foot. She exhaled a long, cleansing breath. *Thank—*

"Mom! You know it's wrong to kill bugs. They're a part of nature, and we're supposed to respect them!"

Loren turned and faced her irate eleven-year-old daughter; the wasp spray canister hung limply in her left hand.

Kara, a self-appointed bug expert, propped her hands on her hips like a furious schoolteacher. She had watched numerous YouTube videos and read articles online about native, Illinois insects. In her spare time, she copied photos and made collages, which she hung up around the house, underlined with dire warnings about the loss of native species.

Loren chewed her lip and rubbed her jaw as if it had been struck. "Listen, young lady, I got stung this morning, and your baby brother got stung yesterday. Insects may have some rights, but I'm the protector of this family and—"

Kara rolled her eyes and wandered away.

Loren clutched the spray canister so tightly that she accidentally sprayed the floor. Marching into the kitchen, she placed the bug spray on a high shelf and then turned to the sound of the dryer buzzing. She glanced at the stovetop clock, dashed downstairs, piled the warm laundry into a plastic tub, tossed the wet laundry into the dryer, shoved the last load of dirty clothes into the wash, set the timers and scurried back upstairs.

Baby Addison screamed as he climbed the last rail of his crib. Teetering on the edge, he nearly overbalanced before Loren dashed into the blue room and scooped him into her arms. "Whoa, Baby Boy, what do you think you're doing? Besides giving me a heart attack...."

After a quick lunch of grilled cheese sandwiches, homemade pickles, sliced peaches, and milk, Loren placed Addison in the middle of the room with enough toys to keep a thirteenth-century emperor ecstatically happy and turned her attention to her computer. Onto the next battle—family finances. *Well, somebody's got to balance the books.*

Two hours and momentous account juggling later, Loren looked up as Kara sauntered in with a neighbor boy. They both had their iPhones so close to their faces that Loren wondered how they had ever managed to walk into the room without bumping into a wall.

Kara peered over the rim of her screen. "Marvin is staying for dinner. His dad and mom had a big fight and started throwing things."

Loren froze, though her eyes wandered over Marvin's bulky frame and unkempt hair. "You want to talk about it, Marvin?"

Marvin shrugged; his eyes still glued to the screen in front of his face. "They hate each other. What's to talk about?"

Loren's head dropped to her chest. She felt tears well up, but she brushed them aside as her gaze swept the room. *Uh, oh...where's Addison?*

Her heart pounding, she stepped passed Marvin, giving his shoulder a little squeeze as she went by. "I'm making fried chicken. You can stay as long as you need."

When she entered the bathroom, she knew what she would find, though she clenched her hands in prayer. *Please, God, let me get it cleaned up before James gets home.*

It wasn't as bad as she feared, though the wallpaper would never be the same. *Thank heaven for disinfectants!*

A car rolled over the gravel in the driveway, and Loren bustled with Addison into the blue room. She changed his stinky clothes at the speed of light, rushed into the kitchen, pulled the thawed chicken pieces out of the refrigerator, sprinkled spicy breading over them, poured oil in the pan, and popped muffins onto a tray. When James entered, she put Addison on the floor so he could toddle right into his daddy's arms, a sacred tradition that James loved.

By the time James had changed and come

back downstairs in comfortable jeans and a t-shirt, the table was set, the chicken was frying, a large tossed salad graced the center of the table, and a pyramid of muffins sat ensconced next to a jar of strawberry jam, front and center of James' place.

At dinner, Addison gummed his crackers and chicken pieces with childish abandon while Marvin chomped on his chicken legs in morose silence. Kara nibbled carrot sticks and muffins slathered in jam, distaining, once again, the flesh of sacred animals. She wrinkled her nose at Addison until her dad told her to stop.

James pushed back from the table and patted his lean belly. "That was fantastic, sweetheart, thanks. His eyes followed Loren as she began to clear the dishes. "Oh, and thanks for mowing the front lawn. I wanted to get to it, but with all the extra work—"

Loren shrugged. "It's fine. I'll try to get to the back tomorrow, but I'll have to squeeze it in before I take Addy in for his check-up."

James swirled his water glass. "Oh, and could you invite Carl's new wife—" he snapped his fingers together with a puzzled frown.

Loren glanced over. "Chelsea?"

"Yeah, right, I can never remember. Anyway, invite her to your next Lady's Tea. I take it that the other wives have shunned her for a—shall we say—checkered past. If you act nice, they might follow."

Loren filled the sink with soapy water and nodded. "Called into diplomatic service once again, eh? You know that's what I first wanted—"

Addison's wail cut short the conversation as James lifted the baby from his high chair and offered to walk Marvin back home.

Later that night as Loren brushed her teeth, she could hear sniffles from Kara's bedroom. She tiptoed into the dark interior, trying not to bang into the desk or the multitudinous science experiments, which Kara laid like traps for her unwary parents. Shuffling forward in low gear, she found Kara's bed and inched her hand up to Kara's shoulder. "What's wrong, honey?" She perched on the edge, knowing full well that she was sitting on at least three stuffed animals.

Kara wiped her eyes with the back of her hand and sniffed. "Jean texted me that I'm nothing but an amateur, and I'll never amount to anything."

Loren frowned. She didn't know Jean, as she didn't know most of the kids that Kara interacted with over her iPod. "Well, darling, you may be an amateur now, but if you study and keep working hard, you may become a professional someday. It all depends on much you—"

Kara waved her hands in contemptuous disdain. "Oh, you don't understand. You'll never understand. I want to be great at something. I don't want to just make a living…or be like *you*."

Loren took the body blow with only a slight grimace. She swept a lock of Kara's hair out of her face and took a deep breath. "You know, I like to think I'm doing something great—here—at home. It may not seem like much but—"

Kara shook her head. "You're just a mom; there's nothing great about it. Millions of women have done it—forever. I want something more, something grand and—"

Loren let her head drop as she listened to her daughter's dreams and aspirations. They all sounded wonderful and noble, something that might make headlines one day. There was so much she wanted to say, to share about her own life and her experiences, which had led her to the edge of her daughter's bed, but Kara wouldn't understand, not now. Maybe someday. When Kara talked herself sleepy, Loren squeezed her hand and tiptoed back into her bedroom and finished brushing her teeth.

Guardian

Originally published on The Writings of A. K. Frailey
9/15/2017

I turned thirteen that summer and had my first real job. Well, it felt real, even though I didn't get paid much. I helped out at the local library, shelving books, cleaning up, and polishing the tables after closing. This was back in the day when libraries bustled with students who plucked paperbacks and heavy resource volumes from designated sections labeled with letters and numbers according to the Dewy Decimal System. They propped their elbows on long, polished tables and turned thin paper pages. It was old-time, but it worked. My heart still thumps with joy at the sight of books stacked neatly on shelves.

We had a hot summer that year. I was late getting home because the library hosted a big summer festival, and someone needed to put the place back together afterward. I didn't mind. Shelving, sweeping, even wiping down the tables, kept me busy and at peace. I would stop and flip open an interesting cover, read the first page, and then let the story linger in my imagination. I felt like a kid snitching candy off a shelf, but I don't think anyone minded. Sometimes my boss, Mrs. Murdock, would smile at me, her eyes twinkling even though she usually kept a serious demeanor about the place.

When I trudged home in that late evening, I didn't know what I might find. When mom was sober, she captivated the house and neighborhood with witty banter and lively open houses. But when she wasn't sober, few saw her except me, and then she was anything but witty.

Since money was scarce and taxes had risen, Mom had taken in a couple foreign students to board for the year. Jamal stayed in the backroom on the second floor, while Mr. Chin occupied the refurbished attic. Jamal was young, energetic, and obsessed with engineering. He never talked about anything else, and I wondered if he dreamed science formulas in his sleep. Mr. Chin was quiet and always polite. He noticed when things weren't right about mom and the house, but he never said anything. He'd just go to the kitchen, make himself a cup of tea, and take it to his room to finish his work.

That summer night, I came in exhausted, longing to collapse on my bed, but the moment I stepped in the house, I knew something was wrong. Mom and my brother, Glen, were in the kitchen arguing. Glen was a lot like mom. Smart and good-looking, he could charm a room full of mountain lions, but when he started drinking, he turned even nastier than mom. When they were both drinking, life turned sour real fast.

I remember standing on the threshold. I didn't want to go in, but it was getting dark, and I had nowhere else to go. Besides, I didn't want them to hurt each other. I had always been the peacemaker. Hell of a job.

Suddenly, I saw Mr. Chin step between them and go around and about the kitchen. He was making himself a cup of tea, acting like they weren't having a big screaming match right in the middle of the room. I thought I'd fall over in a faint. How could he be so calm?

It took a little while, but eventually, Mom seemed to realize that Mr. Chin was trying to get his evening meal. Glen tossed them both a contemptuous glare, grabbed a six-pack off the table, and hustled out. I tiptoed in and helped Mom up the stairs to her bedroom. I knew she would sleep it off. By the time I came back downstairs, the kitchen was clean, and Mr. Chin was nowhere in sight.

I went to my room, dropped on my bed and felt like crying, but being thirteen, I figured that I'd better get a grip on my emotions, so I grabbed a mystery novel, leaned back against my headboard, and tried to relax. Tree frogs croaked in unison like a church chorus, and I could see the night sky filling with twinkling fireflies. My head soon felt heavy and drowsy. Then I heard the front door crash open, furniture scraping across the floor, and my mom and Glen yelling at the top of their lungs.

By the time Mom was back in bed, and Glen had retreated to his makeshift basement room, I could hardly see straight. But I dared not go back to my room for fear they would start up again. Stumbling to the couch in the living room, I settled on the edge, waiting. I faced mom's rocking chair and remembered how many times we had snuggled there when I was little. I held back aching tears and, in time, I must have fallen asleep, for the light was off, and I found myself laying on the couch with a blanket over me.

I remember being so tired that I could barely lift my head off the couch, but I sensed someone was there, sitting on the rocking chair. He wasn't making any noise, just sitting there, quiet, and watching—watching over me. I tried to mumble thanks, but my mouth felt glued shut. Peace settled over me. Someone else was on guard, so I relaxed and finally slept.

It took me a couple of months to get up the nerve to thank Mr. Chin for taking over that night. We were alone in the kitchen in on a brisk autumn evening, and I had settled down with a cup of tea. He sat with a bowl of Chinese noodles before him.

"Thanks for being there—you know—that night Glen and Mom had the big fight."

Mr. Chin chewed his noodles meditatively, his eyes averted like he was trying to remember. But then he smiled, and our gazes connected. "Wasn't me. Must have been your guardian."

I'm sure my eyes couldn't have extended any further from my face if I had been a human-sized snail. "Excuse me?"

He pointed at me with one of his chopsticks. "You have a guardian. Big fellow. Nice looking."

Whoa! I must've paled considerably because suddenly Mr. Chin looked rather alarmed. He waved his chopsticks in the air as if to wipe away my concerns. "I didn't see him exactly; I just know he exists. You have troubles too big to carry alone, and someone has been helping you. So, you see, I know by evidence. Someone watches over you, and he must be big because your burdens are so heavy. And someone that kind must be good-looking—especially around the eyes."

Mr. Chin's face wrinkled in delight at his logic, and I couldn't help but smile back at him. I never knew I had a guardian, but his words made sense to me.

From that day to this, I have remembered my guardian whenever I'm overwhelmed. I feel a presence around me, whether I'm dealing with old family issues or my latest boss' antics. I'm not alone, and my burdens are never too heavy to carry. When I imagine what my guardian looks like, I see a man much like Mr. Chin—smiling, making a cup of tea, and quite good-looking—especially around the eyes.

Same Spirit

Originally published on The Writings of A. K. Frailey
9/29/2017

Mrs. Eula Claymore pushed her glasses up the bridge of her nose and peered at the dessert tray. *Is that a lemon bar or pineapple upside-down cake?* Her gaze swiveled around the large hall lined with long, white tables. Some of the elderly customers lingered over their meatloaf or breaded chicken, but she preferred to accomplish her meal—like ticking a duty off her list—and then enjoy her dessert with coffee. She returned to the tray and blinked rapidly, hoping to discern her choices better.

"Can't decide, dear?" Mrs. Caroline Ramsey smiled graciously down on the old woman as she laid a steaming cup of coffee to her right.

Making a quick grab, Eula ended the struggle. "No, thank you, Mrs. Ramsey. Just weighing my options." Her laugh sounded hollow. *Weighing. Ha! Yes, have to weigh everything these days.* The battle of the bulge was relentless.

Caroline's paper-thin physique and tight smile swayed closer. "Oh, please, call me Carol, everyone does, and it sounds so much more romantic." She raised her eyebrows archly.

Eula suppressed a snort, tapped her sticky fingers together and considered her baptismal name—Eulamay. With a quick thrust, she jammed the sweet treat into her mouth—and regretted it instantly. Her mouth pursed into the fiercest pucker she had ever endured. *Lord in Heaven, where did they get these lemons? The devil's kitchen?* She peered up, her eyes filled with stinging tears. She must have water, or she'd expire on the spot. Unfortunately, Carol had hurried off to another table to intercede in a senior squabble before something got spilled.

"Mind if I sit here?" A large, buxom woman pointed to the seat across from her.

Eula nodded, attempting to stretch her lemon pucker into a smile.

The woman laughed as she pulled out a chair and laid her black handbag on the table. "Oh, you had a lemon bar, too, I see."

With multiple swallows, Eula tried to eke out a sound akin to human speech.

The woman turned and scurried away.

Eula watched the blurry figure bundle off and wondered if she would have done better to stay at home like her friend Lola. Of course, Lola's great-grandkids had visited her over on the weekend, so naturally, she would be prostrate for a week or so.... Eula's thoughts were interrupted as a cool glass slipped into her hand.

"Here, that ought to help. I thought I'd drink the whole Mississippi dry getting that taste outta my mouth." The large woman plunked down in the metal frame chair.

Trying desperately not to slurp, Eula drained the contents in unspeakable relief. She wiped her eyes with her embroidered handkerchief and regarded her savior as best as she was able. "Thank you. I was wondering if I'd be left to die." She waved a languid hand. "Not that it wouldn't be rather appropriate, dying in a community hall, but somehow it wasn't what I had in mind when I came this morning."

The woman's hearty laughter brought a smile to Eula's face, as well as turned several heads. "No problem. We older ladies have to stick together, don't we? So few of us left." She stretched out a hand and leaned forward. "My name's Mary Burns from Dartmouth County—off the blacktop at the end of Vet's Road.

Eula peered up and appraised the woman before. Large, wispy gray hair, an honest, though blurry face, the usual stretch pants and loose flowered blouse—in short—a possible friend. Eula smiled and pressed the offered hand. "I'm Mrs. Eula Claymore from—"

Mary waved excitedly. "Oh, I know all about you. I've lived around here nearly ten years, but my husband, Melvin, passed away last year. Lola Kinsman was so kind. From the church—you know. She thinks the world of you, she does. That's why I came by. She phoned and said she couldn't make it, but she wanted me to introduce myself."

Eula wrapped a stray lock of hair back into her neat bun. "Her great-grandkids visited Saturday. I suspect she'll be laid up awhile." Nodding, she turned and appraised the crowd. "But I'm glad to meet you. I've been coming for years, but I never seem to— Anyway, Lola's always been with me."

Mary sighed. "To be honest, I'm rather out of place. I used to cook for Melvin and the boys, and there were usually hands and helpers about. Our trestle table would be full to bursting, and I managed it every day, seven days a week, but now, after a little slip and a hip replacement, my sons' wives have decided it's too much for me."

She peered around the room. "I don't particularly take to being served."

Eula smacked her lips. "Especially not lemon bars that could suck the life out of you."

The two women hunched forward and failed to suppress their giggles.

Regaining her composer, Eula leaned back. "It's cataract surgery for me. Can hardly see my hand before my face." She gestured to the small crowd. "I served most of these people when I ran the school lunchroom. And I managed the parent group and the sewing circle. Never stopped for a moment, except—"

A racket at the end of the hall pulled their attention forward. One of the men stood stiffly, staggered, jerked, and then fell into a crumpled heap. Eula gasped. Mary rose like a puppet on strings.

Carol rushed across the hall, wended her way through the startled crowd, and took charge. At least three people had their cell phones in hand and were dialing.

After the emergency team had carried off the unfortunate gentleman, Carol circled around and spoke with each table. The crowd shuffled away in turn. When Carol made it to their table, Eula shook her head. "Will ol' Bertie be all right?"

Carol shook her head and wiped a red-rimmed eye. "They said he was dead before he hit the floor." She peered at them and forced a smile. "I guess we all have to go some time."

Eula wrung her hands together. "Bertie was such a fun boy and a hardworking man—but he never wanted to linger."

Mary sighed. "None of us do."

Carol stared down at them. “Don’t talk like that. You’re not lingering. You’re living.” Pulling out a chair, she plunked down and put her head into her hands. “I had no idea what I was getting myself into when I took this on. I thought it’d be fun: serving the ladies and gents in the community, making money on the side, getting out of my empty nest.”

Mary tilted her head at an appreciative angle. “But—”

Carol ran her fingers through her short, brown hair. “But I can’t keep pace. This is the third customer I’ve lost in two months. And I don’t mean that the way it sounds. It’s just...I get to know people, and then I lose them. It feels—useless.” Her eyes brimmed with tears. “Help me out here.”

Eula leaned over and patted Carol’s hand. “It’s not useless. You’re right. We are living—and dying. Hard for young people to understand, but we’re as new to old age, as they are to adulthood, and you are to middle age. Same spirit, greater experience perhaps, but encased in bodies that break down and wither.”

Mary wrapped her fingers over her purse and clutched it to her chest. “I know that the gentleman’s death is tragic, but I can’t go back; I must go forward. Knowing that I can join you, ladies, a couple times a week—well, it’ll make the journey less lonely.” She patted Carol’s shoulder. “Don’t fret. None of knows how to keep pace. That isn’t the point, is it?”

After Mary had lumbered away, Carol stood and helped Eula to her feet. She took her friend’s arm and led her to the door. “Will you be able to make it home, all right, Eula?"

Eula pressed Carol's warm hand and focused her blurry gaze on the woman in front of her. "Yes, I can make it home. See you on Friday—Carol."

Skeletons

Originally published on The Writings of A. K. Frailey
10/27/17

In a cherry picker bucket twenty feet from the ground, Charles Gilmore, heavyset with a small bald spot, wiped his sweaty brow with the back of his arm. He squinted at the intricate arrangement of wires.

Saunders, tall, lean, and dressed in jeans and a blue shirt, stood on the other side of the bucket. He concentrated on the connections before him.

Charles twisted a wire into place and glanced at Saunders. "At least it isn't raining, eh?"

Saunders nodded; his attention focused on the wires. "I just want to tie this."

Charles gasped. A spark caught the corner of his eyes, and he scowled. "Hey, you sure everything's dead?"

Saunders froze. "I turned off the main—"

"Stop, look here. It's sparking! How the—?"

Saunders lifted his hands away and glanced around. "They all go to that main terminal, see, right there. I turned it off securely, or we'd be toast already."

Pressing a lever, Charles lowered the bucket to the ground. "Something caused that spark. I sure as hell didn't imagine it." He labored over the uneven ground toward the main box and surveyed the vacant field. He grunted. "There was a house here once."

Saunders' eyes roved right and left. "How can you tell?"

Charles pointed to his feet. "Look down." He

kicked through the thin grass, exposing a segment of a cement cover. "It's an old well covering. Probably buried when the house was taken down. They must've had a line here."

"And it's not cut off? Don't be crazy. Besides, the main—"

"Look at that old house over there. It's a distance, but it's fed by a different system. Perhaps this one is too. Come on." Charles started to pace away.

Saunders trotted alongside as they crossed the tussocks of grass.

Charles glanced at his watch. "Dang."

Saunders' eyebrow rose. "What?"

"I told Jill I'd be home early. Won't happen now. And she's already miffed."

Saunders marched evenly at Charles' side, staring at the ground. "Wives. Glad I don't have to mess with one."

"It's not all bad, but she's all bent out of shape lately—it's stupid, really." He frowned. "Well, sort of. You see, her mom's getting old, and she forgets when things happened—talks like twenty years ago was yesterday."

"Pretty common."

"Yeah, but unfortunately, she let it slip to our oldest daughter that Jill gave up her first baby—it was a long time ago. Her mom never wanted her to give it up, and now she's asking questions, demanding to see it. So, Jill had to explain."

"Skeletons creeping out of the closet, eh?"

Charles scratched his jaw as he appraised the farmhouse and a lanky dog ambling in their direction. "Yeah, but Jill is letting the past have too much power over her—"

A wiry, old man shuffled toward them, waving. "Anything I can do for you folks?" He called to his dog, and the hound changed course and scuttled under the porch.

Charles explained their work with the electric company.

The old man nodded and hunched his shoulders. "Fine, go ahead. We don't use much electricity during the day, anyhow."

After cutting the power to the old farmhouse, the two men once again rose in the bucket. Saunders peered at the sky and chuckled. "You think you've got skeletons. Everyone has something to hide." He halted the bucket at wire level.

Charles leaned back and tucked his fingers into his belt. "It shouldn't make any difference. Jill's a great mom; her past is ancient history. Just like I'm not the guy I was twenty years ago—no one should care if I did a few stupid things back then."

"Oh, but people do care. Your sins follow you—" Saunders gave a wire an angry twist and faced Charles. "Even if they aren't even sins at all."

Charles shrugged. "I don't let things bother me. Jill is just overreacting. Chrissie will understand that she gave up the baby for a good reason. It's not like it matters anymore—"

"Give me that cutter, will you?"

Charles passed the tool over. "I never judge people. I couldn't care less if you had a dozen affairs and a couple kids on the side."

Saunders turned and pointed at Charles with the cutter. "How about if I was a killer? Would you still feel the same?"

Charles froze. "Huh?" A smile crept over his face. "You're joking, but really—"

"No, seriously. It was manslaughter—ran a red light and killed a woman and her little boy. I hardly did any time—a little over a year and probation. Total accident."

Charles' gaze dropped. "Sorry, I had no idea. I wouldn't have brought it up if I—"

Saunders shook his head. "I've made you uncomfortable; I get it. But just remember, your wife is right. Our past haunts us."

Charles pursed his lips, focused his gaze on the box, and nodded to the wire assembly. "You finished?"

"Yep."

"Okay, let's get the cover on and go home." Charles screwed everything in place and lowered the bucket. He unhooked his belt and tossed his tools into the truck.

Saunders did the same and slipped into the passenger side of the vehicle. He glanced at Charles. "So what time do you want to meet up on Saturday?"

Charles started the truck and glanced at Saunders quizzically.

"Remember—our fishing trip?"

Pulling into the right lane, Charles' eyes darted from side-to-side. "Oh, yeah, forgot. But, hey, I think Jill's got something planned...hate to make her any more upset."

Saunders let his head fall back against the headrest, his gaze staring through the truck roof.

Charles glanced over. "Maybe some other time. You understand?"

Saunders exhaled and nodded slowly. "Sure do."

Addicted to Me

Originally published on The Writings of A. K. Frailey
11/10/2017

"You have no idea what it's like—the whole world's addicted to me."

Dr. Jim Burns merely raised one eyebrow as his index finger tapped the electronic notepad resting on his knee. "Tell me, Sophia, what are you addicted to?"

Sophia catapulted off the leather couch and paced across the luxuriously appointed office.

Cushioned chairs in dark plaid, a wide couch, a teak coffee table with matching shelves accompanied by a large cherry desk set the room's dignified tone.

Sliding one finger down a framed family photo, Sophia smiled coyly. "Me? I'm not addicted to anything—unless you want to count my morning cup of coffee—dark Columbian with a hint of cinnamon. It's all I ask before I go on each morning and face the multitudes."

The doctor's gaze followed Sophia's stroll around the perimeter. His foot jiggled slightly. "Yes, multitudes. I believe that's where we left off last time. You felt you were being—"

Sophia snatched up a polished stone with the word *"PEACE"* engraved on its shiny surface. "They won't leave me alone. It's killing me!" Facing her therapist, her eyes gleamed with frantic fury. "Yesterday, this little ol' thing came toddling after me, waving her handbag, yoohooing to wake the dead, and she swore upon her dearly departed mother's grave that she watches me every single day. G-O-D! I'm the reason they get up in the morning."

Jim closed his eyes and inhaled a long, slow breath. After a brief moment, he tapped the space bar and unclenched his jaw. "You're making several unfounded assumptions—"

Hunching her shoulders in tune to her eye roll, Sophia strode over to a marble counter and poured herself a cup of coffee. "This isn't decaf? You wouldn't dare—"

Rising, Dr. Burns cleared his throat. "Don't be rude, Sophia. I always offer the best—as well you know."

Sophia scooped three healthy spoonfuls of granulated brown sugar into her cup and stirred meditatively. She peered over her cup at her doctor. "I pay you enough."

Placing his notepad on his desk, Dr. Burns glanced at his watch. "How's the show this morning? Sherrill said you've been calmer and—"

"Sh—Sherrill?"

The sound of her high-pitched, hysterical laughter forced Jim to rub his temple.

"Like that woman knows anything about what I have to deal with. She's as high-strung as a bat outta hell. She better not be—"

"Her son has leukemia, right?"

Sophia's dismissive wave tossed that concern aside. "It's the curable kind, and she'd got the money. Don't give me other people's high-drama."

A firm tap on the door froze them in mid-motion. Dr. Burns regained his composure with a deep intoned, "Come in" and stepped to the door.

The door opened, and a man in his late twenties, slim and clean-shaven, poked his head forward. "Mr. Marshall has arrived a little early, but you said you wanted to know...."

The doctor nodded. "Thank you, Carl. I'll be right there." He turned to Sophia. "We'll have to wrap this up early today. I have a pressing—"

"Pressing? More pressing than *me*? I appear before millions every damn day, and you have more *pressing* matters?"

Carl backed out and closed the door.

"Mr. Marshall happens to be my brother-in-law. My sister has been very ill, and they need my help. I'll be out of the office for several—"

The rage in Sophia's eyes stabbed through Dr. Burn's calm demeanor. "You spring this on me now? You know perfectly well that I have *pressing* matters of my own. I never let them get in the way of my meetings with you. I make *you* a priority because so many people are counting on *me*."

Dr. Burns laced his fingers together as his jaw clenched. "I'm sorry this is causing you so much trouble, but I had to choose. I chose my sister."

"Like hell! I pay you to help me, not wallow in your own family escapades." Sophia grabbed her tiny, red purse and stalked across the room. "Don't worry; I'm used to people letting me down."

After Dr. Burns stepped aside and watched Sophia stalk out of his office, he unclenched his hands and set free a long, cleansing breath.

A tall, heavy-set man in jeans and a blue knit sweater shuffled forward. "Sorry about that, Jim, I can tell she's put out. If Jean weren't so—"

Jim shrugged his shoulders as he reached under the desk and pulled out a small traveling bag. "Forget it. Ms. Grant thinks that the universe revolves around her—the truth is a bit of a shock."

"She always looks so happy and self-assured in public. I'd never have guessed."

Jim stared at his brother-in-law as he passed him in the doorway. "Really? It's always been clear as day to me."

Good Deed

Originally published on The Writings of A. K. Frailey
11/24/2017

Richard Tyler knew his own mind. After dashing from his job at the gym to his mom's house, he breezed through the kitchen door with all the confidence of an Academy Award winner.

His mom's eyebrows rose in surprise. "I thought you were having lunch with Kimberly."

Despite the August heat, Richard shivered. "She decided she needs to 'reevaluate her priorities.'" He shrugged off his discomfort. "Guess that includes lunch."

His mom's gaze swiveled from her baloney and cheese sandwich set neatly on a plate with a modest mound of chips on the side—to Richard. She slid the plate across the table. "Here. Sit and eat before your class." She crossed to the stove and stirred a pot of tomato soup.

Richard plunked down in the chair, grabbed the sandwich, and chewed with a faraway look in his eyes.

After pouring the soup into a ceramic mug, his mom slid into a chair across from Richard. "You know, she's only nineteen, in journalism, and you're a bit older, wanting to be an actor—"

Richard stiffened; a frown burrowed across his forehead. "What? Like I'm not really an actor, and she's looking for honest work?"

Mom stirred her soup as she stared into its swirling, red depths. "You might try to see things from her point of view. I mean, she's—"

Richard shot to his feet, scattering breadcrumbs across the table. "Totally selfish and doesn't know what she's doing. Journalism? Ha! Not an ounce of life experience, and she thinks she'll wake up the world's conscience. Yeah, right."

Mom stared at the cup, searching for wisdom. She responded with a shrug.

With a fretful glance at his watch, Richard started for the door. "I gotta go. We're having a guest director today—said to be brilliant. Might make a good connection."

The screen door slammed as it closed behind him. Mom wiped up the crumbs.

~~~

As Richard leaned back in his theater chair, he had to stifle a yawn. The room was stuffy, and the new director had been introducing himself for almost an hour. Suddenly, he felt a jolt charge through his body.

"Hey, you, kid with the big chin and blue eyes."

Richard sprang to his feet.

The director waved him onto the stage. "Come here. I want to demonstrate a point."

Without hesitation, Richard sprang forward and landed lightly before the rotund, thin-lipped director. "Okay. Listen carefully. You've just climbed out of a car wreck, people milling about—horror everywhere. You got a broken rib or something." He pointed to the stage. "Show me."

Dropping to his knees, Richard writhed in pain, moaning. He scrambled forward on one
~~~

arm, the other clutching his middle. His eyes squeezed shut; he rocked and—"

"Stop! Enough. You've made my point."

Panting from his exertion, Richard climbed to his feet, his eyes darting over the other students who studied him with uncertain expectation, waiting to be told whether he deserved approval or scorn.

The director flung a disenchanted arm in Richard's direction. "I see the same thing all the time—day after bloody day. Actors who forget they aren't alone. People! *It's not all about you.* Remember your audience! They pay for the tickets."

As Richard stepped into the strong afternoon light, he blinked in near blindness after hours in the theater's semi-darkness. He felt lightheaded and needed a drink. Starting across the street toward a fast-food stand, he heard a familiar voice.

"Hey, Richard, wait up."

With a groan, Richard turned and faced his girlfriend. "Hey, Kimberly."

Kimberly shifted a stack of books onto her left arm. "Sorry about this morning. I was...I needed some air. Got some bad news." She glanced up and intercepted Richard's glazed stare. "My dad's been diagnosed with pancreatic cancer, stage four. Not much time left." Her eyes filled with tears. "I'm going to focus on him awhile." She nodded to her shoes to see if they agreed.

Richard's gaze fell on the top of her bowed head. "Dang waste." He clenched his jaw as his mind went completely blank.

Kimberly shook her head. "At least we have a chance to say goodbye." She leaned forward and kissed Richard's cheek. "Good luck—in everything." Her books stacked in her arms, she turned and trotted across the street.

~~~

Later that evening, Richard jogged around the campus track listening to music through his earbuds. Nausea and malaise seeped throughout his body and soul, burying him deep in gloom. Running as fast as he could, he scowled at the realization that the sensation grew in proportion to his desperation.

Skidding to a halt, he sucked in deep lungfulls of air. Words, images, impressions kept intruding even as he stared across the dimming horizon. He imagined himself driving along the coast, the windows down and the music loud, accompanied by a gorgeous sunset dispelling the evils of the day. He trotted across the street from his parked car and halted.

A teen, plump with rumpled hair and sagging shoulders, was standing between his beautiful, red car and a battered, old truck. A ragged scratch scarred his car's shiny exterior. Richard closed his eyes, lifted his head back, and smothered a scream. Finally, he squared his shoulders and marched forward.

The kid glanced over and caught sight of Richard. He wavered between evasion and a complete meltdown.

Taking long strides, Richard's gaze flashed from the truck to his damaged car.

The kid, now nearly in tears, lifted his hands. "Sorry, mister. It's all my fault. I'm new at parallel parking—always been a nightmare in driver's ed." He scanned Richard's car wistfully and shoved his glasses further up his nose. "My mom's got
~~~

insurance, and I'll pay with my own money too. So stupid. I should've gone to the lot up the street."

Though the light was failing, Richard's vision cleared. He swallowed back a rising ache and blinked in hesitation. "Listen, it's no big deal. I got a friend who works in a body shop, and he owes me. He'll fix this up in a couple minutes, and it'll be as good as new. Don't worry about it."

The eye-popping relief on the kid's face tightened Richard's throat to a searing ache. He sniffed, regaining a semblance of cool composure—the best acting he'd done all year.

~~~

It was nearly midnight when Richard slipped into his mom's dark kitchen. He plunked down on a chair and laid his head on his arms. A warm hand clasped his shoulder. He didn't need to look up.

"You okay?"

Richard shook his head and groaned. He sat back and stared through the darkness at his mom's rumpled figure in her long, shapeless bathrobe. "The director made me look like a fool, Kimberly showed me I was a fool, and some kid I don't even know gave me a shot at redemption."

His mom chuckled and sat down, her hand sliding over his. "You know, one good deed deserves another."

Richard pressed his other hand on top of hers and grinned with the first joy he had felt all day. "It does."
~~~

Survival of the Fittest

Originally published on The Writings of A. K. Frailey
12/8/2017

Ling believed in wood-folk with her whole soul. The magic of a mid-winter snowstorm over sleeping fields opened a doorway into a world of scheming squirrels and spirit-filled pine trees. A cawing raven warned the tree-stump mouse family of a stalking calico cat while swaying trees forecasted an impending storm.

Though Ling could hear the voices plain enough, their actual words eluded her. The sound of their murmuring sent a warm thrill through her chilled body as she trudged across the newly fallen snow with a bulging backpack slung over her shoulder.

Skipping up the frozen steps to her snug house at the end of the block, she huffed a white plume of smoke into the air. Before turning the door handle with her mittened hands, she turned and bowed goodnight to her wood-folk-friends. No doubt they wished her well through the silent evening glow, and she, in turn, would not forget them.

After tugging off her wet boots and dropping her pack in a heap, she tiptoed down the dark hall toward her father's study. His bent figure leaned over a hardwood desk with a computer screen outlining the edges of his head. Swallowing back her anxiety, Ling timidly tapped on the doorframe.

A shuffle and a snort precluded his slow turn.

Black eyes in a pale face peered at the doorway.

Ling dropped her gaze.

"So, you made it home on time today."

Ling nodded but stayed in place. "Yes, Papa."

He granted permission to enter with a slight beckoning gesture. "Come in." His gaze darted back to the screen. "There's not much more I can do here today."

Ling scuttled forward and placed her small hand on the arm of his chair. Her eyes flickered to the screen. A gorgeous painting of a woodland scene snatched her breath away. Her fingers rose as if to touch the gently swaying tendrils of an enormous weeping willow.

Her father wrapped a loose arm around her waist and drew her closer, his gaze joining hers. "It's for a mid-western university. They want to demonstrate their inclusiveness by commissioning art from every culture in the world."

Ling blinked; the spell broken. "Inclusiveness?"

The old man shrugged. "Art can be a unifying force." He tilted his head. "Of course, it can be enslaved by a propaganda machine just as easily." Ling's puzzled frown brought a tired smile to her father's face. "You are too young for such things. Enjoy your freedom while you may."

Placing her hand on his silky sleeve, Ling pressed his arm in excitement. "I saw a red fox sneaking across the field. He's been threatening the other animals, wants to rule the west woodland. Do you think the—?"

A shrill call cut through the air. "Ling? Come here, child, and bring your school bag."

Her whole body drooping under a sudden weight, Ling stepped back toward the door. She gazed at her father. "You should draw a fox peeking out from behind the tree."

The old man's eyes shifted from the picture to his daughter, surprise on his brow but pleasure in his eyes. "Why?"

She trudged across the threshold, her eyes darting toward the kitchen. "Because—there's always a fox around somewhere."

~~~

After hours of study, Ling's eyes burned with exhaustion. Her blurry vision made it difficult to make out the text before her. Her mother filled the kettle for tomorrow's tea and set it in its designated place on the stove. The immaculate room stood in readiness for the next day to meet the demands of a peak performance.

In her weary haze, Ling wondered if a kitchen could revolt—demand a rest from the never-ending grind of routine preparations. Pots and pans, stovetops, counters, scraping, cleaning, bubbling, oil, smoke, dishes, and grime, wiping—endlessly wiping—it all away, only to start over the next morning before the sun even hinted at the day.

"What has gotten into you, child? You've been sitting there for an hour, and nothing is done. You know your exams are next month. You want to be ready."

Ling nodded.

Her mother placed a damp hand on her shoulder. "You won't succeed unless you work
~~~

hard and try—"

"Mama?"

Her mother stared down, their gazes locking.

An implicit allowance offered Ling courage. "We're supposed to make a family tree and describe our cultural heritage in class next week."

A stiff jerk and the mother's gaze shifted to the wall. "That won't be hard. I have our whole lineage written down, and your father can tell you what each person did for a living."

Ling shook her head, dissatisfaction pressing on her shoulders like a lead weight. "I'd rather take one of Papa's pictures to show. That would—"

Her mother turned and swiped the clean counter with a vicious smack. "Pictures are only illusions. Don't be ridiculous. Our family has survived a great deal—more than most—and we did it by facing facts and working hard."

"But Papa's pictures—"

"Your father makes pictures because he is paid to do so. He is an illustrator. He works at his job—as you will too before long."

Her mother's unflinching gaze squeezed Ling's heart.

"It's survival of the fittest, just like all the books say. And you, Ling, must survive."

Ling's gaze dropped to the floor. A small brown knothole in the wainscoting caught her eye. In sudden wakefulness, she thought she saw a small mouse dart out an inquiring face, blinking a question at her. It seemed to ask, "Why?" But Ling had no answer.

~~~
~~~

Two dozen years later, Ling pushed her father's frail form engulfed in a wheelchair through the wide doors out into spring sunshine. A trailing line of elderly people sat like potted plants on the edge of the retirement property. Small blooms added texture to the scene. She found a quiet corner and pressed the brake lever with her foot. Her father, asleep again, would rest in the mild sunshine for an hour or so, until the nurses collected their charges and set them all in a straight row at the long table for a noon dinner.

A passing nurse stopped and patted Ling's shoulder. "I heard about your mama. So sorry. But your papa is beyond worry now. Just be glad he's so content."

Ling nodded and choked back a rising sob. She let her gaze fall on the surrounding scenery. No one could fault the clean and professional atmosphere. Suddenly, her eyes fell on the swaying branches of a weeping willow in a neighboring yard.

She felt a hand on her arm. Looking over, she met her papa's gaze. "I painted in the fox, but I forgot something."

With wide eyes, Ling marveled at her father's sudden lucidity. "What? What could you have forgotten, Papa?"

His eyes drooped in weariness, though a feeble finger shook in emphasis. "I forgot to paint a little girl—to admire the tree and keep an eye on the fox."

High

Originally published on The Writings of A. K. Frailey
12/22/2017

Hating Libby Lawrence wasn't just self-defense; it was an undiluted, adrenaline high with a clean conscience. In the fifth grade, Libby personified a "mean-girl" before the term had become popular. From the first day when she ordered me with a sneer and a glare to sit on the *left* of our shared desk, promptly told the teacher that I smelled bad, and scribbled a black line through my book report, I knew she and I would never get along. Unfortunately, since I was short, thin, and timid, I didn't stand a chance. To boot, I stopped growing that year. Thanks to some kind of miraculous providence, her parents moved away, and I started growing again.

But from then on, even into my adult years, the name Libby sent chills down my spine. I tried to control my fury when my brother decided to name his first daughter Libby after some relation on his wife's side. I didn't care how great the relation; no child deserved to be stuck with such a moniker. Despite my best on-my-knees entreaties, he went forward with his malicious scheme, but to my surprise, the child grew up to be a pretty decent kid.

Years later, when my dream-teaching job opened up in my hometown, I only paused for a brief moment when my eyes tripped over the principal's name—Libby Macintosh. Couldn't be the same. After all, the Libby I knew could hardly control herself, much less a whole school.

I steeled myself for the long-distance phone interview from California to Wisconsin. I had taught five years at LA Unified and felt that if I didn't get an infusion of the four Midwestern seasons soon, I'd dry up and wither away. I also missed my family and Lake Michigan. What's an ocean I hardly ever saw—much less touched—to a lake that's got miles of open beachfront?

The interview went well. Ms. Macintosh was courteous and clear. She had a third-grade vacancy that needed to be filled for the autumn term. She wanted someone with experience who would be willing to take on a few extra duties as need be. The lack of specificity about the "other duties" worried me, but the school's location—just five miles from my parent's home and three miles from Lake Shore Drive—attracted me like a puppy to an untied shoelace. Daily runs along the lake and easy visits with my elderly parents would be worth a few extra duties. My spirits rising, I felt confident enough to ask a couple of personal questions. "You're a native of Wisconsin? Been a principal long?"

Yes and no was about all Ms. Macintosh had time for that day, but she kindly referred me to her Facebook page where we could connect—if I felt so inclined. Picturing myself on the cover of a Nancy Drew mystery novel, I quickly accepted the offer and gave her my email address so she could send me specifics on the school and the position. I would send my updated resume to her by return email. End of interview.

If it hadn't been for a series of life crises involving a misfit kitten, an exploding dryer, and an elderly neighbor's cries of distress, I would have put on my detective cap that same day. But as it was, it took me the weekend to get my life in order and my laptop to cooperate. Finding Ms. Macintosh wasn't hard. What was hard was swallowing back was my horror at seeing those all-to-familiar green eyes, that pugnacious nose, and the jutting jaw that could clip a hedge.

If my mom hadn't called at that moment, I would have turned off my computer and made a run for the nearest Dairy Queen—despite the fact that it was nearly eleven miles away.

My voice was a slight bit shaky, though I tried to cover myself. Still, moms have a way of noticing.

"You alright, honey? You sound out of breath."

"I—I'm fine. Just—you know—busy. With stuff."

Well, mom was never one to mess around on a long-distance call even though she's got a package deal that—never mind. She got to the point.

"Your father's birthday is next week. And he's not getting any younger."

I could clearly drop my Nancy Drew persona. No detective needed here.

"Well, the plane ticket is pretty expensive, and I want to set up a few interviews before I—"

"Didn't you have a phone interview this week?"

"Uh, yeah...."

"Well, then, just come home, check in on your poor, aging parents, and stop by the school. Never hurts to show a little interest. Besides, it's a lot harder to turn someone down when you've met them in person."

I pictured Libby's furious glare framed by flapping, black ponytails as she pushed herself into my space with a whirling fist at her side. Somehow, I didn't think she had any trouble turning people down. She probably arranged interviews for the sheer joy of knocking prospective hopefuls on their backsides.

"I bet she even sent you an invitation for an in-person interview. They do that, you know. Have you checked your email lately?"

As surprise and anxiety played touchdown football with my innards, my hand reflexively clicked to my email. A cold shock ran through my body when I saw the subject line— *Invitation from Principal Macintosh.*

I don't remember much of the rest of the conversation, but I do know that mom had a list of airline specials for the coming week.

Getting home, celebrating dad's seventieth birthday, catching up with my brother and his brood of three rapscallions kept me busy over the weekend. I actually slept for a few hours each night—after highlighting plans for a perfect revenge.

On Monday, I dressed in my most professional, intimidating gray suit with matching heels, and I toted my very expensive leather briefcase. I dearly hoped she was an animals' rights activist and was deeply offended by my insensitivity. I sniffed back disdain till my sniffer was sore. I had a childhood score to settle, and I had not an iota of an intention of accepting the job. I wanted to see her in person, and after she reviewed my sparking work record, my laudable service in Peace Corps, my glowing endorsements, I would slap her offer into the dust. Only then would I remind her of her left-hand seatmate in fifth grade. And, yes, the past can come back to haunt you.

Why I felt the need to torture myself with a quick detour at the lake, I don't know. I stood on the grassy shore, sucking in lung-fulls of invigorating lake scent, and hoped that Libby hadn't grown much taller since our last meeting. Her Amazonian height was still an issue to contend with. Reviewing the many trials and experiences I had had since fifth grade, I wondered—briefly—if I wasn't letting my childhood mini-trauma get the better of me.

When I saw a little girl and a bully of a big sister pull the child along like a rag doll—my burning resolve reformed itself. No! Justice demanded an honest accounting. I would face this haunting humiliation—or die trying.

Marching up the steps, I passed a group of middle school kids texting one another. I didn't even shake my head. It wasn't worth the effort.

I gripped my briefcase, tapped the intercom, got permission to enter, pushed open the wide front door, charged down the green and yellow hall—my heels clacking officiously—and entered THE OFFICE. It was empty. Since it was going on five o'clock, I hadn't expected a crowd, but I was surprised by the stillness.

There was a counter with a little bell. I looked around, cleared my throat, stared at the half-opened door labeled *Principal's Office,* and tapped my fingers on the counter. Nothing. Finally, in sheer desperation, I tinkled the stupid bell. A call from the office informed me that Ms. Macintosh was in.

"Coming."

I squared my shoulders and straightened my back. Five foot four inches would only take me so far, but I had every intention of making the most of what I had. Deciding that I didn't want to appear too interested, I strolled to the wall and glared at the bulletin board.

I heard an odd sound and a horribly familiar voice. "Oh, hi! You're early. I like that. Thanks for coming, Grace."

I turned, my eyes lifted high to meet those green orbs, but there was nothing there. Until I dropped my gaze. Sitting in an automated wheelchair was the shrunken visage of my childhood tormentor. I tried to control my intake of breath, but honestly, I could have sucked in the whole of Lake Michigan.

Adding a layer of bizarreness on top of my shock, Libby Macintosh didn't seem even remotely surprised. She just waved me toward her office. "Come on in. It'll be more comfortable for both of us."

Since walking was about the only way I could cross the room, and collapsing into a heap didn't seem like a viable option, I followed.

With expert swiftness, she swiveled her metallic armature into place behind her desk, waved to the empty chair, and beamed at me.

"So how long has it been, Grace? Gosh, it's got to be nearly eighteen years."

Yes, my jaw did drop all the way to the floor. Stunned, I could hardly speak. Finally, trying to hide my shaking hands, I squeezed them into my lap, my shiny, leather briefcase forgotten on the floor where it fell when I landed in the chair. "You—you remember me, Ms.—?"

A waving hand and a disarming smile deflected my question. "Oh, not at first. Your mom came by my office a few weeks ago. She helps out in the library, you know. She's the one who told me that you were looking to relocate. It wasn't until she brought along a grade school yearbook and showed me your picture that I put two and two together."

I honestly believe that my brain melted at that moment. I couldn't think of a thing to say. The impulse to get up and walk out the door was the only idea that made even the slightest sense, but before I could arrange my synapses to fire coherent messages to my skeletal system, Libby chuckled.

With bubbling giggles, she wagged a finger at me. "Do you remember what a brat I was? Gosh, I was terrible. I used to go out of my way to make everyone miserable." Suddenly, her laughter died as she dried her damp eyes. "But God got my attention." She gestured to her emaciated legs and the wheelchair in a comprehensive sweep. "Car accident. Just a couple years later. My dad was killed, and my mom never got over the loss—or my crippled legs. She took to drinking. I ended up living with my grandma."

Blinking back sudden tears, I clasped my head with both hands before it exploded. "I doubt God wanted that."

Libby nodded with a slow smile. "You're right. He didn't. But it changed my life. My parents were troubled people. I was a nasty kid, and I would have grown up to make a lot of people miserable. But Grandma had faith that could move mountains, and she taught me to use a wheelchair. She also taught me to think about others and to use my newfound understanding to better the world."

Libby wheeled herself around the desk and arrived on my left. Reaching out, she clasped my hand in hers. "Can you forgive me for being such a wretched brat? I'm sure you must still carry some hurt for the things I did."

I couldn't wipe my tears way fast enough.

She scooted her wrecked body aside, pulled a clean tissue out of a hidden pocket, and handed it to me. "I always keep some handy. Never know." She smiled through glimmering eyes.

Sniffing what was left of my composure under control, I met her gaze. "You know, I came here to teach you a lesson—to show you that I had always been better than you thought. I wanted—" I couldn't go on. It all seemed so pathetic.

Libby squeezed my hand—comfortingly. "You know, when I realized who you were, I went out of my way to ask your mom to follow up with you. I was so grateful for this chance. There were a lot of people I hurt but, thank God, there are a lot of people I help now. And I just thought it would be rather grand—if after our miserable past—that as adults we could work together for the next generation. Would you like to do that, Grace?"

~~~

I worked with Libby for twenty-two years until
~~~

she had a debilitating stroke and had to retire. She asked me to take over as principal, and the school board unanimously agreed. During those years, and every autumn after, we'd start the term with an assembly, retelling the story of our fifth-grade animosity and how, in later life, we became good friends who loved kids and cherished the future.

In the end, loving Libby was the best high I ever had. I have no plans to come down.

A Beggar's Choice

Originally published on The Writings of A. K. Frailey
1/19/2018

Chelsea faced the little hellions on the garage roof; her arms perched akimbo on her hips. "You get down here right this minute, or I'll call your mama and daddy, and we'll just see what they have to say about all your goings on!"

David and Susie grinned and climbed higher on the steep roof.

With a long shuddering sigh, Chelsea decided that there wasn't enough money in the Fredrick's bank account to pay her to babysit these twin wretches. Dusting her hands clean of the matter, she marched inside and picked up her plastic, pink purse—the one her daddy had given her before he left for his overseas assignment. The one he'd never returned from. She sighed again and perched on the couch waiting for the Fredrick's return.

~~~

Ten years later, Chelsea landed a job at Mid-State University Library. She wasn't a full-fledged librarian, but that hardly mattered since she spent most of her days sorting and cataloging files on the computer. She had her own cubicle—that was something. Since her scraggly brown hair always wafted over one eye, she habitually tilted her head as she worked. The crick in her neck had ceased to annoy her.
~~~

A tall, slender man in his early fifties leaned over the cubicle. “Hey, kiddo, I noticed that the coffee pot’s empty.” He jerked his thumb in the direction of the lounge.

Blinking away a grimace, Chelsea nodded and scurried to the coffeemaker tucked into a gray corner. When the filter split and the wet grounds cascaded across the counter and onto the floor, she merely closed her eyes for a brief second and counted to three. Kneeling on the tiled floor, she started the laborious process of compiling the icky mess into a neat circle.

An elongated shadow slanted over the black spray.

Chelsea peered up, her hair falling like a theater curtain to one side.

A plump, young woman grinned and waved a handful of paper towels. “Personally, I think the company that makes these thin filters should be sued—and then drawn and quartered.” With lightning speed, she swiped up the mess, tossed the remains into the waste bin, and clapped her hands clean.

Chelsea stood and faced the energetic, little wonder-woman. She almost put out her hand, but as black grounds still stuck to her palms, she merely clasped them together and attempted a brave smile. “Thanks. Do you—?”

“My name’s Sue. Just part-time—work-study—to help pay the *atrocious* tuition—you know.”

“Ah.” Yes, Chelsea knew. Her student loans sucked any hint of joy out of her financial life since graduation. She unleashed a grimace. “I’ll take my debts to the grave.”

"Ha!" The young woman apparently enjoyed shared desperation. She stuck out her hand, unconcerned about coffee grounds or germs, exchanging pleasantries. "Nice to meet you—?"

"Chelsea." She slipped a new filter into place and poured a small mountain of grounds into the appropriate basket.

"Ooh, nice. I knew a Chelsea once."

A shadow glided passed the doorway.

Sue's eyes rolled. "The old geezer, he's a fright, isn't he? Told me to hurry you up. No mercy—"

As the coffee began to percolate, Chelsea shrugged. "Mr. Howe says I make coffee better than he does."

"Oh, brother!" Suddenly, Sue's eyes widened. "Hey, I think I might know you. Did you ever babysit an unruly set of twins—for the Frederick family?"

Chelsea's throat constricted. She swallowed convulsively.

Pouncing, Sue reached over and gripped Chelsea's arm in a vice grip. "Oh-my-gosh! This is amazing. I've always wanted to meet you again—"

A pronounced throat clearing turned the two women like marionettes.

"Ahem." Mr. Howe stood in the doorway and tapped his watch, his eyebrows raised, lips pursed tight.

Chelsea started forward, but Sue's grip tightened. "After work, okay?"

At closing time, Chelsea slid into a worn brown jacket, shoved her purse strap over her shoulder, stacked files under her arm, and slipped along the bookcases until she was near the front door. She made a quick dash and—froze.

"Hi! I've been waiting for you." Sue's brows puckered. "What? You take work home?"

With a grunt, Chelsea bundled herself through the door into the blustery night.

Keeping a determined pace, Sue marched along at her side. "You know, I never forgot what you did. It meant a lot to me."

Hunching her shoulders, Chelsea ducked her head against the chilly wind and the first splattering raindrops. "I quit."

"Huh?"

Chelsea stopped on the corner and looked both ways, though the street was deserted. "I quit babysitting. I can't see—"

"But it was the way you quit!" Sue gripped Chelsea's arm again. "Look, there's the Corner Café. Let's stop. I'll buy."

Smothering a groan, Chelsea let herself be dragged across the street into the tiny shop. They slipped into the first booth and wiped the wet from their clothes.

A tiny man wearing a bright smile slipped over. "What can I getcha'?"

"Two hot cocoas with plenty of marshmallows and the biggest cinnamon buns you got." Sue grinned as she leaned back into the puffy red booth.

Chelsea's mouth tightened into a firm line.

"So, you want to hear my story?"

Chelsea shook her head and laced her fingers together like a doctor about to give bad news. "Look. I think we've got some kind of memory discrepancy here. According to my data banks, I only babysat for you and your brother a couple of times, and then I quit. No pleasant memories. No story."

Like a released catapult, Sue flung her body forward, her hands slapping the table. "That's why I gotta tell you what happened. I figured you never knew."

Chelsea pulled her stack of files closer and played with the corner edge. "Okay. I'm listening."

"The day you quit changed my life. You told mom that babysitting us wasn't worth all the gold in Fort Knox. I had to look that reference up later. But at the time, I just figured we'd riled you pretty good, which was always our intention."

The host returned and gracefully slid two hot mugs of steaming cocoa in front of the women. Mountains of marshmallows did indeed bob up and down on a foamy chocolate sea. The cinnamon buns looked like they could float a couple of aircraft carriers.

Chelsea's eye rounded. "Good glory."

After taking a deep sip and licking her lips, Sue nudged the bun plate across the table. "Business first. Anyway, I'd never seen my mom turn that shade of red before."

"I remember. She called me a beggar."

"Yes! But you remember what you said back?"

Chelsea shoved her cocoa aside.

Sue leaned forward, her long, blond hair splaying across the table. "You said, maybe beggars don't have *pleasant* choices, but they still have choices."

Leaning back and letting her eyes roam over the mottled ceiling, Chelsea exhaled. "So?"

Sue's eyes brimmed with tears. "So—a few years later, my brother got killed drinking and driving. My parents blamed each other—and they split. I thought my life was over. But your voice came back to me, like some kind of movie voice-over, and I could hear you saying—even beggars have choices."

Reaching out, Sue beckoned for Chelsea's hand. "Some people said that David's death was just an accident. But it wasn't. He made a choice. And so did my parents. But after a while, I realized I had choices too. Even though I felt like a beggar with a ruined family, I could still decide how to live my life."

Chelsea shoved her files aside and took Sue's hands in her own.

~~~

The sky had cleared by the time Chelsea arrived at work early the next morning. In one hand, she held a Corner Café mug of steaming coffee, and with a light tap, she dropped her files on Mr. Howe's desk. In a moment, she settled down to work, humming to herself.

Mr. Howe's shadow fell over her. He shook an empty coffee pot in the air.

Brushing her hair from her face, Chelsea glanced from the pot to Mr. Howe's face.

"Hey, kiddo. I think you forgot something."

With a winning smile spreading from ear to ear, Chelsea lifted her mug of hot coffee in salute. "Not this time. My memory's working just fine."
~~~

Ol' Diablo

Originally published on The Writings of A. K. Frailey
2/16/2018

Among the spruce and maples, surrounded on three sides by vast fields of freshly tilled soil, Joy pushed her baby girl in a swing. Her husband couldn't pass the wooden structure without slapping a beam and grinning. "Solid as a rock!"

In her first audacious foray into play dates, Joy had invited a friend from church and a colleague from her husband's work for an afternoon of fun and frolic. Joy exhaled a cautious breath. *So far so good. The kids are getting along well together.*

A professional in a pinstripe pantsuit, Ginny Hawthorn exuded efficient confidence; while Ruth in a jean skirt and a flowery blouse breathed exuberance—like a full-page, color advertisement for the outdoor life. Ginny's boy, Frank, tossed a Frisbee to Ruth's boy, Ezra. Being the same age, they enjoyed the usual eight-year-old entertainments. One minute they were racing each other across the yard, the next, they were climbing a tree to see who could get to the top the fastest. Ruth watched them with an anxious eye, but Ginny hardly peeled her gaze from her phone.

After lifting her baby from the swing, Joy ambled over to the two women. "I'm so glad the boys are getting along." She pointed to Ruth's round tummy. "Soon, we'll have another little one to join in the fun."

Ruth's face glowed. "I can hardly wait. It's

been so long—I just about gave up hope. But God is good."

With a slight grimace, Ginny slipped her phone into her purse and peered across the yard. "Hey, kiddo, I've got a conference call at 5:00—twenty minutes." She strode over to an Adirondack chair and perched on the edge. "I really appreciate your befriending us, Joy. The kids at Frank's school are such Neanderthals—obsessed with the latest gadget. I'm too busy to play games, so the kid doesn't get much fresh air, and I'm sure he's putting on weight."

Joy shrugged. "I don't know how you do it. I can barely manage with Rick and the baby, yet you juggle a family and a full-time career."

Ruth shaded her eyes as she scanned the yard, a frown building between her eyes. "Is it okay if they play in that dirt over there?"

Joy turned and appraised the scene. The two boys had jumped into a fresh hole and were digging with frenetic energy. "Oh, I don't think they can do any harm. Rick pulled out a fallen tree, and he thought maybe he'd excavate a bit and make a root cellar. He sure—"

A scream sent all three women hustling toward the site.

Frank scrambled out of the hole, holding a large, angular jaw bone ennobled with wide, flat teeth. Ezra ran to his mother and yanked her over. "Look at what we found! It's a skull—think it might be from a dinosaur?"

Ruth's frown deepened.

Ginny leaned in, adjusting her glasses to peer at the skull in her son's hands. "Could be—I've heard of farmers finding all sorts of prehistoric—

”

"Cool!" Ezra jumped forward and stroked the bone. "I wish I could've seen it when it was alive. I would've ridden—"

Frank lifted the bone out of reach. "Don't be stupid. Humans and dinosaurs didn't live at the same time. Dinosaurs had been gone for a zillion years—"

Ezra shook his head and leaped for the bone. "Not true. Men and animals were created in the same week—says so in the Bible."

Ginny laughed. "You've got to be kidding—only flat-worlders believe in that nonsense."

Ruth pulled Ezra to her side. "The Bible isn't nonsense. It's the world of God, and He doesn't lie."

"You can't be serious—"

Joy cleared her throat and tried to steer Ruth toward the house. "Come on, let's not get into a debate. We're friends—"

Ruth's gaze met Joy regretfully. "I'm sorry, Joy, but we have to go. Ezra doesn't need to hear a grown woman spouting misinformation—"

Ginny waved an accusing finger. "Misinformation? Because I teach my kid to use his brain and not believe every—"

A truck pulled into the driveway. Joy sighed and waved. "Rick's home. He can probably identify the bone for us."

Ginny waved Joy's suggestion away. "I've got to go." She patted Joy's limp hand. "Nice try anyway." Ginny nudged Frank toward her car.

Ruth wrapped her arm around Ezra and pointed to their minivan. The boy lumbered away with his head down. Ruth stroked Joy's arm. "I'm sorry, but I can't just stand by while someone tries to shake my son's faith. I have to stand up for what I believe, right?"

Joy nodded and shifted her baby higher on her hip. "Sure. You just have different views."

Ruth shook her head. "More than that. Well, I better go. See you Sunday."

After her guests had cleared the driveway, Joy picked up the bone and drifted toward her husband.

Rick greeted his wife with a kiss on the cheek. He accepted the bone and laughed. "Good heavens, where did you find this?"

"The boys dug it up from the hole—where the old tree used to be."

Folding one arm around his wife and the baby, Rick nudged them toward the back door. A grin broke across his face. "Old Diablo—I forgot we buried him under that tree."

Joy's eyes widened—alarmed. "What? Who?"

Rick stopped and gazed over a distant field. "An old donkey of my dad's—meanest creature ever to set hoof on God's green earth. He called it Diablo because he swore that the devil himself had a hand in creating that creature's nasty tricks."

"So, you buried him by the tree?"

"He fell dead there one day, and Dad dug a hole and pushed him in. He said that Ol' Diablo wouldn't get the last laugh this time." He squeezed her shoulder. "Have a good time with your friends?" He rubbed his stomach. "Boy, I'm starving."

Joy nodded. "Dinner's almost ready." She started up the back porch steps after her husband. “But you know—” she looked back toward the hole, “I think Ol’ Diablo’s still laughing.”

You Don't Look Dead to Me

Originally published on The Writings of A. K. Frailey
3/2/2018

Jack marched over the threshold, slammed the front door with a backward kick, and slapped his phone on the counter. With a groan, he fell onto the couch and buried his face in his hands. *Stupid manager! Idiot clerk. How was I supposed to know the kid was lying? Three grand—gone—on my watch. Blast!*

Rolling onto the couch, Jack stared at the ceiling and considered his existence. *What's the point? I've tried so hard. No breaks. There's always someone ready to mess with your mind—or break your heart.* The picture of his ex-wife embracing his best friend floated before his eyes. He squeezed his eyes shut.

A revolving red siren blared by his window and drowned in the distant cityscape. With a strangled cry, he sat up, his eyes darting around the room like a trapped animal. "I've got to get out of here." He started forward. A magazine caught on his sleeve and flipped to the floor, exposing a full-page, glossy ad. Frowning, Jack retrieved the magazine and stared wide-eyed at his salvation.

Two days later, Jack squatted before a modest fire in an immodestly large national forest. His chin sported a rough beard, and his wrinkled shirt, torn pants, and mud-smeared boots proclaimed their freedom from the usual constraints of formal living. He bit his lip, his red eyes peering intently at the stripped twig bearing his dinner, which he balanced over the flickering flames. Three blackened cinders and an open package of surviving hot dogs bore testimony to his recent culinary adventures.

After achieving the perfect level of brown with only a hint of carbon coating, Jack pulled a white bun out of his portable kitchen sack and sat cross-legged for the first meal of the day. It took three more such examples to settle his stomach into a mere grumble. He rummaged through his bag, grabbed a bag of corn chips, and then snapped open a beer. With a satisfied sigh, he plunked down on the picnic bench in front of his one-man tent and smiled.

A pink and orange sunset melted into the horizon across the lake. "God, this place is beautiful." He rubbed his chin. "I may never go back. Why should I?" The food, the beer, and assorted mental strains whispered together in conspiratorial tones. Before Jack knew what hit him, he fell into a deep sleep before his dying fire.

The next morning after a quick swim in the lake, a change of clothes, and three granola bars, he rummaged through the glove compartment of his car and found his jackknife. Scuffling through many years' accumulations of dead leaves, Jack found a small branch with a quirky knot. He snapped off a section, perched himself on his bench, and commenced to whittling.

The sun sailed over the sky. Jack peered at his food bag. Just as he reached for the trail mix, he paused at the sound of angry voices.

A man and a woman clumped down the trail, their hands flailing and their tempers flaring. Jack retreated to his bench and his half-carved bird.

"It's your fault! You're the one who said that it'd only take an hour. Now we'll be late, and Mom will complain, and Dad will hate you!"

"Your dad already hates me. Being late hardly changes—"

The two pairs of eyes fastened on Jack. The woman blushed as she came to a complete stop. "Oh, sorry. Didn't know we were trespassing. Kinda got lost." She squeezed her mate's arm like a lifeline.

Jack stood and shrugged. "No problem. The road is about half a mile that-a-way." He jerked his thumb to the right.

The man stepped forward; one hand extended. "Thanks. Name's Jansen—this is Colleen. We're getting married next week."

Jack swallowed.

Colleen's eyes rounded into glowing orbs as she focused on the food sack. "You have any water by chance? I'm nearly dead. Jan forgot to pack the water bottles and then led me on this forsaken adventure—"

"Hey! Not fair. Who forgot to bring the snacks—huh? You—"

Shaking his head, Jack retreated to his car, pulled two water bottles from the back seat and then snatched a couple candy bars from his food bag. He tossed them over. "Here. You'll live long enough to get married, okay?" His eyes shifted to the right.

Jansen nodded appreciatively and tugged Colleen aside. "Thanks! You're a lifesaver." He checked his watch. "We'll still make it if we hurry. Come on."

Jack watched the couple bounce down the road, gulping water and tearing into the snack food. Just as he settled back to his bench, he heard a squawk. A blue jay hobbled into view; a bright orange twine wrapped tight around his leg.

Five minutes, three pecks, and innumerable protesting squawks later, the bird flew free into a nearby pine tree.

Shading his eyes from the sun's glare, Jack considered the angry bird. "You might try a little gratitude, you—"

A chuckle turned Jack to the left. The oldest man in creation ambled toward him. "Oh, they've no sense of gratitude. Not a blue jay. They like to complain. No matter what happens, they gotta squawk about it. It's their nature, you know, like some people—bitter to the very end."

Jack cleared his throat, his eyes shifted to his limp food bag. "You need something?"

The old man settled on the edge of Jack's bench. "Naw. Just a second to catch my breath. This used to be my spot. I'd come up here to get away from things and consider my next steps." His aged, lined face wrinkled into a wreath of smiles.

Heaving a deep breath, Jack plunked down on the other side of the bench, his hands resting on the knife and the half-carved figure. "I wish I could. No next steps for me. Just retreat."

The old man surveyed the sky. "Yep. I done that too. It's a good move—while it lasts. But you can't retreat forever. You got to keep moving or lay down and die." With a tilt of his head, his gaze swiveled over to Jack. "You don't look dead to me."

Tears filled Jack's eyes. Snatching up the knife and figure, he set to work.

As he rubbed his beardless chin, the old man surveyed the distant hills. "It was a nice thing you done—helping out that lost couple and freeing that ornery bird. That's how it often works out. Can't help yourself, but you can help someone. Makes life worth living."

Jack's hands froze. He tried to blink away his blurry vision.

The old man stood and stretched. "Well, this isn't my place anymore. I gotta move on, too. But stay and enjoy—till you're ready. You can always come back."

When Jack dared to look up, a breeze rustled the leaves of the trees and rumpled his hair. No old man. No couple. Even the bird was gone. His stomach growled. His eyes flickered from the depleted food bag to the remains of last night's charred feast.

He picked up the knife and the wooden figure and stared into the horizon.

Four hours later, Jack steered his car down the road. A roughly carved bird sat perched on the dashboard, its gaze pointed straight ahead.

Don't Miss a Day

Originally published on The Writings of A. K. Frailey
3/16/2018

Kenny stared down at his sleeping grandson. His hand trembled as he pulled the cover over the boy's thin shoulders. "You'll be alright. It's not a reflection on you. Not about you at all." Slowly, he leaned over, and his arm shook as his weight descended. He bent low and kissed the child on the cheek. "Bye, my boy. We'll meet again someday."

Shuffling into the kitchen, Kenny snapped on a light, and a yellow glow brightened a country décor with wood cabinets, hanging herbs, and matching blue and green striped towels. He pulled open the refrigerator door and rummaged about, looking for possibilities.

"Your appetite back, Dad?" A tall man with a swath of black hair—a younger version of his father—stepped to the counter and plopped down on a stool. He rested his head on his hands, his eyes red and strained, pain peeking up from their depths.

"It never left—my stomach just got bewildered for a bit." Tucking a beer under his arm, Kenny balanced a plate of cold chicken in one hand and squeezed a bag of biscuits in the other. After arranging the food on a napkin, he settled down on a stool across from his son. "Want some?"

The younger man waved the offer away. "So—you sure you want to go through with it?"

Kenny bit into a fried chicken leg and chewed, his gaze roaming the room and stopping on a bright orange clock in the shape of an oversized chicken head. "I remember when your mother gave you that. Cindy hated it—don't deny it. I told Evelyn that such a monstrosity would only perpetuate the evil mother-in-law myth, but—well—you know your mother."

A flickering light flared to life as the young man grinned at his dad. "Cindy loves it. A conversation piece that never fails. Gains sympathy every time."

Kenny chuckled as he wiped his scraggly chin. A two-day-old beard scratched noisily against the paper leaving white specks on his face. He took a long swig of his beer and shoved the chicken aside. "I'm not going *through* with anything. That's kinda the point. I'm letting nature take its course. What will be—will be." Picking up the biscuit, Kenny waved it absently. "Let it go, Tom. Just let it go."

Tom's leg began to bounce as he tapped his fingers together. "Listen, if you won't take the treatment—at least stick around here awhile. I can help you—"

Slapping his hand on the counter, Kenny snapped. "No! Don't you see? It wouldn't work. I'll fall apart just the same. Slow or fast. What's the difference? It's not just about you, my boy." Raising his shaking hand, he pointed to the doorway leading to his grandson's room. "Remember Davy? I don't want his last memory of me being a filthy, decrepit old man hooked up to tubes and wires." His eyes filled with tears. "Or you either—for that matter." He shoveled his food onto the napkin and wrapped it into a tight ball. He shoved it toward his son. "I'll eat later." Easing off his stool, he headed for the door. “God to take me soon. I’ll not step one foot in His way.”

Tom’s head dropped to his chest; his eyes squeezed tight.

~~~

A bright morning sun sent brilliant dust-speckled beams through the kitchen, revealing a different side to her nature. Cindy waved to her little boy through the window as he boarded a yellow school bus.

He waved back, his mittened hand a smidgen of red on the snow-covered road.

Cindy turned and slid a bowl of hot oatmeal across the counter.

With quick steps, Tom hurried into the room, slipping his arms into a heavy winter coat. “Why didn’t you wake me earlier? I’ve got to meet the guys and then—”

Cindy waved her husband toward the door. You’ve got plenty of time. George will have donuts and that horrible fake juice waiting—don’t you worry. It’s what he lives for.”

After a swift peck on his wife’s cheek, Tom headed out the door.

Cindy shook her head. “Men.”

Tom poked his head back through the open doorway. “You’ll keep an eye on Dad? He’ll have to be ready to go by one.”

With a nod, Cindy ushered her husband on his way.

Kenny lumbered into the room and plunked down on the stool. He peered from the hot cereal to Cindy.
~~~

After slinging a towel over her shoulder, she grabbed a jar of brown sugar and slid it in his direction.

"Tom off?"

Cindy nodded and started folding yesterday's laundry. She peered up and watched Kenny slurp his cereal in cautious sips. "You know, Davy will be crushed when he finds you've gone."

Kenny's fingers clenched around the spoon. He laid it down and stared his daughter-in-law into oblivion. "I got to do what I got to do. Davy don't need to see me all ragged and—"

Her chin jutting a mile from her face, Cindy gripped the back of a chair. "Yes. He. Does." She pounded across the room and stood up to the old man, peering into his watery blue eyes. "Listen to me, you ragged, wreck of a man. That boy loves you not one bit less for being rough around the edges. And your son is crushed under by your doubt."

"I don't doubt him. I just want to spare—"

Cindy sucked in a shuddering breath. "Long past that, Kenny." She straightened her shoulders. "Listen to me. You're on the brink of stepping off a cliff. I get that. You're facing the end of your journey here, and you have the right to decide your treatment—or non-treatment. But you don't have the right to tell your family to act as if nothing bad is happening—as if this isn't tearing our hearts out. Because. It is. Ragged or no ragged." Snatching up the towel, Cindy ran it along her eyes, wiping away tears.

Kenny stared into the air. "I just can't bear it. It's bad enough that Evelyn has to stand by and watch. How can I handle an audience?" Kenny laid his head in his clasped hands; his elbows perched on the counter. “God, I just wish it were over.”

Cindy stepped over and wrapped her arms around Kenny’s thin shoulder. She laid her head on his shoulder. “What did Evelyn say when you told her you wouldn’t stay?”

“Called me a coward—but I had that right. Said I could slip into the dark night anyway I want.” Kenny laid one hand on Cindy’s and let his head rest against hers. “That’s how much she loves me. She’ll let me go in peace.”

Cindy straightened up and stepped away. She pointed to the clock on the wall. “You know, at first, I hated that thing. But after a while, I didn’t see the ugliness—I just saw the love that Evelyn intended.” She returned to her laundry. “Life is full of ugly. Davy already learned that when my brother, Uncle Ben died. Car accidents are ugly—let me tell you.” Laying a pair of worn jeans aside, she peered over at Kenny. “If you can’t face ugly in this world, you’ll never get to see the beauty beyond it.”

Kenny peered across the room, his gaze resting on the stack of jeans.

“Don’t let Davy miss a day—even if it’s got some ugly in it.”

~~~

A spring breeze blew across the graveyard, sending a shower of white cherry blossoms wafting through the air.

A nine-year-old boy in a pair of jeans and a plaid shirt stood in front of a shiny monument
~~~

standing guard over a fresh mound of earth. He tilted his head to one side.

Tom ambled up and laid his arm on his son's shoulder. "It's time to go. You have your chat?"

Davy turned and took his father's hand. "Yeah. I told him that I like his monument. I think he'll like it too."

A quizzical smile quivered on Tom's lips. "Any reason in particular?"

Davy swung around and started home. "Well, you know. It's so clean and handsome—like grandpa."

My Love Is Strong

Originally published on The Writings of A. K. Frailey
3/30/2018

Wendy tripped over a block castle, fell against the counter, knocked the coffee maker askew, and apologized. "Whoops, sorry 'bout that!" Grabbing a sponge, she quickly mopped up the spill and darted a worried glance at the wrecked castle.

Ginny, her six-year-old daughter, skipped into the room. "Who you talking to?"

Before Wendy could answer, Ginny's gaze swept across the devastation of her former block-castle glory. Her eyes widened in fitful rage. "What'da do that for, Mom?"

"It was an accident, honey. You shouldn't leave—"

"Hey!" A large, heavily built man with a close-cropped, brown beard sauntered into the kitchen. "You remember me?"

Wendy blinked as wrinkles spread across her forehead. Something on the edge of her frazzled memory sounded a weak alarm. "My husband—right?"

"Very funny." Mitch tapped his watch. "We're going out tonight—anniversary? Ring any bells?"

After swallowing back a gasp, Wendy clasped her hands together. "Yeah, I remember, but earlier—I forgot. I, sort of, invited Deirdre over for a cup of tea." Wendy's hands flew out imploringly. "Her life's falling apart. I thought tea might help—somehow."

Mitch pulled a cup from the shelf and poured out the coffee dregs. "It'll take more than tea to fix that woman." He took a sip and winced. "Sides, I asked for tonight first—about twenty years ago."

Wendy nodded. "Of course. I've been looking forward to it. Did you get Keith off to his game?"

Mitch leaned against the counter and rubbed his jaw. "Like a happy gladiator going into battle. Scary, actually." He peered down at his daughter's pensive face. Reconstruction was well underway. "Who's watching—?"

Wendy froze. "Oh, my gosh!"

Heaving himself into a chair, Mitch sighed. "And I don't suppose you have anything ready for dinner?"

Wendy peered at the ceiling. "The part of my brain in charge of dinner remembered about going out. The rest of my brain forgot." She rubbed her eyes. "What do you think—early dementia?"

"Well, I did notice that you put Patrick's jeans in my drawer. Wasn't till I got stuck somewhere around the knees that I figured it out." Mitch pursed his lips. "How does that kid stay so dang thin? I pay enough for the meal plan."

Wendy slumped into the chair opposite her husband. "He's not coming home like he used to—preoccupied. I think it's a girlfriend or—"

"He'll never make it through college." Mitch rubbed his forehead. "I should've just had him take up a trade."

Wendy shrugged. "He's used to having his own way. Perhaps if he fails—"

"Fails with my money!" Mitch glanced at his watch and stood. "I'll order pizza, and we'll make it an easy night. Maybe watch a movie or something."

Wendy's heart sank as she offered a brave smile. After her husband clumped out of the room, she peered at her daughter. "Time to clean up, honey. Daddy's going to—"

"Can't I leave it here—please? It took me so long to fix—after you messed it up." Gina's large brown eyes implored with every fiber of her being.

"Well, okay. I guess—"

A large, heavy-set woman bundled into the kitchen. "Lord, where's that tea? I'm about done-in."

Wendy's eyes flashed from her friend to the kitchen door.

"Mitch let me in the front. There's a ton of mud in your driveway—it's not safe." Deirdre plunked down onto a kitchen chair and dropped her head onto her hands. "I can't take it anymore. Life is pure hell these days." She peered up at Wendy, who stood frozen in the middle of the room. "I'm thinking of ending it all."

A rumble scoured across the heavens.

Wendy strolled to the window and peered at the dark, threatening sky. She bit her lip and glanced at Deirdre. "I hate to tell you, but tonight's Mitch's and my anniversary and—"

Deirdre dragged her limp body off the chair and staggered to a standing position. "I tell you I want to kill myself, and you toss me aside. Sure—I understand. Loving hubby needs you. Priorities." With a shaky hand, she patted Gina on the head.

Gina glowered.

Lightning flashed, lighting up the descending gloom.

Deirdre shrugged. "Sweet kid." She started

toward the kitchen door, her foot knocking part of the block castle across the floor.

Gina wailed.

Deirdre clasped the door handle and looked back at Wendy; her eyes half-lidded. “You got it all. Lucky woman.”

Mitch’s voice called from the living room. “Hey, honey, you want sausage, pepperoni, or meat-lovers?”

Rain pelted the window.

When the phone rang, Wendy wasn’t the least surprised. In an automatic motion, she pressed the receiver to her ear. “Yes?”

Patrick’s voice whined across two state lines. “Mom, I’m sick. Can you come get me?”

Wendy’s gaze swept from Deirdre—still gripping the door handle—to her sniffling, miserable daughter, to her husband’s frowning face peering through the doorway.

“Mom?”

Wendy didn’t hear anything break, but she felt a snapping deep within. Her gaze darted to a crucifix on the wall. Standing completely motionless, only her eyes widened.

She gripped the phone more tightly. “Patrick, the college has a clinic open twenty-four-seven. Go there and see if they can help. Then call back and let me know.” She pressed the end button.

With a nod, she waved goodbye to Deirdre and watched her friend harrumph her way out the door.

Turning her attention to the block-strewn floor, Wendy pointed at her daughter. “Pick it all up—now—and not a word, or you’ll go straight to bed.” Her gaze swung to her husband.

Mitch started to back away.

"Let's try something new—the Hawaiian or Taco—surprise me."

~~~

As ragged clouds drifted across a waxing moon, Mitch wound his arms around his wife in the privacy of their bedroom. He peered through the dim light and grinned. "What got into you this afternoon—I hardly knew you." He chuckled. "Scared everyone—even me."

Wendy slid her fingers down her husband's bare, muscular arm, her eyes radiating a serious glow. "When I looked at the crucifix—I heard a voice inside my head."

With a startled jerk, Mitch fixed his gaze on his wife. "What did it say?"

Wendy sucked in a deep breath and enunciated each word carefully. "'I said *meek*—not *weak*.'"

Mitch loosened his hold over his wife and swallowed. "Am I in for it now?"

Wendy giggled, leaned forward, and kissed her husband. "My love is strong."

Grinning, Mitch pulled his wife into a tight embrace. "Lord, have mercy."
~~~

So Blind

Originally published on The Writings of A. K. Frailey
4/13/2018

Nancy rested her head on her hands and blocked out the bars of her cell. She could feel the swelling lump on her forehead where she had banged against the dashboard, but otherwise, she couldn't sense any other serious damage. Of course, they had checked if she could walk and if anything was broken before they brought her in. Almost seemed to care. She shook her head and snorted.

"You're awake then?"

Lifting her gaze, she peered at the officer on the other side of the bars. "Never slept. Just lay down for a minute. That's a crime too, I suppose?"

"I could hear you snoring down the hall. The sun's up, and your lawyer said he'd be here by nine."

"Thank God for small mercies."

The tall, thin, brown-haired young man stared at the middle-aged woman before him. "You have a chance to think things over?"

"Think what over?" Nancy wobbled to her feet, clutching her aching head. Her voice rose. "Think about how some damn fool smashed into me, but *you* put me in jail?"

"Plenty of witnesses saw you cross the line. Your car ended up backward in the left lane. And your blood alcohol level—"

"Oh, don't start again! Good heavens! I only had *one* and a half beers. It was a party! I couldn't just sit there acting like I disdained their offerings."

"And their wine? It showed up—"

"A sip or two hardly amounts to anything." Nancy ran a disgusted gaze up and down the young man's form. "You're young enough to be one of my students. You know, I'm not the person you take me for. Not some bit of trash getting drunk at—"

The officer lifted a hand. "I not your judge or jury. Just hoping that you have something to say to your lawyer when he shows up."

Nancy tugged at her collar and straightened her sleeves. "What difference does it make to you? *You're* the reason I'm in here. If you had just listened to me, my son and I would—" Nancy frowned. "Where's Billy? Did Ron get him?"

"He's still under observation at Children's. Nasty wallop he got—"

"It wasn't my fault! It was that crazy woman, that idiot blond with the tight skirt." Nancy swung around. "I've been a teacher for nearly as long as you've been alive, and I volunteer for good causes. No one in their right mind will think I'm guilty. But one look at her—"

The officer's chin hardened as he thrust back his shoulders. "Her baby girl was in the passenger seat."

"See! Made my point. Everyone knows that babies ought to be in the backseat. Stupid woman!" Nancy ran a finger along her bruise and then tucked a stray lock of hair behind her ear. "How's the baby doing? I'll tell my Ron to go see her when he checks in on Billy."

"Wouldn't do that if I were you. The baby's critical. She was facing the wrong direction and the airbag—" The officer looked away.

Nancy flopped down on the rickety cot. "Damn." She squeezed her eyes shut; her lips quivered a moment. "No deserves to lose their baby." After wiping her face, she looked up and wagged a finger at the young man. "She ought to have known better. There're about a million notices everywhere about that very thing."

Another officer marched forward, and the two officers consulted together.

Nancy ran her hands along her rumpled dress and rubbed her stomach. When the two men were finished, she called to the first. "Hey, you." She peered at his nametag. "Officer Raymond. Anything to eat around here? I'm famished, and I don't know how long it'll take before I get a decent meal."

The officer considered the woman before him. His voice dropped to a cold, professional tone. "You'll get fed along with everyone else when the meals are brought over." He turned away, stopped, and then turned back. "I go off in an hour, so you'll be gone before I get back. But I've really gotta thank you."

Nancy blinked in surprise. Her lips curled into a pleased smile. "How's that? I'm probably a model prisoner compared to what you're used to—"

The officer lifted his hand. "On the contrary, I've dealt much better prisoners, men and woman, who were actually sorry for what they've done. You happen to look a lot like someone I know. I always worried I'd lose my perspective if had to I deal with someone that reminded me of a friend. But now—that fear is gone."

Nancy stepped forward and gripped the bars with both hands. “Because I’m so innocent?”

The officer turned away. “Because you’re so blind.”

In Two Words

Originally published on The Writings of A. K. Frailey
10/18/2018

Professor Lana Bentley leaned back in her chair and crossed her legs. Her gaze rolled over the eighteen-year-old woman, sitting ramrod straight before her. She practically glowed with her brightest smile. "So, Irma, are you excited about your first year of college?"

Irma slumped forward, her hands clasping and unclasping convulsively, like sea creatures swishing through the deep. Her grey eyes peered through thick glasses and heavy makeup, imploring the fountain of wisdom behind the desk. "I don't know. I think I am. I mean, I've been looking forward to this my whole life. Always wanted to go to college, ever since I first learned there was such a thing."

A twinge of alarm spread through Professor Bentley. "How old would that have been?"

"Four...maybe five." Irma met Professor Bentley's gaze. "My dad's a janitor, and he got a job at a university. He took us to see where he worked. And—" Irma blushed. "It was love at first sight."

Heat crept up Professor Bentley's face. "Well, that's the best of news." She beamed again. She felt proud of her ability to put others at ease. Beaming was one of her specialties.

Irma frowned; her hands squeezed so tight her knuckles turned white.

Professor Bentley considered the girl's hands.

"But it appears that you're still a little anxious. Is there something bothering you? Worried about your classes or—?"

Irma swallowed a gulp of air, a drowning victim at the end of her strength. "It's just that I'm so afraid."

Sitting up straight, Professor Bentley tapped her computer keyboard and pulled up Irma's file. After scanning the record, she glanced at the girl before her. "Your grades and scores are excellent. You've already won awards in your chosen field of study, and your recommendations are brilliant." She pursed her lips and tapped her fingers together, a serious professional doing her duty. "You have nothing to be afraid of. You'll do fine."

Irma shot from her chair and twirled around behind, gripping the back for dear life. "I'm not afraid of the work. I know I can get good grades."

Professor Bentley snatched a glance at her watch. She stood and stepped away from her desk. "I have a class in fifteen minutes but walk with me across campus. She swung a satchel over her shoulder. "I really want to help—I'm just—"

Irma opened the door and let the professor pass through. Once outside, crossing over the long shadows of an August afternoon, the student tromped alongside her mentor, her shoulders drooping and her hair hanging like a curtain across her face.

A young man jogged by and waved.

Irma averted her eyes.

Professor Bentley smiled, stopped, and laid a gentle hand on Irma's shoulder. "You're worried about making friends...men friends even?"

Irma's eyes flickered to the sky. "Yes...and no.

I make friends easy enough. Everyone likes the shy, smart girl who shares her notes."

Professor Bentley choked, her eyes widening. She started forward again, her heels clicking on the tidy cement walkway. Autumn leaves whirled in a sudden breeze.

Quickening her pace, Irma kept up. "It's just that I've dreamed about this for so long; it's like the best fantasy ever...and I don't want it to end."

Stopping before the science building, Professor Bentley felt a chill run through her veins. "But, Irma, reality is better than fantasy."

Irma shoved her glasses up the bridge of her nose and peered into the eyes of wisdom. "Is it?"

Professor Bentley blinked at the tears starting in her eyes. "Oh, my dear. You just told me the saddest story I ever heard—in two words."

~~~

That evening as Lana sat ensconced in the crook of her husband's arm, she laid her head on his chest and sighed.

George pulled off his glasses and laid them on the coffee table. "You want to tell me?" He titled his head and peered at her lifted gaze.

Lana shook her head, her gaze dropping. "I met a new student today, a friendly mentoring session. You know."

"You've done hundreds. Best there is." A smile quirked at the corner of his mouth, his eyes sparkling.

"I always thought so. But today—I was the one mentored. The student taught the teacher."

"What on earth could an eighteen-year-old freshman teach you?"

Lana slapped her forehead and tugged her
~~~

fingers through her hair. "What it feels like to be eighteen—a dreamer with nothing but dreams to hang on to."

George shrugged. "You've handled that before."

"Yes, and I always challenged it. I always knew best. I—" She pulled away and sat up, her hands clasping in an attitude of prayer. "I just realized—I don't remember what it's like to be a freshman, to be young, to be scared, to be idealistic." She swallowed and met her husband's frank stare. "From the first moment I saw her, I had this girl pegged from her thick glasses down to her skinny jeans. But, really, I have no idea what she dreams of. And if perhaps her dreams are better than the reality I'm offering."

George shifted to the edge of the couch, positioned for a launch. He glanced at the kitchen counter with an array of drinks lined in neat order. "Dreams die in the light of day."

"But somewhere, somehow, isn't their room for a both—a dream to guide and reality to rule?"

Standing, George peered down at his wife, a frown forming between his eyes. "Dreams don't pay bills. You've told me that a million times."

Lana stood and sauntered to the bay window. She stared at the black frame, peering into darkness. "That's true. But when Irma told me she was afraid of reality, she scared me and made me sad." She turned and peered at her husband, her own eyes imploring.

George sauntered toward the kitchen. "You don't kill these kids' dreams. Reality does."

"Perhaps that's why I feel so bad. I've known that all along." Lana turned and faced her husband's departing figure. Her voice dropped to a whisper. "When I dismissed her dreams, I dismissed the girl...and perhaps...a reality that might have been."

Alternative Universe

Originally published on The Writings of A. K. Frailey
4/27/2018

Jim Smith's office loomed in darkness except for a single lamp highlighting a cluttered desk.

A tall man with a black ponytail leaned back on a rolling chair and rubbed his eyes. "Dang, it's been a long day."

Staccato heels clicked across the floor. "Muttering to yourself again, Jimmy-boy?" A grinning brunette with round, jovial eyes tapped the edge of Jim's computer screen. "Time you gave it a rest. Kenny and I are going to grab dinner at the Seashell. Wanna come?"

Leaning on one arm and looking like he might slide to the floor in a puddle of spent energy, Jim eyed his compatriot in exotic studies. "No rest for the wicked, Christy. You ought to know that by now."

Christy leaned in, her smile widening in a challenge. "Even the devil gets time off for good behavior." Swiping a stray lock of hair from her eyes, she straightened and shrugged. "We'll hang out for a bit. Come when you can."

Sliding his fingers down the side of his face, Jim shook his head as he watched Christy's silhouette pass through the doorway. "Gorgeous but never makes the least effort to be logical. The devil—hah!" His gaze flickered to the screen. Under a subheading "Alternate Universe Citations," thirty resources lined the page in perfect APA order.

With the sublime effort of a god-finger reaching toward Adam, Jim tapped the off switch and the screen blinked to black. "Time to feed the cat." He struggled to his feet, staggered, and then, like a ship when the wind dies down, righted his mainmast and headed for the door.

At home, Jim found the cat alive though far from happy. He scoured the shelves and discovered what the cat already knew—the cupboard was bare. "Dang it!"

The cat couldn't have agreed more.

"Guess it's out into the wilds once again." Jim peered down at the feline. "It won't take me long. They have eatables in the shop on the corner." He glanced at his watch. "If they're still open." He rattled through the doorway, clumped down his apartment steps, and plowed his way through the crowded street.

The cat watched from the window.

Inside the market, Jim snatched up a bag of kitty food, a quart of milk, a box of granola, and a sausage pizza. He pondered a can of root beer.

A man, loaded with foodstuffs, stepped next to him. "Excuse me." The man pulled open the glass door and plucked a root beer off the shelf.

Jim glanced over and nearly dropped his groceries.

They peered at each other; both sets of eyes widening in confusion.

Jim's arms began to shake. *Mirror, mirror….* He peered at the items in the man's arms. Kitty food, a pizza—pepperoni not sausage—a quart of milk and a pack of granola bars. His gaze traveled to the other man's round, frozen eyes. He swallowed and stuttered a single word. "H—Hello."

The stranger cleared his throat. "You seem *awfully* familiar."

Like a pricked balloon, they burst out laughing. Jim piled his parcels onto one arm and thrust out a hand. "Name's Jim. Always wanted to meet my alternate universe persona."

The other man balanced his goods on his left arm and grasped Jim's hand with a warm smile. "James." He shook his head. "Never seen anything like this. "He nodded to the checkout counter. "I'm just staying the night at the One-Stop next door. Traveling through. Me and Millie—my cat. We're visiting friends in Milwaukee."

Jim dumped his foodstuff on the counter and faced James. "I live up the block. I wasn't kidding about an alternate universe—that's my thesis. I'm a student at Chicago University."

James lined his foodstuffs in neat order behind Jim's. "Very cool. My dad's big into theoretical science too—time travel, extraterrestrial life—all that."

The two men paid their dues and started for the door with matching sacks hanging at their sides.

Jim opened the door and nodded to the left. "Well, I go this way."

James grinned. "Hey, how about you stop by the motel a minute, and I'll get a picture of us together. My friends won't believe that I have a lookalike."

Jim shrugged. "My cat is about ready to kill me—but sure. I'll take one too. My mom will freak.

She thinks I'm crazy—this'll at least bring some credence to my theory."

As soon as the two entered the dark room, James snapped on a light and dropped his groceries on a table. He pointed to another. "Just put your stuff there—" He fished his phone out of a pocket as his gaze roamed over the matching foodstuffs. "Did you notice? We got almost the exact same things?"

Jim nodded. He bent down and patted a gorgeous white Persian cat. "Well, at least we have different tastes in cats. Mine is a calico." He straightened and peered at James. "So, what do you do for a living?"

James adjusted the camera feature on his phone. "I'm studying to become a Jesuit priest." He peered over the camera and grinned. "Thought my dad would kill me—alternate universe here I come."

With his hands clasped, Jim sniffed back sudden irritation. "What do you mean by that?"

Focusing on Jim, James waved with two fingers to the left. "Take a step—there. Perfect." He tapped the phone and scanned through images. "Take a look at my dad. He's a big man—important in his own way—never to be taken lightly." He turned the phone around so the image faced Jim.

Jim took three steps forward and froze. As if his hand moved by a separate power, it found his shirt pocket, lifted a phone forward, and within seconds, his eyes scanned through multiple images. "Dad hates to have his picture taken—now I know why." He turned the phone around.

James staggered and fell on the edge of the

bed. “Oh, Lord.”

Jim plopped down next to James and rubbed his face. “God had little to do with this.”

Slapping his leg, James stood. He stalked across the room. “So, that explains everything. All the business trips. Gone for months at a time!”

The cat twirled around James’ leg.

With shaking fury, James’ peeled open a can of cat food, pounded to the bathroom, and slapped the container on the floor. “Here, now quit being a pest.”

Jim’s gaze strolled from the cat to James. “It isn’t the cat’s fault.” He shook his head and ran his fingers through his hair. “I should’ve guessed. I always thought his secretiveness had to do with his science—never occurred to me he was leading a double life.” His fingers curled into clenched fists. “Poor mom.”

His eyes closed in pain; James leaned against the wall. “What’s your mom’s name?”

Jim’s gaze flickered over his phone. He found another picture, stood, and held it out. “Saundra.”

James opened his eyes and nodded. “She’s beautiful.” He held up his phone, found an image, and passed it over. “Maria.”

Jim stared at the photo. “Gorgeous.” He slapped his face as he handed the phone back. “Dad always has had a strange sense of morality.” He shuddered a long exhaling breath. “Odd sense of humor too.”

James shook his head as if chastising the floor. “True. I just never thought it extended this far.” He nudged his half-brother. “Guess the joke’s on us.”

Jim stood to his full height and pulled a card out of his wallet. “Call me when you get home, and we’ll arrange a little joke on Dad.” He gathered his groceries into his arms and stepped to the door.

James followed and tapped his card into Jim’s shirt pocket. “I’ve always believed in a supernatural, not an alternative universe. But in this case, I’ll bet by the time we’re through, Dad will believe in both.”

Jim stepped over the threshold. “When our moms find out, likely, he’ll be heading for one—or the other.”

Enlightened

Originally published on The Writings of A. K. Frailey
4/11/2018

"The only thing worse than loving a married man—is loving a dead man."

"Huh?" Patty passed one last cleansing swipe across her baby's bottom, tossed a soiled diaper into the trashcan and bundled the infant into clean clothes faster than her sister could comprehend. She turned triumphantly with a smiling, drooling baby in her arms. "Wanna explain that?"

Megan unfolded her body, rose from the chair and limped across the room. She wiggled inviting fingers, her wide eyes beckoning. "Airplane? Zoom-zoom?"

Baby Sam grinned over his mother's shoulder, but as soon as Megan stretched out her arms, he shrieked and nearly strangled his mom in an attempt to stay out of Megan's reach.

Backing off, Megan lifted her hands high. "I'll stop. Geesh, you'll give me a complex, little one."

"He doesn't mean anything insulting. Just loves his mama. You'll find out." Patty raised one eyebrow and pursed her lips. "What'ya mean by loving a dead man? Sounds creepy." After throwing a clean cloth over her shoulder, she hitched Sam on her hip and speed-walked down the hall to the kitchen. She called over her shoulder. "And don't you *ever* think about a married man. I'd get an exorcist over here so fast—"

Megan hobbled to the kitchen counter and

flopped onto a barstool. “Pu-leez! I was just saying—in effect—that all the good men are taken. I have my choice of men other women already snatched up or dead poets who—though full of soulful sentiments—are now residing in six-foot coffins with only room enough for one.”

Patty closed her eyes and rubbed her forehead. “Lord, where did mom get you?” She opened her eyes and stared at Megan. “Little sister, you need to get over yourself. You think it was magic that got me married to a great guy?”

Megan drummed her fingers on the countertop, her gaze wandering over to her brother-in-law’s hunter-green coat hanging on a peg by the back door. “Well, you did say about a ka-zillion rosaries, and I swear you bought so many votive candles, the church could afford to enlarge the parking lot.”

After sliding Sam into a highchair, Patty dropped a bowl of puréed fruit on the tray and invited him to dive in.

He did. With both hands.

Megan cringed.

Patty literally tossed a salad into a large bowl and shoved it near the center of the kitchen table, grunting. “Silly girl! I wasn’t asking for anything—I was thanking Him—for everything.” Her gaze darted to the door. “I was smart enough to follow the advice of nearly every saint in history.”

Megan sat bolt upright, folding her hands in apparent ecstasy. “Share the secret, oh enlightened one.”

The back door banged open and a muscular man in his late twenties with a scratch along the side of his face, wearing a dirty jacket and carrying a load of lumber, struggled into the warm kitchen. “Honey, I’m gonna work in the basement—it’s too friggin cold out there. My hands keep freezing up.”

Tucking a loaf of bread under her arm, Patty swung the basement door open, toed a stray boot out of the way, and grinned. “Fine. Dinner’s almost ready.”

Megan grimaced at the sound of two-by-fours pounding down each step. She turned and watched as Patty laid the loaf of bread on a plate and set it at the head of the table. “He’ll make a mess. You just barely got the chick pen outta there.”

“Likely he’ll have to put it back and raise the chicks down there...if this weather doesn’t warm up soon.” Patty turned and pulled a steaming roast beef out of the oven and set it on the table. She sniffed in satisfaction as she eyed the well-laid table. “You know, the key to a man’s heart.”

Megan snorted. “So that’s your pearl of wisdom to a poor, unwed maiden...learn to cook and clean...and take care of babies?” Jumping off the stool, Megan winced and grabbed her ankle. “Stupid sprain!”

A hammering racket rising from the basement sent shivers through the house. Patty closed the door, steered her sister to the table, and pressed her shoulder, forcing her to sit. “No—and yes. Listen, the way to a man’s heart is the way to anyone’s heart. Love them, love what they love, and make their lives a little easier whenever possible.”

“Sounds so—Medieval.”

Baby Sam shrieked and threw his half-finished appetizer across the room, sending a splattering of purple goo over the chair, the wall, and the floor. Patty sighed, pulled the dishrag off her shoulder and started wiping. “Ancient maybe but not tied to any particular time or place.” She straightened, snatched a handful of paper towels off the counter, and passed them to her sister. “Here, you help.”

Megan’s lips pouted. “But my ankle hurts.”

Patty frowned as she bent forward and hissed in her sister’s ear. “Life hurts, kiddo. Accept that little fact, and don’t let it ruin your day.” She pulled her baby from the high chair and snorted. “Sammy needs a new diaper.” She pointed to the bedroom “If you’d prefer—”

“No! I’d rather wipe up goo than—” She knelt on the floor, winced, and began wiping.

Patty retreated to the bedroom with the giggling baby on her hip.

Clumping footstep stopped behind her. Megan peered up and stared into the sparkling brown eyes of her brother-in-law.

The large man knelt at her side with a damp rag and began wiping the mess off the floor. He grinned. “Like I always say, you can always tell the worth of a woman by how she treats her sister.”

Innocence

Originally published on The Writings of A. K. Frailey
4/24/2018

Sunrays slanted across the budding woods as Sean dragged a dead sapling along a well-worn trail. He yanked it over a makeshift wooden bridge crossing over a spring-swollen stream. Grunting, he lifted the thick end over his shoulder and hefted it on a mountainous brush pile by a tumbledown old barn.

"What 'cha doing? Building a pyre to the gods of ol'?"

Sean turned, his blue eyes glinting in the bright light. "More like penance for my sins." He pulled off a torn work glove and rubbed his face where a two-day-old beard highlighted the edge of his chin. He offered a quick, half-hearted smile. "What're you doing here, Clive? I thought you were helping out at the McAllen place."

Clive shrugged and started ahead as Sean turned back across the bridge. "Ah, they got the plumbers and electricians in today. I went to help at the Buran building, but Joe said they have enough guys—told me to take the rest of the day and catch up on my rest."

With a snort, Sean yanked on his glove. "So kind of him. Always thinking of the other guy."

Clive stepped off the edge of the bridge and gazed in wonder at the matriarchal old maple cut into manageable lengths. "What's this? Sarcasm from Mr. Congeniality himself?"

Without a backward glance, Sean pulled a

branch free and tugged it to the bridge.

"So, this what you've been up to the last few days?" Clive grasped another branch and followed his friend. He cleared his throat. "I heard about Ginger."

For a brief moment, Sean halted in the middle of the bridge, but then he yanked the branch free of a snag and tromped off to the brush pile, his back straight and his feet unwavering.

Clive hurried after him. "I'm the one who warned you about her, remember? Always said she had a roving eye."

Grunting, Sean shoved the branch high on the pile. "When it was roving over me, I didn't mind so much." He stood back and let Clive heave his branch on the pile. "I should've seen it coming. Stupid of me to be so blind."

Clive's branch rolled to the ground, and both men hefted it back on top. Clive turned and stared his friend in the eye. "You're a trusting sort of guy. Wasn't your fault." He eyed the huge pile and then let his gaze roam the wooded landscape. "You've got enough here to keep your woodstove stocked for a century." He lifted his chin. "You don't really blame yourself—do you?"

Tromping down the path, Sean intercepted a hound that jumped and wiggled for attention. Bending down, Sean scratched behind the dog's ears. "Joseph asked me why his mom moved out." He straightened and glanced back at his friend, his blue eyes appearing grey and clouded.

"I hope you told him the truth—she's a manipulative shrew without an ounce of human kindness—"

Storm clouds entered Sean's eyes as he

stomped back to his friend, the dog following with its tail lowered. “Seriously? You’d have me tell my seven-year-old boy that his mother is anything less than—”

“He’ll find out someday. Besides, you gotta hate her for what she’s done.”

Exhaling a long breath, Sean pulled off his gloves and ran his fingers through his unkempt, brown hair. “She’s hardly my favorite person at the moment, but I don’t hate her, and more importantly, I don’t hate my son. What’da think it’d do to him to learn the truth—if I ever knew the truth.” His gaze stabbed the air before him. “I can’t trust my own judgment anymore.”

A ringtone blared from Clive’s pocket. Clive dug deep and pulled out his phone, his gaze flickering between his friend and the number scrolling across the screen. He sighed, punched the keypad, and lifted the phone to his ear. “Yeah?”

Sean returned to the dead maple, pulled two more branches forward and stacked them on the pile.

Clive trotted up to his friend. “Hey, Joe said they’re ready to finish up at the McAllen place this week—he wants you to come along—needs all the help he can get to finish on time.” Clive glanced at his phone. “Can I tell him you’re coming?”

Sean peered up at the sky and rubbed his face. He nodded. “Yeah. I have to live.” He shrugged. “I can do my penance anywhere.”

A quizzical expression wandered over Clive’s face as he returned to his phone. After a moment, he caught up with Sean returning to his grey house on the hill. “You’re kidding about the penance, right? I mean, we both know it was her fault."

Sean toed an empty dog dish by the back door. "Funny thing about penance, it doesn't have to be for anyone in particular. Just has to be sincere."

Clive stood rooted to the ground; his eyes wide. "But you're an innocent man, Sean."

Sean snorted and opened the back door. "Not anymore." He pointed to his truck in the driveway. "I'll be at work in the morning. Right now, I got to feed the dog and take care of the last shred of innocence in my life."

Clive blinked and glanced at a boy's face in an upper window, peering at his dad. Clive nodded and turned away.

Sean peeled off his gloves, opened the back door, and stepped inside.

Not With His Eyes

Originally published on The Writings of A. K. Frailey
6/7/2018

A yellow-striped spider climbed down from a sparking web amid rainbow-colored dewdrops and a faint breeze. Settling into a shadowed corner, it snuggled down to await its fortune. Two robins fluttered onto pine boughs and squabbled until a Blue Jay sprang between them and ended the conflict with a raucous call. A pink horizon brightened into a burnished red and gold spectrum as the sun crested the horizon, sending rays of light up the porch steps right into Betty's blind eyes.

The tears washing down her cheeks did little to appease the anguish rising in her heart. Wiping them away with the back of her hand, she sniffed and shuddered. The air, tinged with spring's warmth, wafted over her, yet her bones, chilled to the marrow, could not accept even a hint of hope.

"You're up early." Her mother, Kim, dressed in a pair of rugged jeans, a light sweatshirt, and slip-on shoes, strolled onto the back porch. Laying a gentle hand on her daughter's shoulder, she stared upon the same scene and reveled in the beauty. "It's a gorgeous morning."

Betty swallowed back a relentless sob. "I wouldn't know."

Pulling Betty into an embrace, Kim laid her head against her daughter's. "Just be glad you're alive. Those tumors would've killed you."

Reflexively, Betty touched the healing wounds

near her temples. She dropped her face into shadow. "They did—in a way. My old life is quite dead."

Kim took a step away and peered at her daughter's slumped figure. "You've got plenty of life ahead of you. And your sight might return. Doc Mallory said—"

"Doc Mallory is a know-it-all and a snob. Just because she's had bazillion patients, she thinks she understands *me*. She doesn't!"

Folding her arms over her chest and with a slight shake of the head, Kim turned and faced the rising sun. "Nevertheless, you have an appointment today, and she's the best hope we've got." After glancing at her watch, Kim started down the steps. "I'm going to check the cabbages I planted yesterday. Get ready, and we'll leave in an hour."

~~~

As Betty pounded out the clinic door, her mom grabbed her arm. "Stop and listen to me! I know you're upset, but I've got to pick up the prescriptions. The door to the Arboretum is right here—" Kim pulled Betty forward and led her fingers to a metal handle on a wide industrial-sized door with a fancy steel plate entitled *Garden Center*. "Just go inside and wander around a bit. There's staff nearby. I'll be back in half an hour."

With an angry grunt, Betty jerked open the door and stumbled inside. The humidity hit her like a slap in the face. Blinking, she stepped forward with her arms out, searching for obstacles.
~~~

Footsteps jogged forward. "Hi! Can I help you?"

Betty froze. The voice sounded like a young man. She cringed. Blindness humiliated her. For all she knew, her hair was a disheveled wreck, and her shirt was inside out. Squeezing her eyes, she reminded herself that her mom wouldn't let her out of the house without checking her over. Lifting her head, she faced the voice. "I'd like to sit down."

"Sure thing." A gentle hand gripped her shoulder and led her to a bench.

Feeling her way, Betty sat with a relieved sigh. The sunshine warmed her face. Birds twittered and a fragrant scent wafted to her nose.

"You've been to the doctor—or waiting to get in?"

Betty grimaced. "Been there. Old crow."

A snorted laugh made her tilt her head. She grinned against her will. "What's so funny?"

The man sat down at her side. "Let me guess—Doc Mallory?"

Turning as if to stare into the stranger's face, Betty blinked in surprise. "How'd you know?" She could practically hear his grin as he slapped his thighs.

"Ol' Doc Mallory is famous—or infamous—around here. Knows everything, boss of the universe, can tell what a patient's thinking and feeling miles away. Most patients hate her guts."

Betty sniffed. "She's not worth hating. Blindness—now that's—"

A bird flew by and fluttered around the two figures. Betty jerked away, bumping the stranger.

"Don't be afraid. Just a parakeet."

She could sense the stranger lift his arm. The bird flew closer, the fluttering stopped. The voice crooned in a soft undertone.

Shivers ran down Betty's spine.

The man shifted. "Despite her reputation, Doc Mallory's not so bad. She helped to build this place—got the funding for the whole wing—glass ceiling and all. And she brought in these birds as an extra surprise. This one's probably Bather—loves the birdbath and never a bit shy about asking for a little treat."

Betty cocked her head and listened to the various chirping and warbling interplay all around her. "You know all the birds here?"

"Pretty much. I volunteer twice a week. Nice way to meet people and get away from stuff—all the antics of our wild world. You know."

With a shrug, Betty dismissed the notion. "I'm never in the wild world these days—always stuck inside or holding someone's hand."

The man nudged her arm. "That'll change. You'll get more independent with time." He stood. "Well, I better feed the fish—amazing how anxious they get if you're late."

A frown puckered over Betty's brow. "You're kidding—right?"

Though his shadow blocked the sunshine, he seemed to exude his own warmth. "Caught me." He patted her shoulder. "Maybe you see better than you think."

Slouching in sudden loneliness, Betty listened as his footsteps retreated across the garden. Something landed on her shoulder, chirping in her ear. Lifting her arm, she held out a finger and a tiny, feathery body fluttered onto her hand. She could practically feel its heart pounding. "You aren't a bit shy—are you?" Lifting her chin, she listened. The sound of water trickling on her left pulled her to her feet.

Stepping carefully with one hand out and the other aloft with the bird, she finally bumped into the wide-brimmed birdbath. After laying her finger on the edge, the parakeet hopped off. Suddenly, drops of water splashed her face. A gasped laugh erupted from deep within her being.

Footsteps clicked up behind her. "You've been enjoying yourself?"

Betty turned and faced her mother. "It's beautiful here."

Kim sighed, her voice dropped low and soft. "Yes—it is." She took her daughter's arm and led her forward. "Did you meet Melvin?"

"You mean the guy who volunteers here?"

"Yeah. He was here on the day you went into surgery. I thought I'd go crazy with worry. But he set my mind at ease."

"Seems nice enough. Is he still here?"

"I don't see him now. But we better go—dad's waiting to meet us for lunch. Besides, you can see Melvin next time. He's practically a permanent fixture around here. He's Doc Mallory's son."

Betty froze in her tracks. "What? That can't be—not the way he talked about her. He seemed—to really understand!"

Kim pulled open the door and stepped aside. "Oh, I'm sure he does." With a firm grip, she directed her daughter through the doorway. "He's been blind since birth. It's why Doc Mallory built this place—and works so hard." The door swished shut behind them.

Betty choked. "*He* can't see?"

Kim took her daughter's arm. "Not with his eyes."

Betty stumped along beside her mother. "Oh, Lord, Mom! He identified the bird, and I thought—"

Kim patted her daughter's hand. "There are many ways to see, honey."

Betty exhaled. "And many ways to go blind."

Take Over the World

Originally published on The Writings of A. K. Frailey
5/52018

"Artificial intelligence will soon take over the world—you do realize that don't you?"

Sasha popped a red M & M into her mouth and crunched. Her gaze swept across the campus with a practiced eye. "I think it already has."

Barb shook her head as she appraised the harassed throng heading to various classes. "I'm not talking about people glued to their iPhones. I mean that my grandmother just texted me that a storm's coming, and she wants me to email the grocer about delivering extra supplies this afternoon."

Sasha shrugged as she pounded across the grassy courtyard to the library. "What's so bad about that? Technology makes our lives easier."

"Exactly my point!" Barb checked her phone, scrolled through three messages, and muttered. "Professor Gilmore is sick—she said to study chapter nine, and we'd meet next week."

"Lucky you. My professors are health freaks. They know whether it's coffee or tea that'll kill us this week—or is it cheese?"

"You're making my point. We know too much. We have too much power. We can't handle so much information—"

The electronic door swung open, and Sasha set off the entry alarm. "Dang it!"

The deputy security officer strolled over, a wide grin lighting up his blue eyes. "Carrying concealed weapons again—are we?"

Sasha dug into her pocket. “My grandpa gives my little brother all his old camping knives. Which the little idiot promptly uses to carve his initials into everything—so naturally—”

“You take it away and carry it into the library.” His grin widened. “An option.”

Sasha and Barb exchanged eye rolls.

Sasha pulled the offending pocketknife from her pocket and dropped it into the man’s hand. “Keep it, Jared. Carve your initials into something and feel smug.”

Jared stepped aside, flicked open the knife, and peered at a miniature toolkit with a sharp blade, a screwdriver, bottle opener, and file. “Cool—must be worth a fortune.”

Sasha frowned. “Hardly. My grandpa has dozens of these. All the rage when he was a kid.”

Barb nudged Sasha, glancing at Jared. “He’s a virtual-reality kind of guy—hardly ever sees anything *real* these days.” She wiggled her eyebrows. “An honest blade must come as a bit of a shock.” Waving her arm in a mock karate move, she went in for a slice to the arm.

Instinct kicked in and Jared lashed out, jabbing with the open knife.

Barb reeled back, gripping her stomach, blood seeping between her fingers. “Oh, God. I didn’t mean it.” She stared at Sasha as she crumpled. “He didn’t mean it.”

~~~

Sasha watched Jared’s mother, Ms. Franklin, pacing in front of him in the hospital waiting room, her eyes glued to an iPhone.
~~~

Jared sat with his hands clasped, his head bowed, staring at the grey-tiled floor.

Sasha perched on the edge of a chair. "She'll be fine. The doctor said it wasn't deep and won't even need a lot of stitches. It was an accident. Accidents happen."

Jared lifted his head a fraction. "When's her dad coming?"

"He's on the east coast. Said that since she's going to be okay, he'll get the doctor's official report and talk to her in the morning."

"Doesn't he even care?"

"He talked with her on the phone. She told him not to come." Sasha shrugged. "I think she's embarrassed. If he had to fly out here, across all those time zones and everything, he'd be sure to make it into a bigger deal than it is."

"And her mom?"

"Who knows? One of those absentee moms." Jerking to her feet, Sasha bypassed Jared's mother and headed for the candy machine. "You want something?"

Jared shook his head. With a long, exhaled breath, he strolled over to his mom. "You don't have to stay. It'll be okay."

Ms. Franklin peered into her son's eyes, brushed a stray lock of hair from his face, and nodded. With a professional twitch, she straightened her skirt and flung her purse strap over her shoulder. She glanced from Sasha to Jared. "You need anything—just text me—all right?"

They nodded in unison.

Standing before the machine, Sasha tapped the key code and a bag of peanuts dropped with a thud. She snatched it, ripped it open, and passed the bag to Jared. “Have a few; the protein will do you good.”

With a strangled cry, Jared staggered back to his chair. “God, do you hear yourself?”

Sasha swallowed and followed him. She peered at his bowed head. “What?”

“Protein. Text. Flights. Time zones. Absentee moms.” He covered his head with his hands. “I’ve played so many games where I slice up the bad guys—I can beat every opponent out there—long as he’s two inches high and made of pixels.” Jared sucked in a shuddering breath. “I don’t think I’m made for this world.”

Sasha slumped down on the chair. “Listen, you’ve had a bad day.”

Jared glared at her.

“Okay, a really bad day. But that hardly means that you’re doomed.”

“If I am, there’re a lot of guys just like me. Girls too.”

“Funny, but Barb and I were talking about this earlier. She said that artificial intelligence will take over the world.”

Jared shook his head.

A nurse stepped forward, leading a wobbly Barb. “You the family?”

Jared glanced aside at Sasha.

Barb offered a weak wave. “Yeah, kinda like. Sasha’s my roommate.”

Sasha stepped forward. “Jared will drive us back to the dorm. Professor Kim said he’d have a pizza waiting when we got there.”

The nurse looked Barb in the eye. “You’ll follow the directions? The script has been sent in already."

Barb nodded. "I'll be good. Promise."

The nurse smiled and retreated.

Jared stepped forward and took Barb's arm. "I'm really sorry about this."

"You said that a million times on the way over. I get it. Nothing to forgive. It was my fault for starting it in the first place."

Once they stepped into the cool evening air, Barb looked up at the millions of twinkling stars. "Guess I was kind of hard on Artificial Intelligence today. I'm paid back royally for my prejudice."

Sasha shook her head. "How's that?"

"It was modern medicine that fixed me up and modern miracle drugs that'll keep me from dying from a stupid infection. Numbed my pain too."

Jared patted her hand. "No, you had a good point—just got it backward."

Barb and Sasha stared at him.

"It isn't artificial intelligence that'll take over the world—it's a lack of common sense that'll lose it."

Like a Ballerina

Originally published on The Writings of A. K. Frailey
5/19/2018

Lydia didn't know why she had to wait, but since waiting was such a big part of life, she tried to amuse herself by watching the other people in the room.

A young woman tugged at her t-shirt, her foot jiggling as it hung crossed over her leg. The woman's elbow perched on the arm of the chair, and her eyes scrolled over the bent magazine page, but Lydia doubted she was really reading. The woman's gaze kept wandering to the door.

A man in a neat suit sat ramrod straight with a briefcase perched obediently next to his chair. He checked his watch and harrumphed noisily. Pulling out his iPhone, he scrolled with quick, thumb-jerking motions bearing stark testimony to his mood.

Lydia frowned, biting her lip. Her gaze darted to the door her mom had gone through—it seemed so long ago. Her stomach rumbled.

The receptionist called the young woman.

She leaped to her feet like a ballerina, though her face looked more like an acrobat walking a tightrope. Tossing the magazine, the page still folded backward, on the table, she slipped her purse strap over her shoulder and sucked in a deep breath. She strode forward.

A scene from a movie where the main character faced a firing squad flashed before Lydia's mind. She blinked.

The door opened, allowing the young woman

in and an older woman to escape. Her eyes red rimmed, and her gaze wandered the room like a sailor lost at sea. The new woman meandered to the suited man and tapped his shoulder.

He glanced up, still holding the iPhone at eye level. "What'd they say?"

The woman shook her head and glanced around. "Not here." Gripping her black purse like a life preserver, she headed to the door. "We have to talk."

The iPhone disappeared into a hidden pocket, and he gripped his briefcase almost as hard as she gripped her purse.

Lydia watched them traipse out the door. She felt a knot tug her insides. The image of a dog being kicked to the road sent a shudder through her body. She glanced around. No dog. She frowned.

The door opened, and her mom slipped through. She clutched no purse, and her gaze remained clear. Searching the room, she found Lydia and smiled.

Lydia's stomach relaxed, and she smiled back. She straightened up.

Her mom reached out and helped pull her to her feet. Her orthopedic shoes clumped as she stepped forward.

"You were a good girl?"

Lydia nodded. She squeezed her mom's hand. "Why're we here?"

Her mom peered down and then glanced aside. The empty room could tell no tales. "I just had to make sure." She pressed her hand over her protruding tummy.

"You've got the baby still?"

“The baby’s okay.” Her mom started toward the door.

Lydia swallowed. “Not like me?”

Her mom stopped in mid-step. Turning, she bent and peered into Lydia’s eyes. “No one is like you, Lydia.” She ran a hand over her soft hair. “You’re perfection.”

Lydia grinned. The knot was gone. The image of her dad’s open arms brought tears to her eyes. “Is Dad home?”

“Waiting for us.”

Lydia limped to the door—but her soul danced like a ballerina.

Soul Mates

Originally published on The Writings of A. K. Frailey
8/2/2018

Her hair falling to the side of her face and her long denim skirt plastered against her sweaty legs, Zoe hefted a large trash can in her arm and dumped an array of plastics into the "Plastics Only" barrel. She wiped a smear of peanut butter off her plaid shirt and stepped aside, narrowly missing the grey wall.

Another woman, dressed in designer jeans and a white blouse, stepped in and tipped a small can. Plastics of various shapes and sizes cascaded into the barrel.

And one shoe.

Zoe lifted her index finger. "Oh, uh…I think you…uh…just lost a shoe."

The woman peered down at her well-matched feet. Two neon-pink tennis shoes stared back.

Tiptoeing over the barrel, Zoe peered in. She pointed to a black heel poking out of the containers, looking distinctly out of place.

The other woman inched closer as if she thought Zoe might make a weird attempt to dump her into the barrel. Glancing over the edge, she frowned. "Oh, my! That's my best dress shoe. How'd that get in there?"

Zoe bit her lip.

The woman lunged and almost fell in.

Clutching the woman's arm with one hand, Zoe knocked the containers out of the way with the other. She snatched the miserable shoe from its indignity and held it high with a smile. "Got it!"

Accepting the wayward foot apparel, the woman laughed. Her gaze rolled up and down Zoe with practiced care. "My name's Lilith." She considered her shoe. "I should pay you something."

Zoe snorted. "For one shoe? Hardly. I don't get paid till I retrieve a complete pair."

Lilith picked up her can and started for the open parking lot. She glanced aside at Zoe, who lugged the large trashcan in her arms. "You Amish or something?"

Her eyes wide, Zoe looked around as if Lilith was talking to someone else. She realized her mistake and blushed. "Oh, no. Just—" She giggled. "Well, I once went three whole days without a washing machine." She opened her car door and wedged the can in the back seat. "That's as far from reality as I ever want to go." She folded her arms and leaned against her battered Chevy Cruise.

Lilith dropped her can in the hatchback of her silver Honda Accord, turned, and met Zoe's gaze.

"I'm what you might call green—I guess." She shifted and dug her keys out of a deep pocket. "I try to live wisely."

Lilith twirled her keychain. "I'm liberal too. Got a color-coded chart of all my causes at home."

Zoe tripped as she circled around her car. "Really? I'm conservative, but I've got a chart too, except most of my causes have names...David, Stephen, Ellen..."

"Your causes are your kids? How many do you have?"

"Five."

"Oh, God. That's not particularly green…or wise in my book."

Zoe shrugged. "Perhaps. But it's liberal in the best sense of the word." She opened her car door and propped her arm on the edge. "Funny, but I bet it's more the labels we use than who we are that separate us."

Lilith's eyes narrowed. "You really think so?"

Zoe laughed. "Two women who keep color-coded charts could possibly be soul mates." She ducked into her car, started the engine, and rolled down the window. She called over. "Oh, and I have the exact match to your shoe. Except—mine is midnight-blue."

Live Honestly and Follow Your Passion

Originally published on The Writings of A. K. Frailey 8/2/2018

"I could be prosecuted for imitating a seamstress." Kim held up a slanted swimming suit skirt with an unfortunate black zigzag running down one side and blew a strand of hair out of her eyes.

Her mother, Janice, swept a spool of thread and needle into a desk drawer. "Megan is obsessed with swimming, not the suit. She won't care if—"

"You're making my point." Kim rolled the suit into a ball and tossed it on a dusty wooden dresser. "She should care. I should care." She winced. "The world will care."

Janice strolled over and plucked the outfit off the dresser and shook it out. She eyed it critically. "Good thing you never became a surgeon." With a shrug, she let it dangle in one hand. "I'll buy her a new one. After all, she tore it while playing with the dog at my house."

Kim snatched the suit back and hugged it to her chest. "No. I can't afford to buy another suit, and you can't afford to indulge her. She wasn't supposed to be wearing it in the woods, much less racing with your volatile terrier. This might teach her a lesson about actions and consequences."

Janice pursed her lips and strode from the room, talking over her shoulder. "You're just being stubborn. There's no reason in the world the child should wear a ragged outfit when I can afford to buy another without the least discomfort. I'd be happy to."

Trailing after her mother, Kim stepped into the kitchen, swept around the island, and dashed to the refrigerator. "You want some ice tea?"

Janice glanced from the dishes in the sink to a dried ketchup splotch on the floor. "You really need to get someone who can help you clean up around here."

Yanking the refrigerator door open, Kim grimaced. "Even if I could, I wouldn't. Dave and I live simply. The kids study and play. Dave works and does his—" Her gaze flashed to the window and the half-finished swing set in the backward, over to the garage overflowing with bicycle parts. She swung the ice tea container to the table and slid it to the center.

Janice rose and daintily lifted two glasses off the drying rack. "You sell anything lately?"

Hefting a large ceramic cookie jar shaped like a gorilla to the table, Kim shrugged. "A portrait last week." Her eyes brightened. "But one guy wrote up a really nice editorial about my work in the paper." Setting the gorilla's head aside, Kim shoved the jar next to the pitcher of ice tea.

The grandfather clock in the living room chimed three times. Kim glanced at the stovetop. A large metal pot with crusted tomato smudges on the side sat next to a cooling loaf of homemade wheat bread.

Janice followed her daughter's gaze. "Chili? Again?"

Kim poured two glasses of tea and handed one to her mother. "Okay. I don't sell much. Yet. I probably don't even cover the cost of my paints, but we're living within our means, and Dave and I believe in—"

"'Living honestly and following your passion' Yes. I've heard it before." Janice shoved her glass under the ice dispenser. It spat a few splinters of ice and stopped.

Kim rubbed the back of her sweaty neck. "We're going to get that fixed in October." She pointed to a bulletin board with a series of charts, graphs, and lists. "We have it all planned out. We're getting the washer repaired at the end of the week because I'm not Amish enough to survive otherwise. We'll get new tires for the car in September and deal with the icemaker in October."

Janice sipped her tea. "You do realize that you won't need ice in October."

A large yellow bus squeaked to a halt on the street in front of the house.

Kim plopped a stack of paper napkins on the table and arrayed metal cups with handles around the pitcher of tea. She grabbed a gallon of milk out of the fridge and set it by the pitcher.

Four children pounded into the room, each one talking and no one listening.

Kim cracked a grin. Janice smiled.

The kids stopped, glanced from Kim to Janice, shut their mouths, opened their mouths, and ran to their grandmother. They chatted away as Janice patted their heads and pretended she could understand what they were saying.

~~~

Kim strolled down the dark driveway with her
~~~

mother at her side. Muted sounds of a battle between daddy-monster and warrior-kids erupted in screams and occasional yelps from the house.

Janice pulled out her key and pressed the unlock button.

The car flashed its lights.

Kim strolled around to the driver's side, opened the door, and stepped aside. "Thanks for coming, Mom. It's always fun to have you visit."

Janice leaned over the car door and caressed her daughter's face. "You're a remarkable young woman, Kim." Her eyes glimmered. "You've done better than I did."

Kim's jaw tightened. She swallowed. "It wasn't your fault. Dad and—"

Janice waved her comment away. "It hardly matters now." She rested her arms on the car door. "I always fixed everything. Tried to make life easy. I wanted the best for you too."

Kim blinked back tears. "Comfort was never my God."

Janice smirked. "No, you and Dave have chosen a less comfortable road." She shrugged. "But I respect your choice."

"Really? Or are you just trying to make me feel better?"

Janice ducked into the car and scooted into her seat. She glanced up as Kim came near. "I believe in you." She smiled. "To prove it, I won't buy Megan a new swimsuit. I'll leave it to you."

Kim grinned. "Good. I was planning on getting her one for Christmas."

Janice laughed. "I don't doubt it." She closed the door, started the engine, backed out of the driveway, and sped away.

Kim stood on the sidewalk and peered into the dark night. Children's laughter mixed with a man's gruff monster voice brought a smile to her lips.

Beyond the Scar

Originally published on The Writings of A. K. Frailey
9/6/2018

Lacy touched the ragged scar on her cheek and winced. The pain, long since faded, lingered only in her mind. “Z for Zorro.” She bit her lip. “No mask or mascara in the world can fix this, honey.”

“Mom?” Jason stood in the doorway and peered at the reflection of his mother.

She glanced in the mirror and met her son’s worried, forlorn eyes. “Nothing, kiddo. Just—” She couldn’t think of a quip fast enough. Lord, she was weary.

Jason stepped into the room. “It’s not so bad. I mean, you’d have to really look carefully to even notice.”

A laugh jerked in her middle, tumbling over the tears she wanted to free. “Yeah. It’s practically invisible.” A quick swipe and her eyes were nearly as dry as her tone. She turned around and squared her shoulders. “You ready?”

Jason lifted an armload of books and grinned. “Mr. Baxter will love these. Vintage Hardy Boys.”

Lacy ran her fingers through her son’s tumbled locks of curly hair. “No doubt. Being as rugged as the hills himself, he loves the old and familiar.” She grabbed her keys, swung her purse strap over her arm, and led the way to the bookstore.

~~~

A bell tinkled as Lacy entered. Old man Baxter glanced up from a table crowded with
~~~

paperbacks.

Jason hustled ahead of his mom, a grin spreading wide across his face. “Look what I brought, Mr. Baxter.” He edged a stack of mysteries aside and placed the Hardy Boys securely in the center.

Mr. Baxter lifted one book, his gnarled hand clasping the cover with gentle care. Rifling through the first pages, he whistled low and glanced up at the boy. “These are a special find, son. Collectors always looking for vintage pieces.” His gaze strayed over to Lacy.

On autopilot, Lacy offered a little wave. The scar seemed to stand out more when she smiled, so a flashed grin sped by.

Mr. Baxter rose with a nod. “So glad to see you’re up and about again. Car accidents—dreadful affairs.” He waved to the back of the room and swept his gaze to Jason. “I’ve something to show you.”

Jason jogged in the direction indicated, his eyes growing wide at the sight of a glorious double bass standing in the corner. “Oh, man! Can you play it?” He ran a finger along the polished curved wood.

Mr. Baxter ambled up, grinning from ear to ear. Cradling the instrument in his arms, he hefted it out the back screen door and held the frame with his foot. “Come into the light, and I’ll play a little something.”

Jason jogged forward and slipped into the sunshine. Lacy, an ache tugging on her heart, stepped outside and backed into a shadow.

Mr. Baxter plucked the strings, his body swaying to a nightclub melody.

Blocking the bright light with her hand, Lacy watched her young son and old man Baxter as the music floated over the air like a sweet memory. Focusing on Mr. Baxter's face, it suddenly seemed as if years evaporated: his eyes brightened, his mouth turned up in a happy grin, and his skin smoothed. The man stood in his prime, his back arched just so, his legs sturdy, his hands strong, and his vigor restored.

Swallowing back a gasp, Lacy blinked and dropped her hand. Jason and Mr. Baxter could be brothers, their love of books and music binding them stronger than the years that divided them.

As they returned to the car, Jason buckled himself in and glanced at his mom. "You okay?"

Lacy turned the key in the ignition, and the car roared into life. With one hand, she passed her fingers over the scar. "I never realized; we all have scars. Age brings them on in multitudes."

Jason shrugged. "I guess it all depends on what you're looking for."

Lacy pulled into traffic and glanced aside. One eyebrow rose.

"If you look beyond the scar, you might find happiness."

Peering ahead, Lacy smiled.

That's Your Job

Originally published on The Writings of A. K. Frailey
9/20/2018

Gabe pushed back from his luxurious, high gloss mahogany desk and swiveled around so that he faced the floor-to-ceiling plate glass window overlooking the city. A glorious sunset highlighted mountainous clouds, tinting them in gold and pink. The beauty moved him not. Except for the dull ache in his chest, he couldn't feel a thing.

"What the h—'s wrong with me?" He leaned back, clasped his hands over his not-as-muscled-as-it-used-to-be middle, and exhaled a long, slow breath. His therapist said that would help.

It didn't.

A ringtone blared a swinging rhythm that he once loved—until he put it on his phone. Now it sounded stupid. He snatched the phone off the desk, tapped the button, and pressed it to his ear. "Yeah?"

Blair, his eldest daughter, spoke with her usual calm authority. God, he loved her. "Dad, I've got to stay late at the lab tonight. Professor Baughman said that they've got three internships opening in the fall, and if I can get all the paperwork in on time, I should get one. Plus, one of the freshmen got sick in class, and I need to help him disinfect the place."

Gabe chuckled. "Always something—isn't it?" He could almost hear her smile.

"Yep. So, don't expect me back till late, okay? I'm fine. Just working."

Tiny sparks flickered to life in Gabe's middle. "No problem. Just drive carefully. Especially around those d—" He caught himself. "The curves. Okay?"

"I always do."

Gabe waited. He didn't want to say goodbye. He shook himself. He couldn't expect his daughter to fill the hollow void inside.

"Oh, and dad."

"Yeah?"

"Remember, you're making dinner tonight. Johnny hates spaghetti, and Sarah loves pancakes."

Tears flooded Gabe's eyes, stinging them even as he blinked and swallowed the strangled whimper he knew would rise if he spoke too quickly. He sat up straighter. "Got it."

"Love ya." The connection was severed.

Dropping the phone back on the desk, Gabe turned once more to the window. The sun hovered over the skyline. He glanced at his watch. "Blast! They'll accuse me of overworking again."

After heaving himself to his feet, he swung into his jacket and tucked his phone into his pocket. A quick glance at his desk and his unfinished work. "It'll wait. Always tomorrow." A sinking feeling followed him down the hall as he approached the elevator. "I never get enough done. Come early, work late, try hard—but it's never enough." His therapist said it was a perpetual guilt syndrome from his early childhood and that being aware of it would help him grow past it.

It didn't.

~~~

As Gabe loped into his country-style, well-lit
~~~

kitchen, he glanced aside.

Johnny leaned over the wooden table staring at a half-finished puzzle, holding a piece in his hand, his brow furrowed. A stack of folded laundry lay at one end. He glanced at his dad and flashed a grin. “I won it in a contest at school. I’ve read more books this semester than anyone else in seventh grade.”

Gabe pursed his lips. “Shouldn’t surprise me—but it does. You don’t seem like the bookworm-type.” His gaze flickered to the laundry.

Johnny huffed. “I read a whole six books. Hardly makes me a worm. Just nobody else read that many.” He jerked his thumb at the neat pile. “Sarah’s getting pretty good at getting the corners straight.” He returned to his puzzle. “What’s for dinner?”

“Spaghetti, if you don’t move your puzzle.”

With a laborious groan, Johnny slid the puzzle pieces onto a cutting board and carried it out of the room.

Gabe searched through the refrigerator. A package of spicy sausages and a carton of eggs brought a tired smile to his lips. *Thank God.*

A little girl with brilliant blue eyes, fair skin, and a pixie face wafted into the kitchen. Wrapping her arms around a bundle of clothes, she hefted it into a tight embrace. “I’ll put these upstairs and help set the table for you, dad.”

Slicing into the plastic wrapping around the sausages, Gabe nodded. “Thanks, sweetheart.” A painful tightening in his throat and stinging in his eyes warned of a fresh wave of grief. He clenched his jaw and sliced faster. “Dang!”

He rushed to the sink and ran cold water over his bleeding finger. Sarah came back, swished the second bundle away, and trundled off. Gabe couldn't move. He knew that if he took one step away from the sink, he'd start sobbing like a child. Sarah didn't need that. He didn't need that.

"Hey, dad?"

Gabe blinked and glanced down.

Sarah stood there, her hands empty, her eyes as blue as a summer sky. "You think mom's happy now?"

Fearing that he might break his teeth if he clenched them any harder, Gabe slapped off the water, grabbed a dishcloth, wrapped his finger, and stepped to the kitchen table. He plopped down on a chair.

Sarah stood by the sink, her gaze on him. Waiting. He tapped his knee and motioned her over.

Sarah stepped up but only leaned in. No hopping onto his lap anymore.

Gabe put the towel aside and peered into her eyes. "You know, we were separated most of your life." He swallowed, anguish mounting, and forced himself to concentrate. "But I never wished her ill. I always wanted her happy." He shook his head. "We just couldn't make things work. Too different. Set in our ways." He sucked in a deep breath. "She was a hard person to make happy."

Sarah's brow furrowed. "You too."

The sky fell. Mountains crashed. Waves washed over Gabe as tears rolled down his cheeks. His words rose like strangled gasps. "I wish she were still alive. I wish she hadn't died. You still needed her—even if I didn't."

Sarah laid a soft, gentle hand on his arm.

Gabe buried his head on his arm. He couldn't face her tears too.

~~~

Late that night, Gabe sat in bed staring at a page he couldn't see.

A light knock on the door turned his gaze.

Blair stuck her head in the doorway. She frowned. "Heard you had a meltdown...want to talk about it?"

Snorting, Gabe waved her in. "Shhh. I just got Sarah to sleep, and God knows what Johnny thinks of me."

Blair stepped in and perched on the edge of her dad's bed. She laid her hand on his.

Gabe waited, but Blair didn't start. So much like her mother. "Okay. I had a little meltdown. No big deal. I'm going through some stuff." He rubbed the back of his neck. "Just because we were divorced doesn't mean I didn't care. I love you guys—and I know how hard this must be on you."

Sarah scooted back and folded her legs to the side, leaning her weight on one arm. She tilted her head, her gaze direct and unwavering. "In a weird sort of way, I think mom's death is easier on us. We got along and had some really good times together." She shrugged. "I'm not saying that I don't miss her or that it isn't hard. But—I don't know. We're her kids. She sorta lives in us still." Her gaze moved to the window. "I really believe we'll see her again someday." She squeezed Gabe's hand. "Kinda different for you."
~~~

Gabe stared at the ceiling. “She was always trying to make me a better man. Fix me.” He glanced at his daughter. “I only gave up smoking after we split to spite her.” He patted Sarah’s hand. “And for you guys.”

Sarah straightened, unfolded her legs, and swung them over the bed. “Well, she can’t fix you now.” She stood and started for the door. On the threshold, she stopped and peered back. “That’s your job.”

~~~

In the dark, Gabe patted the empty side of the bed. He swished his arm from the pillow all the way to his side. Lots of space...lots of empty space. His therapist said that pain was a good teacher.

It wasn’t.

But then he thought of his kids, and puzzle pieces, a neat stack of laundry, a decent dinner, and a stack of work on his desk. He sighed, curled his arm around the pillow, and closed his eyes. *That’s your job.*

It was.
~~~

For the Living and the Dead

Originally published on The Writings of A. K. Frailey
10/4/2018

Yvonne stopped on the threshold and sucked in a deep breath. *Oh, Lord, have mercy. It never gets any easier.*

A slender, willowy woman with flaxen hair turned, stared, and with her hands squeezed tight, red-rimmed eyes and quivering lips, sat beside an occupied bed.

Frank's feet pointed to the side, his arms limp over the white sheet, his eyes closed. Wrinkles, like signposts of pain, edged his eyes and mouth.

Yvonne didn't need to be told the details. How many bedsides had she visited this year alone? *Too many.* She strode forward, her hands extended. "I'm here, Catherine."

Catherine stood and they hugged. A tight embrace that would've broken an unscarred heart. "Thanks for coming. I wanted you to have a chance to say goodbye." She glanced back, blinking. "It can't be long now."

A shuffling at the door turned both their gazes. Two men stepped in, one tucking away a phone, the other holding a ball cap. They hugged Catherine in turn.

Catherine gestured to Yvonne. "Carl, Ben, this is Yvonne. From my church. She helps arrange things...visitation, the dinner...you know..."

Carl shook his head, his gaze swinging beyond the women to his friend. "Frank was never much of a believer. But if it makes you feel better."

Yvonne's lips tightened. *Not now, Lord, not now.* She took a step nearer Catherine and clasped her hand.

A moan erupted from the bed.

Everyone shuffled closer.

Frank's eyes fluttered open, his gaze searching until he locked on Catherine.

Sitting on the edge of the bed, Catherine leaned in, clutching his hand in both of her own. "I'm here, honey. Anything you want?"

His husky whisper barely rose above the pounding hearts around him. "Sorry...to leave. Don't know...where...I'm going..."

Flinging one hand against her face, Catherine stifled a sob. "You're going home, Frank. You're going to God."

Yvonne laid a soft hand on her friend's shoulder.

Frank's gaze floated to the ceiling. "Don't know..."

Carl bent low, blocking the light from the window, throwing a shadow over Frank's body. "Doesn't matter, friend. You'll soon be outta pain. That's what counts. Like as not, we'll meet up in Valhalla for a drink or two, buddy. Save a seat for me, will ya?"

Frank's gaze wandered. He winced.

Catherine glanced back at Yvonne, her eyes wide with a slapped-across-the-face expression.

Yvonne clasped her hands and closed her eyes. Her prayers would reach God if no one else.

Time passed. Frank closed his eyes; his breathing falling into irregular rasps. Ben paled and wrung his ball cap. Finally, he excused himself. Carl pulled up a chair and leaned over his friend with his hands clasped and his knee bouncing.

A ring tone chimed and Catherine rose, pulled out the phone, pressed the button, and listened.

Yvonne watched her wander from the room, her friend's gaze unseeing.

Taking Catherine's chair, Yvonne clasped Frank's hand and kissed it.

In a blink, Frank opened his eyes. His wretched breathing rose and fell in spurts. Only his eyes could speak. They implored.

Yvonne leaned in and peered deeply into Frank's eyes. "Trust, Frank. You've been a good man and loved deeply. You're loved in return."

Catherine reentered and dashed to her husband's side.

Yvonne stepped back, tears flowing, as Frank gasped his last, and Catherine sobbed at his side. Yvonne glanced at Carl and gestured to the door.

Carl stood stiffly, like an old man. He ambled out and strode to the kitchen.

Yvonne followed Carl and stopped at the sink. She heaved in deep gulping breaths.

Carl leaned on the counter and peered at her through narrowed eyes. "You think you had a right to do that?"

Yvonne turned, a headache pounding. "What?"

"All that, trust in Jesus crap." Carl shook a finger at Yvonne. "There's no way in hell you know where he's going and that's a fact. Offering a dying man a mirage isn't an act of kindness in my book."

Yvonne straightened, her eyes drying fast.

She swallowed back the ache in her throat. “If I’m right...what harm did I do?” Her gaze stayed fixed on Carl, searing into him. “If I’m wrong...what harm did I do?”

Catherine staggered into the kitchen and leaned on the counter. Her tear-strewn face rose as she glanced from Carl to Yvonne. “He’s gone. Beyond our reach, now.” She extended a hand to Carl. “Thank you for being here. I know how much you loved him. He loved you too.”

Carl took her hand and pressed it. A tear slipped down his face. Catherine reached for Yvonne. “Thank you.”

Yvonne embraced her friend and then stood back. “I didn’t do much.” Catherine shook her head, glancing back toward the bedroom. “Oh, but you did. Hope is for the living—as well as for the dead.”

Before the Lights Go Out

Originally published on The Writings of A. K. Frailey
11/1/2018

Kasandra heaved herself up the ramp and plodded into the back room where various set pieces leaned against the wall, waiting, like the unused furniture they were, for their next big scene.

Allan followed close behind, his dark head bent in thought. The smell of old wood, sweat, and a miracle on the brink of bright lights always sent chills down his arms. He chewed his lip, then peered up at the older, buxom woman. "But you're great at what you do. They'll always need women to play your parts—" Kasandra's abrupt laugh short-circuited his thoughts.

"My parts, you say?" She shook her head and marched with determined steps toward the last dressing room on the right. "Look around, child, and get it through your head that what seems to be is all that matters in this world. Whatever body fits the seeming will get the job done."

He trotted along and entered the room close behind. "But you're skilled, and that's a fact. I wish I were half as good as you."

Kasandra flopped down on a hard chair and beckoned to the young man. "Get me my shift there on the back of the door." She pointed to the left. As Allan handed the thin gown to her, she eyed him with a soft smile. "You're a dear, and that's a fact. With those blue eyes, firm chin, and chiseled jawline, you're a man made for the stage—or film. Whichever suits your fancy."

Allan leaned against the dressing counter, his back to the huge mirror. "I'm not special. There're a hundred guys who look as good as me and can make better use of their arms and legs." He chuckled. "I'm learning, but it's a steep curve, and one slip will land me in the mud."

Kasandra peered into the mirror, dabbed her fingers in cold cream, and smeared it over her face. She tilted her head to get every angle. "You're a wise kid if you see that already." Her gaze reached through the mirror and smacked into his eyes. "Gain a few too many pounds, get sick, pick up a bad habit...and you're done for."

With a shrug, Allan pushed off the counter and sauntered across the room. "Could be true for any profession. Most guys—"

"Naw, it's not." She peered back into the mirror. "Well, maybe some. But there's nothing like show business to teach a person their place." She thumbed the counter with the flat of her hand. "No place."

Allan pulled down an oversized feathered hat and slid his fingers along the edge. "How's that?"

"Can't hardly be yourself. Always got to be somebody else to survive. And you got to look the part and act the part all the time, or your audience will think you've gone traitor."

Plucking the feather, Allan grinned. "You make it sound like we're prisoners of our profession."

Kasandra frowned as his fingers played with the feather. "Damage that stupid thing, and I'll get hell for it." She scoured her face and wiped it clean with a fresh cloth. "Prisoners of our bodies, our profession, and our success—if we're lucky enough to have any." She nodded to the door. "You better hurry, kiddo. Time and opportunity are passing faster than you think."

~~~

Late that night, Allan ambled up the steps to his house, strode through the entryway, and frowned at a light glinting from a back room. Stepping carefully, he inched his way forward.

Not a sound.

He poked his head through the open doorway and peered at his father sitting up in bed with a book in his hand.

Allan sauntered forward, a grin warring with a frown. "What're you doing up so late, da?"

The old man glanced up, startled. He laid the book on his lap with a tired smile hovering on his face. "Couldn't sleep. Thought I'd catch up on my reading."

Allan titled his head back, considered the cover, and glanced at his father. He turned the book around. "The Egoist?" He pursed his lips. "Thought you liked the classics—"

Da slapped his hand over the cover. "It is a classic. At least in some circles." He flipped the book over. "It was the title that caught my eye. Thought it might have a few answers."

One of Allan's eyebrows rose. "How to be one—or get rid of one?"

Da's smile reached his eyes. "You're too damn smart for your own good, laddie." He shoved the book aside. "How'd it go today?"
~~~

"Same as usual. I made mistakes, and I learned from them." He sat on the edge of the bed. "You remember Kasandra? You know the big—"

Yeah? What about her?"

"She seems to think that as an actor, I'm in for a life sentence—a prisoner of sorts."

"You think that?"

"I don't know. It could be true. But then, doesn't every profession make demands, have expectations...I could get fired from anything."

"True, but not everyone would notice or care. There's something about becoming a public person that comes with its own set of rules. It's a matter of trust."

"Lots of public figures mess up. Sometimes it actually helps their careers—"

"Careers aren't the person on the inside, son. Don't forget that. It's true, you could be a school teacher and get run through the mill, but the public light burns awful bright. It doesn't care about the person inside." He tapped his chest and leaned back. "You know, I was in the limelight for a good many years. Cost me more than I care to admit. I got paid well, and I got a lot of attention. But..."

"But?"

"Well, in the end, we're all going to die and when you get to my age, that makes a person think. If you live long enough, you get old...and hints come along to remind you that we're not here forever. The lights will dim, the stage door will close, and we'll have to face what every human being throughout history has had to face. The great equalizer."

"Maybe they'll invent a bio-engineered body

when my time comes." The joke fell flat.

Allan flushed.

"Just remember, Allan, a career, no matter how good, no matter how well you're paid, no matter how many people tell you they love you—You're on your own at the end. You better get to know *that* person..." He tapped his chest again. "Before the lights go out."

I'll Always Know

Originally published on The Writings of A. K. Frailey
11/15/2018

"She'll never know."

As I tromped along the cornfield-bordered road, I clamped down on the squirming kitten and stared bug-eyed at my friend-sometimes-worst enemy. "Won't know? As in won't notice another kitten among her whole slew of critters?"

Janet smiled that patronized smile she had—like she was four years older rather than four months. "Exactly." She nudged me in the ribs.

My ribs had taken enough from the pounding of my heart. I stopped then and there. A storm was coming, and the kitty was onto it. That and the fact that we were well beyond my property line. "Listen, I'm not a deceptive person by nature. This whole enterprise—"

"Enterprise? We're not on a starship. We're in the middle of a blinking cornfield trying to do the right thing by this—" She zeroed in on the clawing bundle of black fur. "Fluff muffin." With a hand on her hip and one finger-wagging, she launched in. "You've got another baby on the way, a husband who is hardly ever home, a house that's falling about your ears, and a sick grandmother." She jutted her jaw at the little eye peeking out from under my elbow. "You don't need—that!"

I shrugged. "But it was in with the chickens—in the coop. Don't you wonder if that was a sign…from God maybe?"

The roll of Janet's eyes was positively eloquent. "God has got better things to do. Like, keep people—"

A long rolled "Helll-ooo" stopped us both.

Mrs. Blackstone trundled down the rocky drive and toodle-oooed. "Thought I heard voices. Just coming to check the mail—Al forgot yesterday." She slapped her hands and chuckled as if her husband's memory loss tickled her funny bone. "Not that there's much to see—bills and ads and those obnoxious political adverts. Might as well tell me who to pray to."

The kitten had had quite enough—and since I had tightened my grip—she probably wanted to breathe as well. The scratch she offered in return, set her free and let loose a naughty word on my part. I would've clamped my hand over my mouth, but I was too busy clamping my hand over the long bleeding tear in my forearm.

Janet merely shook her —at the scratch, the freed cat, or my poor literary choices, I didn't know, and at that moment, I didn't care.

Mrs. Blackstone, on the other hand, knew a thing or two about mercy and infections. "Oh, let me take you right in and put something on that. It'll swell up quick if you don't." She peered around. "Was that the black kitten that went missing couple days ago?"

Thunder rumbled in the distance.

I let myself be tugged along like the child I wasn't and glanced at my neighbor. "Was that *your* kitten?"

"Oh, got so many; I lose count. New litters year-round, it seems. Some live, some die, some move on..." She led me up the back steps into a warm kitchen. A stew pot simmered on the stove. "Just sit, make—" She glanced at Janet as if she had noticed her for the first time. “Oh, hi, Jan.” She waved to a back room. “Back in a sec.”

Janet pulled out a chair and plunked down as if she had been the one wrestling a miniature tiger.

I toed a stool forward—my good hand being occupied, trying to stem the flow of blood, which I was certain would cascade down my arm if I took my hand away. I perched on the edge.

“See, I told you. It never was your responsibility in the first place.”

I leaned in and, I’ll admit, my whisper wasn’t gentle. “As it turns out, if we’d left it alone, it probably would’ve wandered home on its own.”

“Not in a million years. You’d have babied it—like you baby everything. Why, you would’ve taken it in at night and fed it leftover hamburger.”

“That’s a crime?”

“How many hours sleep did you get last night?”

“What on God’s green earth does that have to do with—?”

“Here we are.” Mrs. Blackstone waved a vial of dark liquid, a cotton ball, and a package of Band-Aids. “We’ll have you fixed up in no time.”

I sniffed when she unscrewed the top. It smelled faintly familiar but unlike any medicine, I’d ever come across. “What’s that?”

“Oh, a homemade remedy my mama taught me.”

She dabbed the cotton ball in the liquid, motioned for my arm, and grinned.

I was fairly sure I’d make a mess of her floor if I let go of my arm, but her cotton ball commanded compliance, so I flung caution to the wind and extended my damaged limb. You can imagine my surprise when I saw not a flood of leaking corpuscles but rather a long swelling red mark.

As she ran the ointment-soaked swab down my arm, I suddenly knew with blinding certainty the main ingredient in her mama's home remedy. I gritted my teeth against a fresh onslaught of naughty words. "Is that— apple cider vinegar—by—any—chance?"

"Certainly. Kills germs on contact."

It was certainly killing something. I hoped not my will to live.

For the first time, Janet seemed to actually feel something for me other than contempt. She winced and patted the hand I clenched in my lap.

As we sauntered back up the road toward my farmhouse, she nudged me in the ribs again. "Listen. I was just trying to make a point. I didn't expect you to get martyred by an old family cure-all."

I stopped and closed my eyes. Janet was right. I hadn't gotten much sleep the night before...or the night before that...or the night... But it didn't matter. It was my life. I could sacrifice myself in pieces and parts if I chose.

Janet sniffed.

Good Heavens! She couldn't be...crying... My eyes snapped open.

No, she wasn't crying—exactly. Just sad. And looked about as tired as I felt.

"I know you're worried, Jan. But I'm fine. I like extending myself. I love babies and husbands who work too hard...and even killer fluff muffins that show up in my chicken coop."

Janet considered me through narrowed eyes. “You’re giving me an inferiority complex.”

“Am not.”

Janet climbed the front lawn and headed for the porch steps. “Well, when you collapse from exhaustion—you know who you can rely on help you out.”

I sauntered along behind, checking for Bob’s truck in the driveway. He was still home. Good. The back door hinge was loose. I wrapped my arm around Janet and hugged her and then winced at the still searing burn in my arm. “You’re on my speed dial.”

She snorted and waved to the front door. There, sitting as pretty as a picture, sat the black kitten.

I looked at Janet, and Janet looked at me. The kitten didn’t seem to care when Jan picked it up and started down the road.

But I did. And I’ll always know.

Crushed—but Not to Death

Originally published on The Writings of A. K. Frailey
11/29/2018

Camilla sat at the outdoor café and listened to the twittering of the birds and the distant rumble of thunder. How was it possible that the two co-existed yet seemed so oblivious to each other? Did the birds worry about an approaching storm? Not so you'd notice—they flew and chirped in their usual abandon. And the storm clearly wasn't about to alter its course to avoid a flock of happy birds.

"Perhaps it's a grace..."

"Excuse me?"

Camilla glanced up. A man in blue jeans, a white shirt stretched over defined muscles, with wavy black hair, intense sparkling eyes, and a charming grin, stood before her table with a tray in hand. A hot flush swept up her cheeks. *Lord, don't let me blush...please...* Too late.

"Uh, oh, nothing...just talking to myself. Odd. Me." She glanced around. All the other tables were full. A quick glance at her purse loitering on one empty chair and her foot absently propped on the other. *Selfish slob.* She dropped her foot, snatched her purse off the chair, and blushed. Again. "Sorry. Didn't mean to—" *Oh, Lord, he's sitting down...at my...table. Not mine. Just...a table...*

"Do you mind?" He gestured to the unencumbered portion.

She scrunched her books closer. "No, course not." She swished her gaze around the bustling café. *When did it get so busy?* She glanced at her watch. “No, can’t be!”

Arranging his breakfast plate and hot coffee, the man peered up. “Something wrong?”

Camilla swallowed. “I just lost three hours.” She adjusted the glasses on her nose. “I came in when they opened at 6:30, and now my watch is telling me that it’s 9:30. That can’t possibly be.”

After slathering his wheat toast with grape jelly, the man proceeded to take a large bite. He chewed, swallowed, and tapped his watch. “What day is it?”

Frowning, Camilla blinked. The dark clouds and their faint thunder had veered north. Sunshine reflected brilliantly on every surface. “Uh, Friday, November eleventh.” She grinned like she had just won the final match of a tennis game.

“Nope. It’s Saturday, November the twelfth.”

Shock drained all thought from her mind as Camilla shot to her feet. “It can’t be! I’d have missed my class and mom’s evening medication—Oh God!” She practically inhaled her notebooks in one encompassing swish.

A strong hand reached out and gripped her hand. “Sorry! Really.”

The grin was still there, though a little sheepish now. “I was joking. Didn’t think you’d take me seriously. Please. Sit down. It’s Friday. No time warp or anything.”

Camilla thrust her hand against her chest as if she could put it back in place manually. “Lord, have mercy.” She glanced at him as she sat down. *Such a sweet face, too. Kind or cruel...*

He cut his egg into bite-sized pieces with the side of his fork, dropped a bit of bacon onto each piece, and enjoyed it.

Camilla pursed her lips. “You like to traumatize people before you eat?” She thrust out a hand. “Camilla. Just so you know who you almost sent into coronary arrest.”

He swallowed. “James.” Then he took a sip of coffee and leaned back for a moment’s respite from the exhausting labors of eating and teasing. “So, tell me, Camilla. How did you manage to lose three hours on such a glorious morning?”

Clutching her notebook against her chest, one shoulder doing its own little shrug, Camilla glanced across the campus. “I was writing. It’s like that Narnia story where you go into another world for a few days and thousands of years pass back home.” She met his intense gaze. And blushed. Again.

“What do you write?” He sipped his coffee, his hands cradling the cup, but he seemed interested.

Camilla swallowed panic. *He’s really bored. Waiting for his girlfriend to get here. Or his wife...* “Oh, just stuff. Stories that never get published and sit on my laptop languishing for—”

His gaze followed a student as she sauntered by.

Hot lead burned in Camilla’s stomach feeling strangely akin to jealousy. *Don’t be ridiculous. You don’t even know this guy!* She gathered her notebooks. One slid off the top and landed on his jellied toast.

He glanced up and met her gaze. “Why do they languish? Stories are meant to be read.” With care, he used his napkin and wiped the notebook free of jam.

Camilla laid it back on top. She peered at him. "To be perfectly honest, I'm ridiculously sensitive—totally crushed by rejection."

"Not totally." He started on his second egg.

Camilla clutched her books tighter. "Yes. I am. I know how I feel about my writing. I'm sick for days when my professors correct my papers. I hate it when anyone finds fault—"

He took another sip and frowned. "I didn't say you liked it. I said you wouldn't be totally crushed. You'll be a better writer by hearing what others think of your work."

Oh, really? Camilla tried to take the edge of sarcasm off her tone and slipped back onto her chair. She leaned forward; her hands clenched tight around her stack. "I got something published once...in a magazine. You know what happened?"

James bit his toast and raised an eyebrow.

"One reader wrote in and said that my beginning sucked; it was boring and flat. But then, some other guy wrote and said he loved the way it began and thought I had an artistic touch."

James wiped his mouth and drained the last of his coffee. "So?"

"So, readers mess with my mind! I didn't know what to think or who to believe."

"Do *you* like your work?"

"I love my work. That's the problem. Each story is like an innocent child—and when I send them out in the world...they get throttled. Or ignored. Which is even worse."

"Was your next piece a little better?"

"That's generally the goal."

"So, you weren't crushed." He looked around.

"I wish they had waitresses who came around with coffee."

Camilla kept her gaze steady. *I will not roll my eyes...I will not roll my—* "It's self-serve, here."

James stood with his plastic coffee cup in hand. "Yeah. I get that." He glanced at the table and her empty cup. "Want some more?"

Camilla glanced at her watch. "I have a noon class."

"So, you've still got a couple hours—right?" He started away. "You said it. Self-serve. Gotta take a chance. That's what writing is all about— isn't it?"

Swiping up her empty, she trotted to his side and filled her cup with just enough room for three scoops of sugar and a dollop of cream. "How do you know so much about writing?"

"I'm an architect. I plan beautiful buildings and cities and—" Stirring his coffee, James started back to the table. "You know what happens?"

Camilla shook her head, frowning.

"Everyone makes suggestions. Helpful hints. Monetary considerations. Historical reflections..." He slid back into his chair. "No one gets to have it their own way."

"But you're not crushed?"

"Crushed. But not to death."

A shadow dimmed the light. Dark clouds swept in, and a rumble of thunder rolled overhead.

Camilla laughed. She glanced at James. "Perhaps, it is grace..."

With Your Help

Originally published on The Writings of A. K. Frailey
12/13/2018

Leander dropped his head on his hands and slouched on the edge of a metal, straight-backed chair.

The crowded room murmured with low-toned conversations amid a swirl of officious activity.

A uniformed officer paced before him; his hands clasped behind his back. "So, you—what? Give online advice?"

The floor, grey plastic tiles with chipped edges and age cracks, offered not an ounce of inspiration.

Leander peered up, barely lifting his head above his hands. Weariness engulfed him. "No. Not really. I just...chat with people and reflect on the state of things in our world." He sat straighter. "How could that be so wrong? Everyone does it."

The officer stopped mid-pace and blew air into the stagnant room. "People make all sorts of suggestions—demands even. But few listen. In your case, you were unlucky enough to have someone follow your advice and do exactly as you suggested."

Leander stood, his hands waving, imploring. "I only said that we should throw all our guns in the ocean...you know...get rid of our weapons of destruction."

The officer chuckled and rubbed the back of his neck. "So, this lady gets a group of moms, and they gather every weapon they lay their hands on, hire a boat, and go out...and do just that!"

Leander gripped the desk for support. "I didn't think anyone would really do it—not like that."

"Like what—you think?"

"I just wanted to make a concrete suggestion, something people could do to make the world a better place."

"Drop your assorted guns in the ocean?"

"Out of kids' hands! Yeah. Is that a bad idea?" Embarrassment, fear, and anger played touch football in Leander's stomach. "Listen, Officer, I'm not the bad guy here. I didn't mean anyone should break the law or do anything stupid. I figured anyone who read my post would understand what I meant."

"You know, when Ms. Stevens was apprehended, the first thing she said was—'Leander Jones told me to do it.'"

"Oh, God." Feeling faint, Leander dropped back into his chair.

The officer stepped over and crouched before him. "What—you're in your forties; you've got a wife and kids, and you honestly thought you were helping humanity out." He stood. "When she mentioned your name, I read through your blog. Got some nice sentiment there." He stepped away and stared at the wall. "I've seen the aftermath of a school shooting. I know what guns can do. I know how—" He stopped and ran his hands over his face. He turned. "Still—fact is—she blames you."

Lander pulled himself to his feet. "I didn't say anything that Hollywood stars and politicians haven't been saying for years. Guns are dangerous."

The officer pulled out his desk chair. "In the

wrong hands. I agree with you." He sat and glanced up. "So is advice."

~~~

Leander sauntered over to the embankment and stared at the waves rippling over the lake. Kids and adults hustled between picnic tables, arranging and snatching food, joking, chatting, and having a fun Sunday afternoon.

A man dressed in black, wearing a Roman collar, plodded over the short grass and stood next to Leander, facing the scenic beauty. "Love this view. Trees, sky, and water refresh the soul—" He glanced at Leander. "Don't you agree?"

Leander's eyes narrowed. "They should." He sighed. "But I've found that life is nothing but a bundle of contradictions." He whisked a fly off his arm. "You oughta know better than anyone. Blessed are the poor...riches lead to slavery...good intentions pave the way to hell."

Father Peter retreated to a log situated on the water's edge. Propping one foot on the trunk, he crossed his arms over his thigh and watched a flock of geese fly overhead.

Leander faced his priest. "What? No clarification? Aren't you going to explain that God knows our hearts, and we should trust in Him no matter how wretchedly things turn out?"

Father Peter dropped his gaze and met Leander's eyes. "You said it— what's left?"

Leander pounded across the spongy turf and stood before the priest, his hands on his hips. "You know what happened! I gave innocent, well-meaning advice—and I nearly went to jail." Tears
~~~

welled. "What that would've happened to Jeanie and the kids then?"

Father Peter's waited. His gaze steady, his demeanor calm.

Leander flung out his hand and waved a finger in the priest's face. "Really, it's all your fault! Aren't you always preaching about how we should be salt and light in the world? What a world!" He turned and paced away. "The other day, I gave a steak bone to the dog, and he choked!" He swung around. "I gave twenty bucks to a homeless guy, and not ten minutes later, I saw him buying cigarettes!"

Someone called from the distance and waved.

Father Peter straightened and waved back. He returned his gaze to Leander. "So, what do you want to do?"

"Do? Duck and hide—if only I could. But this damned world hounds me. The other day my son came home with a guy dressed like a girl, my sister was hospitalized for alcohol poisoning, and my boss thinks he might have cancer." Leander plopped down on the log. "There's too much grief and when I try to mend a problem, I nearly get sent to Alcatraz."

Father Peter shook his head. "You can't save the world."

"Save? Heck, I can't even apply a decent Band-Aid."

Father Peter chuckled and patted Leander on the back. "The job of

Savior has already been taken."

Leander pivoted on his heel, thrusting Father's hand away. "Ah! There's where we disagree." His face flushed, he felt nearly drunk on fury. “Kids are killing other kids, drug abuse is on the rise, for all our prosperity—the world’s a miserable place.” He glared at the priest. “Doesn’t seem to me that anyone’s safe—or saved!”

His jaw hardening, but his eyes softening, Father Peter lifted his hands in surrender. “You’re right. The world as we know it is pretty miserable. No denying that. But this world is not all there is. We don’t have to be saved —not if we don’t want to.”

“Stop being so sanctimonious.”

“Stop trying to be God.”

The two men glared at each other. A shuffle turned their gazes.

A little boy hovered near, his eyes wide. Fear scrawled across his face.

Leander closed his eyes and rubbed his temple.

Father Peter crouched and beckoned the boy over. “It’s okay, Davy. Your dad and I are just having a little discussion.”

Davy hesitated, glancing from one man to the next. He finally settled on his dad. “Mom said lunch is ready. Eat now cause she’s not fixing anything else.”

Leander opened his eyes and nodded. “Be right there.”

The boy turned and scampered away.

Father Peter turned to follow but glanced over his shoulder. “Everything you said is true, Leander. You’re not wrong. But you’re not completely right, either.”

A sob welled up inside Leander as he peered into the distance and watched his son tug on his wife’s arm, probably babbling on about how dad was arguing with the pastor. “So, what, in Heaven’s name, am I supposed to do? How do I live in this crazy world?”

Father Peter sighed and waited. “Do the best you can. Remember, you’re a man. Not the Creator of the universe.”

Leander shuffled forward. “There’s a new world waiting for us—and God’ll make everything right in the end?”

Father chuckled, patted Leander’s arm, and moved on. “With your help—yep.”

Leander snorted, shook his head, and headed for lunch.

Sister-O-Mine

Originally published on The Writings of A. K. Frailey
12/27/2018

Giles slid onto the driver's side of his compact car, buckled the strap over his lap, focused on the tight maneuver needed to get into the flow of traffic, and felt his stomach clench.

Once he roared the motor to life, gripped the wheel and flipped the music on high, he made an expert swing into the proper lane. His fingers began tapping a lively dance, and his head started bopping to the rhythm. Blood pumped and his stomach unclenched. He grinned.

He sped onto the highway and pictured Esmeralda's face. Lovely woman. Beautiful eyes. He suspected...beautiful everything. Well, from what he knew of her. Online chats can only take a man so far. One phone call. Lovely voice. Husky...just the way he liked it.

Once at the Millard exit, he turned off and scaled the hill to his sister's house. Sadie had said she wanted to "talk." His stomach tightened again.

After he rang the bell, Sadie swung the door wide and beckoned her brother inside with a languid half-wave. "Dan took the kids to a movie, so we have at least two hours of uninterrupted chat time."

Giles pursed his lips as he slid one leg over the kitchen stool by the counter. "Why do we need"—he made quote marks in the air—"'uninterrupted chat time' together?"

Sadie rounded on the refrigerator, pulled out an ice-cold soda, swung to a high cabinet, flipped open the door, shuffled with her fingers, and pulled down a red bottle. After filling two tall glasses with crushed ice, lemon-lime soda, and Chardonnay, she handed one to her brother. She lifted her hand in salute. “Cheers, brother. Do I need a reason to chat with you?”

Giles leaned back, perching his foot on the stool rung. “Usually, you have a reason.” His eyes widened. “Is something wrong with Dan…or the kids?”

Sadie leaned on the counter, savoring her drink. “No. They’re fine.” She looked straight into Giles’ eyes. “As the older, wiser sibling, I just want to catch up with my little brother. Anything wrong with that?”

Giles snorted. “Seventeen months! You’re only seventeen months older, girl.”

Sadie straightened and clutched a platter of brownies. She slid them onto the counter. “Hard as rocks. Wilda made ‘em. First attempt. Not bad if you don’t break a tooth.” She tilted her head. “So, tell me all about Izzie.” Her eyebrows wiggled.

Giles bit into the brownie and froze. They were indeed hard as rocks. He tapped his tooth, laid the brownie aside, and glanced up. “Izzie? Who—?”

Opening the refrigerator, Sadie grabbed a bag of baby carrots. She pulled one out and crunched. She talked around munches. “You know…your online friend.”

Giles’ eyelids dropped to half-mast. “Her name is Esmeralda. And we’re just getting to know each other.” He shrugged. “What’s so wrong? You met Dan through a Catholic dating service.”

Sadie took a sip of her drink. "That's my point. I knew something about Dan before we met. I knew he was Catholic, and that says volumes."

Giles grimaced. "Screams loud and clear." He wrinkled his nose and stared at the carrot held like a cigarette between Sadie's fingers. "How can you eat a carrot and drink a wine cooler at the same time?"

Sadie shrugged. "Easy. But don't roam off topic. Listen, brother-o-mine. I love you dearly, but I think you're making a humongous mistake. You don't know anything about this woman...and worse yet...she doesn't know a thing about you."

"I know she's gorgeous." Giles smiled. "I'm not bad looking...What else matters?"

"Is she funny? Does she handle money well? What religion is she? Any ax-murders to her credit?"

Rolling his eyes, Giles labored to his feet and sauntered into the strangely clean-living room. He glanced back at Sadie, who followed him. "What happened to all the toys...and the mess?"

Sadie punched Giles in the arm. "Listen, buddy, one time you show up *unexpected* and the house looks unfit for human habitation, and you act like that's my usual routine." She eyed him as he plopped down on the sofa. "You still got dust bunnies ruling the roost at your house?"

Giles set his drink on the end table and covered his ears. "Dang it, Sadie. I told you never to mix metaphors in my hearing. You know how that makes my skin crawl."

"Sorry, Editor. Didn't realize you wore your English Grammarian badge during off hours."

Giles lifted his hands. "It's a curse I'm

learning to live with." He smirked as Sadie sat on an overstuffed chair opposite him and threw her legs over the arm, just like one of the kids. "I know you *think* you're helping me out...but I'm having a good time with Esmeralda. It's a fling. Fun time. Nothing more."

"You told her that?"

"Pretty obvious, I should think."

"Obvious to who?" Sadie tapped the rim of her glass. "I know you, brother. You're still dealing with all the baggage from Janet." She took a long slurp, finishing off the contents. "You need to get an annulment before you start anything new."

His eyes nearly popping out his head, Giles leaned forward. "Annulment? Lord, Sadie. The priest who married us is dead and gone, and I'm not Catholic anymore. Janet doesn't even believe in God. I don't think we really need to bother some overworked Canon Lawyer with the hideous details of our failed marriage."

Sadie set her glass down with a click and leaned forward. "I think you do. I think you'd be a fool to start anything new without figuring out what went wrong last time."

Giles shot to his feet. "Well, don't worry your pretty little head about it, sis. I know exactly what went wrong."

Sadie held her position. Only her eyes followed him as he paced across the room, turned at the television, and faced her.

"We were kids...stupid kids overloaded with hormones." Giles shook his head and chuckled, his gaze dropping to the brown carpet. "Your Catholic God is the funny one." He lifted his finger and mimicked a voice from on high. 'Be perfect as your heavenly Father is perfect!'" His voice returned to normal. "And then He gives us bodies and sensual joyrides." Giles retrieved his glass and swallowed the last drops. "Joke's on us—eh?"

Sadie rose and stepped closer; her gaze fixed on her brother. "You got hurt—really hurt, Giles. I know you did. Divorce is hell, no matter what." She laid a hand on his shoulder. "Listen to your older, wiser sister, will ya?" She tilted her head and peered deep into his gaze. "I love you, idiot. And I never want to see you in so much pain again."

Giles dropped his head to his chest.

Sadie swung away. "I don't care how hot she is...now." Sadie ran her fingers along the edge of a crib set against the wall. "You know perfectly well, looks fade or get ravaged." She glanced back. "Remember mom?"

Giles' jaw hardened; his moist eyes darkened. "Don't go there, Sadie."

"Listen, Giles. Every relationship you have with a woman is colored by every other relationship with women—mom, me, Janet...and all the little flings you've had...online or in person." She lifted her hand. "Don't pretend innocence. I'm not stupid."

Giles plunked down on the couch and buried his face in his hands. "Why are you making my life so damn complicated?"

"It's a sister's job. Actually, it would've been mom's job...if she hadn't—" She swallowed and turned away. "Don't forget, Giles, this gorgeous woman you like so much is someone's daughter...maybe someone's sister." She strode over to an iPhone lying on the table. “These tech toys help us forget—but we’re dealing with real people. Not just names. Not just faces. People someone else might love just as much as I love you.”

Giles rubbed his face and stared across the room with vacant eyes. “I’m not a creep, you know.”

“I never thought that for a moment.” Sadie returned and knelt at Giles’ side, folding her hands prayer-like on his knee. “But you are unguided. You could use some help to make a real relationship work—better than Mom, better than Janet. Heck, she could even be better than me.”

Giles reached out and brushed a strand of hair from Sadie’s eyes. “Not possible, sister-o-mine. Not possible.”

Leopold

This story was originally published on The Writings of A. K. Frailey 1/10/2019

"If ever you go to the North Country
Where the oak and the ash and the rowan be,
And the ivy bosses the castle wall
You must go to Edenhall..."

Miranda wrapped her arms around her middle and traipsed through the winter woods, tugging her coat tight, her gaze meandering. Not that there was much to see. Snow dusted the trees and covered the leaf-strewn ground. Barren. Empty. Aloneness personified in foliage.

A bird called. What was it saying? She could almost make out the tune, but it was too distant. A raucous crow rose, cawing, and flapped away.

She trudged back to the bright-lit home she shared with her cousin, Edna, and her husband and their kids. Turning at the door, she stared at the scene. The glorious woods silhouetted black against the white evening sky stabbed her heart.

The after-dinner routine, raucous as usual, soon settled into an evening of books and board games. Miranda knitted, sitting on her chair by the lamp and watched Edna settle with the baby in her lap and the toddler tucked under her arm. She balanced an illustrated bedtime story between them. Joe played Memory with the older two boys and groaned grandly every time they made a match.

By the time everyone marched up to bed, Joe stretched and yawned, saying that he'd hit the hay early since he had to get up before dawn the next morning. Edna switched off the lights, shut down the computer on her work desk, and started after him.

Miranda continued to knit.

Edna stopped and glanced back. She frowned. Miranda heard her cousin's footsteps draw near, but she didn't look up. She didn't have the heart to.

Edna's shadow slanted over the knitting.

Miranda sighed and let the half-finished blanket fall flat on her lap.

"Something wrong, Miranda?"

Willing herself to face her cousin, Miranda shoved all pain aside and peered up. "Nothing's wrong. How could it be? I have a perfect life."

Edna tugged a footstool over and plunked down. "Normally, I'd agree. But something feels...wrong." She perched her head on her hand. "You know, I always envied you."

Miranda snorted. "Good Lord, what for?"

"You traveled...saw the world. You were a useful human being. Nursing the sick all over...helping surgeons. Teaching. Advising." Edna sat up and spread her hands wide. "Why, you were a regular modern hero. None the like I ever met before in real life."

Miranda picked up her knitting and squinted in the dim light. "The operative word there is 'were.' I *was* all those things." She shrugged. "Now I'm just an old lady knitting in a corner and walking through the woods to while away my empty days."

Edna slapped her hand on the edge of the footstool. “Not so! You help with the kids and keep me from madness. I consider that a worthy endeavor.”

A momentary squabble on the second floor filtered down but was soon checked by Joe’s command to ‘settle down—or else.’

Edna narrowed her eyes. “Besides, you’re not exactly old. Not by today’s standards. Still in your fifties. You’ve got years ahead of you.”

“Sixties looms ever nearer, and the years ahead look pretty desolate to me.” She adjusted her glasses. “Listen, you and I know perfectly well that the nursing profession slipped away while I took care of Jack, and my boy lives in Singapore. Not exactly around the corner. Today the world is connected in ways I can hardly fathom. I don’t recognize half the things your kids say. I’m what they call ‘out of the loop.’” She shook her head. “My glory days are quite gone.”

Edna clasped her hands and rose from the footstool. She paced across the room and then turned and faced her cousin. “Those days— yes—I agree. They’re quite gone. But—”

“I’m too tired to go back to school and start over, if that’s what you’re thinking.”

“Not school necessarily. But change...a trade...a skill...a new environment.” Edna marched forward, her hands on her hips. “Don’t you see? It’s all in how you look at your life—forever ending or forever beginning. You decide.”

~~~
~~~

The next day dawned bright and clear. Cold swept in from the north, but Miranda wasn't one to be detained by the threat of frostbite. She knew how to dress warmly.

After the older kids were off to school, Edna settled the little ones down with activities and started in on her daily online routine.

Miranda bustled out the door with a quick nod to the perfect order of the little corner of her world and braced herself for the cold. But she didn't feel it. She hurried into the woods; her gloved hands sunk deep into her heavy coat pockets.

A bird landed on a branch before her and started in its usual song. Leopold...Leopold...tweet, tweet, tweet...

Miranda frowned and knocked a bit of snow off a tree trunk. "Stupid bird. Always calling to your Leopold, but he never answers, does he?" She stumbled forward, fury building little an interior steam kettle.

The bird hopped along, calling the same plaintive song. "Leopold...Leopold..."

Her nerves strained to the breaking point, Miranda turned and screamed. "Stupid idiot. Stop waiting for Leopold!" She shook her fist at the snow-speckled trees. "Go make a nest and do your own thing...live your own life. Don't ask for no—"

A choking sob welled up from Miranda's middle, and tears burned her eyes. She wiped them away, brushing snow across her glasses. "Dang it!" Nearly blinded, she plucked her glasses off her face and carefully paced her way to a fallen log. She plunked down, not caring that she'd wet her clothes through to the skin.

Taking off her gloves, she pulled a tissue out of a pocket and wiped her glasses dry.

The bird drew near once again.

"Leopold...Leopold...tweet...tweet...tweet..."

Miranda blinked as she watched the little bird hop before her. "Oh, God." She held out her hand. The bird hopped close, then proceeded to peck at the tree bark, intent, and perhaps content, with something besides Leopold.

A thrill rushed through Miranda. "Could it be?" She laid her hand open.

The bird lifted its beady eyes and stared at her. It hopped nearer, almost touching her hand.

"Good Lord. Am I—Leopold?"

~~~

Later that evening when Edna returned from taking all the kids to their dentist's appointments, she stopped dead in her tracks.

The boys finished divesting themselves from their winter coats and then set to work on helping the little ones.

Edna swallowed and entered the warm, yeasty-smelling kitchen, following the sound a happy tune. She stared at her cousin.

Slicing into a hot loaf of homemade wheat bread, Miranda called to the kids. "Snacks are ready and on the table in five minutes, boys. Be sure to wash your hands." She glanced at Edna. "I've made enough to go with supper; don't worry.
~~~

I also made a nice hot stew for everyone."

Edna shook her head. "You're feeling better, then?"

Miranda stopped and met her cousin's gaze. "Yes...and no. I just have to find myself again. Not easy. But the first task is always the hardest."

Edna crept into the room. "What's that?"

"You got to figure out where you are." She drew a dish of butter near and laid a knife beside it. "And go from there."

Tears welled in Edna's eyes. "I'm glad." She surveyed the brown bread and sucked in a deep breath. "My, but that looks good!" She perched on a stool and slathered a piece with a healthy dollop of butter. "What was that tune I heard you humming when I came in?"

Miranda blushed. "Oh, it wasn't anything...just a birdsong you sometimes hear in the woods. "Leopold...Leopold...I'm here; I'm here."

...But do our best and our most each day,
With a heart resolved and a temper gay,
Which pleasure spoils not, not frights appall—
Though we never see Edenhall—
~Edenhall~

by
Susan Coolidge

What Do You Know?

Originally published on The Writings of A. K. Frailey
1/17/2019

If Catherine had known what the day would bring, she would never have gotten out of bed.

"Well, that's not entirely true," she murmured as she flopped down on her bed that evening. The old-fashioned ceiling fan was covered in dust, and she wondered why she'd ever thought it was a creative choice. "Probably doesn't even work. Like the freezer...the mixer...the stupid thingamajig on the dashboard." She sighed, sat up, and rubbed her eyes. Lord have mercy; she was tired.

Boot steps clumped up onto the kitchen porch. One of her mongrel dogs started barking. Heaving herself free of the embrace of the bed, Catherine swore under her breath, her eyes darting to the purple sunset out the window. "Who on earth—?"

The dog she referred to as Sally, though she hated the name, upped her barking to frenzy mode. A shiver ran over Catherine's arms as she hustled into the room. What if it was a crazy man? Or worse yet, someone selling something? Or—nightmare image—a religious cult member wanting to share the good news with her?

A man's voice murmured in the darkness. Soothing words. He chuckled.

Sally's barking stopped. Instantly.

Alarmed, Catherine swung wide the kitchen screen door. Oh. Great. There lay Sally on her back, her legs splayed, with an idiotic grin on her face, getting a tummy rub from a total stranger.

Man's best friend, maybe but certainly not

mine. Catherine gritted her teeth and peered through the dim light at the stranger who had straightened up and stood to face her.

He was tall, his dark hair swept low over his brow, a little long, but not unkempt. He wore jeans and a black jacket over a rolled up long-sleeved shirt exposing a serious tattoo, and his heavy boots had traces of mud on them. A working man.

Catherine frowned. He was bigger than her and perhaps two or three years older, but she didn't feel threatened. Not exactly. She met his gaze.

"Sorry to bother you, but my car died at the end of your lane, and I'd like to call someone for help if you don't mind."

Suspicion flooded Catherine like a tsunami. "Why can't you use your cell phone? Don't tell me you don't have one."

He ran a hand along his jawline; a long red scratch marred a fading tan. "I tried, but either my cell's out of juice, or there's no reception around here."

Catherine winced. She knew perfectly well that reception was spotty. She glanced at the mountainous clouds gathering overhead and made an impulsive gesture. "Well, alright. I still use a landline since my cell phone reception is as unreliable as a man on a first date—" *Oops! I didn't just say...* She closed her eyes and stepped aside.

He swept past her and stopped in the middle of the room, looking around.

Thunder rumbled.

Catherine blinked and pointed to the far wall

where an old-fashioned telephone, 1950's style, sat ensconced in a wood frame.

He strode forward, picked up the phone awkwardly, and dialed a number.

Catherine lugged her school bag to the wooden kitchen table and dumped an array of papers, books, pencils, colored pens, and various school paraphernalia over the surface. She sighed and murmured, "It'll take me all weekend..."

Throat clearing turned her around. She looked at the man in the bright glare of the kitchen. He was good-looking. Not classically handsome but familiar somehow. His deep-set eyes looked weary, and something around the corners made her think he'd had troubles of his own. Good grief. He looked like a man who had known deep sadness.

Catherine bit her lip. Still, he was a stranger. A man. Like her ex-husband. Like her brother. Like her father.

This morning when she caught a junior high student cheating and brought the fact to the principal's attention, she had been told she was too sensitive and needed to be more caring. Later, she discovered that the principal had a very friendly arrangement with the mother of said cheater. In the lounge, all the teachers had laughed when she protested the injustice of it all. Leanne even told her to "get a life and stop acting like a self-righteous old nun."

Lightning flickered in the windows.

Heat burned Catherine's cheeks.

The man looked around at the country-style kitchen that Catherine had labored so long to decorate.

"Nice place." He held out his hand. "My name is Clem. Sorry about intruding like this." He flipped out his phone and grimaced. "Not a bar on here."

"It's the trees...and the fact that we're in such a low spot...and out in the middle of nowhere." Catherine wanted to slap herself. *Shut up, you idiot!*

Clem smiled.

My lord, how the smile changed his face.

"I'm out behind the McCarthy place. I just moved in...and no one mentioned that reception was so bad. I guess I should've done some research."

"Well, with the storm—"

A thundering crash of rain pelted the metal roof.

Glancing at the sprawled mess of spelling tests and math quizzes, Clem grinned. "I used to be a teaching assistant in Utah...corrected papers faster than a speeding bullet."

Catherine snorted. "Anytime you feel a hankering to mark off atrociously misspelled words in red ink, you just let me know."

Flashing lights vied with the pounding rain outside the doorframe.

Clem hustled forward. "It's my friend; he lives next door. Only other person I really know around here. He'll take me home." He shuffled his feet. "If you don't mind, I'll come back in the morning and get the car." He peered down at her as if asking permission...as if it were her lane.

Her throat, suddenly as dry as the Sahara, made her voice sound huskier than she ever intended. "That's fine. It's a dead end. No one goes down this way...except to check on the cows...in the pasture." With a shake, she peered at him. "What were you doing...if you don't mind my asking?"

He shrugged. "Just getting my bearings. I got work down at the power plant. As I was heading home, I realized that this lane is just behind my house. I had nothing better to do, so I thought I'd investigate. Didn't expect my car to die." He snorted. "Or my phone to quit...though..."

She didn't need him to finish the thought. "Yeah. Me too. One of those days." She met his gaze again. "Don't worry about the car. It'll be safe enough." She stepped toward the flashing lights.

Clem followed and opened the screen door. He hesitated. "Thanks. I appreciate your trust. I was afraid you'd set your dogs on me." He grinned as Sally whined and tried to smuggle her fat body between his legs.

Catherine rolled her eyes. "Lord, save a woman from marauders with that specimen of canine protectiveness."

Chuckling, Clem scratched Sally behind the ears. "I don't know. I think she did all right. Glad she didn't eat me." He stepped out onto the porch, waved to the bright lights from the car parked in the driveway. He turned back to Catherine. "I'll be back in the morning. Mind if I stop in and say hi? I'll bring my red pen..."

Her heart jumped to her throat. Catherine swallowed. *This does not happen in real life. Not to me.* She sucked in a deep breath. "Sure. No, I mean, that's fine. I have a pot of strong coffee about 7:30—sleep in on Saturdays..." She wanted to slap herself again.

"Great. See you then." He stepped off the

porch into the rain and disappeared into the waiting car. The bright lights swiveled as the car turned and drove away.

Catherine limped back to her room on shaky legs, her whole body radiating a heat she could hardly explain. She flipped the fan switch and plopped down on her bed. The blades turned smooth as silk and sent a delightful breeze over her skin. It suddenly struck her as enchanting. Even the dust looked rather quaint. “Well, what do you know? It works.”

I Need the Practice

Originally published on The Writings of A. K. Frailey
1/24/2019

Kent stared at the white streak speeding across the evening lavender sky and wished he could be up there...heading west...anywhere but standing on the front porch of his wife's mother's new house. He couldn't refer to Eula as his "mother-in-law" out loud. She had screamed the first time he used the word, a high-pitched shriek that raised the hairs on his arms like a warrior encountering a deadly beast.

Today her welcome echoed her former shriek, but with laughter lines around it. Her clutching embrace and a quick shove through the doorway stiffened his spine. He wasn't sure, but he thought he might have been passionately loved and tossed away at record speed.

Bright lights and happy chatter crashed against his ears.

He knew perfectly well that this day would come. He'd have to meet all the relatives...and the relatives of the relatives...and the friends involved with said relatives. He peered ahead at the loud, mingling throng. A man with a fluted drink squeezed by a cloud of women, grinning like a Cheshire cat.

Good Lord, everyone, including third cousins, must be here!

As the only child of parents with no siblings, Kent's life had always been simplified to minimalist family interactions. Frankly, they were lucky to scrape up a great, great granduncle once removed to invite to any particular holiday gathering. Not that they had a lot of those. Work—and more work—held a prime position in the academic hierarchy of the Stevenson family.

Laughter burst from the high-ceilinged living room. Kent shivered. *God save me.*

Tina grabbed his arm and squeezed. "You're going to be fine. They'll love you."

Kent dearly hoped not. He couldn't take that much love. Not in one day. Not even in a lifetime.

He marched forward like a condemned man facing the executioner's block. *I will live through this...*rippled through his mind like a mantra. *I will...*

"Tina!"

New shriek. But familiar somehow. Ah. Yes. Tina's older, wiser, and classically gorgeous sister, Beth? Bella? Berta?

"Haven't seen you since the wedding!"

Kent felt his other arm being snatched with relentless good cheer. "You've been good to her? Of course, you have!" She waved across the room to a clutch of elderly women. "Or they'd eat you alive..."

Tina chuckled, slipped her hand under Kent's sleeve, and caressed his arm in that way she knew drove him mad.

He swallowed hard.

Tina's voice dropped to a purr. "Oh, he's good all right. No worries there."

Oh, just take me, Lord. Kent smothered a groan and unclutched his arms. "I'll get us something to drink." Ambling toward the bar set up in the ultra-modern kitchen, Kent bumped into the men's department of said family gathering.

"Oh, there you are, ol' boy!" Booming laughter. Perhaps one sneer.

There wasn't much to say to such an obvious assessment, so Kent sidled up to the makeshift bar.

A man dressed in formal wear with an even more formal expression merely raised his eyebrows. After ordering his wife's favorite wine, the same for his sister-in-law, and a beer for himself, Kent realized he didn't have enough hands or the dexterity needed to carry three drinks through the mingling throng.

"So, I hear you're a journalist."

Kent turned and faced two men, one tall and lean and the other looked like an aging football coach. He cleared his throat. "Yep. I plod along as best I can..." He lifted the two glasses of wine from the counter and stepped forward. Hint. Hint.

Oblivious, the tall stranger laughed. "You don't have to carry drinks around, kiddo. There's plenty of help going around doing that sort of thing."

Feeling his face flush, Kent couldn't think what else to do but deliver the stupid drinks, even if a dozen helpers swirled about the place.

"My name's Davies. William Davies. Chicago side of the family. This is my partner in crime, Shell Beck." The tall man thrust out his hand.

Oh hell. Kent put the glasses back on the counter and shook each man's hand in turn. He forced an innocent smile. "So what crime are you involved with at present?"

Shell snorted. "Same as everyone. Making a living in an insane world." He scowled. "Surely you've heard of Davies and Beckman industries?"

"I thought you said your name was Beck."

"Got to have some anonymity, you know. This way, I keep my professional and private life separate."

"Ahhh..." Kent just barely suppressed an eye-roll. *Doing a great job.* He snatched his beer and took a long swig.

William wagged a finger. "You know, I've read some of your stuff. Sure write a lot. You're either rich or damn poor. Why do you pump out so much?"

Kent took another gulp and wiped his mouth. His gaze flashed to the doorway as Tina caught his eye and grinned. "I need the practice."

By the time they were ready to leave, Kent had drunk more beer than was good for him, but Tina was as sober as the day she was born. Lucky for him.

~~~

After a hot shower and a strong cup of coffee the next morning, Kent attempted to process his first clan gathering. He stared open-mouthed as his wife dug into a stalwart breakfast of bacon, eggs, hash browns, and wheat toast. As she slathered grape jelly on her toast, he grimaced. "I suppose your family doesn't think much of me, eh?"

Tina crunched, chewed, and swallowed with obvious relish. "Oh, honey, of course, they like you. As much as anyone."

"Is that supposed to be comforting?"

She reached across the table. "Dear Heart,
~~~

you're worried about nothing. You've got to understand, they're far more interested in what you think about them than in what they think about you."

Kent blinked. He remembered the Cheshire cat and wondered if he had actually dropped through the rabbit hole. "Say that again?"

Building a towering forkful of bacon, egg, and hash brown, Tina crunched her brow in concentration. "It's like when I went to see your family and your mom showed me her China plate collection, and your dad shuffled those stuffy academic journals on the coffee table, and your great uncle whatever...told me all about his DNA test and how his genetic code is exactly split between Eastern Europe and the Iberian Peninsula." She plunged the entire forkful into her mouth and grinned.

Kent's stomach roiled.

After chewing, Tina handed him a piece of jelly toast. "Eat something, and you'll feel worlds better."

Kent felt his blood pressure rising. "My family adores you. But your family—?"

"Kent... Do you remember what happened when that stupid editor wrote that scathing review of your work, but so many readers wrote in to say that they loved it, and he had to recant his statement?"

Kent nodded.

"You remember your reaction?"

Kent nodded.

"You said that you write like you live—the best you can—and you keep at it because you need the practice." Tina rose from the table and carried her plate to the sink. She glanced back. "Oh, you'd better hurry up, or we'll be late."

Alarm shivered over Kent's body. "Late?"

"Yeah. Remember? It's Sunday. After church, we're going to the picnic and jamboree. There will be quite the crowd, so put on comfortable shoes."

Slowly, Kent rose and plodded to the window. A red bird perched on a branch and chirped its heart out. Almost seemed to be laughing. Kent shook his head and hunted for his shoes.

And Everything in Between

Originally published on The Writings of A. K. Frailey
1/31/2019

"Being rejected isn't exactly the end of the world...just feels like it." Gertrude heaved a long sigh. "Silly of me...to think that...but, you know, it's...life. Beginnings...and endings."

She launched herself from her partitioned, tan and grey workstation, pulled on her heavy winter coat, and plodded to the check-out counter.

Dressed in a blindingly white parka with a fake fur fringe around the hood, her friend, Kamila, smiled as they punched in their work numbers and timed out. "Got plans for the weekend, Gerty?"

Gertrude closed her eyes, sighed, and then straightened her shoulders. Focusing, she met Kamila's teasing gaze. "Nope. But I'll make some. And you?"

Kamila grinned. "Timmy is coming over for the weekend. We're going out on the town and have some fun!" She did a little arm shake with a hip wiggle and laughed.

A stab of pain made Gertrude wince. Her stomach clenched. "You be careful, Kammy. People get hurt...driving around and partying...you know."

"You're such a worrier!" Sauntering out the main exit, Kamila shivered in the cold blast of winter air and linked arms with Gertrude. "You need to have more fun. Besides, people get killed sitting at home too. Heart attacks, cancer, random acts of violence—no one's safe." She tugged at her zipper. “Might as well live while you got the chance. Can’t stay at home all the time.”

Her plaid coat buttoned to the top, Gertrude pulled her keys from her purse and punched the unlock button as she neared her Cruise. “No safe place in this world, I agree. But it’s just plain dumb to beard the lion.”

“I don’t even want to know what that means.” Kammy waved as she scrunched into her tiny sports car. “Get a life, girl, not a proverb.” The engine roared, and the tires squealed out of the parking lot so fast, passersby had to scurry aside.

Gertrude shook her head and murmured under her breath.

When she got into her apartment, Gertrude tugged herself free from her coat and peeled off her work clothes. She stood under a hot shower for a full five full minutes and then dressed in her comfortable, well-worn jeans, fluffy socks, and a long shirt. It had a tear at the neck when she had caught it on the latticework reaching for a hard-to-reach cluster of grapes last summer, but she figured that no one would see her and who would really care anyway?

Just as she settled down on the couch wrapped in a knitted blanket, a hot cup of tea near at hand, and a mystery novel on her lap, the buzzer rang long and loud. She glanced up, a thrill of fear racing through her. *It’s just someone looking for a donation...or some lady looking for a friend...or—*

The buzzer insisted.

Frowning, she set the book next to her teacup, tossed the blanket aside, and jogged forward. The buzzer raged for the third time. Irritated, she swung open the door. “Hey, unless someone’s about to be murdered, you can lay off the buzzer."

Short and stocky, Ben stood before her in a crumpled EMT uniform, his brown hair disheveled and a wild look in his eyes. "You're okay?"

Gertrude scrunched her face like she was looking at a pink armadillo. "Yeah. You care?"

Passing through the doorway, Ben tromped to the couch and flung himself down with a long sigh. He ran his fingers through his hair, standing it up in a scattered array. "Good Lord. You know what you've put me through?"

Gertrude blinked. "I. Put. You. Through?"

"When they reported the accident, I recognized the vanity license plate. I called your office, and they said you'd just left. I thought you were with her!"

Gertrude slapped her cheek, all warmth draining from her body. "Kamila?"

"Burned beyond recognition. At least her car is...it'll take time to sort through the mess..."

Swaying on her feet, a roar swelled into Gertrude's ears. Strong arms grabbed her and led her to the couch. Ben crouched at her side and stroked her hand. "Sorry, I didn't mean to shock you like that. I was just so worried. There's been one emergency after another... Crazy days. I've been working overtime..." He shook his head. "But when that call came in...I didn't even ask. I just ran out the door."

Before she knew what she was doing, Gertrude was sobbing on Ben's shoulder.

By the time she had a fresh cup of tea, the blanket wrapped over her legs, and Ben's arm around her shoulder, she had wiped the last of her tears off her cheek. "I must look awful."

"Not to me. You look just fine. Alive. The way I like you."

Gertrude dropped her gaze and tugged a loose yarn string. "I got the impression that...you know. You were tired of me. Too busy all the time. Working."

"You do realize that I save lives, right? That I work hard to earn a good living...so that maybe one day we can..."

"So, you're not avoiding me?"

Ben grinned. "You know, it'd make things a lot simpler if you just ask me next time."

"You didn't return my messages..."

"Yeah. There is that. My fault. Sorry. Just so blasted busy. You know...I see it all the time. Misunderstandings. Couples going at each other. Kids wanting to kill themselves."

Gertrude felt her throat tighten. "It wasn't a misunderstanding today. Kamilla is dead. I tried to warn her...but..."

Ben harrumphed and clapped his hands together as he sat forward. "Kamilla drove like a speed demon. She was on the track to self-destruction long before you met her." He dragged his hands over his face. "I can't save everyone. And neither can you." He pulled Gertrude into a tight embrace. "But I'm here now and...you know...we might make a life together. Despite this crazy world. Despite misunderstandings..."

Gertrude snuggled into Ben's arms, her heart aching yet comforted. "Kamilla was going out on the town today...and I thought something in me had died. Guess it shows...we don't really know. Life. Beginnings and endings...and everything in between.

Die Hard Optimism

Originally published on The Writings of A. K. Frailey
2/14/2019

Agnes couldn't decide which skirt to wear. Not that there was much of a selection. Her choices consisted of a black skirt reserved for funerals and formal church events, an autumn floral thing that she always tripped over because it was a hand-me-down from her sister, who was a good three inches taller than her, a severe gray pencil skirt, which made her look like a desperate job applicant, or a green knee-length accordion skirt that made her feel like she was back at St. Robert's grade school.

She sighed and wondered if her daring pair of form-fitting black slacks would work. Not that she had ever actually worn them. She bought them in the hopes of one day *needing* them. Could this possibly be their call to duty?

She plopped down on the bed and let the weak rays of a February sun pour over her. "Good heaven. I'm agonizing over nothing. No one will notice what I'm wearing. They'll only notice me if I trip the waiter and spill everyone's drinks." She shuddered at the thought.

A plaintive cry turned her attention.

"Come in, honey."

Lenora, her six-year-old daughter, wandered in, looking very much like a rumpled, exhausted princess. She had the tiara to prove her identity and the unsteadiness of a child woken from a sound sleep.

Agnes wiggled her fingers. "Come here,

sweetheart."

Her brightly speckled costume, a gift from Grandma last Halloween, sashayed and shoo-shooshed as she toddled over. She crawled up on the bed and curled into her mom's arms.

Agnes ran her fingers through her daughter's unruly tangles. "I'm going out for a bit, sweetie, and Grandma is coming by. She's bringing pizza. Rumor has it that it might be pepperoni..."

Lenora hunched her shoulders as if she'd never heard of pizza and couldn't care less if the whole world turned into a pepperoni.

With the sensation of a knife plunged into her chest, Agnes rolled off the bed, yanked open her dresser, pulled out her back slacks and a silky button-down blouse that rippled over her hips, and marched to the bathroom. "You know, I'm not the bad guy here."

When she peered at the reflection in the mirror, she had to admit, she wasn't the bad guy or a bad woman for that matter, though age had taken its toll. She wasn't a spring chicken anymore. A hen? She turned from the mirror; best not to think about it.

By the time Grandma Mimi hustled through the front door and hung her coat on the rack, Agnes had Lenora bathed and in her best PJs.

Mimi practically swallowed the child alive in a one-arm hug and handed a frozen pizza to Agnes. "Take the wrapping off and don't forget the cardboard. Oven at 400."

With a half-satirical salute, Agnes marched into the kitchen.

Mimi followed.

Agnes could feel her mom's eyes boring into

her back. “Okay. What?”

She turned around and ran her fingers over her slacks as if she could iron them by hand.

“Nothing. Much. Just wondering why you’re going to a work-related fundraiser dressed like a woman...”

Agnes felt the heat rise through the roots of her hair. “Because I am a woman, maybe?”

“Your husband isn’t dead. He’s just missing in action.”

“If only!”

“You know what I mean.”

“Mom, you know he’s not coming back. I know he’s not coming back. That’s all there is to it.”

“But not all there is to you, apparently.”

“What’s so wrong?”

Lenora tiptoed into the room with her hands clasped above her head, twirling like a ballerina.

Agnes clenched her jaw and closed her eyes against tears.

Mimi led Lenora out of the room with cooing encouragement and pulled a small box out of a large pocket. “I brought a puzzle we can put together if you open it up and lay out the pieces on the coffee table. Okay, Sweetums?”

Agnes felt her mom’s firm hand on her shoulder. Then a gentle squeeze. “You’re a strong woman, Agnes. I’ve never thought otherwise. But I know how it is. You get lonely...and it takes more than a woman can stand to be both mother and father every day...day after day.”

Agnes blinked back her tears and focused on the kitchen table. Mismatched socks still lined the edge. She scooped them into a bundle and dropped them on the counter. “I didn’t think these slacks were such a big deal. I just wanted to look..."

Mimi set the oven timer. "I know. But you're still married. At least in the eyes of the church. If you want to change that..."

"There's always the chance—"

"Is there?"

"I'm caught between worlds, Mom. Stuck. Never really married and never really free. I can't move forward. Or back, for that matter."

Mimi rummaged through the refrigerator. "You got any salad fixings? A side dish would go well with the pizza."

Agnes pursed her lips, leaned in, yanked open the crisper, and pulled out a bag of lettuce and a soft tomato. "Good luck getting her to eat anything healthy. She'd rather die of the plague."

With quick, efficient motions, Mimi tore up the lettuce and diced the tomato. She kept her eyes on her work.

Agnes got the message, sighed, and retreated to change her clothes.

~~~

It was late by the time Agnes stepped into her living room. The lights were dim and her mom was sleeping on the couch with an afghan thrown over her legs. The same afghan Mimi had given her on her wedding day. The irony struck her as funny, and she giggled. The one beer she sipped through the evening might have helped.

Mimi sat up and rubbed her eyes. "You're home safe. And giggling?"

"Yep. Safe and sound."
~~~

Mimi patted the couch next to her. "Tell me about it."

Agnes tucked the green skirt under as she plunked down next to her mom. "Well, I had an epiphany as I sat at the gloriously set table and listened to people's conversations. One woman bullied her husband mercilessly about not getting their garage cleaned out, while another couple sat in stony silence. Then there was this kid who kept screaming at his dad, saying that he wanted to go home and watch a movie and eat real food. One girl sat pathetically by the wall, her eyes searching for someone, while a crowd circled around a handsome bearded guy like he was the greatest thing since the invention of the iPhone."

"Sounds like a dull crowd."

"Average. That's what struck me."

"That people are average?"

"That even at an expensive club, wearing the best clothes, eating sumptuous food, drinking whatever, and all for a noble cause...most of us poor human beings weren't happy."

"Grim observation."

"Yeah. But freeing too. I get it now...better than before. Jim's abandonment nearly killed me, and deep down, I know that he's not coming back. I have to accept it. We've got more cause for an annulment than most...neither of us had a clue what marriage meant...and we were drunk on dreams. But most of all, I see now that my life is what I make of it...right now. Today. What's before me. You know, even when God— Creator of the Universe—lived on Earth, we weren't happy. If He couldn't make us happy..."

"So, you aren't striving to be happy anymore?"

"Nope. I've decided to reach a little higher...go for contentment."

Mimi stretched and pulled herself to her feet. "Well, tell me about the view when you get there. Right now, I need to find my bed and collapse. I'm leading three junior high classes through the museum tomorrow. If the effort doesn't destroy the rest of my brain cells...I'll be delighted."

Agnes stood and hugged her mom. "I knew I got it from somewhere." She stepped to the front door and handed her a floral-patterned jacket from the rack. "Be careful on the way."

"I only live down the street." Dressed in her winter best, Mimi opened the door, shivered, and stepped over the threshold. Her eyebrows puckered as she glanced back. "Got what?"

"My die-hard optimism."

After shutting the door, Agnes smiled and climbed the steps to bed, her green skirt rippling over her bare knees.

Where Is My Hope Now?

Originally published on The Writings of A. K. Frailey
2/21/2019

Kevin stared at the red tube going from the pole into his arm and knew that he was going to die. At forty-five, he was still young enough to feel that he still had way too much ahead of him to quit now. *But then,* he sighed, *I've had a better life than many others. Still...*

His mom's gray head poked through the doorway. "You decent?"

With a snort, Kevin shook his head. "If you don't mind the sight of blood flowing into my veins...I'm decent enough." He peered down at his stained sweatpants and ragged shirt.

Ginger tiptoed into the room, her gaze roaming from side to side. Three other patients sat slumped in a line of chairs in various stages of intravenous feedings...blood, medicine...chicken soup, for all she knew. Swallowing back the ache in her throat at the sight of her son pale and drained, she squared her shoulders. *No time to be weak now. Be strong, old woman.* Still, her hand shook as she patted her son's shoulder. "The nurse said you're almost done, and you can go home as soon as they've made sure you're not going to faint." She looked around. "They give you crackers or anything?"

"Juice and crackers. Deluxe treatment." Kevin winced. He didn't mean to sound so sarcastic, but his back was killing him. Three hours was way too long to sit in a chair.

"Well, I've got coupons for the family

restaurant next door. I thought we'd grab a bite before we head out into the wilds of—"

"I'm not hungry, Ma. But you can—"

"I'm not hungry either, but that hardly matters, does it? We don't eat just to make ourselves happy. We eat to stay alive. And you need to stay alive a little longer. Hear me?"

Kevin clenched his jaw. He knew it was absurd to argue with his seventy-eight-year-old mother. She had a long-standing tradition of repeating herself until he gave in. He merely nodded and glanced over as the nurse came in and started to unplug him from the technology that saved his life each week.

After they settled in a red booth and the waitress took their order, Kevin pulled out his phone and scrolled through. There were three messages from his friend Dave at work. He frowned and pushed the redial.

Ginger pointed to the lady's room and toddled off.

His eyes following his mom's careful maneuvers around the café, he listened as Dave picked up the call.

"Kevin? That you?"

With a snort, Kevin laughed. "Yeah, what'da think? I was just getting blood, not a new heart or anything."

"Oh, well, I've got news..."

Kevin felt a ripple of fear shoot through him.

David cleared his throat. "Hey, man, you sitting down?"

A headache building between his eyes, Kevin tapped the tabletop in staccato fashion. "In a booth at an overcrowded family diner, if that's any comfort. What's going on?"

"I hate to tell you this over the phone, but the news has it all over..."

Kevin's hand shook, and a thousand bees buzzed in his head. "What?"

"Rhonda was in a head-on collision after work today. Five-car pileup. Three dead, two critical, and one kid survived without a scratch. But Rhonda..."

The bees began stinging. Kevin's whole body trembled, and he wondered if he'd puke his crackers and juice all over the floor.

Dave's voice rose. "You okay, Kev?"

Kevin dropped his head onto his arms, the phone slipping off his ear. He could hear Dave shouting. "Kev? Where are you, man? I'm coming—"

He felt the phone plucked from his weak grasp and his mom's shaky voice. "Hello? Oh, Dave. Yes, just saw it on the news. So tragic."

Silence.

His mom's voice dropped to bedrock. "I see. Terribly sad. For all of you. Rhonda was a dear girl...woman. Don't worry. I've got Kevin with me. I'll get him home now. If you want to meet us—"

Silence and then an assenting "Yes, that's a good idea."

Kevin had little memory of the drive home or how he got into bed. He only remembered the sensation of falling. And not being able to save himself.

~~~

When he opened his eyes, Kevin realized that
~~~

he had slept through the night and a good part of the next morning. Groggily, he raked his fingers through his hair, shuffled from his rumpled bed to the bathroom, stripped, and took the longest, hottest shower he could stand. He stood naked and grimaced at the pile of dirty laundry on the wet bathroom floor.

He heard Dave's voice on the other side of the door. "You want something bright or dark?"

Kevin shook his head. "Black as hell, if you can find it."

As he dried himself, the door opened a crack and a pair of dark blue jeans and a black turtleneck sweater flew through the air and smacked him in the head.

"Best I could do. You have the worst selection of clothes this side—"

Ginger's voice piped up. "Oh, leave him alone, Dave. You know how he is. Platypuses have more fashion sense." She lifted her voice as if he was in Siberia rather than the bathroom. "Breakfast is ready. Better hurry before it gets cold."

Kevin winced as he pulled on his jeans, mumbling under his breath.

When he sat down at the kitchen counter, a large platter of bacon, eggs, and toast was set in glorious array before his wondering eyes. He couldn't believe that his stomach rumbled in salubrious joy. Traitorous things...stomachs.

Dave pulled up a stool and perched on Kevin's right with a large cup of coffee, a faint aroma of cinnamon wafting through the air. His mom bustled about his tiny kitchen like she owned the place.

Dave watched him eat with absorbed interest.

Finally, Kevin nodded to his mom. "She can make you a plate—"

"Naw, I already ate." He glanced at the bustling homemaker. "You ever want to trade moms, just let me know. I'd even pay extra..."

An image of Dave's fashionable mother as she commanded underlings at city hall sent a shudder through Kevin's body. Then he remembered the news and dropped his fork. "Oh, God. Rhonda."

Ginger turned and gripped his hand. "It's awful, honey. But—"

Nearly leaping from his seat, Kevin felt his pulse racing. "But what? We have to accept what we can't change? She died mercifully quick—God, I hope so!" A sob struggled to free itself from his throat. "But where is my hope now?"

With tears coursing down his cheeks, Dave took Kevin's other hand. "Where it's always been, man. Right here. With us. With Joe, Dan, Kelly, and all the others at work. With the nurses, the doctors, your mom, and..." He swiped the rolling tears away. "Oh, God."

Ginger lifted her chin. "Listen, if you'd have been at work yesterday, more than likely you'd have been in that car with Rhonda. And you'd probably have died then and there. But instead, you were getting your treatments...ones that save your life one week at a time."

Ice coursed through Kevin's body. "But not forever."

"No. Not forever. Not for you...not for me..." Ginger glanced at Dave. "Not for any of us."

Kevin sucked in a deep, shuddering breath and slumped on the counter. He covered his face with his hands. “So much pain.”

Dave gripped his arm. “But you’re not alone.”

Kevin looked up and met his friend’s honest gaze.

Dave nodded in Ginger’s direction as she returned to the sink. “She needs you. So, do I. And everyone at work misses your ugly face.”

As Kevin felt his friend’s hand grip his arm, he could practically feel fresh blood flowing into his veins.

Like Dreams upon Waking

Originally published on The Writings of A. K. Frailey
2/28/2019

"You've checked your watch five times in the last fifteen minutes. Would you stop already?" Greg grabbed a handful of chips from the bowl on the coffee table, leaned back on the plush sofa, and pointed to the big screen TV centered on the back wall. "You'll never enjoy the game if you keep this up."

Tom crossed his arms, plopped down on the easy chair on Greg's left and glared at his best friend. "You have no idea what I'm going through."

Greg chomped on a chip, swallowed, and wiped his hand on his jeans. "I have a daughter, too."

"She's four!"

"Yeah, but she'll grow up and probably date some guy with tattoos and a shaved head, and I'll be cool enough to shake his hand, point to my gun rack, and remind him of the curfew. I'll leave it at that."

"Ha! If I know anything about you, buddy, you'll barricade the door until he leaves the names and addresses of his closest kin. And even then, Sally-Ann will be wired for sound."

As if called by magic, a little girl scampered into the room and flew into her daddy's arms. "Give me a ring-a-round, Daddy!"

With a groan, Greg pulled his daughter into his arms, centered himself in the living room, and began to spin her in a wide arc.

Tom grinned as Sally-Ann squealed in delight.

Speeding up, Greg edged to the couch and deposited his daughter on the cushions. "Enough. If you throw up, your mama's going to blame me."

A woman's voice called from another room. "Sally-Ann, get your backside into your room and pick up these toys like I told you."

Tom and Greg froze.

With a fresh squeal, Sally-Ann raced out of the room.

Tom peered at Greg. "So, you think Joan will interview the prospective dates when Sally-Ann gets of age?"

Greg nodded and stroked his chin. "Might work." He frowned. "Sorry, man. I know you're on your own. If you want...Joan could come over and..."

Tom checked his watch, his foot tapping. "It's barely eight. I gave them until eleven. It's only a school dance, but if the guy doesn't act like a perfect gentleman—"

"Like you were?"

Tom squeezed his eyes shut a moment and then ran his fingers through his hair. He stood up. "I think I'd better go."

"But the game!"

"I can't relax. Besides, I have things to check out." "Such as?"

"You don't think Kami would mind if I stopped—"

"You'd have more to fear than death itself. Don't go there. Literally or figuratively."

"Maybe Joan could go undercover?"

"Joan happens to trust your daughter enough to babysit our kids. I doubt she'd spy on

Kami...even for a good cause. Like keeping you sane." Greg spread himself on the easy chair and nudged the chips in Tom's direction. "Have a healthy snack and sit down. Put your mind on the game and just live through the next few hours. Okay?"

Tom plunked onto the couch and closed his eyes. "Only because I know I couldn't stop myself from stopping at the school if I left now."

Greg snorted. "A little self-control, man. Just a little."

Tom opened one eye and peered at Greg. "I'll have my revenge one day. You realize that, right?"

Greg laughed as he reached for another chip. "How do you figure?"

"Sally-Ann's so enamored with her daddy...she'll pick a man just like you."

Leaping from the chair, Greg knocked the bowl over, and chips scattered like dreams upon waking.

For the First Time in Months

Originally published on The Writings of A. K. Frailey
3/7/2019

Standing outside the huge garage door, Madge fumbled with her keys and then handed them over to the serviceman.

Without a word, he took them and nodded.

Buttoning her coat against a bitter late winter wind, Madge forced a grin. "Sorry, I'm so clumsy. I was out at the zoo, showing the school kids the monkeys—kind of funny how they play off each other—but dang, my hands get so cold, I could probably freeze water, like one of those superhuman types on TV."

The service guy grinned and started away. "Well, if you want to sign for the order inside, we can get things moving so you don't have to wait too long." He stopped by her car, frowned at the tires, circled around and shook his head. He opened the service door and stood aside.

Nervous anxiety rippled through Madge's body as she traipsed inside. She tossed her bulky purse onto the high counter. She glanced at the nameplate with Rick written in bold letters, next to a family photo with a pretty wife and two adorable kids.

Rick punched numbers into a calculator.

Marge swallowed back her fear. "So, before you get too far, you want to tell me what I'm looking at? I mean, it's just the oil change, right?"

Rick looked up, an appraising expression on his face. "Truth is, your two front tires are as bald as any I've ever seen. I'm surprised you made it through the winter on those things. Your steering wheel has more tread on it."

Madge's courage fell to the cement floor. "Well, I've been hoping they would make it to June. I only have to drive into the city twice a week, so I figured—"

The horrified look on Rick's face forced her to grip her courage with both hands. She swallowed hard. "You're right. It's not safe. For me or anyone. Okay, I'll get new ones. Can you get something a little better than what I have now? These only lasted a couple years..."

With obvious relief, Rick nodded and started tapping the calculator again. "We'll take you up a step and with the oil change we're looking at..."

Marge knew he was looking at a number larger than anything she had in her checking account. Or would likely have in the near future. When he was done with the detailed costs, tax, she sucked in a fresh breath and pulled her bag forward. "Do you mind if I call my bank? I'll transfer what I have from savings...and then" —she squinted as if the light hurt her eyes— "maybe you'd let me make monthly payments on the rest? I'm good for it. It'll just take three...four months, tops. My job...well...it's not one of those high-paying ones."

Rick nodded. "That's fine. I'll have to order these now, and when they come in, we can get everything done at once. Will that work?"

Pulling her phone from her purse, Madge exhaled. "Yep. I'll call the bank now and pay you what I can, and then—"

A man behind Marge cleared his throat.

With a frown, Rick peered over Madge's head.

Marge started for the door. “I’ll go outside. I can’t get any reception in here anyway.” The wind had died down, and Marge soaked in the noonday sunshine. Her heart pounded as she pressed the phone to her ear. A tap on the shoulder turned her attention.

Rick stood before her, a strange expression on his face. “Hey, don’t worry about it. Just go home, and I’ll call you when I have everything set. Okay?”

A fresh blast of frigid air careened through her thin coat. She peered at the service door. “You sure?”

“Yeah. No problem. I’ve got some things to take care of right now, but I’ll call you about arranging the balance and payment.”

As Marge gave Rick her phone number, she wondered if she had accomplished anything. She marched to her car, her keys biting into her grip.

~~~

Once at home, Marge made herself a hot cup of tea and settled on the sofa with her checkbook and a pad of paper. She had to rethink her options. She sighed and took a tentative sip. Lipton’s best wasn’t nearly so good without sugar, but hey, it was better than just hot water.

Her phone rang. Dragging her purse by the long strap, she yanked it closer and sifted through myriad objects. Once she had her phone in hand, she tapped it on. “Yeah?”

“Marge?”
~~~

Marge waited. *Oh boy...* Exhaustion seeped through her body.

"Sorry, I don't mean to bother you...and I suppose I acted a little odd when you left. But, you see, the guy in line behind you told me that he overheard our conversation, and he offered to pay for your tires if we ate the cost of labor and the tax."

Marge froze. She wondered how long she could go without breathing. When conscious thought returned, she blinked and stared at her worn black bag slumped on the floor. "Who? Did what?"

"The gentleman behind you...well, he heard about your situation, and when you went outside, he offered to pay for your tires... but he didn't want you to know it was him. He said he doesn't know you or anything. Just his good deed for the day sort of thing. So that's why I told you to go home."

Tears filled Marge's eyes. "I never...I mean...I can't believe..."

"We told him okay; it's a deal. So, I ordered your tires, and you can bring your car on Friday at noon. We'll have everything done by three. That'll work for you?"

"But I'd really like to thank him...whoever he is. And you too, of course. I can't believe..."

"Don't worry about it. Just bring your car on Friday, and everything will be taken care of. Free of charge. Sometimes life is good, you know."

Marge swiped the tear from her cheek. "People are good, Rick."

As she dropped her phone back into her purse, Marge realized that not only weren't her hands cold, but her whole body felt warm for the first time in months.

Start in the Clouds

Originally published on The Writings of A. K. Frailey
3/14/2019

"Just put me out of my misery now, would you?" Wearing a pair of worn work jeans, a plaid shirt, and mud-splattered tennis shoes, Kevin pushed back from his laptop desk and swiped a large coffee mug off the side table. "I might as well try fishing for tuna at the Skinner's pond."

His bulky frame positioned before his ancient computer, George grinned and thrust out his empty mug. "Since you're getting a refill?"

"What do I look like? A serving—"

"Ah, ah! Careful. Don't lose your nice boy demeanor the moment you get offline. After all, a good woman can smell a fraud all the way across the cyber universe."

"Sure, she can smell fraud...but can she see decency, kindness, and everlasting patience?" Kevin plowed his way through the cluttered office, scattering stray papers in his wake.

The overhead light glinting off his bald head, George leaned back on his chair, the rollers squeaking in useless appeal, and propped his scuffed boots on the corner of his desk. "I told you that this online dating thing was a waste of your time and talent. No good woman will put her face on a dating site. And those that do will only see you're an unmarried farm boy with four kids. Not a romance in the making, my boy."

Sloshing coffee into his cup, Kevin shook his head. He yanked a paper towel from the rack and wiped up the spill. With a steadier hand, he filled

George's mug brimful. "Look, this isn't exactly St. Louis. Small town America has lots of land and sky but few people. Not a lot of unmarried options around here."

"You could try the big city...visit your friend...the cool one with the long ponytail and suave attitude. He's probably got women lining up—"

Passing George's mug safely into his friend's hands, Kevin perched on the edge of a ripped couch and blew on the steaming coffee. "Not really. He's struggling as much as I am. Says that every woman he goes out with has this list...an impossible list by the way. A guy has to split the bill...or he's a Neanderthal. Except for the ones who expect him to pay for everything, or he's a selfish jerk. And women like beards...or hate them. Got to have a decent job that pays well, you better revere your mother, and God forbid you have a strong opinion about religion or politics."

George snorted. "Just to be fair..."

Kevin stared over his cup. "Yeah? What?"

"Well, I happened to notice that you put on your profile that you live with your mom."

"She's sixty-eight years old and would be in a nursing home if I wasn't helping her out."

"Not exactly chick-bait, my friend." He swallowed a sip of coffee and shrugged. "Though I admire your honesty, did you have to mention that you got laid off last year?"

"The harvest was terrible. Besides, I picked up carpentry work and made more money in the long run..."

"I know and you know...but listen, buddy... You're going to have to explain every bloody detail or learn to leave some stuff out."

"I suppose I should leave my kids out?" Kevin's jaw hardened as he returned to his desk.

"Naw. I think you should tell the truth about them upfront. Your wife died. You've done a great job with the kids...and any woman who isn't open to that isn't worth your time anyway."

"Like anyone wants to deal with..."

"What?"

"Anyone's real life."

George sighed and dropped his feet to the ground. "Now, I think you've hit the nail on the head." George folded his hands in his lap and leaned forward. "Look. Back in my day, a guy met a gal at a school dance or got set up by a friend...or maybe saw a nice girl at church or something. Heck, it just sort of happened. We had movies and stuff, but we knew that wasn't real. Least most of us knew."

Kevin propped his head in his hand. "But now?"

George flicked a finger at the computer screen. "Well, now, everything is done online. Shopping, banking, even this dating thing. And it's all in the head. Works for numbers...but not so good for the heart. How many women have you reviewed just this week, say?"

Kevin shrugged. "Maybe twenty profiles..."

"See? That's exactly what I mean. Twenty! Lord, have mercy; they all get to looking alike after five. No one can get excited about meeting woman number seven or eight...or fifteen. We're just not built that way. We're social beings...our attraction is filtered through our senses. All you got to go on is a few pictures and a carefully worded bio."

Kevin dragged his fingers through his hair. "Times are a changing, my friend. I'm long past school dances, my friends are married—hanging on for all they're worth—or divorced and bitter. And the average age of women at my mom's church is about seventy."

George squinted at Kevin. "You looked at twenty profiles? Really?"

"Or so..."

"And not one of them caught your eye?"

"Several did...but one gal had a weird sense of humor, another was three years younger than me, two were going to nursing school so they'll never even think about staying home with kids, and besides...can you imagine the school loans? And the rest either had kids or had ticking clocks or—"

"Sheesh! And I thought women were picky!"

"Aw, quit! I just don't want to get entangled in another messy family. You remember Brenda's sister? Issues, man. Major drama. And I'm hardly in a position to take on anyone's financial mess..."

"Do you happen to hear yourself when you talk?"

Kevin tapped his keypad and glared at George.

"Hey, just saying... You've decided all this stuff without one conversation, right? Or maybe one or two conversations..."

"Who wants to wade into quicksand?"

George snorted and glanced at his watch. "You do, pal. You do. You want a relationship with a woman...expect quicksand. Expect drama, financial stress, scary family closets, sick kids, bad-mood days, lonely nights, and a few headaches to boot."

Kevin stared at his screen. "Sounds charming."

"Yeah. But that's only part of it. There are also the quiet talks on the couch, holding hands, smiles from across the room when you both know what the other one is thinking, the kind of hug that holds your heart in place when nothing else in the world can..." George stood and plodded across the room. He patted Kevin's arm. "Hell, look at us. You hate how I decorate the workspace, whine about my filing system, undermine my authority every chance you get, and act like an overgrown puppy half the time. Do I mind? Yeah. But do I put up with you? Sure. And we make a great team." He leaned down. "Now add in a great—"

George put his hand in front of Kevin's mouth. "Stop now. Save yourself. And me." He shifted and glanced at his friend. "I get it."

"Good." George put his empty mug on the sideboard and headed for the restroom. "After work, check out a couple profiles, chat to some lucky woman. And bring yourself back to earth, man. Even if you do have to start in the clouds."

Kevin watched his friend stride out the door. He shook his head and grinned.

It Makes All the Difference

Originally published on The Writings of A. K. Frailey
3/21/2019

As far as I was concerned, the whole world was on a fast train headed for destruction, and I didn't want to watch. Humanity might *party* on the way, but the crash wouldn't be pretty. It would be painful. Very painful. I couldn't think about it.

So, I did the next best thing. I invited myself over to my sister's place in the country. She has one of those mini-farms with cute domesticated animals, a huge garden, fruit trees, and a stack of firewood big enough to make Paul Bunyan envious. And, yes, they and their assorted young'uns eat bacon, eggs, and pancakes with homemade maple syrup every Saturday morning.

I got there on Friday night, just to be on the safe side. Right off the bat, Leslie laughed at me. I carried a cup of herbal tea to the counter, pulled up a wooden stool, and harrumphed. "Hey, I'm being serious. The planet is being poisoned beyond repair... we'll likely nuke ourselves soon...and then aliens will decipher one of our stupid transmissions and figure that we really ought to be decimated just to end the drama."

With complete indifference to my dismal prognostications, Leslie sloshed her hands into a sink of dirty dishes, steaming water, and soapy bubbles. "You need to lighten up. Tonight, you can bunk with the girls; they don't snore much. In the morning, we'll all eat a healthy breakfast and then, while I brandish a chair and whip to keep the kids from following, you can take a long rambling walk in the woods. After that, I'll put you to work helping me clean the basement, we'll play a rousing soccer game, afterward, go to Mass, and by the evening, Jasper will join us for a family-feud Ping-Pong tournament. By Sunday, you'll be a new person."

Heck, I thought, by Sunday, it won't matter where the world is heading, I'll be dead.

~~~

True to her word, the girls didn't snore. Much. With carefully placed pillows smashed against my skull, I managed to fall into a deep sleep in the wee hours of the morning. When Leslie clanged the outdoor bell calling her screaming kids and a much too happy husband to the breakfast table, I managed to stumble down the stairs with a modicum of composure. The fact that I felt like road kill didn't appear to dampen anyone's spirits.

But a glorious breakfast and a strong cup of coffee worked a miracle. For the first time in days, I actually felt glad to be a human. With Jasper's assistance, Leslie managed to hold the kids back while I made my escape, and I practically skipped across the cow pasture, carefully sidestepping unmentionables, into the woods. A fun fantasy escape just for me.

Except it wasn't.

Deer inhabited the woods and terrorized my thumping heart into regions it did not honestly belong. Stupid deer. Who knew such innocent creatures could look so darn ferocious up close and personal?
~~~

Brandishing my water bottle, I backed up toward the old Tobin place and decided to investigate the ancient ruins dating back at least...well...fifty years. It was a squirrel that ruined everything. That little scoundrel scurried into a hidey-hole by the back entrance, enticing me to follow, when I suddenly felt my footing give way.

After I found myself flat on my back at the bottom of a muddy, brick-lined—thank God not-full—well, I said words I'm glad my nieces and nephews weren't around to hear. Then I tried to sit up and found that I couldn't. I tried to breathe instead.

That accomplished, I felt a tiny bit better. But I was still on my back at the bottom of a well, far from human habitation. Even if I could yell, no one was around to hear me. Well, I figured, no use straining myself. Just lie still and wait for someone to rescue me.

Did I mention I was feeling a little depressed before I fell down the well?

By the time the sun set, I was suicidal. And really hungry.

As the stars flickered on one by one, (I knew they don't actually flicker on...but I was practically hallucinating at that point, so I wasn't picky on the details) I wiped what I was certain would be my last tears off my face. I discovered that if I tilted my head just so, I could see more stars than I had ever seen in my life. The Big Dipper shone in splendor and since I'd never been one to stop and stargaze, I was rather amazed it actually existed. I'd heard of it, of course, but I'd never stopped to actually see it—outside of the kids' picture book anyway. It took my breath away.

At that moment, I was glad I had breath to take away.

Then something ran across my hand. I shrieked and sat up. I'm sure I surprised whatever it was that scurried into the blackness. But even more, I amazed myself. I had been convinced that I was broken beyond repair.

Apparently not.

Did you know that stars actually move? That the sky turns? That you can see the universe from the bottom of a well?

When I heard voices calling my name, I winced. Part of me was ready to kiss the first person that pulled me out of the hole. But part of me felt a pang of regret. It was like I had made friends with some unseen universal force that sat with me, glimmered and danced before my eyes, silent yet speaking of wonders I could barely grasp.

Turned out it was a nice fireman who helped me out of the hole. And, yes, I did kiss him. On the cheek.

My sister hugged me so tight; I knew that if I hadn't broken a rib in the fall, I broke one then. But I didn't care. I was alive. I could breathe. And I had seen the stars for the first time in my life.

As I now stand on my apartment balcony, remembering snoring kids, bacon and egg breakfasts, rambling woods, and scary deer, I can't help but stare up at the faint night sky. I can't see the stars like I did at my sister's place. But I know they are there.

And it makes all the difference.

A Connection

Originally published on The Writings of A. K. Frailey
4/4/2019

Selma was freezing. As she rubbed her frozen fingers together, she stomped her booted feet on the floor and started humming a lively tune she used to sing to the boys when they were babies. Ach! It wasn't helping. *Dang ice storm, falling tree branches, and downed power lines!*

"Mom, I've got to get to work. You know…keep the pipes from freezing and the food from thawing."

Selma waved her son away with a nod. "You're a one in a million, boy."

Her son laughed as he headed out the door. "You know my motto— Take no excuses, give no excuses." He glanced back with an impish grin. "Sides, Bradley is already there, and he'll give me hell if I don't show up."

The light was fading and her hurricane lamps were just about out of juice. There wasn't a chance in the Kingdom that she'd be able to get more light or heat before tomorrow. She fed the dogs the last of their Alpo—as yet unfrozen—and wandered around the lonely, dark house. Icy branches swayed from the gleaming trees and powdery snow blew ghost-like swirls along the ground.

Once back in the kitchen, she filled her icy mug with the dregs of her cold coffee and peered at a large bag of old newspapers in the corner. "Wish we had a fireplace; I'd make the biggest bon—" She blinked.

In the backyard, the brick-lined fire pit

staunchly faced the bitter winds without concern. Selma bit her lip. She could barely feel her fingers or her toes. Ice was crusting around the edge of her cup.

Without further thought, she dragged on her heavy coat, snatched a bottle of kerosene and a pack of matches from the cabinet, and lugged the bag of old papers out the back door to the fire pit. She dumped the sack in the center, squeezed the remaining Kerosene on top, and managed to light one match, which she flicked into the dark mess.

Instant bonfire!

She raced back into the house, got her mug and practically danced around the fire, turning around and around so as to warm her outsides and her insides and thaw her coffee in an orderly manner.

"Ahhh...you okay?"

Selma froze, her cup held out to the licking fingers of the flames like a devotee making an oblation to a fire god. She glanced aside and forced a grin.

Her neighbor, Jason, a respectable man in his forties, stood facing her—his eyebrows up, his legs jiggling, and his hands tucked into his armpits. "You don't usually have a cookout this time of the year." He stuck out one finger. "What you trying to do?"

Selma straightened and held out her mug. "Thaw out my coffee."

The man blinked and peered into Selma's backyard. "That your power line laying on the ground?"

"Sure is. The tree decided to shed a few limbs before summer and the line got in the way." She started turning again. “So, I gotta do, what I gotta do to get a decent cuppa before I settle in to freeze for the night.”

Jason trotted forward and threw a wave in Selma’s direction. “You’re coming home with me for a decent cuppa. Joyce and the girls are playing Monopoly and killing their old man. I could use a good excuse to get out of jail.”

A tug of shyness tugged at Selma’s composure. “I don’t want to interrupt…I know how you value your family time.”

“Oh, hell, family time includes freezing neighbors, don’t it?”

~~~

As she entered the brightly lit and gloriously warm kitchen, Selma noted the clean counters, the colorful row of assorted coats hanging on wall pegs by the door, a sterling sink unencumbered by dirty dishes, and an empty coffee pot sitting by its lonesome on the edge of the counter.

Guilt washed over her. “You probably have everything set for tomorrow. I hate to—”

Like a cat batting a ball of string, Jason swiped the air. “Forget it. We’re a social family, as you know. Not a Friday goes by that we don’t have people over.”

“But this is Sunday.”

Jason nodded to the living room. “So? Jeanne picked Friday for our socials. I pick Sunday to rescue neighbors.” He shrugged. “Seems fair to me.”

Selma perched on the edge of a stool and peered into the living room. When Jeanne glanced
~~~

up, Jason bellowed. "Her power's out. I'm making a cup of coffee to thaw her hands so she doesn't have to set the neighborhood on fire."

Jeanne called back. "Sounds good. You're still in jail as far as we're concerned."

Jason snorted. "Every man's dream wife."

Selma's throat tightened as she watched Jason prepare the pot.

Clicking on the red button with a little flourish, he grinned. "Takes two minutes."

He pulled up a stool and leaned across the counter. "Your boys at work?"

Selma nodded, unable to speak.

Jason sighed. "They're good kids. Hard-working as all get-out. I like that. Don't see that in most kids these days." He swept his hand toward the living room. "Care to give any parting advice? My girls are a little...shall we say..."

With a quick glance over her shoulder and a rush of embarrassment burning her face, Selma cleared her throat. "Can't give any real advice.

My boys work hard cause they have to. Their dad cut out years ago, and I only work part-time. So, if they want to eat and live in a decent place..." She shrugged.

"Where's he now?"

"Dead. Suicide. A troubled man. Still, I loved him...once. He was the boys' father." She peered into her clasped, chilled hands. "Never made any sense to me."

Jason returned to the coffee maker and tapped the pot as if he could make it work quicker. "Sorry. Shouldn't have asked. I just wondered..."

"Nothing to be sorry about. Just..." The

exhaustion of battling the cold and darkness swept over Selma. "You know, experience is a great teacher, but it doesn't give a lot of answers. The thing with raising kids is that they got to see a connection between themselves and the world around 'em. You give them love and support, but they gotta know that they aren't in control all the time. But still, they have to be responsible for their part."

The rich aroma of coffee filled the room as the black liquid poured into the empty pot. A cheer rose from the living room, and one of the girls giggled.

Jason's smile wavered as he glanced from the living room back to Selma. "You want to spend the night here? We've got a perfectly good couch." He poured a cup of steaming coffee and handed it to Selma.

Selma shook her head. "Naw. This is great. Thanks. But I've got to keep the water running to keep the pipes from freezing and check on the dogs and...you know. I want to be home when the boys get back."

Jason nodded and poured himself a cup.

~~~

As Selma heard the boys bumble through the front door, down the cold hallway, and into their frozen beds late that night, she pictured the warm house next door. The clean kitchen. The kids playing with their mom. Jason and his gentle kindness.

Though the coffee had only warmed her for a bit, she knew as she settled into bed wearing five
~~~

sweaters and two pairs of sweatpants that she would sleep well tonight. The bonfire had burned out quickly. The power company had promised to be their first stop in the morning, and her boys were safe and sound. For the first time in months, she felt warm all over.

One Aisle at a Time

Originally published on The Writings of A. K. Frailey
4/1//2019

Wilson stared at the blinking cursor and couldn't think of a thing to write. His brain seemed frozen, unable to articulate one creative thought. All he could do was lean back on his swivel chair and let his gaze wander around the room. A midsized wooden bookshelf with five extra books arranged awkwardly on top. Lamp, coffee mug, printer, window, landscape painting hanging slightly crooked, dusty calculator, a crumpled stack of receipts, notepad, frogman...the one Sami had given him on Father's Day—

Oh, God!

Searing pain clutched his innards. He closed his eyes and turned away. "This will kill me. A month after the funeral, and I'm still a mess." He heaved himself out of his chair and paced across the room. He stopped at the doorway. Where could he go? To the kitchen? What for? He had no appetite. The thought of food made him nauseous. To the living room? Why? The couch was empty. No stuffed animals. No half-completed pictures. No fourth-grade math book shoved under the pillow.

His phone buzzed. Clenching his jaw, he returned to his desk and snatched up the phone. "Yeah!" He knew he sounded like an angry bull, but hell, he couldn't help it. He *was* angry. Disgustingly, furiously, blindingly angry.

"Wil?" Camilla, his wife. She sounded strong. Too strong. Damn. She had no right to be strong. He swallowed and sucked in his cheeks as if chewing his own flesh might help him maintain a modicum of composure.

"Yeah, honey, what's up?" His shoulders sagged as weariness enveloped him.

"I'm at the grocery store, and I forgot the list...could you get it for me and read it off as I go along?"

Before he could give his brain any formal directions, Wilson found his feet padding into the kitchen. Yep, sure enough, there was the list, written in his wife's beautiful but tiny cursive. He'd be lucky if he could read it. "Got it." He squeezed the phone between his chin and his shoulder and held the list out with both hands, far enough to read but not as steady as he would've liked.

Her voice, calm and parental, enunciated her next request. "Great. I made it past the chips and cracker aisle, and now I'm stuck between peanut butter and cereal."

Wilson frowned and leaned against the counter. "Yeah? It says peanut butter and cereal on here..." He shook his head. "Look, you've done this every week for years; you've got to have the entire store mapped in your head. Dang it, woman, you could do this in your sleep."

Silence.

Wilson's heart began to pound. "Honey?"

It was the softest sniffle in the world, but it nearly crushed Wilson's will to live.

Camilla's voice wavered through the air, into the phone, and pierced Wilson's broken heart. "I just don't know *which* peanut butter or *what* cereal..."

Flummoxed, Wilson felt a scream rise from his

chest. "The ones you *always* get."

A ragged breath brushed his ear and sent prickles of terror racing down his spine. "But we always got crunchy...because that's what Sami—"

"Oh, God!" The phone clattered to the floor.

Waves smashed against his composure, heaving rocks at his innards. Black water smothered his airways. Vaguely in the distance, he could hear his wife's plaintive voice calling from the floor.

"Wil? Please, I need to know. What kind of peanut butter? What cereal do I get—?"

Every ounce of his body wanted to grind the phone into smithereens with his heel, but his hands chose differently. He dropped down on a kitchen chair and pressed the phone to his ear. Camilla was crying. There were no sobs or wails. But he knew. She was probably just standing there in the middle of the aisle, gripping the cart with one hand while tears poured down her face.

He leaned on one hand and waited. Muffled conversation rose over the distance. Camilla was talking to someone. Another woman...soothing words, a gentle tone... He pressed the phone harder. "Who the—?"

A voice rose. "Lost my son five years ago...hell on earth. Couldn't pass his bedroom without breaking down and forget going out in public. Took me a whole year before I could go shopping by myself. Terrible. Yes, it is. God have mercy on parents who lose a child. Doesn't matter how it happens...or how old. Just hell."

Silence.

Tears streamed down Wilson's face and

meandered over the phone before they fell like miniature pools on the smooth kitchen tabletop. Then, like a tidal wave on the rise, his shoulders heaved and his whole body rocked with searing, overwhelming pain. God, the pain.

After a few moments, still clutching the phone, he heard Camilla sniff. And then a sigh. An embarrassed—giggle? "Cam, what's going on?" Wilson sat up.

A distant conversation. "Yeah, I'm okay now. Thanks." Camilla blew her nose.

Loudly.

Wilson's eyes widened.

He wiped his face with the back of his hand. "Wil?"

Teardrops smeared the phone. Wilson snatched a paper napkin, wiped it down, fumbled, and then smashed it against his ear again. "Yeah. You okay, honey?"

"No. But I'm...better."

He could imagine her shyly ducking her head, winding a strand of hair behind her ear.

"A lady here...she understood...gave me a hug. It's what I needed."

Wilson nodded as his tears flowed again. He choked out his words. "So, what're you going to do?"

Camilla cleared her throat and undoubtedly squared her shoulders. "She suggested I try the smooth peanut butter and pick out a new cereal, one we never had before. So, I grabbed a banana-strawberry granola mix." Her voice dropped low, like a child begging for understanding. "Will that be okay?"

Wilson sniffed and grabbed another napkin.

He wiped his nose. “Sure, honey. That’s perfect.” He swallowed back the ache in his throat and sat up. He fumbled for the list. “You want to do the rest of the shopping now or come home?”

Camilla’s voice steadied. “I’ll keep going...as long as you stay with me.”

“Course, honey. We’ll just take it one aisle at a time...”

~~~

A half-hour later, Wilson returned to his desk. The curser was still blinking. He lifted his hand over the keys and tapped out five words.

One Aisle at a Time...
~~~

Face the Cranberries

Originally published on The Writings of A. K. Frailey
4/18/2019

"Cranberries are the best food on the planet. And aliens are set to invade Earth any day now."

I waited; my hands clasped around a bag of red berries in an attitude of perfect composure and watched my dearest husband add the final touches to his miniature boat. Well, it was Johnny's boat. Or so the story goes... The perfect gift for an eleven-year-old boy who was all thumbs. A boat building kit. His dad couldn't get the box open fast enough.

I cleared my throat. "Jack?"

"Huh?"

His big brown eyes peered at me as innocently as I'm certain he felt.

He had no idea he was ignoring me. Or that I had a rotten day. Or that Jonny couldn't care less about boats. He was simply focused. On his work...or his hobby...whatever.

I wanted to whap him with my bag of berries. But he wouldn't have understood that either. Time out.

"I need some sugar. Going to Beth's place for a bit."

That caught his attention. "Way over there? She's not a grocery store. Besides, I'm getting hungry and—"

"The chicken is in the oven, and there are crackers and cheese on the table. Have a snack. I'll just be a bit." Feeling ever so justified in leaving him to his newest pet project, I sauntered out the door and roared off in my mini-van with music blaring right through town. The only reason I didn't close my eyes to deep cleanse my psyche lay in the curvy road and the glory of swiftly passing spring fields.

Beth had amazing kids. One was a doctor, another an astrophysicist, and the middle kids were all-purpose miracle workers. The youngest two stayed at home and managed the farm while her husband recovered from a...broken arm...or was it a leg? Appendicitis? Something.

Anyway, no matter how bad my day might have been, just stepping into Beth's house offered me perspective. Like a clown on an analyst's couch, I knew she'd listen to my dire groans and sprinkle witty inspirations and clever parenting tips upon me no matter how ridiculous I looked.

Or maybe not.

When I swept into the kitchen, Beth's red-rimmed eyes bespoke some kind of serious dark matter in the Kilroy universe. My heart skipped a beat. "Something wrong?"

Beth's eyes widened. With horror or stupefaction, I couldn't tell. She seemed so surprised. *I* was surprised. After all, I'd been barging into her house, getting free analyst sessions for years. We were close friends. Like sisters. No warning phone call. No knock on the door. No loud call from the foyer. Just—

Beth broke down, lumbered over to me, and started sobbing on my shoulder. The sky could've fallen, and I wouldn't have noticed.

I half carried, half dragged her to the kitchen table and maneuvered her into a solid wood chair. Always loved those chairs. Practically indestructible. Sorry…I digress.

I put on a pot of water for the clearly needed cup of tea. "Herbal or something stronger?"

Beth looked up and waved a limp hand. "I don't care. Whatever."

Gee. That wasn't like her at all. Body snatchers? My hands shook as I assembled the cups, brown sugar, and perched the English teabags in the cups just so. I leaned over and peered into my friend's swollen eyes. And waited.

"Terry wants a divorce."

The jolt that ran through my system could have electrified a city. "What? That's crazy. Terry loves you. You love Terry. You love your kids. Your kids love you…" I sat back; my gaze stuck on her face.

"He's not the man I married. After his heart attack—"

That was it!

"He says he wants to retire and travel to exotic places, have some fun…live before he dies." She dropped her head onto her hands and sighed. "What have we been doing all these years? Play acting?"

The irony of our role reversal was not lost on me. Being the one expected to offer helpful advice pricked my conscience like angry hornets. After all, my oldest kid was only a teen, and I had three compared to her six. And Beth had been married nearly thirty years while Jack and I had a mere fifteen anniversaries tucked under our marriage belt.

I slumped down on the chair and tried to gird my loins. Ridiculous phrase but being biblical, it seemed to fit. I certainly needed supernatural assistance. *Any time, Lord.*

"I can't believe that Terry told you that he wants a divorce. It's just not like—"

"Oh, not in so many words. Of course not! He just scattered pamphlets, brochures, travel books all over the place and started listening to Spanish radio. He went shopping and bought casual shirts and jeans, for crying out loud! Jack never wears jeans. He's an office man who can't leave the office—even when he comes home."

I blinked. Suddenly I saw the universe from an entirely new angle. "Uh, Beth darling, do you think that perhaps you are misreading Jack? I mean, perhaps he is kinda tired of being the office guy and wants to have a little fun. Doesn't mean he wants a divorce. Why would he scatter the travel paraphernalia under your eyes if he wanted to leave you behind?"

"Why didn't he just tell me?"

"Have you ever mentioned an interest in traveling?"

"I've been too busy raising kids for thirty years. And doing a darn good job of it, I might add. Who's got time for frivolity?"

My throat had gone as dry as Mars. The singing kettle saved me. As I poured the steaming water into our mugs, Beth skedaddled to the counter, snatched a handful of pamphlets and slapped them on the table.

"See what I mean?"

I stirred sugar into my tea with one hand and browsed through the offending material with the other. Hmm... Yep. Terry wanted a little fun. Looked like a lot of fun. I tried not to turn green with envy.

I took a long sip and sat down. Then I reached over and patted my friend's hand and said the only thing that might save her universe. "Go have fun, Beth."

Beth's eyes widened.

I stirred two scoops of sugar into her cup and nudged it closer. "If it makes you feel any better, you can learn Spanish before you go." I leveled my gaze at her. "But go."

~~~

I didn't turn on the music on the drive home. I need to think and pay more attention to my pounding heart than a pounding pop song. By the time I stepped into the kitchen, my brain was clear enough to take in the wonderful aroma of cooked cranberries.

Jack stood at the head of a table, which apparently had been set by visiting gremlins since the knives and forks were scattered at awkward angles and the plates and glasses marched up wobbly lines on either side of the table. But a roast chicken and mashed potatoes did sit comfortably in the middle of the table near the glorious bowl of cooked berries.

I glanced at my husband. My throat had returned to Mars. And after three cups of tea, too. "Uh, Jack?"

Jack smiled at me through such proud eyes I thought my heart might burst right through my chest. "The kids and I fixed dinner. Course, you had the chicken in the oven already. But we did the rest."

Standing around the table, the kids looked
~~~

like miniature versions of their dad. It took me a moment, but I did eke out a coherent, "Thank you, guys!"

Jack peered at me, his smile fading. "You okay?"

And at that moment I knew with unerring certainty what I needed to do to make my universe perfect. "Yep. Everything is great. But I do have one request."

Jack and the kids looked at me. God only knows what they were thinking.

"Show me your boat after dinner, okay?" Jack's smile returned, and I could finally face the cranberries.

New Life Into Her Soul

Originally published on The Writings of A. K. Frailey
4/25/2019

The end of a pier is a lonely place. But sometimes you have to face the deep before you can face your life.

The little bandage on Mary's breast didn't hurt, just felt odd, like a scab that needed to come off. She peered down. Her chest looked the same as always. But it wasn't. She knew the truth. Under her bright yellow shirt, neat stitches marked the spot where a tumor had grown, threatening her very existence.

"There's always hope," the doctor had said. A thirty-something woman who had served in the military and brooked no dissent. Even her smile demanded obedience.

Mary didn't have the heart to argue. Sure, the tumor was gone, and new treatment plans prolonged life. But what years? Who wants to live through dying?

She stared at the rippling water. *Am I already dead?* Her parents had passed away a decade ago, and her only brother lived on the coast of Main and practiced yoga. The fact that they shared the same DNA still amazed her. Her co-workers sympathized, but they didn't understand.

A flock of honking geese flew in for a landing, sending a party of ducks flapping toward shore. Their startled cries sent the whole park into an uproar. Even a couple squirrels chattered in noisy complaint as they chased each other across the treetops.

With a sigh, Mary shivered. There was no point hanging out at the end of a pier. She had to go home and eat something. Just live until...

"Excuse me?"

Mary turned and blinked at a man's figure silhouetted against the setting sun. She shaded her eyes and waited. She hardly had the energy to speak.

The man stepped aside. A big guy. Tall with a healthy build, wearing jeans and a button-down blue shirt. "You happen to see a book there?" He pointed to the edge of the pier. "I think I left it..."

Mary turned and considered the wooden planks as if she had never seen them before. To her surprise, white pages glinted in the evening light and fluttered in the breeze. The sound of their flapping awakened her from the torpid stupor. She stepped over and gently lifted the book. "To Kill A Mockingbird?"

The man reached out; his tanned, rough hand exposed his outdoor lifestyle. "Yeah. My wife read it to me when we were first married. I thought it might bring back..." He dropped his gaze, his thoughts apparently falling into the rippling water.

Mary swallowed back fear. Her words rushed out like an avalanche trying to bury a mountain of pain. "I read it in high school. Really left an impression. I always wished I had Atticus as my dad."

The man snorted. "I wish *I* was Atticus. Instead, I'm more like Boo Radley."

Mary squinted. "You don't look like Boo Radley." She attempted a smile. "You're much too tan." Her hands wouldn't stop shaking, so she clasped them behind her back. If only her stomach would stop rolling.

A sheepish grin spread across the man's face. "Well, I wasn't going for a literal interpretation." His humor vanished as his brows furrowed. "You okay?"

With an uneven step, Mary gripped the slimy post and sucked in a deep breath. "My first dose of chemo. Does wonders for my disposition."

The man grabbed her arm and helped her regain her balance. "Cancer? Oh, God. What kind?"

A surge of strength swept over Mary, and she found she could stand, her breathing calmed. "Breast. Early stage. The doc says I'll be fine..." She squared her shoulders and panted like a runner about to start a marathon.

He led her away from the post. "Early stage is good...your doctor might be right."

Mary nodded toward the parking lot. "Mine's the blue cruise."

He kept his arm fixed at her side and matched her pace as they maneuvered to the parking lot. He pointed to a Ford Focus. "That's mine." He helped her rest her weight against her car. "My name's Brad. Lost my wife to cancer three years ago. Hell of a thing..."

The warm metal comforted Mary's cold bones. "Yeah. You've got that right." She peered at him. "Sorry about your wife. Not easy being the survivor, I suppose."

Brad's gaze swept across the road. "There's a fish and chips place over there. You want something to eat before you go? Might do you some good."

Mary considered the possibility. The faint smell of fried fish wafted in the air and sent demanding ripples through her body. "Yeah. It might do us both some good." She eyed the book still gripped in his hand. "I always wanted to read that story again."

Brad took her arm. "It's a remarkable tale...tells it like it is. Lots of ways to die in this world."

Mary nodded. "Yeah. Lots of ways to live, too."

After they ordered, Brad hunched forward and pressed open the novel to the first page. He cleared his throat. "When he was nearly thirteen, my brother Jem got his arm badly broken at the elbow..."

Mary leaned back and closed her eyes. The pier faded. A small southern town appeared, and a new vision breathed life into her soul.

Romantic Soul

Originally published on The Writings of A. K. Frailey
4/2/2019

Kathy loved hot tubs. But she couldn't admit that to a living soul. She also loved chocolate chip mint ice cream, but she rarely indulged. And as for mystery novels...well, if there was a bit of romance thrown in, so much the better. But God forbid anyone ever caught her reading a trashy novel. No, she kept those squashed under a tower of historical biographies detailing the late-greats of the nineteenth century. So far...no one ever caught on.

It was a perfect spring day. The cherry and peach trees were in full bloom, and if the sky glowed any bluer, she'd break into song...and that would never do. Lord have mercy. Kathy's heart swooned, but her body stayed as ridged as a cliff facing turbulent ocean waves.

Elliot had no idea what he was doing to her insides. But then Elliot had better things to do than worry about his frazzled Catechism assistant. As a director of social services for the county, he had people with real problems to deal with. Unwed mothers, abused kids, out-of-work fathers, drug-addicted teens. The list was endless. People's problems were endless. Yet Elliot always managed to smile at his hyperactive class of Catholic kids and act like he was having great fun just being with them.

Kathy's heart melted at the mere memory of Elliot's face. She pulled open the door to the Sacred Heart Community Center and stepped into the quiet interior. No one else had arrived yet.

Good. That gave her time to arrange the material for today's class and set the player on the right episode for tonight's theme—Who Do You Say That I Am?

As she brushed by the front desk, she noticed a half-empty water bottle. Elliot's? Probably. No one else used this classroom during the week. She picked it up and stared at it as if its previous owner would magically appear to take back his property. She jumped at the sound of a woman's voice.

"Staring at it won't bring it to life, honey."

Kathy turned around and faced the matronly figure of the Pro-Life Director.

In her early fifties, with salt and pepper hair that she kept tied in a neat bun on the top of her head, Chika might look like a schoolmarm of old, except that she wore jeans, hiking boots, and an oversized plaid shirt, which would have fit a lumberjack.

A blush spread over Kathy's cheeks.

Chika moved into the room like a ship's captain taking the helm. "I'll be delivering the main address today. Elliot asked me to come in and highlight some behavior issues he's concerned about."

Kathy bit her lip. "I thought we were doing Who Do You Say That I Am?"

"Well, we are...sort of. Just add in the consequences of unregulated lust and rampant promiscuity, and we'll have tonight's theme."

Kathy thought her face might have caught on fire. "Oh?"

Chika grinned. "It's a talk the kids need to hear...but, not you. In fact—" She wandered to the front of the room, pulled a key out of a deep pocket, and unlocked the cabinet. "I think you could do with a little *more* romance in your life...not less."

Embarrassment combated with fury as Kathy stood before the chalkboard. Undiluted anger won. "Oh, really?" An edge sharpened her voice as it rose to a squeak.

Chika shook her head. "Come on. Be honest with yourself. You like Elliot. And I think he likes you...but you give that poor man not an ounce of encouragement. It's time to step off the sidelines and make your move."

"That's hardly my place! I'm a modest woman and I—"

"What's modesty got to do with it? Look in the Bible, honey, and get with the times. God made man and woman for a reason!"

"I'm perfectly well aware of that fact, but I'm hardly about to throw myself—"

Chika grinned. "No one is suggesting anything radical. Would be amusing to see you get a little radical, I'll admit. But—" She leaned in closer. "Since you're the two shyest people on the planet when it comes to romance...I'll just ask God to do His thing and give you two a little nudge." She nodded to a foot-high statue of Jesus with His sacred heart glowing in his chest. She grinned. "Author of romance, don't you know?"

Completely flummoxed by this unorthodox reasoning, Kathy snorted a tiny puff of dragon's breath and retreated across the room.

The sound of pounding feet turned both women to the doorway.

His eyes wide with anxiety, Elliot rushed into

the room. “Call 911 and get Jason’s mom. He’s having an asthma attack. I can’t calm him down.”

With flashbacks of her own childhood asthma trauma flooding her brain, Kathy rushed to the hallway and found Jason slumped against the wall. His face flushing bright red and his hands fluttering in a panic as he dragged a ragged breath from his chest.

Kathy dropped to her knees and braced his body upright. She stared into the boy’s face. “Look at me, Jason, and squeeze my arms. Breathe. Slow in...slow out...look at me...everything is going to be okay. I’m here. You’ll be fine. Relax. Let your breath come...one in...two out...”

His shoulders relaxing as he clasped Kathy’s arms, Jason closed his eyes and exhaled.

A bustling movement forced Kathy aside. She got out of Jason’s mother’s way. The harried woman handed an inhaler to the boy, who gripped it in both hands and soon had it pressed to his mouth, his mother continuing to count out slow breaths.

Kathy stepped aside and stood alone as the blare of an ambulance sounded in the parking lot. Her heart pounded, but she sucked in a deep breath and then exhaled, releasing the tension. A firm hand pressed her shoulder.

Elliott leaned in and whispered in her ear. “You’re amazing. Thank you.”

With only a slight turn of her head, Kathy met Elliot’s gaze. A blush warmed her cheeks. The smell of chocolate-chip mint ice cream filled her imagination. As she swallowed hard, a figure across the room caught her attention.

Chika raised her eyebrows, a knowing smile on her lips. She pointed to the figure of Christ. A rose lay at His feet. Kathy blinked...and then squinted. It was one of the plastic roses used to decorate the room. Well, okay, it was a romantic gesture...giving God a rose.

Elliot's hand still rested on Kathy's shoulder. It felt warm and comfortable there.

A shocking thought raced through Kathy's mind, sending a shiver down her back. *Does God have a romantic soul?*

Perhaps He likes chocolate-chip mint ice cream, too.

Topic Sentence

Originally published on The Writings of A. K. Frailey
4/23/2019

Kimberly wondered if there wasn't an easier way to earn a living. Not that she was earning anything beyond a few get-out-of-purgatory-free days and a mammoth headache.

As a volunteer tutor at a local college, she happily offered her writing skills to those in need of literary assistance. Her gaze shifted from the screen in front of her to the student beside her. Kimberly clenched her jaw and tapped her lips. Hmmm. How does one tell an anxious student that you can barely make out the meaning of her first sentence?

Kimberly cleared her throat. "Could you tell me what you're trying to say here? I mean the general point of the paper?"

The girl was about twenty and apparently—from the way she kept writing her hands—desperate to get her paper reviewed in a hurry.

"It mean, like, we all God's children. Science not know that. Can't test faith. You know what I mean?"

Oh, yeah. Kimberly nodded. Yep. She understood perfectly. Clearly English was a second, maybe even a third, language. So, what to do?

The girl smiled. "It's kind of you. To help me. I know it's bad..." She shrugged. "Never got practice much."

Squaring her shoulders, Kimberly faced the sentence again. Yeah, it was tangled in a heap of words...but tangles can get untangled. Her fingers hovered over the keyboard. “So, let’s start with your topic sentence...”

~~~

As she settled onto the couch with a hot cup of tea and a glorious chocolate chip cookie, Kimberly glanced up.

Her husband, Ron, entered the room, tossed his work bag on an end table, and groaned, “I love my job...I love my job...I love my job.” He stumped to the couch, flopped next to Kimberly, threw back his head, and slapped his hands over his face.

Kimberly licked the crumbs off her lips and nodded. “So, what you’re saying is—you love your job.”

Ron dragged his fingers down his face and glanced aside. “Yep.”

“Well, that’s a great topic sentence. Care to offer any supporting evidence?”

Ron practically melted as he stretched out, his legs sprawled under the coffee table and his arms limp at his sides. He looked like a beached whale. Kimberly figured she wouldn’t mention this fact at present.

Spluttering a long-exasperated sigh, Ron, obviously using the last bit of his strength, lifted a feeble hand, a finger slightly raised above the others. “One, I have a great boss.”

Kimberly took another bite out of her cookie and suppressed an indecent groan of pleasure.

Ron’s second finger wavered upward. “Two, my co-workers are terrific people.”
~~~

A sip of tea almost undid Kimberly's composure. Who knew that Earl Grey could burst with such savory perfection?

Like a depleted Olympic long-distance runner barely making it to the finish line, Ron's third finger joined his digital mates. "I actually like commercial design. Creative. Fun. A constant blast of innovation."

Kimberly peered at the last piece of her cookie. Should she share it? She pursed her lips as she glanced from the pathetic figure to the chips gleaming from the cookie crust. Dang, it smelled so good. She hesitated.

Ron glanced over and fixed his gaze on the sweet treat. "Any more of those?"

Kimberly popped the delectable morsel into her mouth and chewed quickly. "Uh, well..."

With a near sob, Ron hoisted himself off the couch and stared down at his wife.

She grinned in innocence. "I didn't want to ruin your appetite. Dinner'll be ready in an hour or so."

"Yeah. And you love me, too. I get it. Thanks." He slogged his limp body toward the kitchen.

A tug of regret pulled at Kimberly's cookie-happy tummy. "Wait. You never told me the summary."

Ron propped himself in the doorway. "The what?"

Kimberly sat up and brushed incriminating crumbs from her shirt. "You know. How it all ends. To restate how much you love your job."

"Oh, yeah." Ron rested his head on the doorframe. "Did I mention that my company has been bought out, I'm getting a new boss, a completely different position, one I know practically nothing about, and nearly all my co-workers are being transferred overseas?"

Kimberly closed her eyes. The savory sweetness in her mouth had turned dry as dust. She stood there, guilt and grief tangling her thoughts. Footsteps padded near. She felt strong arms wrap around her.

Ron murmured in her ear. "I may have lost the job I love and missed the last bite of cookie, but surely, I have something left to live for?"

Kimberly snuggled into her husband's embrace as a distinctly new sweetness swept over her. She opened her eyes and stared into his eyes. "Certainly, my love. Glad to help. Now, let's see if we can write a new topic sentence..."

If You Want To

Originally published on The Writings of A. K. Frailey
4/30/2019

Edith never had any intention of painting her forearm olive green. It just sorta happened to happen. She stood under the afternoon sun and stared at the husky-built man before her with utter defiance seething through her pores.

Aden only laughed.

"For your information, I was helping my son spray paint his crossbow." Edith flicked her finger toward the woods behind the man. "He wants to blend in with nature. Makes perfect sense to me."

Shaking his head, Aden strolled across the grass to a camp chair set before a fire pit. "His idea makes sense. Your arm, on the other hand... Don't you ever read directions?"

Edith stomped across the yard to the brooder house. "I read them. But they never mentioned anything about accidentally brushing your arm against freshly painted crossbows."

Aden plunked down on the folding chair before the flickering fire, stretched, and leaned back. "I can't leave you alone for a few hours without some kind of mishap or another."

Edith stopped at the chick house door and considered her retort, but her eldest son, Cal, strode forward carrying a load of wood and dumped it at the base of the fire pit. "This should keep us for a while." He peered at her arm. "Hey, what happened to—?"

Edith waved him off. "Don't ask. I was just helping Nick with the manly arts of crossbow decoration—something you could've been doing—big brother."

Cal blanched, his gaze flickering to Aden. "Hey, I mowed the lawn this morning, straightened the barn door, and turned on the outdoor well pump." The young man crossed his arms in an attitude of defiance.

"And he got us an armload of wood. I'd say the kid has earned his pay for the day." Aden gave Cal a nod of approval.

Edith shot Aden a sneer. "Unlike some people..."

Aden's grin widened. "I'm here on vacation; remember? You're the one who said that country life would relax me...take all the tension outta my overstressed body." He clasped his hands behind his head. "Well, I'm relaxing. And you're right; I'm not feeling a particle of stress at the moment."

Edith rubbed her forehead. He had her, and she knew that he knew, that he had her. How could she admit, even to herself, that she had been entertaining fantasies of leaving her to-do list in the dust as they played games of volleyball or went to the movies? She glanced at the half-mowed yard and sighed. "I gotta take care of these chicks, or they're going to expire, and we'll have to eat pork chops all winter."

Cal nudged Aden. "Want something cold to drink? I'm going in for a soda; I can bring one out."

Aden nodded. "Sounds good." He grinned as he met Edith's gaze. Edith swung on her heel and smothered a string of naughty words.

~~~
~~~

As the sun sank below the horizon, painting the summer field crimson and sienna, Aden stacked an array of used paper plates and tossed them on the low burning embers. He collected four crushed soda cans and lined them on the nearby picnic bench.

Edith watched his slow, deliberate motions as if viewing them from Mars. Her whole body ached in weariness, though it was a pleasant ache, like a drug-induced state of utter relaxation. Her body could take no more, so she simply had to give in to rest. As she licked the last crumb of chocolate cake off her upper lip, her eyes meandered over his muscled arms. "Uh, oh. You're working... I thought that was against the rules."

Aden chuckled. "It's not work if you want to do it. I happen to like stacking paper plates and lining up soda cans." He dragged his camp chair near hers and plopped down, the fabric straining against his weight. He lifted her limp hand and caressed her fingers. "You know, not all physical exertion is work."

Edith groaned. "Don't play with my mind."

"It's not your mind I was thinking about..."

Edith forced her body into an upright position and stared at Aden.

"You've been here the whole weekend, and you're clearly feeling better."

Aden nodded; his gaze focused on the horizon. "That'd be putting it mildly."

"Good." With a sigh, Edith leaned forward and clasped her hands.

"You know, I only want what's best for you. But it never dawned on me that for us...I have to want what's best for me as well. All work and no play make Edith a grumpy girl."

Aden sighed.

Edith pushed through her hesitation. "When I visit, you work like a madman to manage your job and keep me and the boys entertained. When you come here, I run the situation in reverse."

A hound dog ambled over and nudged its nose into Aden's lap.

"Seems like there should be a happy medium somewhere, doesn't there?" Aden rubbed the dog's head, his gaze wandering to the first stars blinking in the firmament. "Maybe we should do some projects together?"

Like a puppet yanked by invisible cords, Edith flopped back onto her chair, a boulder pressing on her shoulders. "Like Habitat for Humanity sort of thing?"

Aden snorted, rose to his feet, and stepped around the dog. He scooped the cans into an empty box. "No. Well, maybe down the road we could do something like that. But in the meantime, I could help you here, and you could help me at my place. Seems silly to be always trying to entertain each other when we've got more work than any single person can do."

"It's not work if you do it together? Is that what you mean?"

Aden stepped behind Edith's chair and rubbed her shoulders. "I watched you scurry about this place like a rabbit running from a fox. Cal's a great kid and even Nick helps out. But I couldn't help but wonder—am I running through my days rather than living my life?"

Warm peace seeped into Edith's body. "Join the club. Human beings need to justify our existence...one way or another."

"Though pleasant distractions also work well to pass the time." He rubbed Edith's shoulders a little harder.

Cal stepped into the faint circle of glowing light. "Hey, hate to break up your fun, but it looks like Nick might have stopped up the sink. Something about washing the leftover instant potatoes down the drain."

Edith slapped her forehead. "Oh, Lord. I knew I should've made baked beans."

Aden stepped away from Edith and clapped Cal on the shoulder. "Come on, kid; I'll show you a new trick. It's called plumbing with potatoes."

Cal snorted and marched alongside Aden, his gaze focused on the kitchen light ahead, his smile widening.

Edith rose with a groan. In a state of happy exhaustion, she peered at the gloriously star-speckled sky and shook her head. Her life rotated with the universe—work, rest, and plumbing with potatoes.

She laughed.

The Difference Between Us

Originally published on The Writings of A. K. Frailey
6/6/2019

Auden stared at his friend through narrowed eyes. "You broke up over what?"

Delano shrugged. "It was a snail that started it. My first insightful clue into her real personality. But it took a Tsunami to really clarify things."

Auden harrumphed as he lifted a log from the truck bed and carried it to the neat stack. He fit it carefully into place.

Delano laid long pieces on top, like a kid arranging his toys on a high shelf.

Auden cleared his throat as he ambled to the truck bed. "You wanna clarify that?"

An insulated coffee mug sat in the cup holder in the front seat. Delano reached through the open window and pulled it out, took a long swig, and eyed his friend. "Well, when she screamed and promptly fainted at the sight of a snail I saved from being utterly and literally crushed, I knew that she and I weren't seeing nature from the same perspective. "

Auden swished wood chips from the truck bed and slammed the back end shut. He chewed his lip and then cleared his throat. "And the Tsunami?"

"When they put that alert out after the earthquake...you remember, last week...that big 7-pointer with the epicenter in the middle of the ocean and all those warnings went off?"

Auden shook his head in disbelief. "You can

take a thought and drag it out beyond all reason."

"Don't get huffy. That little gal didn't even know what a Tsunami was. She thought I was mispronouncing pastrami and confusing the issue with some kinda food poisoning alert."

With a snort, Auden pulled his coffee mug from the car and twisted the lid. He sat on an upturned stump, sipped, and rubbed his dirt-smeared chin with the back of his hand. "You have a long, boring history with women, my friend. Always the same thing. They're wonderful, gorgeous, funny, kind, generous, spirited, loving, and the best thing to come along...until..."

"Hey, I'm not seeing anyone else."

"But you're thinking about it. I know that look in your eye."

"What if? No fault in finding someone better suited to my tastes.

Someone I can really hit on all cylinders and feel comfortable with."

A squirrel scampered down a maple tree, eyed the two men, turned tail, and scampered back up the tree, chattering as it went.

Auden took another long swig and pointed his index finger at Delano. "Not a problem normally, except you're never satisfied, man. Problem with you is you want to make a life-altering commitment without ever altering your life. You want a woman to fit perfectly with you, but you'll never budge an inch to fit with her."

Delano raised his hands in mock surrender. "Hey, I've made huge sacrifices for the women in my life."

Auden recapped his cup and tossed it into the truck cab. "You pay for dinner and take the lady dancing a few times. Buddy, you don't know the meaning of sacrifice."

Irritation flashed in Delano's eyes. He poured the dregs of his coffee on the ground, shook the empty cup, slapped the cap back on, and popped it back into the cup holder. "You're such an expert, huh?"

"I got dumped by a woman with the exact same mentality as you...makes me insightful."

Delano shrugged, the fury fading from his eyes. "She didn't understand you. It was her loss."

"Yeah. That's what I tell myself. Except for one thing."

Delano stumped over to the wood stack and shifted a log for a tighter fit. He grabbed his gloves and slapped them against his thigh. "We better get back. There's a storm coming in tonight."

Auden nodded and headed around the truck. He strapped on his belt and started the truck as Delano slid into place.

Delano sniffed as he buckled in. "What thing?"

Auden sighed. "I would've moved heaven and earth to make things work with her."

With a puff of air, Delano dropped his head back onto the headrest. "You don't think any of...well...none of mine really cared *that* much."

Pressing his foot on the accelerator, the tires spit gravel, and Auden sped onto the main road. "Comforting thought, buddy, but not necessarily true."

Delano closed his eyes.

His hands clenching the steering wheel, Auden glanced aside. "Funny thing, Delano. You'd never treat me like that. So, I can't get too mad at you."

Delano sat up and leaned forward. "But you're my friend, man. I'd never hurt you."

"Yeah, I know. And there's the difference between us."

So, What'll It Be?

Originally published on The Writings of A. K. Frailey
6/13/2019

Margery stared at her reflection in the mirror and wondered if the hairstylist could read her thoughts. Naw...

Good thing, too.

At the moment, she was battling a strong desire to call her boss and quit her job. And then there was the issue about dating three guys at once. Who knew that would get so complicated?

Eeney...meeney...miney...moe...

"So, what'll it be?"

Margery lifted her gaze and met Shasta's piercing blue eyes. "Same as usual. Just a trim."

Shasta snipped the scissors, her eyes fixed on Margery. "I mean...the choice you're trying to make. Come to a decision yet?"

A shiver ran down Margery's spine. "Whatda' you mean? What choice?"

"Look, honey, people come in here every day wanting a new look, a fresh style, a whole passel of unrealistic expectations. Hey, I cut hair, you know? But you, you come in and just want a trim...but I can see in your eyes...you're contemplating something serious. Deep. You know what I mean?"

Yep. Margery knew. Uh-huh. She had been reading self-help books and posts with themes like "Managing Your Life, So You Can Fall in Love Without Regret." But even though they often made sense, she had a hard time applying popular wisdom in her particular orbit.

Shasta started to snip. Apparently, she didn't need answers to cut hair.

A woman with a model's figure, holes in her jeans in all the right places, a glorious tan, a tank top that could knock Miss Universe off her pedestal, and a perfect pout swung onto the chair next to Margery.

Jealousy never reared its ugly head. A sudden desire to evaporate— maybe.

Shasta snipped her fingers in the newcomer's direction. "Be with you in a minute. You're early."

The walking advertisement for beauty shrugged. "I've got nothing better to do. Thought I'd bug you for a while." She dropped her head onto her sculptured hand. "Get so lonely sometimes...you know?"

Margery strangled the scream rising in her throat. She just managed to eke out the words, "Lonely? You?" She let her eyes roll over the woman's figure to highlight her point.

Shasta tapped Margery's shoulder. "Hey, don't judge a book by its cover, hon. Gale here deals with a lot."

Margery lowered her eyes and clasped her hands. "Sorry. That was rude. I just figured that with your body...lots of guys..."

"I try too hard. Scares men silly. Actually, I've got a degree in social work and a minor in Spanish, so I have a good job, and I make friends easy enough. I dunno...I just can't seem to keep things going over the long haul. People get too serious or move away...or have a crisis of some kind."

Shasta tapped Margery's head to get her to tilt it to one side. "It's this dang modern technology.

Everybody's so plugged in they forget to touch base...and they lose what's really important."

Gale wrinkled her nose like a rabbit about to sneeze. "That's the trendy answer. But really, it's the same ol' same ol'. People don't pay attention to anyone else. They want everyone to pay attention to them."

Margery glanced in the mirror and stared into her own eyes. Yep. Convicted. She might as well have a sign with a number on it hanging around her neck. Though most prison photos didn't look this good. She pursed her lips. Whoa. For a second there, she actually looked hot.

With a nudge, Shasta made it clear that her job was done.

Margery stood and brushed off her shoulders.

Gale slipped to the edge of her seat.

Shasta held up a finger. "Hang on one sec while I sweep up this mess. She reached for her broom and began to tidy up.

Gale climbed to her feet and faced Margery. "You're a pretty gal. I bet you don't get lonely."

Margery ran her fingers through her hair, shaking off the cut ends.

"Funny, but I do. Or at least, I get bewildered. If only someone really understood me..." She glanced from Shasta to Gale. "But that's not really anyone else's job, is it?"

Shasta laughed and dumped the dustpan full of clipped hair into the trash. "You know how it is...we search for what we're afraid to find cause we love the chase more."

Gale plopped down onto the waiting chair as Margery pulled a couple bills out of her wallet and laid them on the table.

Shasta snipped her scissors. “What’ll you have today? A whole new look or—”

Gale glanced at Margery. “What did she have?”

“Just a trim.”

“Then give me a trim. It’s time I stick with something for once in my life.”

With a nod and a wave, Margery turned and strode out the door. The sun shone and the breeze rippled her hair. She didn’t need to look in a mirror to see that she looked almost exactly the same as when she went in.

She grinned. *But then again, you can’t judge a book by its cover.*

Hidden Under Irony

Originally published on The Writings of A. K. Frailey
6/20/2019

"I've lost my sense of humor and all reason to live."

Sylvia closed her eyes and sighed. *Lord in Heaven, if it is possible, let this cup pass...*

The shattering sound of crockery shocked her eyes open. She made a one-eighty and stared at a splintered flowerpot, spilled dirt, and a pathetic Dahlia sprawled like a wounded soldier on the floor. She glanced at her assistant dressed in a long-flowered skirt, a light blue blouse, and lacy sandals, wincing at what she knew she would see.

Yep. Karen had one hand over her wavering lips as she blinked back tears. What a mess. Sylvia stepped forward with a raised hand. "You get the broom; I'll save the bloom."

Karen's expression hardened, her eyes drying like a swimsuit under a hot desert sun. "You think that's funny or something?"

Sylvia swallowed back a retort with a cleansing breath. "I had no intention of being funny or even alluding to an alliteration..." *Oops. What the heck?* "I'm not trying to speak in rhymes today..." She paused, perched her hands on her hips, and stared at the woman fifteen years her junior. "Look, I know it's been hard. Breaking up with your fiancé, the loss of your grandmother, the move to a new city...you've had a lot on your plate. Life is challenging. But you can't let things get you down. You just gotta face the day and be strong—"

"I'm not an infant. I'm a grown woman."

Keeping her face impassive, Sylvia nodded. "Yep. Got me there."

A cat padded near and sniffed the dirt.

Scuttling forward, Sylvia shooed it away. "Don't you dare track this mess all over my clean store." She glanced up. "Get that broom, would you? I'll repot the flower and put it in the south window. That way, you won't have to knock anything over when you water it."

Karen retreated, taking her personal storm cloud with her.

With a shake of her head, Sylvia carried the limp plant to the back room, passing the classics section, the romance nook, and finally, the kids' corner. Books of all shapes and sizes perched on shelves, sat on end tables, cluttered corners, sagged comfortable couches, tottered in towers, and even hugged the walls in uneven stacks.

She pulled a tall clay pot off a shelf and, with dexterous fingers, dug through the soft potting soil and laid the afflicted plant in its new home.

A familiar thrill swelled in her chest as she glanced around. Her crowning glory, this beautiful bookstore, thriving despite economic downturns and all the nay-sayers' dire predictions. She hadn't closed within a year...or even ten years.

After pouring a comforting stream of water over the buried roots, she cradled the pot in her arms and retraced her steps, quickly arriving at the south end of the store. Like a mother showing off her prodigy, she set the plant just so in the window seat between a first edition Harry Potter and the framed picture of Tolkien's Middle-earth.

Next Monday, she would celebrate ten years as proprietor of the most successful bookstore in the city. Perhaps in the whole country. Any why? Because she—

"Excuse me?"

Sylvia peered down. There, standing before her, had to be the tiniest woman she had ever set eyes on. Considering her own Amazonian stature, this was something of a novelty. Out of the corner of her eye, she saw Karen wiping the floor with a damp towel. She certainly had cleaned up the mess—gotta give the girl that.

"Are you busy?"

Sylvia shook herself. "No, of course; what can I do for you?"

"Well..." The tiny, well-dressed matron jutted her chin toward the old-fashioned teapot sitting on top of an antique dresser with an ornate mirror reflecting the glory of happy book buyers.

A round table dressed in lace and surrounded by plush chairs announced a comfortable corner for any book lover just needing a place to cozy up with his or her newest acquisition and a spot of tea. To the left, a no-nonsense black coffee maker stood at attention on a low table with a carafe of creamer, a dish stuffed with a variety of sweeteners, and a jar of luscious cookies, available at the reasonable donation of seventy-nine cents. The jar was stuffed full of one-dollar bills. It was so much easier to drop in a bill than to dig through one's wallet for the needed four pennies.

After settling the elderly matron in a chair with a warm cup of tea and a cookie, Sylvia waited. She clasped her hands on her knees, one eye following Karen, though she couldn't help but be curious about this commanding little personage. Of course, old women were notoriously lonely, and they frequently begged a cup of tea and a moment's "rest," which often involved relating all sorts of stories about relatives that Sylvia didn't honestly care a fig about. Still...

"So, are you from around here? I don't think I've seen you in the store before."

"No...you haven't. Not, at least, if I could help it. I mean, I've been here...a few times. Checking up, so to speak. I came first, years ago, before you even bought the store."

Prickles raced over Sylvia's arms. "Oh?" She sat up and tried to keep her heart from galloping through her chest.

"Yes. You see, I wanted to know if you were the kind of person who could make a go of such a thing."

Sylvia wondered if an earthquake actually rocked the room or if it was merely her imagination. "What do you mean, exactly?"

After wiping her fingertips free of cookie crumbs, the woman stretched out her hand. "I'm your birth mother. Matilda Scott. I gave you up for adoption when you were just a wee thing...but I never lost track of you. I've followed your progress through babyhood, high school, college and right into this business here. In fact, I was the anonymous donor who helped to pay for your tuition, and I also spearheaded the citywide revitalization project, which is what gave you the support you needed to do—" She waved her hand at the posh space. "All this."

The expression, "You could've knocked me over with a feather," suddenly embodied Sylvia's very existence. She stared hard at the old lady, wondering if the person before her was a psychotic illusion. "You must be—"

"Oh, don't say mad. That wouldn't be very nice." She pulled her little black purse onto her lap. "I have all the proof I need, right here. A copy of your birth certificate, the adoption papers...even clippings from every—"

"Oh, God!" Sylvia shot to her feet and wondered if she would make it to the back room before she threw up. Her whole body trembled as her self-image tottered on the edge of an abyss.

Matilda reached out and, with surprising strength, gripped her arm. "Take a deep breath, and calm yourself. I know this comes as a shock, but it's not exactly the end of the world."

Sylvia could not open her eyes any wider. She blinked to return the world to some sense of normalcy. "Are you sure?"

Her eyes twinkling, Matilda chuckled. "See! That's why I knew you could do this. Your humor and your tenacity are a rare combination. It comes from your dad...and me, I suppose. We were a rare combination too. Until he died. I knew that I could never take care of you. Unwed...and all that. But I knew you had our blood flowing in your veins. Our spark in your soul. So...I've always believed in you."

A sob rose and burst the dam of Sylvia's self-control. "Oh, Lord in heaven. I knew I was adopted...but I never knew...not a thing about you...or my father." She plopped down on the chair. "My biological parents, I mean. My real parents were—"

"Yes, I know. And I've stayed out of the picture all these years to give you space to live...to...how shall I say...to discover your own identity."

"But why—? Why tell me at all?"

"Through the years, I'd stop in now and again. Look and listen. See how you're getting on. Discover what kind of woman you're turning into." Matilda glanced aside at the dropping figure behind the counter. "I overheard your comment today. How your young friend shouldn't let things get her down. She hasn't been so lucky as you. She's lost a great deal in a short time."

Sylvia swallowed a lump in her throat.

"You see, you've been watched over and cared for in ways you've never known. But that girl there...maybe she hasn't been so lucky. Maybe life is impossible for her. Maybe she has lost her sense of humor...for good reason. And perhaps, she might wonder why she's alive."

"But doubt and despair won't help. No matter what the situation, I did the hard work...no matter what. Like you said, it was my spark...my humor and tenacity—"

"Yes, but also my love and your parents' compassion. Your words were right...but your attitude is wrong." Matilda laid the stack of yellowed papers on the end table by the cookie jar. "I'll leave these for you to look over when you have time." She glanced at the old-fashioned clock on the wall. "I should go now. But don't worry, I'll be back, and we can chat again." Her gaze peered into Sylvia's eyes. "If you want me."

Sylvia nodded. Her voice lost in a whisper. "Yes. Please."

Matilda toddled to the door, smiling at Karen as she passed.

Sylvia scurried ahead and tugged open the ornate glass door. She stepped aside.

Matilda patted her daughter's arm and grinned. "It's been lovely to meet you...after all these years. I've dreamed about this moment...and it has not been a disappointment." She waved to the tea table. "Oh, but a word of advice...make the donation offering a dollar."

Sylvia's world swirled again. "Why?"

"Because, my child, it's what you really mean." She turned and stepped into the summer sunshine.

As the door shut, Sylvia turned and met Karen's gaze.

Karen pursed her lips into a twisted smile. "I think I just found my sense of humor."

Sylvia sighed. "I bet you have. Hidden under irony, I'm sure."

Blue Ink Flowed

Originally published on The Writings of A. K. Frailey
7/4/2019

Edna watched the fly buzz around her kitchen with all the intensity of a warrior spying out the movements of the enemy. Finally, the devil's minion dared to land on her clean counter. Ah ha! With a victorious slap, she smashed it. Barbarian exultation surged through her.

Her phone chime, a song her father had loved, drew her attention to the living room. She scampered to her work desk and swiped up the phone, one hand still brandishing the swatter in case of any enemy retribution.

Her sister's name flashed on the screen. A groan erupted from Edna's middle. She pressed the phone to her ear, her gut twisting. If she had to hear one more rendition of how Tabitha's recent fling, Marvin, used her and dumped her and how men were all cheats and liars, she'd—"Yeah, honey, what's going on?"

"Hey. Just wanted to let you know that Dave was in an accident over the weekend. Drunk driving."

Edna's heart stopped beating. She was sure of it. "The kids?"

"They're fine. He was out with his buddies, and the kids were with a sitter. Actually, he picked a good one this time. Real responsible girl. She called me right away and then found Dave's mom's number and sent her all the info from the police. I went over, got the kids and figured I'd let Dave die on the emergency room table. He deserved it, right?"

Edna wasn't sure if she had pulled the chair out, but she was grateful when her behind hit the firm seat, and she didn't land on the floor. "Is he...did he—"

A strange tone entered Tabitha's voice, one Edna had never heard before. "No, he's just got a few scratches. But it scared the hell out of him. And it's going on his record. His boss called and told him that he's fired. The firm can't allow this kinda stuff."

Silence.

Edna swallowed and took a deep breath. "So, what now?"

"Ya know. I hate the guy. He was always a jerk. Well, after a couple good years...he revealed that he was a jerk."

Edna rubbed her temple. *Here it comes...* She waited.

"But funny thing, he started crying. Real tears. His mom came and got him, and I went by this morning to check in."

Edna felt waves of turbulent water splashing about her ears. "What about letting him die on the table?"

"Huh? Oh, yeah. That's what I thought. At first. How I felt. But then, you know, turns out that Marvin has cancer...something with his pancreas. He didn't tell me because he was afraid I'd dump him."

A pad of paper sat squarely in her desk corner. Edna grabbed it and flicked a pen point down. If one was facing crazy, might as well doodle. She murmured, "And so..."

"So, it hit me, that perhaps, I might hate the

men in my life for the wrong reason."

The doodle became a black storm cloud. "I'm not sure I'm following."

"Well, Dave drank like an idiot when he was with friends, but that's not why we got a divorce. I divorced him because he was so selfish. He never thought about me...not really. He just lived his life with me in it. And then, you know, Marvin was the same. So, I figured, all guys are blithering fools."

A painful cramp seized Edna's hand. She switched the phone to the right and continued the parade of raindrops from the storm cloud with her left. Wobbly raindrops...but she didn't care. She exhaled. "And so?"

"So, as I watched Dave meltdown in his mom's house and how his mom just shook her head and put her arm around him, I thought...I'd do that if it was one of my boys. I'd love him even though he acted like a complete jerk. And I thought of Marvin getting those test results and never telling me...because...you know...he figured I wouldn't really care *about him*. I'd just be mad because he was sick."

Silence stretched over the miles between Colorado and Illinois.

Edna didn't dare breathe. Her hand froze. The raindrops had become a river at the bottom of the page.

"So, it dawned on me. Maybe, I hate 'em because they remind me of me."

A splash brought the river to life and blue ink flowed. Edna wiped her eyes. She swallowed the ache in her throat. "It's hard to love like you want to be loved."

"Yeah. That's what I think. Kinda what dad told us before he died. Remember how he wanted that song? It irked me because I thought it was so stupid. But the words spoke to me today. Ya, know...letting go of the bad and keeping the good."

Edna sniffed, laid the pen aside, and wiped her nose with the back of her hand. "I remember."

"Sorta like what you've been doing with me all along, eh?"

The river became a torrent. Edna wrapped her arm around her face and stifled a sob. After a monumental struggle, she lifted her head and found her voice. "I've tried. Though I haven't always succeeded. "

"But, at least, you tried."

After the last bit of conversation and a final, 'talk later,' Edna laid the phone on the table and stood. She stared at the pad of dribbled blue ink. It didn't look like the original anymore. She ought to crumple it and toss it away.

A fly landed on the paper. Pure instinct incarnate, Edna grabbed the swatter and lifted her hand. This devil deserved to die.

But the picture didn't.

She waved her hand and the miniature demon flew off to annoy her another day.

She laid the swatter aside, picked up the picture and taped it to the refrigerator. It wouldn't last forever. But it would outlast the flies.

A Real Smile This Time

Originally published on The Writings of A. K. Frailey
8/1/2019

"I have seen alternate realities..." Megan believed it, too. As sure as shootin', she'd spout off the latest and greatest in how life could've been...fantasies...everyone.

I wanted to shoot something myself. But it would have landed me in a reality I didn't want. A small, windowless, jail cell reality. So, I did the next best thing. I started humming a bizarre childhood tune. Couldn't for the life of me remember the words.

We both loved novels and sweet treats, so a Saturday browsing books shops and getting ice cream on the village square seemed like a prelude of heaven. If only...

The sky blazed in mid-summer blueness, the sun scorched my already-tanned-to-a-crisp skin, and the humidity index was near a thousand, but Megan breezed along the quaint street, stopping only long enough to pat a Rottweiler tied to a fire hydrant on its ferocious head. How on earth she managed to get away with such antics, I'll never know. When I sidled past a canine, even with my best smile plastered on, the quadruped sized me up as lunchmeat, and inevitably, the damn thing lunged.

I skirted the beast, returned to my humming, and tried valiantly to steer Megan's brain away from fantasy towards something more profitable. "So, how are the kids?"

Megan pulled the shop door open, her delicate

muscles bulging attractively with the effort. Somehow, she managed to stay slim yet develop an awesome physique. With me, it was a straightforward choice: stay thin and weak or eat like a horse, pump iron, run marathons, and watch my body morph into a hulk-like structure, which caused my husband no end of unease.

I slipped past her fully aware that my plastered smile was still frozen in place. I mentally thwacked myself over the head. What was wrong with me? Jealous? Never. No.

Megan rushed to the last open booth and waved her hand to the empty seat, offering me the honor of sitting with her. Her smile, so sweet and sincere, Anne of Green Gables could've taken a lesson or two.

I mentally thwacked myself again. And then slid into place with the odd sound of hot, sticky legs skidding over hard plastic. I rubbed my forehead and wondered if an alternate reality might be a good idea at this point.

She browsed the menu for a nanosecond, tossed it aside, clasped her hands on the table and leaned in, staring deep into my eyes. "The kids are great. I'm doing wonderful. Jim is the light of my life. But you, Honey? How are *you* doing?"

What was this? I was the one who stuck to my daily duty, lived hardcore realism to the max, allowed myself only enough fiction to put me into a good night's sleep, and nailed my friend's feet to the ground every chance I got with apt advice. And she's asking how I'm doing with a hint of concern in her eyes? Harrumph!

The fact that my parents, in a fit of complete

idiocy and flower-power egoism, named me after a viscous food substance produced by bees fed my belief that life started out unfair and never got much better. I was named Honey at my birth, but I spent my life living it down. Becoming hard as a rock. Strong as iron. Solid as... You get the idea.

The waitress sashayed over, took our orders, and clumped away. Apparently, one didn't need to look as good going as coming.

I returned Megan's stare. "I'm doing brilliantly. Exhausted but such is life. Carl is good. Usually. The kids all have jobs now. I hardly see them." I twiddled my thumbs. Hmmm. This wasn't sounding as wonderful as I intended, even to my ears.

Megan reached out and stilled my busy fingers. "You're not happy. It's clear as rainwater."

I played with that image. Rainwater? Like in a creek?

Megan continued as if I wasn't straying from the field. "You need help."

Whoa! "Me? Help? Like a doctor? A therapy group?" My voice had risen to a squeak.

The waitress practically skipped over with our ice cream Sundays. Her eyes sparkled with the delight of a hound on a new scent. Gossip never failed to attract.

With the cool hand of a surgeon, Megan accepted her dessert, inserted the spoon just so, and took a modest bite.

I plunged my spoon to its depth and nearly cracked the glass dish.

After an appreciative, "Hmm, that's so good," Megan resumed her dissection of my imperfect life. "Actually, I was thinking that you might do well with a friendly counselor or a spiritual director. You know they have people available through the diocese."

The idea that I'd rather skydive into Mount Doom sizzled across my brain. I slurped my chocolate chip ice cream savoring not a bite. It took every effort to swallow the gooey delight. Finally, out of sheer desperation, I sucked up a deep breath, dropped my spoon, squared my shoulders, and faced the boogeyman in the closet. "Why? What's wrong with me?"

Pity and honesty poured from Megan's eyes. Okay, not literally. But you know what I'm saying. Megan exhaled sorrow. "You're so angry. All the time. Everyone knows how I like to fantasize about other worlds, make up scenarios, joke around with the kids and stuff. Well, it's my break from reality. All the stuff that gets me down. Life is hard. So much duty that's not fun...every day. Even the news depresses me. But I toss the bad over my shoulder every now and again and enjoy a change of scenery—even if it's only in my imagination. Maybe it's cheating, but it keeps me happy."

I sat back and clasped my hands over my aching belly. "Your point?"

"You need to remember why you are a wife, a mother... a friend. You need to get away, take a break, and find your joy. Talk to someone who isn't a part of it all."

"You think I'm crazy? Or too weak to manage my life without running to a hippy-land like my parents?" I shoved the empty dish across the table; only somewhat glad it didn't fall over the edge.

Megan rested her spoon inside her dish and nudged it to the side. "Listen, Honey, I love you for *not* saying the cruel things that run through your mind. Your eye rolling, grimaces, and sarcastic tone speak more than your words. You are so fed up with life; I'm surprised you haven't..."

Tears flooded my eyes. Honesty pervaded my being. The boogeyman stomped up, grabbed me by my shirtfront, and demanded that I listen.

"Your parents were messed up. But they weren't all wrong. They wanted to be happy. That part was right. They just didn't know how to balance their needs with others' needs. That doesn't mean you have to be the sacrificial goat here—"

Despite the ice cream, my insides boiled in fury. There was so much that I wanted to say, but my mind blanked. Which, in the end, was a very good thing. Once said, it's impossible to put words back in the unsaid bottle. All I remember was sliding out of the seat, turning without a word, and walking out the door. I didn't even offer to pay the tip.

It was months before Megan and I met up again. At the grocery store. Both our carts were full to bursting. She flipped a stray lock of hair from her eyes and sighed as she nodded at my cart. "You've been busy."

There was so much I needed to tell her, to explain, the stuff that I had unbottled and set free. But it was late afternoon, and I knew her husband and kids were waiting, as were mine. I just patted her shoulder and smiled. A real smile this time. I was so glad to see her. "We should get some ice cream this weekend."

Megan met my gaze, her face a frozen mask. "It's the middle of January."

"Yeah. That's when it tastes the best."

A grin hovered on Megan's lips. "In an alternate universe, maybe."

"Yep. Want to join me?"

The Loving Choice

Originally published on The Writings of A. K. Frailey
8/15/2019

Jamie switched off the fire under the canner, wiped her tomato-splattered forehead, and wondered if Dante's Inferno got as hot as her kitchen during canning season. She rolled her shoulders and flipped open the large wooden cabinet door to her pantry.

Her assembly of last year's canned goodies had been whittled down to a couple of jars of pickles, three salsas, and one pear jam. This year's strawberry jam had pride of place in the front row on the right. The kids had already made dangerous inroads to that line of preserved fruits. If she didn't hide a few now, there would be none left for winter, much less next spring when everything felt old and barren. A jar of bright red strawberry jam could make all the difference between surviving February or succumbing to the inevitable late-winter blues. She shoved the strawberry jam way in the back and dragged the pear jam to the front. What's wrong with pear jam anyway?

The sound of whistling broke through the humid air. Jamie's lips twitched. Who in their right mind could whistle in this heat? Her adult daughter, Chris, practically bounced into the room. "Hey, Mom. How's life?"

Blinking in the glare of Chris' sunshiny mood, Jamie pulled out a kitchen chair and plopped down. "Life. Is. Hot." She waved the tomato-scented air with one hand in front of her face as if that might help. Somehow.

"There's a storm coming in tonight. It'll cool things down. We're looking at the end of August and the beginning of September in just a couple weeks. You should be happy."

Staring at the sink like a desert wanderer wondering if the oasis ahead was just another blighted mirage, Jamie pulled herself to her feet. "Who says I'm not happy?" She snatched a glass from the cabinet and ran the cold water, hoping against hope that ice cubes would suddenly pour forth from the faucet. No such luck. She sighed, filled the glass half full, and pretty much poured the entire contents down her parched throat.

Chris shook her head, her voice rising. "Mom, you can get cans of fruits and vegetables from the store at a reasonable price. I don't get why you put yourself through this every year."

Now that her body had something to work with, a glorious sweat broke over Jamie's body and cooled her considerably. Her gaze strolled over to the cookie jar. She chewed her lip.

Without a by your leave, Chris grabbed a potholder and lifted the steamy canner top. She peered inside. Her eyebrows jackknifed. "Whoa! That's a lot of salsa!"

On autopilot, Jamie swiveled to the counter, pulled a towel off a triple line of cooling jars and dragged the center one forward. She popped the top, marched to the cabinet, ripped open a bag of corn chips, and shoved the salsa jar and the chips forward. "Try one...or ten."

A smirk played on Chris' lips. "I know; it's the best batch yet." She slipped a crisp chip from the bag and dipped it ceremoniously into the bright red mixture.

Jamie folded her arms and leaned against the counter, waiting. Her eyes narrowed as she followed her daughter's chewing motions and eventual swallow.

Chris' eyes rounded. "Oh, my! That's hot. I mean, that's good!" She snatched her mom's glass, flew to the sink, filled the glass to the brim, and gulped the contents without a break. Then she wiped her mouth with the back of her hand, grinning in delight.

Jamie wiggled her fingers like a robber about to break into the bank vault. She lifted a chip, dipped it three times into the salsa, and popped it into her mouth. She chewed with a thoughtful expression, allowing her palate to discern the merit of the new batch. "Hmmm. Well, it's pretty good. Should keep winter germs at bay."

Chris dipped another chip. "Anyone who eats this will have a super immune system all winter." She crunched and then licked her lips. "Plus, it makes a good gift. A delicious way to say 'I love you—stay healthy for the next seven months.'"

Jamie sauntered to the cabinet and waved at the empty space. "But you know, it would be a lot easier just to fill these shelves with sale brands from the store."

The bright red flush that worked up Chris' face matched the salsa almost perfectly. She took another chip and waved it in the air. "Yeah. Easier. But life isn't all about doing the easy thing, now is it, Mom?" She dipped her latest chip and paused. "I could've stayed at home and read a book, but I decided to come to visit you instead. Not the easiest choice, I might add."

Storm clouds darkened the room and a rush

of cool air ruffled Jamie's hair. As her body relaxed, her heart warmed and her mood lightened. "But you made the loving choice, kiddo. The loving choice."

I Think I'll Live

Originally published on The Writings of A. K. Frailey
8/29/2019

Sometimes silence cuts deeper than words. Philip laid his phone aside and stared at his desk. It was a half-day Friday, so his students had gone home early and the other teachers were busy in their rooms, doing whatever setup they still needed to accomplish before the full academic season started in earnest. He could hear someone stapling in the hall. Putting up the "Welcome Back!" bulletin board, no doubt.

He swiveled in his chair and did a one-eighty, surveying his classroom from one end to the other. Everything looked neat and well organized. Luckily, this year he had been assigned the end room with windows facing southeast. So, there would be plenty of bright sunshine for his grumpy morning students, but it wouldn't face the worst of the storms coming in from the west.

He should be thrilled. Well, he should at least be happy. But his gut felt tight and his chest leaden. A whole month had passed since Kelly had stopped talking to him. Ghosted him was the new slang though he hated the term. She wasn't a ghost. Just someone he had loved and lost. Simple as that. Life moved on.

Or it should.

A knock on the door turned his attention. Brent, his colleague in the math and science department, stood hesitating in the doorway. A grin swept over his face but was quickly replaced by a concerned frown. "Hey—just wondered if you'd like to grab some lunch."

Philip climbed to his feet, feeling every bit of his fifty-five years. He had been married to a lovely lady who died suddenly from a brain aneurysm twelve years ago, raised his four boys as a single parent to the point where they were now on their own and doing great, a testimony to their creative spirits and his hard work. He loved teaching, been doing it for more years than he cared to remember, but this year it seemed stale and tasteless. Like so much of life. He met Brent's gaze and forced a smile. "Sure. Sounds good."

When they entered the small-town diner, Brent nudged Philip toward the red booth in the back. "Might as well get a break from all the noise. We'll get enough of that starting Monday."

Philip shifted his body into the booth and looked around. Nothing had changed since the last time he had been here—springtime—when his world was bursting with life and new adventures. Now, late August, he wondered at his naiveté. Who was he to think he could fall in love like a kid and start a new life? He shook his head and flipped open the menu.

Brent made a humming noise as he perused his choices. He tapped a spot and glanced up. "You ever have the Rueben?"

Philip shrugged. "Yeah. It's okay. Nothing to write home about, though."

Brent nodded and continued his search. He tapped the menu again. "I'm craving red meat and something salty."

Philip's stomach clenched. He had lost five pounds this month, and he knew he needed to eat, though nothing tasted good anymore. Still, a hamburger and fries might restore a modicum of balance to his system. "I'll have the cheeseburger, steak fries, and a cola."

Brent waved to the waitress and ordered the same. He watched her tuck her pad into a pocket and saunter away, then he stared at Philip. "So, you going to tell me about it?"

Philip shrugged and wrapped his fingers around the full water glass the waitress had brought. Condensations dribbled down his fingers. He took a sip and pushed the glass aside. "Nothing much to tell."

Brent leaned back and lounged in the booth like a guy about to tell a long story.

Philip winced. He knew darn well what was coming.

Brent's gaze floated to the ceiling. "So, you remember my sister, Krista?" His eyes rolled over Philip's slight nod. "Well, she was an adorable kid. A real sweetheart. But she had the unfortunate luck to marry a louse. A jerk beyond redemption."

Philip's eyebrows lifted, but he kept his mouth firmly closed.

"So, after the divorce, I took her aside and gave her a little advice. She listened, and she's been happily married to a great guy for..." Brent closed one eye in concentration. "About twelve years now."

The waitress sauntered up with drinks, napkins, and silverware they didn't need. Only the clattering of the cold glasses hitting the Formica table and a tiny hum she apparently carried with her filled the booth.

As she turned away, Philip met Brent's gaze and sighed. "So, okay. I know you'll die if you don't...so go ahead. Tell me."

Philip leaned forward and clasped his hands. "I told her to think of the best men she had ever known in her life...our dad...a teacher she respected...me, of course...and then figure out what she liked about those guys. Then look for those qualities in a man she might like to date. Ignore looks, education, style, money. Just find a guy who she liked and trusted. Then she'd find she find a real husband."

Philip nodded. "I found a woman I liked and trusted. It just turned out I was wrong to do so."

Brent shook his head. "You found a woman you wanted to like and trust. Big difference, man. Real trust takes time. Everything real takes time."

"You think I was too quick to trust her?"

"With your heart. Yep. But that's not a fault really. Just a painful lesson. Funny thing is...Krista's second marriage is so much better than her first. Probably because she really appreciates him, and he really appreciates her."

"Our wounds make us weaker. More uncertain." Brent whistled low.

The waitress pursed her lips tight as she centered the plates on the table before the two men. She darted a glance from one to the other, measuring their moods. "Everything okay?"

Brent smiled. "It's lovely."

With a hesitating smile, she swung away.

Brent lifted his burger and inspected it like a scientist doing a data check. "Think this will give me a heart attack?"

Philip shrugged. "Only if you inhale it and five more like it."

"Wisdom of Solomon, man."

They ate in relative silence while the rest of the diner bustled in noonday chatter. A tired mother shoveled food into her mouth while bouncing a toddler on her knee. Two teenage girls laughed behind their hands, their eyes darting to four construction guys perched on stools at the counter, their bare arms coated in dirty sweat. One middle-aged man, his left hand stretched out holding a phone, appeared to be scrolling through messages...or the day's news. His face remained impassive though his right hand carried a soupspoon to his mouth, and he swallowed a mouthful at all the right intervals.

Philip dropped his half-eaten burger on the plate and shoved it aside. He took a long slurp of his soda and tapped his fingers on the table. "I really should get back."

Brent wiped his mouth and shook his head. "Where? You got some hot date waiting?"

Philip's jaw clenched.

Brent washed his last bite down with the soda. "Look. I'm not trying to be cruel, but you've wasted enough time, waiting for what ain't gonna happen. She made her choice. So, you gotta move on. Now, I know you still feel a bit sore about things...but I do have another sister...and she's..."

Philip's eyes widened. "You've got to be kidding!" He waved his hand at the diner as if encompassing that part of the world. "This whole thing was a setup?"

"Not exactly. But...just let me say this. Sometimes other people can help us see things more clearly than we can see for ourselves. If you get what I mean. I could've told you that Kelly wasn't your type. Or rather...you weren't her type."

"You could've, huh?"

"Yep. And being the decent, good-hearted man that I am—a friend indeed—as they say. I think I might know a good match when I see one."

"So? What's the condition? I know you've got something..."

"Just give my sis, Ronda, a chance; that's all I ask. She's not a beauty...on the outside. Kinda the runt of the family. Real shy because of it. But she's got a heart of gold, is smart and knows how to get things done. She's got love to give...but too many guys are looking for that magic chemistry...that cute chick. The spark. You know what I mean. They don't know how to make a friend and fall in love with a beating heart."

Philip took a fry and chewed it thoughtfully. He took a sip of soda and stared at Brent. "So, what...you set us up on a date? Wouldn't she feel kinda weird about going out with a perfect stranger?"

"Naw, nothing like that. Just come around to dinner tomorrow. She always comes on Saturday nights and helps out. She's a good cook—if that interests you."

"I'm a good cook...I don't need... But...yeah, what the heck. It'll be better than sitting home alone."

Brent polished off his burger and fries with relish. He waved at the waitress for the check. A grin spread wide over his face as Philip took the last bite of his burger and slurped down the dregs of his soda. "You liked it?"

"Yeah. It was surprisingly good. Best thing I've

eaten in a while." "Guess you're going to live, eh?"

Philip nodded and stretched, his stomach full for the first time in months and his heart a touch lighter. "Yeah. I think I'll live..."

If the World Were Any Better

Originally published on The Writings of A. K. Frailey
9/12/2019

"You are so blessed brilliant; it makes my head ache."

Two adorable brown eyes peered up at his mother.

"Yeah?"

"Yep. And you know what happens to brilliant people?"

"They become CEOs and run the corporate world?"

Maura sighed.

Calvin II tapped the keyboard and ran the cursor along the edge like a gymnast ready for his next acrobatic feat.

Not for the first time did Maura wonder why her husband chose the name Calvin for their only son. There couldn't be two more polar opposites than her husband, Calvin the first, the exact replica of the comic book Calvin who constantly dangled poor Hobbs over the edge of reality, and their son, Calvin II, a child whose precocious intelligence and unassailable good sense often knocked the wind out of both their sails. What parent dared to misbehave when they had a responsible eleven-year-old eyeing their every move with a cunning appraisal? They knew darn right well he'd tell Santa Claus. God, too, for that matter.

But really, she wondered, what on Earth would her little boy do with his good sense and brilliant intellect when he grew up? Who wants to run a major corporation and make a ton of money when every other mother's son (or daughter) will elbow him aside in an effort to outdo him? Why invent cool stuff, when some evil despot will use his research to blow up the planet? Or discover the cure for cancer when an insane scientist will incubate a deadly virus in order to wipe out even more people in less time?

"Mom, quit that. Please?" Calvin II huffed. He hated it when she sighed.

Maura hugged him like it was their last day on the planet and pointed to the door. "You've saved my computer from an early demise once again. Now get outside and save your cardiovascular system. Go run around in the fresh air."

Dark thunderclouds swirled out the window and Calvin II grinned. He liked storms. A snack called from the cookie jar, so he snatched three packed with raisins and chocolate chips and swung out the back door with all the pent-up energy of a kid who has been released from mortal combat with a cyber monster.

Heaving another long sigh, Maura swiped crumbs off the counter, frowned at the jam drips she had missed at lunchtime, and bit her lip when her husband charged through the door with a huge grin on his face.

"Hey, Sweetie!" He jerked his thumb backward. "Calvin looks like he's ready to do battle with a Greek god. He's got that look on his face."

Maura knocked the cookie bits into the garbage pail. Depression settled in; even a clean counter couldn't soothe her spirit. "Greek, Roman...or New Age. He could battle them all.

The boy ought to get some kind of reward for sparing my computer yet another breakdown."

A puzzled frown spread over the older Calvin's forehead. "I'd think you'd be thrilled by our son's intelligence and generosity. Isn't this the third time he fixed your computer this month?"

Maura straightened and locked eyes with her husband. "He's terrific. That's the problem."

No rest for the weary cookie jar. Calvin the first fished around, and by mere good luck, pulled out the two largest and promptly began to chomp.

Maura poured a glass of milk and slid it across the counter.

The milk followed the cookies to their natural destination.

Calvin II's voice pierced through the evening stillness as he raced a neighbor boy around the backyard.

"So, why do you want our son to be dumb and lazy?"

Maura turned from her husband and wrung the dishcloth with an extra firm twist. "I just wish he had a better world upon which to bestow his brilliance and goodwill."

"Huh." Calvin the first stretched out his arm.

Soon the cookie jar would show its bottom. A sad fate for any worthy container.

Her husband drained the last dribbles from his glass and popped the final cookie bit into his mouth. He spoke around a chew. "Seems to me that if the world were any better, it wouldn't need our Calvin so much."

With that thought, Maura's husband leaned over, pecked her cheek with a brief kiss, peered into her eyes a lingering moment, and grinned again.

A reflecting grin forced its way over Maura's face, accompanied by a slight eye roll.

By the time Calvin II swung back into the warm house, night and a bit of rain had fallen. A roast chicken with sides of mashed potatoes, carrots, and a Greek salad sat side by side proudly on the table.

Maura leaned against the counter and watched as her son sloshed water across the counter in his efforts to wash his hands before supper.

Calvin II turned and dropped the defeated drying towel on the back of his dad's chair. "You know, Jensen said that his mom paid a tech guy three hundred dollars to fix her computer."

Maura plunked sliced bread on a cutting board and set it beside the chicken. "Sad reality that not everyone has a kid like you, hon."

Calvin II shrugged. "Not really. I already told her that her computer isn't worth saving—too out of date. But she didn't believe me." He peered at his mom. "You know...sometimes people just have to figure things out for themselves."

Maura nodded. Yep. She knew.

Wouldn't You?

Originally published on The Writings of A. K. Frailey
9/26/2019

Henrietta Huber wanted to know why a dead cat lay across her doorstep. Animals didn't normally pick her abode to succumb to death's tyrannical fate. Nor humans, for that matter, thank God. Still, the fact remained; a stiff body sprawled awkwardly before her front door.

She lifted her gaze and peered around her quiet, respectable neighborhood. She lived in the center of her cul-de-sac. It had always felt like a privilege, being snug in the middle of her neighbors; a dark brown ranch house to the right, and a two-story brick dwelling on her left. Upper middle class. Very. But today, her quaint neighborhood emitted the faintest odor of disease. Or was that the cat?

Not one to let fate have its way with her, Henrietta trotted a few steps down the street.

A fancy board painted with red fruit dangling from thick boughs and fancy lettering which spelled out "Apple Valley," announced the entrance to their neighborhood, though only one pair of apple trees stood guard on each side of the road, and no valley could be seen for twenty miles. Still, doctors, lawyers, teachers, and a pleasant assortment of craftsmen lived here. It was not a place to be sniffed at. Especially not today.

She chewed her lip as she returned to her front step. These simply were not the sort of people to drop a dead critter on a neighbor's doorstep. On the contrary, Henrietta knew several with speed dial who would gladly report the slightest hint of animal abuse.

She frowned at the insinuation of less than stellar animal care at her feet.

Could this reflect badly on her, perhaps? Had she left some antifungal spray, insect killer, or some other ugly reminder of nature's imperfect reality in a place where this critter inadvertently killed itself upon her carelessness?

Sheesh! One faced deadly peril at every turn these days.

A neighbor's door opened, and a head poked out.

Henrietta stepped in front of the circumstantial evidence and mumbled to herself. "Oh, blast, Lindsey Jenkins. Good Lord, I'll be hauled before the county judge and sentenced to twenty hours of community service if this gets out."

Lindsey, without delay, skittered across her neatly manicured yard, practically leaped over the prickly bush border, and with wringing hands prostrated her forlorn figure before her bewildered neighbor.

Considering that Lindsey was nearer seventy than sixty and usually worked her mouth more than her legs, Henrietta was duly impressed. She dragged her eyes off the thorny hedgerow and interrogated her elderly neighbor with her eyes.

Lindsey, clearly in a hurry to immortalize herself in some kind of unforgettable apology, gushed her words. "Henny, so sorry about the cat carcass, but I really had no choice."

In her attempt to draw her neighbor away from prying eyes, Henrietta tripped over the cat.

Lindsey clasped her friend's arm and, with surprising strength, ushered Henrietta inside the pristine abode.

Once safely ensconced on the beautifully embroidered divan, Henrietta, forgoing common decency, waited for the tale to be told before she offered a morning snack. She arched her brows.

Leaning back with one hand slapped against her cheek like a surprised matron finding the cook and the butler in a compromising position, Lindsey inhaled enough breath to begin. "You see, my grandkids simply adore my cat. Or rather, they adored it. Until it died. When I told their mother, my daughter-in-law, Myrtle, who was bringing the kids over for their usual visit today, that Cleopatra had finally succumbed to old age, she insisted that I tell the children before they arrived."

Henrietta could not for the world imagine where this was going. Despite herself, she felt intrigued. The morning news could wait. Heck, if the world were on the verge of collapse, she would lift a hand in command that it wait a few moments so she could hear this before falling to its inevitable doom.

Henrietta didn't need to prod. Lindsey knew what was expected. "And so, I did what any decent grandmother would do. I told a wonderful tale of how Cleo sprouted angel wings at the moment of death and flew off to her celestial reward."

If someone had actually dropped a bar of hot lead in Henrietta's lap, she would not have been more surprised. She shouldn't have been so amazed. But that was the way of things. Being caught off guard by the obvious. They all lived in a fantasyland of sorts. She knew *that* perfectly well every time she steered her tiny car onto the speeding highway. But this? Angel cats with wings? Ascending into heaven? No wonder children dress up as zombies for fun. Why pretend anything makes sense?

Lindsey shook her head as if in sympathy with Henrietta's perplexed expression. "When I heard the car drive up...and with Cleo still unburied...I knew I had to do something fast. I had no idea they were in the neighborhood when she called. I couldn't think what to do!"

Henrietta grunted to her feet and strolled to the front door. She peered through the glass. Ah, yes. The prickly hedge hid the offending lie. She turned and faced her devious neighbor. "And now?"

With a swipe across her brow, Lindsey chuckled. "Well, the kids have gone off with their mama, and I'm in the clear. I told Jake to get the cat as soon as he gets a break and bury it out back somewhere. Maybe under that sugar maple we all love. It'd be fitting. And well out of the way."

Remembering her manners, Henrietta offered a cup of tea and a little something, but Lindsey supposed that she better get home. She stood on the threshold and stared down at the remains of her once-loved pet. "I know I told a ridiculous tale and made a fool of myself trying to keep the kids in ignorance of the hard facts of life. But," She glanced Henrietta's way, a hopeful gleam in her eyes. "You'd do the same for your grandkids, wouldn't you?"

As Jake scooped the stiff body onto a

wheelbarrow and then wobbled it toward his backyard, Henrietta considered Lindsey's question. "Would I?"

As Mom Used to Say

Originally published on The Writings of A. K. Frailey
10/24/2019

Richard wanted to kill someone. It wasn't his usual state of being, but at the present, it was undoubtedly for the best that he stomp into the wilderness and get some space between him and the rest of humanity.

A squirrel scampered across his path, halted, raised itself on its hind legs, and stared as if considering the possibility between a snack and sudden death.

Richard clenched his hands in his pockets, crunched a snack bar in one and gripped his phone in the other. He pounded forward.

The squirrel high tailed it to the nearest tree and clawed its way to the top.

Richard, who normally enjoyed wildlife, grunted and smacked a branch out of his way.

The branch smacked him right back.

The squirrel, chattering from a high limb and holding a couple of notes longer than usual, warned the entire animal kingdom what kind of man approached.

"To heck with it." His calf muscles burning and his lungs screaming, Richard aimed for a bench set on the edge of the wooded path. As he neared the resting spot, his joints thanking him profusely for the privilege of living through another day, Richard stopped short. A new sound broke through the air. He peered up.

The treetops, devoid of chattering squirrels

and cawing birds, had nothing to add to the faint call or whine that Richard was sure he had heard. An injured dog?

"Awww—hell!"

It was a woman's voice. A woman in pain, by the sound of it. The term "damsel in distress" crossed Richard's mind. He swatted it away with the autumn insects.

Heaving his robust frame, a little larger in the tummy than he would like, though he had to admit his legs looked great in shorts, Richard lumbered back the way he had come.

Yep. There she sat, crouched like a kid on the playground when the other girls got mean, holding her ankle and...swearing like a sailor?

Richard scratched his head and glanced up. *Really?* Retirement had been nothing it was cracked up to be. He traveled for the first six months, took up volunteer work for the next six months, and recently got into a tangle with an idiot from his church who insisted that predestination was part of their faith system and would not allow any new members to join unless they had paid-up life insurance policies.

The woman—somewhere in her late forties—stopped rocking, and thankfully, stopped swearing. With a sudden intake of breath, she lurched to her feet, yelped, and hopped on one foot until she smacked into an oak tree, which managed to hold her in a partially upright position.

Richard snorted and practically pulled out his hair as he ran his fingers over the top of his head. So, like something his first wife would've done. Stubborn as the day was long.

The woman glared at him. "So glad you're

enjoying my plight."

"Hey, I would've helped you up..." Richard looked around. "You want me to call for... assistance?"

Despite an October breeze rustling through the trees, sweat beaded on the woman's brow. "Sure. My phone is dead as a doornail."

Richard's ears twitched. He pulled his phone from his sweatpants pocket and punched the keypad to life.

The woman lifted her hand. "Hey, stop. Really. It's not that bad. My car is only a mile or so back. I can make it. I hate to have paramedics come all the way out here. I'd feel like a fool. Besides, they might have someone in real need somewhere else."

Richard stepped forward and shrugged. "You can use my arm if you want to hop that far." He tilted his head, peering at her, and offered his elbow.

She shoved off the tree, balancing on her good foot, and listed like a sinking ship. "Thanks. My name's Sigrid." She huffed at his quizzical expression and gripped his elbow. "From a Scandinavian author...my parents were literary fools. I forgave them long ago." She limped at his side. "Like an idiot, I decided to get in shape and start jogging, and look what happens!"

Richard nodded. Her hand felt firm but strangely familiar on his arm. He always went for women in trouble. Soft heart, his friends said. Soft mind, his mother told him. Good ol' mom. Richard chuckled.

"Am I still amusing you?"

Sigrid's tone carried an edge, but when he glanced at her, there was a light in her eye and a smile hovering on her lips.

"No, mam. Sorry. I was just remembering something my mom told me long ago."

"Care to share? I love a good quote."

"Well, my mom liked history. Made me something of an eccentric among my peers since I would quote obscure historical facts while throwing together financial plans for my clients. Anyway, she loved to remind me that those who don't learn from history are doomed to repeat it."

Sigrid nodded and stopped, catching her breath. "Just a sec. I'm not trained for the hop-Olympics quite yet." She leaned more heavily on Richard's arm.

Richard pointed to a hefty tree trunk lying near the path. "Here, let's stop a minute."

Sigrid plopped down on the log and wrapped her fingers around her ankle, wincing. "Dang, but I am such a klutz. My daughters ordered me out of the kitchen because they say I'll break dinner instead of make dinner."

Richard snorted. Then, as the mental image washed over him, he laughed outright. It felt so good to laugh again. He peered at her left hand. No ring. "Your husband doesn't help with the cooking?

Sigrid hooted. "Well, that was subtle!" She lifted her ring-less hand. "Divorced seven years. Then, using air quotes, she smirked. "We're friends." With a shrug, she shoved the topic aside. "Two college-age girls and a married son. Their dad sees them when he wants. I keep busy with work and—" She rolled her eyes, "Keeping in wonderful shape."

Confession time? Richard wondered why he felt like he should order a drink from the bar.

"Divorced ten years. Retired one year. Two grown sons who live overseas. Do lots of charity work and slowly losing my mind to boredom.

"Hah! You sound like my ex. Always doing other people a good turn but never satisfied with himself."

Oh, brother. Richard figured he'd cut this short. "I'm an introvert, Aries, non-denominational Christian, and sleep without a pillow."

Clapping her hands over her mouth, Sigrid nearly exploded in laughter.

Four birds escaped with their lives from the leafy foliage.

Sigrid stood and beckoned Richard with a sly glance. "Come on, Mr. Aries, you gotta walk me to my car so I can get home in time for dinner and tell my girls that I've had the best jog of my life."

Richard rose and offered his arm. "But what about being doomed to repeat history?"

Sigrid grinned. "Ah. But as *my mom* used to say, 'Live and learn.'"

A young squirrel, probably still in adolescence, froze directly in Richard's path. It rose with a hopeful expectation in its eyes.

"Aw, heck." Richard pulled the broken candy bar from his pocket, peeled off the wrapping, and slung it at the quadruped.

Duly grateful, the squirrel grabbed the treat and sped away.

Richard slipped the sticky wrapping into his pocket, stuck out his arm, felt the weight of her hand, and strolled back to civilization.

Unless You Give Up

Originally published on The Writings of A. K. Frailey
11/7/2019

Grant dutifully signed the electronic notice declaring that his son was getting mostly Cs and two Ds—in English and Math, of course—on his mid-term report and wondered what it felt like to not fail. Not that grades meant everything, and C's were respectable enough, especially considering Jon's disabilities. But he could hardly meet Ms. Berg's direct gaze.

He nodded in all the right places. "Yes, mam. He has a quiet study place. No, we don't allow that sort of thing in the house. Uh-huh...his sister helps him all the time. Yes, I know. She's a bright little thing."

Named after the General who helped to win the Civil War, Grant vowed at the age ten, when he read a biography of the hero, to never drink. But as the Parent-Teacher Conference wrapped up, and he gathered his two kids from the gymnasium, he wondered if perhaps the General had the right idea. After all, why not take the edge off reality?

Judy was a bright little thing. For some reason fathomable to God alone, she never grew beyond four feet six inches, but her brain—as well as her mouth—outran everyone in the eighth grade. Jon respected her academic abilities but hated her bossy "tude." Grant dearly sympathized.

The drive home remained quiet as Judy was shushed every time she started extolling the virtues of her teachers, her wonderful grades, or the fact that school made life worth living.

It wasn't until bedtime, while Grant sat on the edge of his son's bed, folded his hands, and listened to their prayer time routine, that he realized that Jon was upset.

"And God, if you could just make me good at something—anything—I'd appreciate it."

Grant frowned. He watched as the lanky young man, a freshman whose brain got stuck somewhere along 5th grade, climbed into bed. "You're good at things."

Jon reached for a dog-eared comic book. "My dad is still putting me to bed. How good can I be?"

Grant climbed to his feet and stared down at the boy. "What? I just figured that since I hardly see you…what with work and school…and sports…and…" He shrugged. "Praying with you hardly means I'm putting you to bed." A flush burned his cheeks.

"You think that you have to check on me all the time." Jon shook his head and slapped the comic book on his lap. "You don't do that with Judy."

"I never have to worry about Judy. She always brushes her teeth, puts on clean clothes, says her prayers, and gets up on time."

"And gets all As."

Exhaustion warred with frustration. Grant had suffered through a tedious meeting at work, waited through long lines at the grocery store, mentally calculated the years until his retirement, knowing all the while that he'd probably die in harness, and blindly stuffed aching loneliness to the furthest reaches of his mind. He started for the door.

The muffled words, “As usual.” stopped him in his tracks. He turned around. “What?”

Jon crouched forward peering at the comics like the nearsighted kid he was. His whitened fingers crumpled the edges so fiercely it would never lay flat again.

Grant stomped back and towered over the bed. “Say that again.”

Jon threw the comic book across the room. His eyes blazing, red-rimmed with tears, and his cheeks flushed, he thrashed his way free from his sheets and pounded to the other side of the room. With shaky hands, he rattled through his dresser drawers until he slammed one open and pulled out a sketchbook from between dingy pairs of socks.

Grant felt his heart racing. His latest story—unsold—sat quietly on a writer’s blogging site with only a handful of comments. He bit his lip.

Jon tossed the notebook at his father.

Too stunned to react, Grant watched the book flutter to the floor. He raised his eyes to his son as he picked it up. Then he leafed through the pages. The pictures were good. Not great...well...there was one. It held promise. Certainly creative. He frowned and looked up.

Jon had retreated to the far end of the room, leaning against the wall. The mast listed to one side after the bulk of the ship has gone down.

Honesty was hell. Vulnerability was worse. But watching his son die inside would kill him.

Grant dropped his head to his chest and exhaled a long slow breath. He lifted his hand in a wait-a-moment signal and left the room. He retreated to his room, picked up his laptop, and returned to his son's room. "Here."

Jon glanced over. Bored. "What? A new learning tool?"

Grant felt the smile even though he knew it probably wasn't showing on his face. He needed to cry too much. "No." He shoved three plants he had never noticed before aside and set the computer on Jon's desk. Clicking on a link, he pulled up the writer's site and scrolled through until he found his name. He clicked it, and his most recent story popped up with comments attached. He turned the computer so Jon could see.

If spent balloons could walk, they would look like Jon as he approached the table, flopped down, and crouched forward for a quick read-through.

But he wasn't quick. He returned to the top and read the story again.

Grant's heart clenched so tight he wondered if he was facing cardiac arrest.

Jon's fingers hovered over the curser at the bottom of the page. He peered up at his dad. "You never told me."

Grant shrugged. "I'm not very good."

Jon shook his head. "But it's creative. I think it's good." He pointed to the last comment. "This guy thinks so too."

Grant swallowed the ache of loneliness and wondered where it was going. He crouched beside his son. "You know, there's an art site where you can post your work. It helps to get other people's opinions. Usually."

"But I fail at everything."

Grant rubbed his hand across his mouth and smothered a chuckle. “You won’t fail—unless you give up.”

Trying to Be a Hero

Originally published on The Writings of A. K. Frailey
11/21/2019

Susanne shivered. Rain had settled into a steady drizzle, and dark clouds hid any vestiges of the evening sun. One of the very last pink and golden leaves of the season fluttered in a gentle breeze and then, without warning, careened from the heights to land on her head. She tried not to take offense as she plucked off the ragged symbol of autumn beauty and held it before her eyes. She glanced up. “Trying to tell me something?”

Her car, tilted at an odd angle, sat before her like a shopping cart that had lost a wheel. Without premeditated thought, she kicked the flat tire and immediately regretted her actions. “Oh, holy cow, that wasn’t so smart!”

“I’d say not. It might decide to kick back, and then where’d you be?”

Susanne glanced across the road and met a strange woman’s gaze. Embarrassment and a tinge of fury ran laps around her insides. She knew perfectly well that she looked pathetic. She certainly felt pathetic. But heck, no one need make snide comments. Widening her stance like a prizefighter preparing to enter the ring, she ignored her toes yelping for immediate attention and faced the stranger. A scene from the OK Corral flashed through her mind.

Apparently, the strange woman had never seen the movie, didn’t comprehend body lingo, or she simply didn’t care how terrible Susanne’s day had been since she breezed across the street as if it were mid-summer and the sun was shining.

"Flat, eh?"

Susanne peered at the outstretched hand. Like now was a perfect time to say howdy and make friends!

"I'm Georgia. Visiting my niece this week from Michigan. I saw the flat and hoped the owner might be some muscled guy who worked for an auto station." Her eyes roved over Susan's petite form and shrugged. "Guess not." Her eyes continued their stroll and landed on the elementary school. "You're a teacher?"

Mental fibers started to snap, but with a mighty yank, Susanne gripped her emotions and demanded that they stay in line. "Office secretary. Terrific job. Just, I can't get home with a flat tire."

Georgia pointed to the trunk. "You got a spare in there?" She shrugged. "I've never actually changed one myself, but I watched my sons do it three or four times. How hard can it be?"

Bundled in a winter coat over a thick sweater, it was hard to tell Georgia's body build, but Susanne guessed it to be somewhere between a heavyweight wrestler and Highland Dwarf. "Well, we can try, I guess. I hate to call the service station. So bloody expensive just to take it a few miles."

In the style of a Commander and Chief taking charge of his army, Georgia flipped open the trunk, swept back the cover, lugged out the spare, dropped it handily on the ground, snapped open the enclosed tool kit, and plopped down on the wet ground, fitting the crank under the car. "I think it goes here."

The word "think" sent another shiver down

Susanne's spine. But since Georgia seemed to be on a roll, she had no desire to interrupt. When it came time to unscrew the bolts, Susanne regained a modicum of self-respect by remembering "lefty-loosey" and thus saved her rescuer heaps of time.

The sudden downpour didn't seem to affect Georgia like Susanne thought it would. In fact, it appeared to have no effect on her at all. The gray-headed woman unbolted the flat, switched out the tire, and then bolted on the spare with the same calm composure one would expect from a surgeon doing his fiftieth appendectomy. The painful tangle in Susanne's middle began to loosen. Just a bit.

Once everything was put away and Georgia slapped her hands free of street grit and broken leaves, Susanne felt her newly assembled composure disintegrate. "Can I pay you for your— I would've—"

Georgia waved the suggestion away. "You would've called a tow truck and paid a bundle. How far you live from here?"

"Oh, just a few miles. It'll be fine. I really..." As Susanne pictured her empty apartment, loneliness galloped over confusion and ran it into the ground.

"Well, before you go, I want you to come in and have a hot cup of tea. My niece is off on one of her trips. God knows where this time. That's why I'm here. I saw her for a few hours and off she ran. I stay and watch the house for a week. She's got an old Tomcat that can't find his way from the yard to the food bowl without help. So, I got the job." She shrugged. "At least it's something to do…" She grinned at the replaced wheel. "In my declining years."

~~~

Embracing a hot cup of tea like a rescue buoy and ensconced on a very comfortable chair, Susanne wondered why this stranger felt like the best friend she never had.

Georgia plunked down, set her cup on a side table and leaned forward, clasping her hands over one knee. "Seems to me that you'd already had a bad day before you even saw your flat tire."

Susanne's sudden tears surprised her. But it was her own wracking sob that unhinged her.

Georgia sat comfortably in her chair, waiting, not cajoling or trying to hurry the process. She simply let the strange woman before her cry her eyes out.

Susanne could not have been more grateful. After she wiped her eyes with a tissue that seemed to spring out of thin air, she sat back, took a long sip of her lukewarm tea, and sighed. She lifted her gaze.

Georgia munched a fig newton. Completely at ease. No agenda. No tapping foot or imploring expression. Just calm acceptance, as if to say, "So this is how today is going. Huh."

Susanne exhaled, pulled her feet onto the couch, and wrapped her arms around her knees. "I lied today. Have you ever lied?"

Georgia grunted. "Oh, yeah. Of course. We all do. Sometimes on purpose with lots of planning. Sometimes on the spur of the moment, without thinking. We usually have a fairly good reason. Or
~~~

at least, we think we do."

"Well, I lied for one simple reason. To get back at someone who hurt me. I wanted her to feel bad. The details don't really matter. Maybe she deserved it for the way she treated me. But the lie was all mine. I knew it was wrong. But I did it anyway. And what's worse, I did it over and over again so that this woman's reputation will now be forever shattered. Or at least questionable." The tears started again. "I wanted to punish her, but I punished myself far worse."

"And then you got a flat tire." Georgia snorted. "Bet you thought *Someone* was trying to tell you something, eh?"

Nausea rose and started an open rebellion in Susanne's stomach. She couldn't look up.

"Listen. You did an awful thing. No matter why, you knew it was wrong, and you did it anyway. So, deal with it. You admitted it to me. So tomorrow, go tell the people involved that you lied. Apologize to your enemy, regain your self-respect, and stop hating yourself."

Susanne blinked, her eyes stinging with the effort. "It's not that simple. I'm the nice person. Everyone looks up to me. They trust me. She's the witch everyone hates. If I do that, they'll think I'm some kind of blithering idiot trying to be a hero."

"Well—in a way—you are."

A cat appeared on Susanne's right. It crouched, sprang, and landed on her lap. She yelped in surprise. And then, as the truth of Georgia's words hit home, she laughed.

Georgia grinned. "You like cats?"

"Not usually. But this one—" She peered into the orange-eyed calico as he kneaded his paws into her lap and started his engines full throttle. "He's fine."

"Good. I'll leave him in your care while I go warm up the kettle. I think one more cup is in order before I send out into the rainy night."

Susanne leaned back against the chair and felt the cat curl up in a contented ball. Her shoulders relaxed, and warmth spread throughout her whole body.

It Might Have Been

Originally published on The Writings of A. K. Frailey
12/5/2019

A wrong number. Not a scam. Just some innocent woman looking for her sister Pearl. Jason assured her that he wasn't Pearl, hit the end button, and slid the phone across his desk. He dropped his head onto his hand and tried to concentrate.

Inventory. Yay!

Even mental sarcasm fell flat. He should be pumped. The holidays approached with days off for leisure time, sleeping in, parties with assorted junk food, and perhaps a chance to head out to the park for a little fun and games. The image of a woman clad in a tight winter sweater and black leggings danced in front of his eyes. Heat licked his body.

The phone chimed. Jason tapped his fingers. Answer? Not answer? Hardly a life-or-death decision. He tapped the green button and slapped the phone against his ear. "Dad?"

"Jas?"

Carol? Cold water doused the flames. Oh heck, anybody but his stepmother. He'd rather have root canal. Not that she wasn't a perfectly nice person. It's just that with a root canal, you know what you're getting into. With Carol, Russian roulette seemed tame. Besides, he hated it when anyone shortened his name. *What? Two syllables asking too much? Ja-son. Oh, forget it.*

"Hey, Carol. What's up?"

"Jas, I don't want to take up your time, so I won't beat around the proverbial bush, but your dad's not doing too well. He's really struggling, and I just want to give you a heads up before you come visit."

Very subtle. Okay. It had been a while. A few weeks. Jason rolled his eyes over to the wall calendar—the one his wife had bought for him. Landscapes with hymns scrolled over the top. Oh yeah. Something safe that would keep his mind on celestial matters. Instead of other things.

Pine trees and a little manger scene. Hmmm...that time already?

He leaned back and let his chair fall into relaxed mode. His head tilted, he considered the state of his office ceiling.

"You caught me, Carol. It has been too long. Waaay too long. I need to get my bu—, I mean, I should get Dinah and the kids and head out your way. Christmas season and all." He grimaced at the thought of driving through snow and ice into Wisconsin but then the possibility of escaping Dinah's family...

Carol ran roughshod over his thoughts. "You know, your dad always said that nothing mattered as long as his kids were happy. He still knows who you are. He recognizes me. Most of the time. But if you wait..."

Jason's feet hit the floor with a slap. "What do you mean? He didn't have any trouble recognizing me or the kids last time we were there."

"A year ago."

Jason smacked his forehead. He leaned in, peered at the calendar, and squinted. *Was it*? "Hey, you know. You're right. I need to talk with Dinah and set something in motion. I'll call you back, okay?"

"You won't forget, now, will you?"

The snarky tone mixed with anxiety roiled Jason's stomach. "No. I won't forget."

Once home, Jason perched on a stool at the kitchen island and outlined a quick road trip. Dinah listened in empathetic understanding. Such a generous spirit. Of course. She visited her parents every month. Good woman that she was. He couldn't go most of the time, despite the fact that they lived only twenty minutes away, because, well, you know. He had a hell of a honey-do list and getting older wasn't a picnic; let me tell you. *Hey, I need some me-time, too.*

His mind wandered back to the woman he'd met at the park last week. Gorgeous. Funny. Didn't quote scripture while they strolled along the path. She wore a ring. He wore a ring. But still...

Dinah rattled on. "It's all settled then. Next weekend, we'll leave early Friday and be back by Sunday night. I'm sure your dad will be pleased. He loves you, you know." His eyes lingered on his face, like she was sending some kind of coded message.

Sheesh. Lay on the guilt with a trowel, why don't you?

All evening, images of the park woman meandered through Jason's mind. In frustration, he cuddled up to his wife in bed, but she was already asleep. *Or so she wants me to believe. Great. Now I got nothing but a lousy trip to look forward to.* He yanked the blanket to his side of the bed, exposing his wife's slumbering form to the cold night air. *She probably doesn't even notice. Martyrs never do.*

Images of the park woman slithered through his mind. Her perfect form, flashing smile, the teasing glint in her eye. Then, out of nowhere, his dad appeared on the opposite side of a busy street. The old man tried to cross, but trucks and cars whizzed by in city traffic madness. The old man locked eyes with Jason, bewildered desperation peering from the depths. He waved and called, "Ja-son!"

Jason dropped the woman's hand, his heart pounding. "Dad? Hey, don't try to cross there. It's crazy traffic. You'll get—"

Dinah's scream ripped through the air as she ran out from behind, shoving the park woman aside. She dashed across the street, stopping traffic like magic. She reached her father-in-law's broken body. In true superwoman form, she carried the old man across the street, tears streaming from her disappointed, despairing eyes.

Her words shot Jason like bullets. "All yours."

Suddenly another man, a shrewd well-dressed gent with clever eyes and high cheekbones, stepped forward and swept everyone else away. He pointed toward a wide doorway. "If you please."

Heat flickered through Jason's body, but he shivered uncontrollably. "What's this?"

"What you wanted."

"Wanted?" Jason wrinkled his nose at a strange stink. "I never get what I want! Seems to me that I have to pay a pretty steep price for everything."

The gentleman chuckled. "Think so? But it's all free. Free will and all."

Jason looked around for his father, his wife, his home, anything familiar and comforting. "But I wanted to see dad. I could've—"

Laughter rang in Jason's ears. "The saddest words man ever penned were the words..."

Jason bolted upright. Sweat beaded across his brow. He shivered. "Oh, God!"

Dinah murmured and rolled over. She reached out. "You okay, honey?"

The Sahara Desert had filled Jason's mouth. He couldn't utter a word.

Dinah sat up and leaned in, her fingers stroking her husband's arm. "Worried about your dad?" She cuddled closer, pulling the blanket around them both. "It'll be okay. He's a good man. He's made his life and even if he doesn't remember now, when he dies, he'll know the truth. Besides, he's not dead yet. You still have time."

Jason hugged his wife, tears streaming down his face. The words, "It might've been..." rang in his ears.

About the Author

As a teacher with a degree in Elementary Education who has taught in big cities and small towns, Ann Frailey homeschooled all of her children. She manages her rural homestead with her kids and their numerous critters. She writes books and a Friday blog alternating between short stories, poetry, book excerpts, and her *My Road Goes Ever On* series.

Her nonfiction work focuses on the intersection of motherhood, widowhood, practicing gratitude, and rediscovering joy.

Her fiction novels expand from the OldEarth world to the Newearth universe—where deception rules but truth prevails. She earned a Masters of Fine Arts Degree in Creative Writing for Entertainment from Full Sail University.

In her spare time, she serves as an election judge and as secretary/treasurer of her small town's cemetery.

She is currently finishing a new science fiction novel in the Newearth world. To check out her stories, novels, inspirational books, and her film and tv scripts, visit https://akfrailey.com/

www.ingramcontent.com/pod-product-compliance
Lightning Source LLC
Chambersburg PA
CBHW060632310726
48982CB00003B/743

* 9 7 9 8 9 8 7 4 0 4 7 6 8 *